GUARDED *dreams*

LJ EVANS

This book is a work of fiction. While reference might be made to actual historical events or existing people and locations, the events, names, characters, places and incidents are either the product of the author's imagination or are used fictitiously, and any resemblance to actual persons, living or dead, business establishments, events, or locales is entirely coincidental.

Published by LJ Evans Books

www.ljevansbooks.com

Cover Design: © LJ Evans Books
Cover Images: © Unsplash kiwihug and Deposit Photos ninanaina / MaslovaLarisa / Olga_Bonitas / MarinaErmakova
Copy Editing: Jenn Lockwood Editing Services
Developmental & Line Edits: Evans Editing

Library of Congress Cataloging-in-Publications in process.
ISBN: 978-1-962499-02-6

Printed in the United States

Playlist

https://spoti.fi/2W5cesF

Part 1
Chasing

Sunrise, Sunburn, Sunset – Luke Bryan
Fly – Maddie & Tae
I Met a Girl – William Michael Morgan
Groovy Little Summer Song – James Otto
Speechless – Dan + Shay
Perfect Day – Lady Antebellum
Wild Child – Kenny Chesney w/ Grace Potter
Kiss You Tonight – David Nail
Little More Summertime – Jason Aldean
Breathe – Taylor Swift

Part 2
Falling

Craving You – Thomas Rhett
Whatever It Is – Zac Brown Band
Get To You – Michael Ray
Blue Ain't Your Color – Keith Urban
Love Is Looking For You – Miranda Lambert
Singles You Up – Jordan Davis
I Could Use a Love Song – Maren Morris
Just a Kiss – Lady Antebellum
I Think I Fell In Love Today – Kelsea Ballerini
I Run To You – Lady Antebellum
Heaven – Kane Brown

Part 3
Reviving

Come a Little Closer – Dierks Bentley
Bless the Broken Road – Rascal Flatts
Written In Sand – Old Dominion
Words Are Medicine – Tim McGraw
The Stars – Lady Antebellum
In Case You Didn't Know – Brett Young
This Kiss – Faith Hill
Die A Happy Man – Thomas Rhett
Girl – Maren Morris
Sweetheart – Thomas Rhett
Oh, What a World – Kacey Musgraves
Once In a Lifetime – Keith Urban
The Rest of Our Life – Tim McGraw & Faith Hill

GUARDED *dreams*
LJ EVANS

Dedication

To my sister. For reading all my words first.
To all the authors who painstakingly
write their own words.
To all the readers who make "the writing words"
profession something worthy of pursuing.

Chasing

SUNRISE, SUNBURN, SUNSET
Performed by Luke Bryan

Chapter One

Eli

GIRL LIKE YOU

Performed by Jason Aldean

The heat and humidity assaulted me as I stepped out of the rented truck and looked up at the house on the shore of Aransas Bay. I groaned inwardly. I was so screwed. The guys weren't going to let me live this down.

Somehow, the house had escaped Hurricane Harvey with only a few dents and bruises, but there'd been some reconstruction needed. The remnants of that renovation were obvious in the oversized trash container full of debris outside the two-car garage that took up the bottom floor of the home.

The house desperately needed a paint job. The color was, at the moment, a crazy mix of beaten yellow, raw wood, and left-over white. That was what the guys and I were here to do: paint the house.

I heard Mac and Truck grumble as they slammed the doors behind me.

"Holy fuck, Els-worth, what have you gotten us into?" Mac threw out. He only broke out the Els-worth when he wanted to make a point. He knew I hated it. Call me Eli, or Wyatt, or hell, even my full name of

Elijah James Wyatt, but just don't call me what the asshole lieutenant had our freshman year.

I turned to both of them. Mac was built like a linebacker. He barely fit in the cargo shorts and T-shirt he was wearing, looking as if he might go all Hulk any moment and tear the things apart. You could barely see his normally black hair under the crew cut he sported. His muscles flexed as he reached into the bed of the truck to pull out the military-style bag that we all had with us.

Truck—well, really Travis, but no one had called him that since freshman year—just shook his head at me. But his brown eyes were already flashing with mischief beneath the shaved head that made his ice-blonde hair practically invisible. His square frame was just as built as Mac's, but he'd earned the name Truck for a reason. He blew through anyone and everyone that challenged him…just like a semi-truck. Together, they were Mac Truck. No one messed with them.

Except me. I couldn't help it. I'd been born to razz them. Especially with their "ship-like" nickname that everyone called them when they were definitely not in a relationship.

If I harassed them too much, they'd try to give me shit back, and my frame might not be as thick as theirs, but I had enough of my own muscles to more than hold my own. For some reason, neither of them felt it a requirement to challenge me very often. But this…this house was going to make them challenge me for the entire eight days we were there.

"You said you wanted to stay on the beach as cheap as possible. Free is as cheap as it gets," I retorted.

"But I didn't say I wanted to work my ass off for eight days. We'll be doing enough of that on the Kennedy," Mac said.

He was right that the cadet cruise on the TS Kennedy that Texas A&M's Maritime Academy made mandatory during the summers was nonstop work. I loved it, but not everyone did. For me, it was a glimpse at what I'd been striving and hoping for since I was a kid…to be on a boat, with a unit, making a difference.

I shrugged. "It's a little paint. We'll do a couple hours in the mornings and then take the afternoons off."

"You think eight mornings are going to get this job done?" Travis stared at me incredulously.

I had to admit, now that I saw the house, I had my own doubts. Two stories. Two thousand square feet on the top floor where three bedrooms and two baths stared out at the bay. But the supplies were already here, including a spray gun, so I thought we could manage it.

Professor Abrams had insisted we could do the job in the days we were here while still having time to decompress before the summer "cruise" took off. It was debatable if he was right, but if I needed to put in some extra hours while the guys played, I didn't really mind. I'd rather keep myself busy than sit at a bar drinking and eyeing the local girls, anyway.

We headed up the stairs, and I opened the door with the key that Abrams had given me before we'd departed.

Inside, it smelled like new paint and new furniture. Because everything *was* sparkling new. The wood floors were polished to a shine you could see yourself in. The walls were a mix of white shiplap and gray paint, and the kitchen spoke of money and trend all rolled into one.

Truck whistled.

"Didn't know Abrams had this kind of dough."

"Just don't break anything, asswipes. We don't have the nickels and dimes to pay for any repairs."

I headed down the hall to the bedrooms. Two shared a Jack and Jill bathroom. The third was the master suite that stared out at the bay. I put my bag down by the dresser in the suite.

"Why do you get the master, Els-worth? It's not like you're going to be bringing any girls back here to show off." Mac was still whining and still using the damn nickname, grating on my nerves.

"Did you make the arrangements? Do you want to suck face with gratitude to Abrams when we get back to school in August?" I asked.

Mac scoffed. "He's the one who should suck up to us for doing this job for free."

"In your wet dreams, douche," I said.

He walked out to pick a room off the Jack and Jill.

I left my bag where it landed and went to the French doors. I opened them, stepping outside so I could breathe in the salty air and hear the waves crashing on the shoreline.

The ocean and me, we'd always been a thing. Twined together like almost nothing else in my life. It talked to my soul like some people said music or art talked to theirs.

I'd been on the water with my dad since I could crawl. And after…when he was gone, it was still the place I felt closest to him. It wasn't the entire reason that my life goals surrounded the Coast Guard, but it was an undeniably large part of it.

"We need supplies," Truck said, joining me on the deck.

"Abrams already bought everything we need. It's in the garage."

Truck laughed. "Not those kinds of supplies, asshole. We need food. Beer. You know, the two necessities."

I sighed and headed back into the bedroom.

"Let me unpack, and then we'll go into town."

♪ ♪ ♪

When I pulled the black rental into the driveway of Abrams' house after getting groceries, there was a beat-up red Honda sitting there.

We all grabbed the bags from the back and headed up the stairs. Truck and Mac were already discussing the grilling duties for the night. I was still eyeing the car that they didn't seem to have noticed or cared about.

We heard the music before we even hit the top of the stairs. Loud. Country music. It was blaring out the open windows, letting the air conditioning cool the humidity instead of the other way around.

The guys and I exchanged a curious look.

I opened the door in time to see a blur of dark hair and tan skin jump off the coffee table, guitar in hand, strumming and screaming along to the lyrics.

Except it wasn't really screaming. It was the huskiest, sexiest female voice I'd ever heard. Her hair was a tumble of dark curls and waves that flung out about her as she continued to move, swaying with the guitar and the lyrics. Her frame was all lean muscle with small curves in all the right places.

Her shorts barely covered those curves on her rear end, and a striped shirt was tied so that it bared her midriff, showing off more bronzed skin and muscles.

She was dancer and singer and girl all rolled into one. She hit me to my core and wouldn't let me move. The guys were equally stunned, standing behind me, watching her perform for an audience she hadn't even registered was there yet.

When she finally turned, mid-strum and mid-word, I was hit once more. This time by the intensity of her eyes that stared at me beneath dark lashes. One eye was as blue-green as a Caribbean island bay, while the other was almost muddy green like a Louisiana swamp. They didn't match. And yet, they fit her perfectly.

The joy that radiated across her face from her performance slid off, just as her hand slid off her guitar at the sight of us.

"What the hell?" Her husky voice, full of surprise, washed over me in a wave that told of unsteady seas. Of beauty and desire and storms. And I knew I was in trouble.

"Who the hell are you?" Mac asked, and I had to put a hand holding a bag of groceries out to prevent him from striding toward her.

Her face had closed down, the moment of joy disappearing behind a stone wall. A beautiful stone wall.

She slid the guitar behind her, the strap emphasizing her breasts that were small and pert and barely hidden by the knot of the shirt that sat below them. Tempting me. Tempting all of us.

She should have been intimidated by three muscled men at the door. She should have been unsure and maybe a little shaky, but she wasn't.

Instead, she climbed back onto the coffee table and, from there, stepped onto the couch so that she could get closer. She glared down at me from over the back of it. On the couch, she was barely taller than my six foot three. She put her hands on her hips, balancing on the soft cushions as if she owned it.

"Great. My dad's asshole recruits. Did he send you to retrieve me like some AWOL cadet?" she asked.

I heard her words, but it was difficult to register them because I was still awash in the waves of emotion that she'd sent through my body. Like being tipped over in an unseen current when you swam into a wave.

"Your dad? You mean Abrams is your father?" Truck asked.

Mac started laughing. "Holy shit, that would mean someone was actually brave enough to have sex with that bastard."

I dropped the groceries and slammed a fist into his shoulder—not hard enough to be a threat, but hard enough to make a point. "Asshole, that would be her dad you're talking about."

She laughed. A sound that was reminiscent of wind chimes lost inside a windstorm, muffled, but still strident. Sinking into your soul. "It's okay. I often wonder the same thing. What must my mom have been like if she was really willing to put up with him for eight years?"

We all just continued to stare at each other—her on the couch, us with our groceries by the door. "You'll literally have to drug and hog-tie me if you expect to take me back. Or you can just tell him you failed in your mission and enjoy the ocean view."

There was a moment where I think uncertainty crossed her face, a flash of something that wasn't confidence, but it was so quickly replaced with a rebellious look that I wasn't sure I'd even seen it.

"We weren't told you'd be here at all." I finally found my voice.

"I mean it. I'm not—Wait. What?"

"Professor Abrams gave us the place for eight days before our summer cruise in exchange for painting it," I explained.

She took me in then, really seeing me for the first time. She started at the top with my short hair that needed a cut, then traveled down to my hazel eyes before moving down to my snug T-shirt and tan skin from being near the sea. Once she'd traveled the length of me with her eyes, she returned them to mine, and my stomach flopped over. I wondered, vaguely, if this was how girls felt when my asshole friends looked them up and down in a bar.

She laughed, that husky tone reverberating down my spine once more. "Figures. Just my luck."

She flung herself down on the couch, her mirth filling the air. Truck, Mac, and I all exchanged a look. We weren't sure if she was an angel, or a demon, or just simply crazy.

Finally, she seemed to get ahold of herself, and she sat back up, her dark locks of hair swinging wildly about her face, her two-tone eyes taking in the three of us again. A smile brought her pink lips up at the edges in a way that made me want to touch them.

"I'm Ava. And it seems I've run away from home at the worst possible time."

Run away. Shit.

"How old are you exactly?" I growled. I didn't know if I was growling at her, or my own body's reaction to her, or at the guys who were staring at her like she was the best thing since dry clothes.

She waved at me like I was asking something inconsequential. "Don't worry. I'm not jailbait. I'm nineteen."

That didn't make her less jailbait in my mind. Messing with a professor's daughter was always out of the question. No cadet would ever look at a faculty member's child—girl, guy, or otherwise. It was the unspoken rule. You didn't shit where you slept.

More than that, though, I wasn't going to do anything that would get in the way of the life I saw for myself. Nothing.

"Not that I plan on sleeping with any of you, so y'all can pick your chins up off the floor," she said.

"What exactly did you mean by running away then?" Truck asked.

She looked at our supplies.

"Is that Corona?"

She leaped over the back of the couch, snagged one from the bags I'd dropped, and headed to the kitchen before any of us could really register that she'd even moved. Or that she'd ignored Truck's question.

It was evident that we were still in shock, because we just let her take the beer. At nineteen. Beer that we'd bought. That was a hell of a lot higher on the list of to-not-be-dones than sleeping with a professor's daughter. Aiding and abetting the delinquency of a minor. No. Not minor, but underage? All my knowledge of the law was stuck in a no-man's-land that was called Ava.

She turned back, the Corona open at her lips. "Do you have any limes in there?"

"Duh," Truck said. He was the first of us to move. He dropped his bags on the kitchen counter and started unloading them. When he found the bag of limes, he handed them to her.

She smiled at him, that gorgeous smile with lifted corners twitching, and I almost wanted to slam my best friend into the cabinets—for getting the smile, and for handing her the limes instead of taking the drink back.

Mac exchanged a look with me before shrugging and taking his bags into the kitchen. I was the last to follow. I was still lost in curled lips and a sexy voice and the threat to my unstarted career in the U.S. Coast Guard that was going to have me reaching for her beer and pulling it from those gorgeous lips.

Chapter Two

Ava

FLY

Performed by Maddie & Tae

I pulled a knife from the drawer and sliced the lime apart into wedges, squeezing and then stuffing one into the top of the Corona bottle.

I could feel them watching me. Mostly the tall, dark one. The man in charge. I hadn't even needed them to speak to know that he was exactly that. I'd been around my dad's corps of cadets enough to be able to spot the leader easily.

The leader was always the one in front. The one with an almost casual stride and stance that hid the coiled strength underneath it.

The blonde followed me into the kitchen first. After he'd opened his own beer and stuffed a lime inside, he put out his hand. "I'm Truck, that's Mac, and the attitude over there is Eli."

I couldn't help but bust out laughing. They all gave me that is-this-girl-really-crazy look, but I didn't care. "Mac Truck, really?"

Truck grinned and pulled Mac to him with a muscled arm.

"No one messes with the Mac Truck. We're like the superheroes of the cadet world."

"That's like saying you're the world's greatest sidekicks."

Truck faked a wounded grimace.

"Are you two…like…you know?" I asked, because who gave themselves a shared nickname in today's day and age unless they were a couple.

Mac pulled out of Truck's hold and said curtly, "No."

I chuckled. "There's nothing wrong with that, you know. If you are. I mean, I think you'd still get a lot of flack for it in the military, but—"

"We're not." Mac turned back toward me with a wicked smile that I bet many ladies adored. "I mean, there's nothing wrong with it if we were, but we're not. I don't think we'd be opposed to working out something with the three of us, though."

"Knock it off, Macauley." Tall and silent, Eli, finally spoke with a not-so-hidden warning in his voice.

Mac smiled at me with a shrug.

Eli made his way into the kitchen and quietly started putting the groceries away. I hopped up on the counter and watched them. Him.

He was leaner than either of the other two with a tattoo that peeked out from the back of his tight T-shirt at the neck. He was really more Jenna's type than mine: tall, dark, brooding. Normally, I was all about guys like Truck, with mischief in their eyes and blonde hair. But somehow, I found my body actually leaning into Mr. Silent when he opened the pantry beside me.

"I promise I won't bite you in the middle of the night," I teased, surprised as the words slipped out of me. There was something about this guy that pulled at the edges of me, daring me to push him. Push myself.

He met my eyes with hazel ones the color of wheat in the summer sun. We were both caught there for a moment, sea and sand and grains of straw mixing together in our eyes.

"There isn't going to be a middle of the night," he said.

If I was daring to disobey my father's commands just by being there, I certainly wasn't going to be forced to obey this man's. Not that I intended to spend the night with any of them. That wasn't why I was there. I was there because I had a couple days before I could head north, and I refused to spend it in the same house as my father. I couldn't do one more day without losing it. After trying to get past what he'd done earlier this year, the latest catastrophe I'd discovered had pushed me past the yellow, to green light, go.

Those thoughts brought me back to the beach house and the beer in my hand. I sighed and took a sip.

I was surprised when Eli pulled it out of my hand.

"You aren't twenty-one," he growled. It was an actual growl. Like one a guy in one of Jenna's sexy novels would do. It made my insides tighten in an unfamiliar way.

"You only know that because I was honest about my age. The license I have in my wallet says I'm twenty-two. Will that make you feel better?"

I jumped off the counter, landing closer to him than I'd been before. I went to grab the beer back, but he brought it to his lips and chugged it down instead.

I watched the movement, his Adam's apple moving underneath the smooth skin beneath the stubble that dotted his chin and cheeks in a way that it wouldn't if he was on duty.

When he was finished, his eyes turned down to meet mine again. There was something there. Not just desire. Something more that I didn't want to identify. Dad's cadets and I were like pineapple and pizza. They didn't belong together.

I had plans that were a long way away from cadets, and military colleges, and Texas. I didn't need anything getting in the way of that.

But I'd also had enough of people controlling my life, so I wasn't going to let this cadet dictate for me what I could and couldn't do. I moved away, taking another beer from the six pack in pure defiance. Like defying my father after he'd tried to take my future away. I stuffed another lime inside the bottle and moved out of the kitchen.

When I finally looked back at him, after sitting on top of the small dining room table, he was watching me. I just smiled and raised the beer to him before taking a sip.

I could see his whole jawline clench. I felt sort of bad. It wasn't his fault that he'd caught me in the middle of one of my worst weeks ever. Scratch that. Worst few months ever.

I took another drink while he eyed me. I wouldn't finish it. It would make me play sloppy later at the bar, and I never wanted that. I wanted to feel every moment of being onstage. It was what I lived for. I was determined to not let my dad, or anyone, or anything take that away from me again.

Maybe after my set it would be good to get drunk. Maybe it would allow me to forget, for a few hours, just how shitty things had been. But without Jenna, I wouldn't be able to get too drunk. We'd always been each other's safety valves. Only one of us drank at a time so that neither of us woke up having had something happen that we hadn't wanted.

I ached to call Jenna. The only remorse I had about what I'd done was leaving without telling her, without giving her my new number. I didn't want her to have to lie to my dad when he questioned her. She'd be his first line of attack once he realized that I wasn't at graduation. That I wasn't sitting in the chairs waiting for them to call my name like every other dumbass senior at that dumbass school he'd forced me to attend.

He'd be furious that I'd embarrassed him.

The three men finished putting away most of the food they'd bought in silence while I fought with my emotions, the pleasure of leaving tainted by the age-old fear and despair that came whenever I went against him. I had to remind myself there was nothing more he could do to me. Nothing I wasn't prepared for.

My country music was still blaring. It didn't seem to bother the cadets, but it was making me itch, making me want to pull out my guitar and start strumming along to forget everything but the music. So, I jumped down and went over to where I'd left my phone after syncing it to the expensive equipment Dad had recently bought for the home he rarely visited.

I switched over to a random playlist that Jenna and I used when we were getting ready to go out. Upbeat. Eclectic. Oldies and newbies mixed together.

Hoping it would chase away some of the anxiety that had crawled over my skin.

When I turned back to the men, they'd moved on to preparing dinner, working as a team with minimal communication on a simple meal of hamburgers and tots. Eli moved past me to the deck and the expensive, built-in barbecue.

I followed and watched as Eli lit the briquettes. The smell sent my brain into a swirl of memories of parties that Dad had held at our home in Galveston. Parties for his fellow faculty members. Sometimes his favorite cadets. I'd never seen these three among them. That either meant he didn't think they were connection-worthy, or it meant that they were smart enough to see Dad's slime for what it was.

Greediness. A need to be connected to someone who would make a bid for some high-powered government position someday. Someone he could ride along with, like he'd once tagged along behind my grandfather. Before I could remember. Before my mom and grandparents had been taken away, leaving me with just Dad.

I hated that I couldn't escape my thoughts of him today. I wanted so much to be free. Free of everything that was him.

I hopped up on the railing and slyly took a picture of Mr. Silent so that I could send it to Jenna later. She'd be all drool and no cool when I shared it. I already missed my best friend more than life. It was something I was going to have to get used to: life without Jenna beside me. Jenna was a typical Texas wildflower. Blonde. Blue-eyed. Perfectly done. She'd been my sanity since middle school, and now I was leaving her behind. I didn't think she'd be surprised, but I knew she'd be as sad as I was.

Eli finished stoking the fire and then turned, stopping when he saw me on the rail. His eyes squinted together in disapproval. I wanted to laugh. He belonged in the military. He was going to be a natural.

"I don't think you should be up there." His voice was still deep and guttural. Maybe I brought it out in him, or maybe it was his natural tone. My body liked it even as my mind protested.

"Does what you think always matter?" I asked.

A flicker of emotion went through his eyes. He hid it well behind his control and authority. Maybe like I hid my torn heart behind my sass and music.

"Just not interested in picking up blood and bones today," he said.

I looked down. Below me was the shell pathway that led out to the dock and the water. I wouldn't even be there on the deck or on the rail if I'd had another choice.

The room I'd sublet wouldn't be ready until the end of the week, and I didn't have enough money in my measly bank account to stay at a hotel and still pay my first month's rent. So, I'd come here because Dad didn't know that I knew that the renovations were done. That meant he wouldn't think about coming here until he'd run out of the possibilities closer to home. I intended to be gone before he did.

Now, my plans were in jeopardy because of the arrival of three muscled men. Cadets who might tell their professor about the arrival of his wayward daughter. Apprehension filled me.

"How worried do I need to be?" he asked.

His voice at my side startled me. I hadn't even heard him move. I wobbled on the rail, and he grabbed my waist before I could rebalance myself. His rough hands on my bare skin scorched me. They sent waves of desire and heat through my entire body, and when I met his eyes, I could see that it wasn't just *my* body that had reacted to our touch.

He removed his hands, tucking them into the pockets of his cargo shorts. Shorts that didn't seem to fit him as much as—I would bet good money—his uniform did. He backed away, taking my beer with him one more time.

"As long as you don't sneak up on me, there's nothing to worry about," I said, jumping down.

"Then what are you running from?" he asked. I could feel those hazel eyes taking me in, but I just turned to the ocean. The humidity filled the air and my lungs with every breath. Like it was a part of me. Part of this life that I was trying to leave behind. Weighing me down when I needed to be light so that I could fly away.

"A future that isn't mine," I said, looking back at him.

I could tell he was considering my words, assessing them. As if that was something he did with every comment anyone made. Careful consideration. Planning.

Mac made it out to the deck with a pile of burgers. He handed another beer to Eli, eyeing the one on the barbecue that Eli had taken from me, and then went to work at the grill.

"So, Ava, is Daddy going to show up pissed at the three of us?" Mac asked without looking at me.

I didn't blame him for asking. It was more than just the standard, "don't get involved with the professor's kid." Dad's reputation for reprisals was well-known and well-earned.

"I figure we have a couple days before he even thinks I might be here. He'll want to exert the least amount of energy possible in order to retrieve me, so he'll call before he shows up," I told them honestly, hoping they wouldn't rat me out.

"You're not staying here," Eli spoke up from his position leaning up against the doorframe.

I laughed, thinking he was joking, but then I saw his serious expression, and I knew he wasn't. I wondered if he ever joked about anything. "Look, jerk, this is my house, not yours. You can't kick me out. If you don't like that I'm here, then run along and get yourself a hotel."

"I told Professor Abrams that we'd paint the house," Eli said matter-of-factly.

"You can still do that while staying at a hotel," I responded.

Mac shifted uncomfortably.

They didn't have the money either. Staying in a hotel at the beach in the middle of the prime summer season was unlikely to be anything that three measly cadets could afford.

I just let the whole subject drop, but Eli was still watching me, waiting to see what I'd do. I just watched Mac at the grill.

The burgers smelled good. And I was hungry. I hadn't had anything since the caramel latte I'd grabbed at the gas station after making my escape. Food hadn't been on my list of priorities. Getting away had.

My stomach growled loudly enough for both the guys on the deck to hear it. Mac smiled, Eli almost smiled, and I chuckled.

"You going to try and kick me out before you feed me?" I asked.

They weren't kicking me out. They didn't know how stubborn I could be, but they'd find out. I wasn't planning on going to blows or anything—not that I could ever hope to fight off three muscled guys—but I wasn't going to be around enough for them to argue about it with me.

"Nah. You can eat with us," Mac said. I could tell Eli didn't like it. He wanted me gone. He didn't want me anywhere near their beach adventure regardless of how our bodies had reacted when he'd had his hands on my waist.

I didn't really want me anywhere near them either. For many of the same reasons.

Truck joined us on the deck.

"Tots are ready."

"Did you burn them to a crisp again?" Mac asked.

"No, wedgie-face, they're appropriately crisp."

"I didn't know cooking tater tots required a culinary degree," I teased, trying to lighten the mood. Lighten the heaviness inside me.

Truck gave me a serious look. "Tater tots are an art form, honey. Don't let anyone tell you otherwise."

I laughed, and he pretended to look offended.

No one said anything when I joined them in making up a burger and scooping tots from the pan. I was the first one to make it back out to the deck, and I found a spot on the top of the table. All three men stopped at the door when they saw me there.

I'd always felt more comfortable on top of things. It drove my dad crazy when I'd sit on the coffee table instead of the couch. Or the back of the couch instead of the cushions. Maybe that's what had encouraged it. Pushing the limits on the little things that I could get away with without being reprimanded.

None of the guys said anything. They just found seats in the chairs. So predictable. I'd give my right arm to find a guy someday who would join me atop the table. Like Michael Schoeffling with Molly Ringwald in *Sixteen Candles* that Jenna had made me watch. I didn't consider myself a romantic. And I definitely didn't want to find love yet, like Jenna had, because I had bigger plans for myself. But someday…someday, I'd love to find someone who would see things, even momentarily, the way I did.

The guys were a quiet group. It was something I was unaccustomed to. The boys I was usually around were rowdy and obnoxious, striving to gain attention and top-dog status at a high school that was considered the next coming of God. But really, they were all bottom dwellers. More reasons for me to not want anything romantic with any of them.

I'd take this silence over the stupid teen jokes any day of the week. Plus, I guessed these men were used to being silent during mealtimes. Military code everywhere they went at school. Not exactly your normal American college experience.

Once I was done, I slid down and brought my plate back to the kitchen. I could hear their hushed conversation but not the words. Even so, I knew it was about me.

I cleaned up the kitchen a bit as a thank-you for the meal and then walked back to the doorway. Their conversation halted.

"Well, it's been nice Mac Truck and Mr. Grumpy, but I'm outta here. I'll catch you later."

I grabbed my slouch handbag, my guitar, and my phone and headed out the door. I could feel their eyes on me when I got into my car and did a three-point turn to get around the black truck parked behind me, using the seagrass as a drive-way and probably leaving tire tracks where Dad wouldn't want them.

I rolled down the windows, waved my hand, and drove toward town. They didn't know, but "later" was going to be tonight when I needed a place to crash my head. I didn't have a choice about it, but for now, they could think I was gone.

Chapter Three

Eli

I MET A GIRL

Performed by William Michael Morgan

We all watched in stunned silence as Ava did a remarkable move with her car in order to get out from in front of the truck and then drove off into the setting sunlight. The whole place felt quiet in a way that it hadn't earlier. It felt like it was missing something. It wasn't just the music that had disappeared with her phone. It was that Ava had brought something to life inside the place.

"Well, hell, that's disappointing," Mac said.

I kicked him under the table. "Don't even think about it, dickwad."

"Too late. Anyway, she's gone," Truck said with a smile.

"Last thing any of us needs to do is get in the middle of some goddamn fight between Abrams and his daughter. And we definitely don't need him showing up here with her in any of our beds," I said and cringed, knowing they wouldn't let the "our" slide. And they didn't.

Truck grinned at me. "Visualizing it too, oh Captain my Captain?"

Mac kicked me back under the table. "Even this priest couldn't help but get his penis in a rise over her. Hell, you'd have to be dead not to respond to that."

"Again. Off limits."

"You can't tell my dick how to behave, Captain Prude," Mac continued to ride me.

I wasn't a captain, and I certainly hadn't been one when they'd started calling me Captain Prude. It wasn't that I didn't like girls or sex. I'd had great sex in my four years at A&M, but it wasn't with random chicks that I picked up in a bar every time we were allowed out of our cages like these two bozos.

I wasn't a relationship guy either, but I had a couple girls that seemed okay with being friends with benefits. It worked when we were all under a lot of pressure to perform academically and in the corps. Everyone needed to let off steam sometimes.

"I'm going to take a run on the beach."

I left them drinking their beer and drooling over Ava in a way that was bugging the hell out of me for no reason that I could justify.

I changed and headed down to the sand where I beat a track as far south as I could before I headed back. It helped me get my head refocused on how close I was to getting what I wanted and not on a girl with dual-colored eyes. The Coast Guard was so close to being a reality that I could almost feel the joy of signing the enlistment contract. One more summer cruise. Two more semesters. Months away. Almost close enough to be able to count it down in days.

The humidity, even as the stars started coming out, was enough to have me dripping. We were used to it from doing runs in Galveston, but it never made it pretty. I stunk like I'd been out to sea for a week by the time I returned to find the assholes watching an old eighties flick, *Goonies*. Truck's grandparents had owned a video store back when those were a thing, so he'd acquainted us with all the eighties and nineties classic movies during our time together in the dorms. If he wasn't watching some old movie, he usually had the American History channel on.

"Shit, I could smell you from the stairs, Elsworth," Mac said when the door swung shut behind me.

I shook my shirt out on him in response, and he jumped up, spilling his beer and screaming like a girl.

I chuckled as I headed down to the master suite and the shower with the two showerheads. Those two showerheads brought my dumbass male body right back to what I'd tried to escape: thoughts of a bright-eyed brunette with a lithe body and a sexy-as-hell mouth.

♪ ♪ ♪

I fell asleep somewhere around midnight with the French doors open and the sound of the ocean soothing me as it always did. There was no moon, and the house was far enough away from town and other residences that there was very little in the way of light pollution, so I could barely see my hand. It was like being below deck in the middle of a blackout.

When I woke, it was still dark, and I wasn't sure what had jerked me from my sleep with an unsteady heartbeat. Then, I heard a quiet curse that had me sitting all the way up. I heard another movement from out in the great room and was at the door and down the hall before I could really process it.

I was silent as I moved.

What I found was a drunk Ava. She smelled, from across the room, like booze. She was standing on one foot while she held the other in her hand, rubbing her big toe. As I watched, she swayed and would have hit the wood floor if I hadn't moved forward in a rush of movement.

I caught her, and she seemed as surprised as I was. As surprised as we both had been when I'd had my hands on her waist before dinner. The smell of her, like citrus and ocean, hadn't escaped me then or now. It was hidden at the moment, underneath the mask of booze, but it was still there, calling to me in a way that I hated and loved simultaneously.

She giggled. Although, with her husky voice, it almost didn't count as a giggle.

"Thanks," she said. She pushed off me, her hand searing my bare chest. I had to force my hands away from her as she sank down on the nearby coffee table.

"You're drunk." It was a stupid statement. Obvious. And it sounded accusatory when I had no right to be. I didn't know if I was upset that she had been out on her own, drunk, or if I was pissed that she was back and threatening everything that I held dear in my life.

She looked up at me, and I swear I could still see the difference in her eye color, even in the dark.

"And you're in your boxers," she said back.

Shit. I was. And tonight, I'd put on a ridiculous pair that my mom had sent me as a joke. I needed to do laundry.

"Are those Santa Claus-zes? Ses?" she asked with a slur and another chuckle.

"Did you drive back here?"

"No, *Dad*, I didn't drive. I took a CarShare."

I sighed, running a hand through the little stubble on top of my head that was longer than I could wear next week when I was back on duty.

"That's hardly better, is it?" I asked. "Where the hell did you leave your car?"

She slurred her response. "God, you really are going to make a great father someday."

It wasn't the first time someone had said that to me, but it was the first time I didn't know how to respond to it. A mix of emotions filled me from Ava saying it. I liked that I'd always had my head on straight. Focused. Living by the code of honor in the military before I ever became a true part of it. It was a way of honoring my dad. But a part of me ached at the thought of this free spirit seeing me as a father-like figure. Nothing was right about that. Not when my body was reacting to her like it was.

In fact, it was a fight to keep my body's reaction from becoming visible in a way that I'd never had to fight it since high school and Becky Anderson.

She pushed herself up from the table and headed down the hall in a drunken walk. She bumped into walls and made so much noise that I was sure Mac and Truck were going to come out of their rooms ready to start a fight.

"Where are you going?" I asked as I followed her.

"To bed," she said and entered the master suite.

"Not in here, you're not."

She was already on the bed, feet going under the sheet that was the only thing that I'd been using as a cover.

"Mac and Truck are in the other rooms, right?"

There was no need to confirm the obvious.

She had her head on the pillow that I'd been using. The king-sized bed was huge, and yet, somehow, she'd landed in the exact spot that I'd been lying in.

"Ava," I said her name for the first time. It sounded strange. Throaty. Like a word I shouldn't be saying.

Her eyes popped back open at her name, or the way I'd said it, or both. Those damn eyes stared at me. I had to fight off every nerve in my body that was demanding I jump into the bed beside her. Not that I'd ever sleep with a girl who was drunk. Not that I had any intention of sleeping with her. But Jesus, it was hard to ignore her.

I filled my head with visions of a contract on a table before me and a pen in my hand. That was what was real.

"There's plenty of room, Mr. Grumpy."

It sounded like an offer. An offer we both knew that I wasn't going to accept. She patted the bed behind her as if to reemphasize her point.

"You won't even know I'm here," she continued.

There was no way in hell I was climbing into that bed. Just as there was no way in hell I wouldn't know that she was there.

When I moved toward the bed, her lips curled up in a sly smile as if she actually expected me to join her. I reached over her and grabbed another pillow.

"Sleep good, drunkard, because tomorrow your sweet little ass is out of here."

I saw surprise register in her eyes before I turned away. I grabbed my phone and my water from the nightstand and headed down the hall to the couch.

It was still more comfortable than my bunk on board the TS Kennedy would be. It was long enough for my tall frame, and with the French doors open, it provided me just about the comfort I'd had in the master bedroom.

Sleep evaded me, though. The thought that she'd been out on the town, alone and drunk, wouldn't leave me. The possibilities of what could have happened to her in that state drove me nuts. The fact that she was here, in the house with the three of us, drove me nuts. My heart clenched at the thought of Abrams showing up with her in the bed…drunk.

Shit. She really needed to leave.

Eventually, when my phone finally showed four a.m., I just gave up. I slunk back into the bedroom. Ava was curled up in the exact place I'd left her, sheet wrapped in her hand, brilliant eyes shut, dark hair tumbling over the pillow and her face. Lying there, quiet, seemed contradictory to her nature. It seemed as odd as catching a hummingbird at rest instead of a flutter of wings you couldn't even see.

I shook myself out of my reverie and turned to the dresser. I quietly pulled out a pair of jeans and a T-shirt, grabbed my tennis shoes from the floor, and headed back out to the main room.

I dressed in the kitchen and pulled out a mixing bowl, filling it with half the box of Frosted Mini-Wheats that I'd bought at the store. My brain was still on Ava in ways I couldn't prevent.

Why was she here? *Escaping a future she didn't want*, she'd said. But we didn't live in the 1800s. It wasn't like her father was setting her up to marry some fifty-year-old duke or anything. It was the twenty-first century. She could be anything she wanted. Unless he refused to pay for her college, and even then, she could find ways to pay for it herself.

I shook my head, trying to clear out the thoughts of her, and drifted down to the garage where I started setting up for our morning of painting. We'd have to mask off a lot of the windows and doors. It would probably be easier to do a side at a time. I figured we might be able to get through one side a day. Especially if I started as early as this.

It was six before Truck joined me. Our early hours as cadets were hard to shake. He handed me a cup of coffee. I nodded my thanks, and he looked at the work I'd already done in turning the house a deep teal color that reflected the ocean.

"You got a big start. What put the burr in your butt this morning?" he asked.

"Ava." It still seemed strange to hear her name on my lips. Wrong and right and everything in between.

"Man, she twisted your dick up hard."

I realized he still had no clue that she was inside, in the bed I'd chosen, threatening all of our careers by simply being there.

I punched him hard on the shoulder, and he cussed at me.

"Dude, she's laying in my bed."

And hell, that sounded equally right and wrong.

Truck's smile increased to the size of the whole fricking state.

"Dude, Captain Prude stuck his dick in?"

"Asswipe, she came back drunk as a skunk. I slept on the couch. I'm surprised neither of you douchebags heard her come in."

"I might have had one too many myself," he admitted with a shrug as he rubbed his shoulder.

I'd already filled the spray gun twice by the time Mac saw fit to join us, and the backside of the house, top and bottom, was almost done by the time we caught sight of Ava. She was showered with her wet hair pulled up in a nest of a bun atop her head. She was wearing nothing but a red and white polka-dotted bikini. The three of us stood there, staring like the goons we were, as she came down the steps in her flip-flops with a beach chair, a towel, and a mesh bag in her hand.

She stopped by me first, her scent wafting over me again. She looked at the house, and I tried to ignore every thought I was having about her nearly naked body.

I forced myself to envision my contract. Signing the contract.

"Nice job, boys." The deep quality to her voice kept catching me off guard. It crept down my spine, continuing to call my nerves to attention.

"I'm off to the beach. You know what John Kennedy said about it, right?"

We all continued to watch her without comment. "'We are tied to the ocean. And when we go back to the sea, we are going back from whence we came.' So I guess I'm off to join my past with my future."

None of us responded. We were confused by her words and floored by her body and her confidence. It wasn't like we hadn't seen a sexy woman in a bikini before. It wasn't like we hadn't seen sexy women in our bedrooms completely naked, but there was something about Ava that dumbfounded us all.

Maybe it was her lack of discomfort at her almost nakedness, or her sureness in her own skin, or maybe the fact that she was stunning and completely off limits.

When none of us had responded, she just shook her head and headed down the cracked shell path to the dunes and the dock just behind the house.

Truck was the one to find his voice first. "I think it's time to call it a day and hit the beach."

Mac grinned.

"Hell, yeah."

They handed me their equipment and took off into the house. I sighed, cleaning up our mess, Ava's words ringing in my head. I was tied to the sea, just like she'd said. It was my past and my future, too. Twelve years of hard work wasn't going to be thrown away because of one intriguing nineteen-year-old.

I was still cleaning up when Mac and Truck had the nerve to walk by me in their own swim trunks with beach towels and a cooler in hand.

"Hey, assholes, thanks for leaving me with the cleaning."

"Hey, shrunken penis, thanks for signing us up to paint the goddamn house at all," Mac hollered back with a smirk that I wanted to wipe off his face.

An hour later, I had showered and changed into a clean pair of jeans. I was on the deck outside the master bedroom. I could hear faint laughter coming from the dock and the private beach that belonged to the Abrams property.

It was calling to me. In jealousy as much as desire. What were they saying that was making her laugh? Not that it seemed like she needed much to make her laugh. But Mac and Truck weren't exactly a comedy team. They were all stupid male charm.

Anger flitted through me. At them. At her for even being here. As if to prove my point, my phone buzzed. It was my mom and, thankfully, not Professor Abrams. I just let it go to voicemail because I didn't want Mom to hear in my voice all the things that were in my head.

My thoughts turned to what would happen if it really was Professor Abrams calling. I'd have to tell him she was here. I didn't have another choice. If I lied, he could end my future.

Still, I heard Ava's voice in my head about escaping a future that wasn't hers. I understood wanting a future that you desired. I understood putting that first. She wasn't exactly underage. If she didn't want her dad to know where she was, what business was it of mine?

Regardless, I knew I'd tell him she was there. I had to make her see that it was best for everyone if she left.

I changed into a pair of my own swim trunks, made sandwiches in the kitchen for everyone, and then headed down to the beach. The three of them had beers in hand when I got there. Ava was sitting on top of a rock, her beach chair abandoned to Truck. Mac was juggling a football in one hand and his beer in the other.

"Dad! You decided to join us," Ava called out.

This got both the guys' attentions as they looked in panic up toward the path as if they expected

Professor Abrams to actually be standing there—which was exactly my point. None of us would survive if he showed up. When they saw it was me, they both smirked their approval of Ava's nickname.

"Dad, did you make us lunch?" Mac asked with a smile.

"Dude, you shouldn't have," Truck said.

As they both reached for the sandwiches, I pushed them off. "Buzz off, bugs. These are all mine."

Ava's laugh rang around me. "You really going to eat eight sandwiches?"

I shrugged and then smiled at her before offering her the stack when I should be starving her so she'd leave. Instead, I was goddamn feeding her. "Ham or turkey?"

"I'm not picky," she responded. I hated that response. I wanted her to be extremely picky, but I just plucked one off the top and handed it to her before handing two to each of the other morons on the beach.

After we'd eaten in silence again, Mac, Truck and I hit the sand, tossing the football around while I tried to figure out what to say that would make her leave. Mac was showing off both his muscles and his prowess with the pigskin. If it was for Ava's benefit, it was useless. She had her head in a notebook, pencil in hand, scribbling inside. She'd pause occasionally, sticking the pencil in her mouth while looking out at the ocean, and then go back at it with an eraser and then the tip again.

After quite a while, she smiled. Whatever she'd written pleased her. She stuck the pencil up into the mess of her bun and tossed the notebook onto the towel at her feet.

She bounded off the rock and approached Truck who had made the mistake of turning his back on her. She easily stole the football from him, twirled it in her hands as if it was something she did every day, and then tossed it back to him as she moved toward the ocean.

"Going in. Any of you Hulk wannabes think you can beat me to the buoy and back?"

She was in the water, striding out toward the buoy with strong, perfect motions like she did everything, before Truck dropped the football and raced after her. Mac was behind him in two breaths. I shook my head. They were going to kill themselves competing over her.

For some reason, it didn't bother me the way it had the day before when they'd talked about sleeping with her or even when I'd been up on the deck listening to them on the beach. Maybe it was because, since I'd been on the sand with them, Ava had done nothing but treat them both like two big brothers. I hadn't seen one moment of connection between her and them like the one that had zipped between us when we touched.

Which was the problem. Nothing should be between me and a girl who I'd known less than twenty-four hours and who was a bigger danger to my future than anything ever had been in my life. Even my mom's disapproval of my career choices had never threatened my future in a way this one girl did.

I followed them into the water but didn't even bother to join the race. Instead, I dove in, letting the calm waves of the bay drift around me. Once I was far enough out, I took a breath and sunk as far down as I could go with the waves pushing and pulling me.

I was under there a long time, thinking about my future. Thinking about Ava. Thinking about ways to get her to leave. Suddenly, a pair of muscled girl legs and pink toe-nailed feet landed before me. I pushed off the bottom and came up in front of her, the water spraying off me and all over her.

"I thought you drowned," she said as I looked down into her eyes.

"I told you not to worry," Truck hollered out at her from the buoy.

She flipped him the bird without ever taking her eyes off me.

"You were under there a long time," she said quietly, eyes taking me in as if she was trying to get underneath my skin and understand every thought that was going on inside me.

"Training."

She rolled her eyes. "Of course. Stupid cadet corps."

"Why do you think it's stupid?" I asked, not quite offended but something close. The Corps was not only my home, it was my future and my past twined together.

She shrugged. "I don't, really. I mean, my experience is probably just tainted looking at it through my dad's eyes."

I reached out toward her, and she watched my hand almost like she had last night when I'd reached for the pillow. There was expectation and hesitation and something else in her eyes.

I pulled out the pencil she'd stuck into her bun. I wasn't sure how it had survived the water and the swim, but it was still tangled there, and it took me a bit to remove it.

"I think you might have ruined your pencil." I handed it to her, and she took it, her eyes still on mine as our fingers collided.

We stood like that, staring at each other, feeling the tangle of desire that was floating around us in almost the same way as the ocean was ebbing back and forth around our waists.

"You're different from the rest," she said quietly, eyes never leaving my face. Most people couldn't maintain eye contact for that long. With Ava, it was like she purposefully extended every look, waiting for something in yours. It was intense and freeing at the same time.

"Nope. I'm just the same," I told her truthfully. Just another cadet. Just another guy trying to get ahead in this crazy world.

Her pink lips turned up at the corners. One of the corners always tucked deeper into her cheek when she smiled like this. It was the reason I wanted to touch it. It was on the same side as her muddy green eye. Like they belonged together.

She turned away and started walking through the waves toward the shore. "Keep telling yourself that, Mr. Grumpy."

I watched her as she made her way to the sand, untangling the bun on her head, shaking it out, her body and curves moving with the motion. She gathered all her belongings and headed up the path to the house.

Mac Truck joined me. We were all watching her again. It was like a repeat motion from every time she left us.

"She's gonna give some guy a serious heart attack someday," Mac said. I heard the tone in his voice with relief. He'd already thrown in the towel. If a girl was too much work, it was never Mac's thing. He wanted quick, easy, and painless. He wanted to be in and done.

Truck smacked me on the back of the head, Gibbs style. We all did it to each other. It was one of our things. "I think Captain Prude might just be having his own heart attack over her."

I rolled my eyes and slammed my fist into his shoulder, causing him to stumble in the water. But he was laughing and smiling. He'd thrown in the towel, too. Maybe because he could see the attraction that I felt and knew that I rarely got that way over a girl.

Truthfully, though, I'd never thrown my hand into the game. I wouldn't. I couldn't.

Chapter Four

Ava

GROOVY LITTLE SUMMER SONG
Performed by James Otto

By the time the three guys made it back to the house, I had my country music blaring from the speakers again, and the place smelled like tacos. I had made dinner for everyone out of the supplies they'd bought the day before. I even had a pitcher of margaritas sitting ready on the counter.

It was probably a little presumptuous, but I meant it as a peace offering, hoping they'd not use their muscles to throw me out of my own house.

"Do you clean, too?" Mac asked with his normal snark, and I responded with a finger just like I had earlier. Seemed to have become our thing over the course of twenty-four hours. It felt strange that I'd only been with them that long. In some ways, I was as comfortable with the three of them as I was with Jenna. That was unusual. The only time I was usually comfortable with people was when I was onstage.

We all made plates of food and went out to the deck again. I took the same spot on the table top as I had the day before. Most sane people would be pissed that my feet were on the table near their food, but none of the boys even made a comment. In fact, Eli seemed engrossed by my toes with their chipped nail polish from my time in the sand and the sea.

We ate quietly again. It was weird and not weird. I finally broke the silence.

"Who does the truck belong to?"

"It's just a rental," Eli responded with a shrug.

I took him in, surprised. He didn't look old enough to be able to rent a car. "You're twenty-five?"

He shook his head. "Nah, I'm only twenty-two. I just have connections at the rental car company."

"Interesting," was all I could respond because it was. Who was his connection? Why would they let someone who was not old enough rent a truck? What other rules did they break for him? My guess was that it was someone of the female persuasion, because I'd bet he could get a lot of women to break rules for him. He made me want to break my own rules. But he didn't seem like the rule-breaking type.

"Why do you ask?" His eyes lifted to mine, and I got lost in them a little. The wheatlike hazel had turned dark, like whiskey filtering through a gorgeous bottle. He was like the alcohol—strong and bitter but gorgeous.

I pulled myself back from his eyes and back to the truck. "I need a ride into town, but if you have plans, I can CarShare it."

"You going out drinking again?" he asked, and I couldn't help but smile at the slightly accusatory tone that was there.

"Why do you care, Dad?"

He didn't get a chance to respond, though, because Truck responded for him.

"Eli owes us a drink at the bar. We can take you."

Eli shot him a glare.

"Cool." I jumped down. "I'm going to go shower."

I headed inside toward the bedroom that Eli had claimed but relinquished to me the night before. Their voices halted me before I got too far.

"Was that an invitation?" Mac asked.

"Not for you, asswipe," Eli snapped back.

Mac laughed. "For you, Captain Prude? Would you even know what to do with a girl like her?"

"Not me either, Macauley," Eli said.

Mac groaned. "Please. Not that."

"It's at least your name. That shit you call me isn't anything close to my name."

"Am I getting on your nerves, oh Captain, my Captain?"

"Cut it out, or I'm gonna have to put you in a headlock."

I could hear the humor in their voices. The friendship. I just shook my head and continued into the bedroom.

I had showered, changed, and was putting on a coat of lip gloss that I rarely wore when Eli finally made it into the bedroom. I knew he wouldn't be able to put it off forever, because his things were there.

I was sitting on the bed in my shorts, a pair of cowboy boots, and a slouchy top with a tank underneath. If the top ended up bugging me enough when I played tonight, I'd just lose it for the tank.

I'd left my hair loose, too. It was more likely to irritate me than the top would. For now, I let the curls swing down to the middle of my back, cascading around me in the way that Jenna told me suited me best. I'd never been sold on it completely. Especially when it got tangled between my hands and my guitar strings.

Eli seemed to appreciate the look, and it made my stomach flip in excitement that I knew I shouldn't feel. That I didn't want to feel for a cadet at Dad's school. I watched him over the handheld mirror I was using as he took in my hair and my outfit and then back to my hair.

He was both easy and hard to read. Typical guy, responding to typical girl things like hair and boobs, but he never had the same reactions that most of the guys I knew had. My last boyfriend—could I even call him that?— always dragged me onto his lap whenever he saw me with my hair down and shoulder bared, but I was never comfortable in another person's embrace. It felt awkward and unfamiliar.

Marco had been okay to fool around with. Not that I ever let it go too far, because I wasn't going to get all emotional over some guy who would tie me to Galveston—like Jenna and all the girls I knew had gotten completely wrapped up in the guys they'd lost their virginity to. That wasn't going to be me. I had bigger things in the works. Bigger dreams.

I wonder what fooling around with Eli would be like, though. If the intensity I felt every time his hands touched me was anything to go by, it would be over-the-top insane. Something I might lose my head over like my friends had. Yet another reason to make sure it didn't happen.

"You done in there?" He nodded toward the bathroom.

"Would it matter?" I quirked back just to get a reaction from him, and I was rewarded with him squinting his eyes in disapproval. I chuckled. "Yes, Mr. Grumpy, it's all yours."

He grabbed his clothes and shut the door behind him. I heard the lock click, and I couldn't help but laugh. I knew he heard it, but I didn't care. What did he think? That I was going to go barging in there and leap into the shower with his naked butt? Even though it had looked pretty amazing in his swim trunks. He hadn't worn the typical baggie swim shorts like so many guys I knew. His had been more like what an athletic swimmer wore. It made me wonder if he did swim at A&M.

I'd left the bedroom behind and was teasing Mac Truck when Eli came out of the bathroom in a pair of jeans and a tight T-shirt. His T-shirt had the Coast Guard symbol over his heart. It was the same symbol that I'd seen tattooed on his back when he'd been shirtless at the beach. Except the one on his back had some words written around it that I'd been too far away to read.

It surprised me that he was going into the Coast Guard. At least, that's what I was guessing. Most cadets from the academy hit up the Navy or the Air Force, trying for the iconic SEALs or NASA astronaut program. Going for glory.

Applying to the Coast Guard was usually a last option, not a first. It made him stand out even more. It made me want to ask a million questions that I knew he'd never answer. He didn't share. And I was leaving…tonight. I couldn't stay and put us all at risk from my father's reprisals. I just needed the dollars from tonight to be tucked into my new bank account that my dad didn't know about.

Mac Truck gave me the front seat while they squeezed into the tiny back seats. I protested, but they just ignored me.

When we pulled downtown, I directed Eli to the Bay Grill Bar and Restaurant where I'd left my car the night before after leaving Lacey and Andy. The good thing about having an old, used Honda was that I could pretty much leave it anywhere, and no one bugged it. There wasn't anything to want from it.

Mac and Truck headed for the mahogany doors of the bar. Eli swirled the keys around on his fingers while he watched me unlock my car and throw my purse inside. My guitar was tucked into the trunk where I'd left it the night before.

"Where are you going?" he asked.

"Does it matter?" I answered and turned to take him in.

God, he was heartbreakingly gorgeous. And I was definitely starting to see the appeal that Jenna had for tall, dark, and broody.

"Are you leaving?" It was said without a trace of emotion, but the expression in his eyes didn't match. There was emotion there. Relief mixed with disappointment.

"Gonna miss me already?"

He looked away. Most people looked away. I'd been practicing the long stare for a while now. Ever since I'd read *180 Seconds* by Jessica Park. The longer you stared, the more you saw in people. I'd learned a lot that way. But the fact that he looked away, when he hadn't before, confused me.

"You know what Dolly says, 'If you don't like the road you're walking, start paving another one.' So that's me. Paving the new road," I told him.

"What should we tell your dad?"

My turn to feel disappointed, and it curled through my gut like too much candy. He just wanted to know how to cover his tracks with my father. The truth was, I didn't want them getting in trouble because of me, it was part of the reason why I was leaving now instead of at the end of the week. My dad could make life hell for anyone that got on his wrong side; I knew that in the harshest ways possible. I didn't want that to be them.

"Tell him whatever you want," I told him with a shrug and went to get into the car.

I didn't hear him move, but then he had a hand on my arm, gently halting me. I was surprised enough that I fell into him again, like I had several times since he'd entered my life.

He steadied me but didn't remove his hand. Energy soared around us as thick as the humidity. Sewing us together in a way that was like my notes and lyrics. In a way that had caused me to write a whole song on the beach while he and the boys had played with the football.

I looked up, and his eyes had darkened again, his almost black eyebrows furrowing together. "Ava, are you okay?"

My heart stopped.

Was I okay? When was the last time anyone but Jenna had asked me that? I couldn't remember. Was I okay? I asked myself that question a lot. I didn't really have an answer, even for myself. I met his stare. I wouldn't be the one to look away. Didn't he know that yet?

"Why do you ask?" I finally breathed out continuing to watch the movement of his irises as they took me in.

"Just…you said you were running. And you're here. And talking about the sea taking you back… and drinking…" His words trailed off as if he wasn't sure what else to add, but his eyes still remained on mine, the pupils widening slightly, his eyes moving down to my lip-gloss-coated lips and then back to my eyes. I was slightly amazed that he'd listened to the John Kennedy quote I'd thrown out about the ocean. I wasn't used to anyone really listening to my quotes. Even Jenna flew past them most of the time in our conversations.

I thought a moment more before I gave him a response.

"I'm better than I've been in a long time," I told him. And as I said the words, I realized they were true. I was better than I'd been in years. Because, for the first time, I was free. Free of guilt and expectations and regrets. I was free.

I think he could see the truth in my eyes. He nodded.

"Okay," he said, and he backed away as if it was costing him a lot to do that simple action. He took me in, from head to toe, and a smile hit his lips. A full smile that I hadn't seen yet. And it was stunning. It changed his whole face. Instead of hard lines and hard expressions, it became this glorious softness. I'd heard the expression before that a smile changed a face, but I'd never seen it until then. On Eli.

He took a step toward the bar door. "If you need anything, will you call me?"

The smile was gone again, but there was still a remaining softness lingering in his expression.

"I don't have your number, Dad," I teased. I saw him flinch at the name and wished, immediately, that I hadn't used it.

"You do." He left, entering the building and leaving me stunned.

I got into the car, pulled my phone out, opened the contacts, and saw, instead of one, two. The first one was called "Girlie" and that was the one that I had entered with Jenna's number. The other was called "Mr. Grumpy" and had an area code that I didn't know.

I didn't know how to react to his having put his number in my phone. Some guy I barely knew. Some guy who lived by a code. I shook it off. I was sure he put it there because if something happened to me, he'd want to be able to tell my dad he'd done his best to look after me.

I started the car and drove down the street. I wasn't leaving yet. I had a gig tonight, but I planned on hitting the road afterwards. It was almost a thousand miles to Nashville. That was my destination. I had a new life waiting for me there. Dad didn't know that. A job, a room, and a course at a Tennessee junior college. It was just temporary. It wasn't the end game, but I'd have to wait for the fall before I could reapply to Juilliard. This time, I wasn't going to screw it up. Dad wouldn't be there to screw it up for me.

I drove down the street, turned twice, and ended up at Andy and Lacey's Salty Dog Bar, not far from where Eli and Mac Truck were. But the guys wouldn't know I was there.

I pulled in, got out my guitar and my playlist, and went inside. Andy was on the stage with the house band. When I joined them, Ben and the other guys in the band waved at me while Andy frowned and said, "You're late."

I laughed. "By two minutes. And no one here is expecting live music for another hour."

"You're lucky I'm letting you play at all this year." He was almost as grumpy as the cadet I'd left down the street.

"You love it when I play." I kissed his cheek, right above his salt-and-pepper-colored beard. "You make good money when I play."

"I keep waiting for someone to take that ego of yours and douse it with a good reality check," he muttered.

I'd had reality. Every day of my life living with my dad. But regardless of what my dad told me, I knew that the music inside of me was meant for something that my dad couldn't see. Didn't want to see. Refused to see. But I could see it. My dream. And I was going to go after it no matter what. Even if he said that it was going to be my ruin just like chasing dreams had been my mom's ruin.

I just smiled and turned to Ben and his band.

"Night two and no dad coming to bust us up?" Ben asked.

God, I hoped not. Last summer, Dad had caught me coming to play, and he'd thrown such a hissy fit that I thought Andy was going to get his liquor license pulled. But I'd been eighteen. There wasn't any law against me playing in a bar as long as I wasn't drinking.

Dad had his own way of thinking, though. I'd ended up without my guitar, phone, or car keys for the rest of the summer. It wasn't the first time he'd taken my guitar and phone away. He knew they were the things that caused me the most pain. Unable to hear my music, except in my head. Unable to talk with Jenna, who was my sanity.

"Thanks for letting me sing with you again, Ben," I told him. I was pretty sure that Andy gave him and his band the same amount of money they normally got when I sang with them. It was the only thing that made it okay for me to take some of their stage time as I knew that Ben used the money for his daughter's dance lessons. A father supporting his daughter…I would never get in the way of that.

"We're always glad to have you, Ava. The crowd really goes up a notch with you leading the way," Ben said.

It made me smile. That Andy and Ben believed in me.

"Don't be giving her a hard time, Andy," Lacey, Andy's wife, hollered at him from the bar. I smiled at her as Andy waved her off. Lacey winked at me. I blew her a kiss.

Thank God she'd been with me the night before when I'd gone to the Bay Grill after playing. I'd wanted to be drunk, and I'd done a good job of it, and she'd understood. Understood what running from Dad was costing me as much as it was giving me.

I was on my own. Monetarily as much as physically. Emotionally, I still had Jenna, who I was still aching to call but didn't dare yet. This next year was going to be a true test of all my survival skills. I wasn't sure how, but I'd make it.

I forced my thoughts back to the band, focusing on the thing that I could make a difference with tonight…the music. The band and I went through my song list. Soon, I'd forgotten all about Eli, and the cadets, and my dad. Soon, I was just lost in the notes and the lyrics. It was me, the band, and the stage. Just the way I loved it.

Chapter Five

Eli

SPEECHLESS
Performed by Dan + Shay

The bar that Ava left us at was packed with tourists. A crowd that was shiny and spoiled and worth way too much money for my taste. It wasn't a bar you could sink yourself into, and it surprised me that it was where she'd gotten drunk the night before. It didn't seem like the Ava I'd come to know over the last…twenty-four hours.

Shit. It seemed so much longer than that. Like I'd been around her for a month already. It didn't matter. She was gone. Relief filled me but also disappointment. I didn't understand it myself. She was bad news for all of us, and it was good that she was gone. Yet, I couldn't help worry that she'd gone on a journey to who knew where at nineteen, by herself.

It was why I'd made the huge leap that most would consider border line psycho and put my number in her phone. She had another number in there, and she could easily call the person she'd labeled "Girlie," but I'd still felt compelled to do it. At least, that's what I was telling myself—that it was the obligation to Abrams that had me doing it and not the strange attraction I'd felt for her pulling at me since she'd shown up.

When we ordered off the tap and declined the oyster appetizer, the waitress slunk off in a huff. She could see her tip dwindling away even though she had been flirting with Mac. She was just his type—all Texas blonde bombshell.

We nursed our ten-dollar beers because none of us were really into the thought of losing a hundred dollars on alcohol we could have for a dollar back home at a college happy hour.

"I'm ever so slightly disillusioned," Truck said as he drank the last swallow and set down the glass.

He was looking around. He meant he was disillusioned in what he and Mac liked to call "the talent." Because this crowd wasn't going to be into a muscled cadet who still had a year left of college. Maybe if he was actually in the Navy and in his white dress uniform, he would have attracted some of their attention. Instead, this crowd was much more about the sailboats in the harbor and the expensive Lighthouse Inn down the street.

"There's got to be a better local hot spot," Mac added.

We each set down our share of the tab and left behind the rich atmosphere. Mac and Truck argued over the passenger seat, and then, we drove around the little town of Rockport. A lot of the stores and restaurants were still open, allowing the tourists to wander around shopping as the light refused to fade from the sky. It was humid and hot, but we had the windows down, enjoying the atmosphere.

We found a pizza joint and a semi-permanent taco truck that we agreed we'd come back to another time.

We were just about to call it a no-go and return to our store-bought beer at the beach house when I spotted Ava's car.

She hadn't left town at all. She'd ditched us for another bar. It looked like a place the locals definitely hung out. Not quite a hole-in-the-wall, but close. There was a bouncer at the door and a small crowd waiting to get in with music blaring from the doors. Country music.

I swung the truck into the parking lot, sliding into the spot beside her car. We all got out without having said a word. We got in line, and I could already hear her voice. Husky. Sexy. Filling the street with it. Goddamn. She'd ditched us for not only a better bar, but so that she could play a gig.

The disappointment I'd felt earlier at the thought of her leaving turned into unwanted waves of anticipation at seeing her again—when I hadn't expected to ever see her again. And then I felt slightly pissed, because not only was she still here threatening everything I held dear, but I'd also basically poured my heart out to her, telling her that I was worried about her, and she'd left me to go play at some bar, wearing her short-shorts and a shirt that wouldn't stay on her shoulder. With her hair cascading around her in a way that would have tempted Satan himself.

By the time we reached the door and were finally allowed to pay the ten-dollar cover to get in, I was in a surly mood. And when I saw her, it didn't get better.

Because she was glowing. And every sexual being in the place was drooling over her. She was onstage, guitar swung back behind her, accenting her breasts again. She was letting the band behind her play the music while she crooned into the microphone that she had left on the mic stand and was all but caressing like a lover.

I didn't hear a goddamn word, but it all went directly into my body. Heart. Soul. Dick. I couldn't help but respond to her like everyone else was. Maybe more.

She was like a sea nymph. Something you knew in your rational brain that you needed to avoid at all costs but couldn't help but be drawn to when you saw her.

"Damn," Truck muttered beside me.

Mac came up on the other side, and we all watched as she crooned into the microphone while the crowd ate her up with their eyes and their hearts.

We were at the back of the room. No way she could see us with the lights in her eyes, but every time she glanced our way, my heart would surge hopefully. Stupidly. I hated myself for feeling it. There was nothing to hope for. Nothing here, and yet, I couldn't tear myself away from her.

Ava was in her own world. Like she had been when we'd walked in on her singing on the coffee table. She was the music. It was her. Like the sea was me and I was the sea. So, I understood why she was there, on that stage, but I also found myself getting angrier with her.

For not telling us that she was coming to play. For letting me believe she was leaving.

At the end of the song, the crowd erupted like thunder. Mac and Truck moved off to a table in a back corner, flagging down the waitress to get a beer. I stood where I was, in the exact spot that I'd been in since I'd first seen her onstage.

She drank from a goddamn beer that someone in the band handed her, high-fived them, and then turned back to the microphone. She pulled it from the stand and spoke into it.

"I think it's time to speed things back up. We got a space there to dance, right? I want to see all of you on your toes now. Don't let me down."

It was a cover song. Something upbeat that everyone knew except me because I'd never been overly into music. It was almost always just background noise to me.

I watched, fascinated, as she flipped the guitar around and strummed some chords with the band before going back to singing. The energy was coming off her in waves, like an undertow, and I was going down.

She reached the end of the stage beside the bar, and I watched in horror and wonder as she leaped from the stage to the top of the bar in one fluid movement. Cat-like. Effortlessly. Still singing. She moved down the bar, swinging her hips, twirling, singing down into the faces of the scruffy-looking locals that were lucky enough to be sitting there.

She wasn't showing off anything. Everything was covered, even if she had lost the slouchy top for just the tank top that had been underneath. Nothing was on display, yet I couldn't help but feel like she was entirely on display. That she was more naked singing on the bar than she had been in her red polka-dotted bikini on the beach with us.

She stayed on the end of the bar, away from me, and she had hopped back onto the stage before I could even think of moving. She finished the song, smiled at the applause, and dove into another song that had the crowd two-stepping—or whatever the hell it was called—on the makeshift dance floor that had been made by pushing tables away.

I heard my name and looked over to where Mac Truck sat. Truck was waving me over with a confused look on his face. Mac was flirting with some woman who'd had the unfortunate luck to be sitting at the table next to him. I ignored it all and remained where I was, turning back to the stage. To Ava.

To the girl who had said she was leaving behind a life that wasn't hers. And I think I finally understood. She was running away from normal. For this. To turn her normal, glorious self into something even brighter.

She sang another fast-paced song, the crowd loving her, the band loving her as she interacted with them and the audience.

"Okay, folks, my time is almost up," she said, and the crowd groaned. "I'm gonna sing one more thing for you while the band takes a break."

Cheers.

She started on her guitar by herself as the band behind her filtered away for water and the break she'd mentioned. Her song was a yearning note that built slowly. Her eyes were closed, and she started to sing about wanting more. And I didn't know if it was supposed to be about wanting more of one person, or more of life, or just more, but the throaty, sexy way her voice sang resonated with every person in the room.

My anger had all but dissipated, leaving in its wake a longing that I'd never had in my life for anything but the sea and the Coast Guard. A longing that had the possibility of surpassing the longing I'd had for those things. The unexpected threat to all my dreams that I'd seen her to be. I couldn't let her pull those dreams apart, and yet I couldn't walk away. I'd never felt so torn in my entire life as I did watching her sing about wanting more.

She took the guitar off, its notes fading as she took the mic from the stand again and sang to no notes. To no music. Just her and the mic. And she jumped again from the stage to the bar, and for the first time since I'd entered, my feet moved toward her. They led me to a vacant spot at the bar top, and when she reached me, I couldn't help but reach out my hand as if to help her down off the damn thing.

She looked at me, surprise registering in her eyes. Then she smiled, that smile that had me wanting to touch those lips, and this time, not with just my fingers. I wanted to devour them with my own, even though I knew that doing so would put everything at risk.

She shook her head ever so slightly at me, but I wasn't letting her walk away from me twice in one night. I reached out and grabbed her cowboy boot by the ankle.

The old guy at the bar frowned at me, but I ignored it as he watched to see what Ava's reaction would be. If she wanted to, she could kick me in the face with those pointed boots, and I was sure I'd have a broken, bloody nose. She could take care of herself easily from our positions, but she just smirked at me. When I pushed my free hand up to her again, she took it.

Our fingers twined together, the heat scoring me, as I steadied her as she stepped onto the barstool. Then, she caught me off guard by wrapping her hand around my neck and sinking into my arms like I was carrying her over the threshold.

She continued to sing, her voice a little breathy now. Caught by our movements. Caught, I hoped, by the effect I had on her, because she sure as hell had affected me.

When the song ended, she smiled her heart-stopping smile and said into the mic, over the applause that was bursting from the room, "Say hello to Mr. Grumpy, everyone."

There was laughter and more applause.

She turned the mic off, and the room stared at us, frozen by the bar with her still in my arms and me unsure of what the hell had happened and what I should do now. Eventually, the bartender took her mic, and the band started playing, and everyone moved on, even if they did still turn every so often to watch us curiously.

"Are you going to put me down, or do I need to jump?" she teased.

She didn't ask, "Why are you here?" or "Why did you grab me?" Instead, she was full of her normal sass. Like this had all been part of her every-day norm. It was nothing close to the norm for me. It was the complete opposite.

"You told me you were leaving." It sounded angry even to my own ears. And I knew that I really had no right to be. None. I wanted her gone, and I wanted her to stay. So ridiculous. I was mad at her for both, leaving and staying.

"I never said that, but to be fair, I did allude to it."

She pushed on my chest, and I let her slide down, her body touching every piece of me in ways that weren't good in a crowded bar. When her boots hit the ground, she stepped back, looking up at me with her eyes flashing different colors and different emotions.

"You can't leave now. You've been drinking." It was a poor excuse. I knew it. She knew it. I didn't know why I said it. The opposite of what we both knew I needed—for her to be gone.

"Do you want me to stay, Eli?" It was the first time she'd said my name. Not dad or grumpy or ass. Just my name. And it sounded like the last song she'd been singing as it left her lips. Yearning and desire and wanting more.

I couldn't respond because my throat was clogged with emotions that I'd never known I could feel. Had never felt. I gave her the briefest of nods, uncertain as I was never uncertain. But because she never looked away from my eyes, because she had that uncanny way of staring until she could see your real feelings, she saw the nod and smiled.

"I gotta go get my gear and my money. I'll be right back," she said before leaving me. It felt like I'd stepped onshore after being on the boat for weeks, like my sea legs hadn't quite caught back up to the land.

Mac Truck joined me. Truck cleared his throat, unsure of what to say to me, but Mac wasn't going to let any of it slide. "What the hell was that, Wyatt?"

I couldn't meet their eyes; I was still lost in blue and green ones that had departed with the citrus smell that surrounded her. I couldn't answer even if I wanted to. I didn't know what had happened.

"Truck, I think our captain has finally found the girl that will do him in."

"Fuck off." I finally found my voice.

"Dude, it was like *Coyote Ugly* and *Officer and A Gentleman* all rolled into one," Truck teased.

"Of course you'd be naming chick flicks," Mac ribbed him, giving me a moment to compose myself.

"You like the chick flicks," Truck said. "You never leave when I put them in."

"That's just because I'm used to them being on. I grew up with three older sisters. What's your excuse, asswipe?" Mac tossed out.

He shrugged. "I have a mom."

Mac busted into loud laughter. "A mom. You're telling me you sat in front of the TV watching those girlie-ass movies with your mom? What, we gotta call you Mama's boy now instead of Truck?"

Truck had had enough. He moved quickly and had Mac in a headlock so fast that Mac choked in surprise.

Ava walked up with her purse, a portfolio, and her guitar case. "Boys, boys. You don't have to fight over me. I've already told you: I'm not sleeping with any of you."

Truck exchanged a quick look with me and then let Mac go. Mac pushed his shoulder, and they playfully continued punching each other as we walked out of the bar into the muggy night air.

I fished the rental keys out of my pocket and tossed them at Truck.

"I'm driving Ava," I said. They both smiled as if they knew what the hell I was about, but they didn't. I had no desire to sleep with Ava and leave her.

Except, shit, I did want that—to sleep with her. Make love to her. Make her moan and say my name. But I also didn't. I was so royally screwed up.

She unlocked the car, and I stopped her before she got in. "Let me drive?"

She flashed me that smile. "I really haven't been drinking. Couple sips from a beer."

We eyed each other for a moment, but she pushed past me into the driver's seat. I had been drinking. More than her, it would seem, so I went around the car and sank down into the passenger seat, banging my knees on the dash and swearing.

She laughed. "Sorry, Jenna is the only one that ever sits there, and she's like an elf."

"Who's Jenna?"

"My best friend."

"And how does Jenna feel about you running away?"

She was quiet. "We haven't talked yet."

I watched her as she drove. She glanced over at me.

"What?" she asked.

"I thought girls told their best friends everything," I said, looking for her reaction. It was there. Small, heartbreak.

"I will. But I don't want her to have to lie to my dad."

She hit the button to open the sunroof and threw one hand out into the night sky as if she could catch the air and tame it. Somehow, I believed that Ava might just be able to do that.

"You have questions, just ask them. It's so much better than pussyfooting around," she said with a barely concealed smile.

"I don't pussyfoot."

"What do you call this?" She waved a hand between us.

"I don't know you. I don't really have a right to ask."

"You put your number in my phone, you're staying at my house, I kicked you out of the bed you chose, and I landed in your arms tonight, so I think we've crossed the line of know and don't know," she teased.

"You didn't kick me out. In fact, if I remember, you invited me into bed," I responded to the one thing I could.

Her smile got wider. "Did I? I don't remember. I was pretty drunk."

"That was pretty stupid, and you don't strike me as being stupid."

She nodded in agreement, not even a little upset.

"It was, but to be fair, I was with Lacey, and she wouldn't let anything bad happen to me."

"Lacey?" I asked.

"Andy and Lacey are the couple who own the bar you were just at."

"The guy who wanted to kill me when I had my hand on your boot?"

She nodded.

The humid night air filled her car. I couldn't escape it this trip. I probably wouldn't escape it until we were out to sea again in a few days. It didn't bother me most days, but sometimes I just wanted to breathe without feeling like I was being dragged down.

"Are you really nineteen?" I asked quietly.

She nodded again.

"It can't really be running away, then. What's your dad going to do?"

She laughed, a bitter laugh. "You truly don't know my dad very well, do you?"

She was right. I didn't know him well. I'd been lucky enough to avoid his classes until this last semester. I'd heard stories about what a prick he could be and warnings not to get on his bad side. Which is why, when I'd had no choice but to take his advanced military history class, I'd been sure to use extra sirs, turn everything in early, and stay under the radar. I'd bit my tongue when I disagreed with anything he said and just got the hell out. When he'd posted the offer to paint the house in lieu of a free week's stay to everyone in the class, I'd seen it as a bonus to lasting a semester with him.

When I didn't respond, she continued. "For starters, let's just say that he was probably pissed as hell when he showed up at graduation to find that I wasn't in the chairs."

"Wait, you walked out on your own graduation?"

She laughed, lighthearted. Free. It was her freedom that sucked me in.

"Wow," I said.

"Go ahead, ask it."

"What?"

"Why are you nineteen and just graduating?"

"Okay. Why are you nineteen and just graduating?"

"Dad got angry when I purposely flunked history in sixth grade to spite him—the history professor. So, he held me back against all my teachers' objections, moved me to a private school, and had weekly meetings with the faculty until I got to high school."

I took all of that in. It made me feel smothered, and I didn't even live with him. My mom had always given me room to breathe. We might keep things from each other, to protect each other against more pain and hurt, but we still had a relationship that was full of love.

Ava took in my silence, and then shrugged it off. "It kind of backfired on him, because I met Jenna that way, and I got to escape with her a lot."

"Escape. Running away. You act like he had you locked in a room," I said, half joking, only to have that turn to terror inside me because you heard things like that all the time on the news. Girls locked up. "Wait. He didn't have you locked in a room, right?"

She shook her head in the negative but didn't smile.

"Why'd he let you go off with Jenna then?" I asked.

She smiled weakly. "Now you're getting closer. Jenna's dad is one of our state representatives."

"So?"

"Dad is addicted to anything close to power. You know Professor Slughorn?"

"Who?"

"Harry Potter, Professor Slughorn?"

I tried to remember my Harry Potter books. I'd read them so long ago that they were a faint memory. I shrugged.

"You're hopeless," she said, exasperated. "Professor Slughorn 'collected' all these students from powerful families or who were powerful themselves so that, later, he could get favors from them and rise in his own fame because of that association."

"And that's your dad?"

She nodded.

"I feel slightly offended now that I've never been invited to any of his little soirées."

Ava laughed, filling the air with her huskiness.

"I'd say you've escaped the guillotine."

"It's well known that I want to join the Coast Guard, and that isn't the way anyone makes a name for themself."

"The Coast Guard is pretty amazing," Ava said.

I nodded. I agreed. It just wasn't a story I wanted to go into tonight—just how amazing they were. Because being with her threatened that very thing.

Instead, I said, "No one sees that as a power play, though. They consider the Coast Guard as a sellout or for people who couldn't hack it in one of the other branches of military."

She considered that and didn't respond.

We pulled into the beach house, parking behind the two goons in the pickup. I waited by the car while she locked up and took the guitar from her hand as she walked up the stairs. She looked over at me with a smirk.

"Don't go all gentlemanly on me now, Mr. Grumpy. You've given up your right to claim half the bed."

I smiled at her in return. "I wouldn't claim it back now, even if you begged."

We both knew it wasn't true. We both knew that if she begged, I might just cave. But she wasn't drunk tonight, and she was leaving. It was a fact that we both knew—the fact that we both needed her to leave and that seemed to put a damper on her own careless abandon. It made my chest ache. Because I kind of adored the careless abandon.

Chapter Six

Ava

PERFECT DAY
Performed by Lady A

I woke with the sun in my face, the muggy air already filling the bedroom from the open French doors like cotton balls stuffed in a jar. I kicked off the covers and stared out the windows at the ocean.

I could hear the paint gun running and the yammering back and forth that had to be Mac Truck. Eli didn't talk that much. Except last night, when he'd talked a lot—or asked a lot—in the car on the way home from the bar.

When he'd shown up at the Salty Dog last night, I'd been surprised. Not many people had the ability to surprise me, and he had several times. My body's reaction to him was a surprise. His control and constraint at twenty-two was a surprise. The way he'd been able to command acquiescence from me, so that I'd stepped down off the bar into his arms, was a surprise. Because I didn't spend time in anyone's arms…ever.

This strange song that Eli and I were dancing to was the reason I was staying when I needed to leave. Selfishly, I wanted to explore the feelings and reactions I'd never had a bit more, even though I knew it was threatening us all the longer I remained with them.

All my plans seemed more muddled than they had the day I'd left Galveston. I missed Jenna. I wanted to talk to her about all of it. The emotions. The boy. The escape.

I reached for my phone and, with fingers shaking because I knew she'd be pissed, texted her.

ME: Girlie, it's me. You alone?

Her response was so fast that it shocked me.

GIRLIE: Jesus Christ! Are you okay? Did some serial killer steal you and cut you up into pieces? Do I have to come get you? Where are you?

ME: I'm sorry.

GIRLIE: You could have at least told me you were going.

ME: This way you didn't have to lie to anyone.

GIRLIE: My dad barely stopped Ethan from forcing an APB being put out on you.

Jenna had always called my dad by his first name. She was one of the few people who did. I honestly thought it was because she didn't want to show him more respect than she felt he deserved.

ME: How'd he stop him?

GIRLIE: The cops told him you were nineteen and had to be missing for longer than a couple hours, and when he kicked up a fuss, Dad took him outside to cool off. I think Dad suspected you'd flown the coop on your own.

ME: I can't believe he actually called the cops!

GIRLIE: He'd rather you be a serial killer's chop bait than have the truth be that you chose to leave him in the stands at your own graduation...with a whole party planned.

ME: You're right.

GIRLIE: Where are you, really?

ME: I can't tell you. I still don't want you to lie.

GIRLIE: I can't tell them you texted me, anyway. They'll just want me to show them the texts, and then they'll get your location off the GPS or some stupid random location device on our phones.

ME: I have all my GPS locked down tight on this new one.

GIRLIE: You know they'd find a way.

*ME: **pic of Eli*

GIRLIE: Holy Hottie! Is this why you left

now? He's gorgeous. And so much more my type than yours. How is this even fair?

*ME: **laugh emoji. Don't let Colby hear you say that.*

ME: He isn't why I left. He was a pleasant surprise.

GIRLIE: How pleasant? Like finally lost your v-card pleasant? Like spent the night moaning his name pleasant? Wait. What is his name?

ME: Can't tell you that either.

GIRLIE: Excuse me? BFF here.

ME: I'd be putting him at risk.

GIRLIE: WTF. He's one of your dad's collections?

ME: Not in his collection but at the academy.

GIRLIE: You are just full of random surprises today.

ME: How was graduation?

GIRLIE: Exactly what you said it would be. People crying because they'd never see me again when they'd hardly spoken to me all year. Best thing was the car Mom and Dad bought me and taking it parking with Colby.

ME: YOU GOT A NEW CAR!!!

*GIRLIE: ** pic of Audi convertible*

ME: Damn. How did you "park" in that?

GIRLIE: We were very, very creative.

ME: I miss you.

GIRLIE: I miss you, too. I wish you could come back. But I know you can't.

ME: Once I'm set up, you can come see me. There won't be anything he can do then.

GIRLIE: There's not really anything he can do now either.

ME: I know, but he could take it out on the "surprises" that I found.

GIRLIE: Wait. There's more than one? Picture please.

*ME: ** pic of Mac Truck at beach*

GIRLIE: Dammmmmmmnnnnn girl, when you go off the cliff, you really go OFF THE CLIFF!

ME: LOL. They're all perfectly harmless.

GIRLIE: Then you're doing it wrong.

ME: I'm only here for a couple days. I have to get going. No reason to go burning the midnight oil with any of them.

GIRLIE: According to you, that would be the perfect reason to burn the midnight oil. There'd be no time to build an attachment.

No attachment… I wasn't sure I could say that. And according to Eli, I'd invited him into bed with me. I didn't really remember it. Getting drunk had been as stupid as he'd said. Thank God Lacey had put me in a CarShare and sent me home.

A knock on the bedroom door startled me out of my thoughts.

ME: No comment. But I gotta go.

GIRLIE: Please don't EVER go two days without texting me again. I need to know you're okay.

ME: It's a deal. Take care of you.

GIRLIE: Take care of you.

Jenna and I had started saying "take care of you" to each other after she'd made me watch all the classic romance movies with her in middle school. *Pretty Woman* was at the top of her list. The main characters were two friends looking out for each other, and that was us also. The words were extra meaningful now that I was leaving her just like Julia Roberts had left Laura San Giacomo.

Another knock.

"Yep?" I hollered out.

Eli's head appeared around the door hesitantly, as if he was afraid I'd be naked or something. Or maybe hoping I was naked? Or maybe that was just me. Hoping that he was hoping.

"Morning," I said with a smile. I was cross-legged on the bed in a T-shirt and panties. It covered more than my bikini had the day before, so I wasn't really worried about it. Besides, there was nothing on my body that he hadn't seen on a million other girls, I was sure.

I was never one to get hung up on my body. It was what it was. I wasn't going to hide it or flaunt it. It was just part of what made me me. I looked way more like my mom than my dad—not that I ever knew my mom since she'd died when I was six months old in a plane crash that took her and both my grandparents. But I looked like the pictures of her that I'd seen, and my dad threw it in my face all the time that I looked and acted like her. He always said it as if it was the worst thing I could have ever done. Be like her.

Eli, however, didn't look like he thought my minimal apparel was nothing. His eyes raked over me and then darted back out the window. It was cute and so unlike the image that he portrayed to the world. Authority. Command. Control. With me, I could see the pieces of him that would come undone if he let go. It made me wonder why he held on so tight.

It made me want to stay and find out. Which really was the reason I needed to go. If I had anything to say about it, my dad would be the only man to ever have had any control over me.

"I just wanted to get some clothes and go shower in the guys' bathroom."

"Are you guys already done painting for the day?" I asked.

"Already? It's eleven o'clock," he said.

I looked down at the time on my phone, surprised once more. I hadn't slept that late in my whole life. Dad would never have allowed it, and my body was trained now to his hours. It seemed like the last few weeks had taken a bigger toll on me than I had thought.

"Wow, I guess it is. You don't have to shower in there, though. Use this one. I'm just gonna change and hit the beach."

I stood up, and I caught him glancing at my legs and where the T-shirt barely covered my butt cheeks. It made my heart hammer louder that he looked. His gaze shifted away when he realized I knew he was watching me.

I grabbed another bikini from my bag and then stood, waiting for him to move in one direction or the other. His eyes caught mine. He looked down at the turquois strips of fabric I held and then back to my eyes, his all squinty.

"What is it now, Dad?" I knew my calling him Dad would jerk him out of whatever awkward mood he was in, and it did. He didn't like me calling him Dad. Truth be told, I didn't either, because he was nothing like my dad. I should have started calling him an old man instead. It was more accurate.

"Nothing," he said as he crossed to the dresser he'd commandeered the use of. He took out some clothes and glanced at me one more time.

"What?"

"Do you want to go first? Change?"

I laughed. "No, I'll change here once you get out of my hair."

He swallowed.

"In here?" He glanced toward the open windows.

"Jesus. There's nobody for miles. It's all ocean. No one is going to see, and if they do, it's not going to be anything they haven't seen before. Do you want me to show you?"

I reached for the bottom of my T-shirt, and he actually paled before flushing a color so beautiful that it made me want to run my hands over his cheeks.

"No! Shit. Wait till I go inside," he said and stormed toward the bathroom door.

"Chicken," I called after him quietly.

"I learned not to play that game a long time ago," he said back, but I swear there was a tone in his voice that stated he wanted to play very badly. It made me smile. It lightened my mood from my sadness at leaving Jenna behind. And it continued to make me want to stay.

I heard the shower start before I undressed. Then, I took my notebook, my chair, and a water and headed down the path to the beach when I really should have been heading my car toward Tennessee.

♫ ♫ ♫

The boys joined me again. They played football and taunted each other into doing stunts off the dock. Flips and twists and all sorts of typical guy stuff. They mostly left me to myself on the other end of the dock, with my feet in the water, scribbling my notes. My music.

It was nearing dinner when Mac threw out a challenge. "I bet music girl could do that flip better than you."

I heard Truck guffaw, but it was Eli's silence that got to me. I looked to their end. Eli's eyes were hooded as he watched me. I couldn't tell his assessment. Did he think I could or couldn't do whatever the hell Mac had challenged Truck to?

I put my stuff down and joined them at the end.

"Okay, pansy boys, what's the challenge?"

Eli crossed his arms across the wide expanse of his chest. Muscled. Contoured. All three of them were built that way from the military exercises they did at the academy.

Mac grinned. "Run, jump, somersault, land without a splash."

"Seems pretty basic. What did you do, dumb it down for the girl?" I asked.

Truck swallowed, and I could tell I'd made him nervous. Little did he know, I couldn't do any of this. I could swim. Swimming was demanded by my dad. I'd been on a swim team until I was fourteen when I'd used my period as an excuse, making him blanch a pale white I'd never seen on him before. It had been a small win that I wasn't used to having. He'd punished me for it, though. I'd stopped swimming, so he stopped paying for my guitar lessons.

"Who's going to judge?" Truck asked.

"Me," Eli said.

Truck laughed. "Well, hell, we both know you're going to pick her."

"Mac then," I said.

"No way. He would pick anyone over me."

"Who do you suggest?" I asked.

Truck eyed the shore. Down a ways on the beach was an elderly couple. They had binoculars and a book in hand as if they were birdwatching.

"If you can get them to agree, I'll even give you a point advantage," I teased, knowing already that I was a lost cause. What did an extra point matter?

Truck was off down the beach at a jog. We couldn't hear what he said from where we were, but he was gesturing with his whole body and pointing to the dock, and I knew without even seeing it that he was grinning that huge Truck grin.

When all three of them started back toward the dock, Mac swore and Eli laughed. It was like his smile. Unexpected, stunning when he did it. I looked up with my own smile into his eyes.

"You don't have to do this, you know." It was a statement instead of a question, but there was still a smile on his face. I liked the smile. I wanted it to stay there.

"I'll just follow the wise words of Gail Sheehy who said, 'I dare to do things - that's how I survive.' What could go wrong?" I told him with a shrug.

When the elderly couple got on the dock, it was obvious that Truck had already explained the situation. The man looked slightly dazed, but the woman was smiling an impish smile.

"Young lady, you challenging these boys to a duel?" Her voice was wavery but full of humor.

"More like they challenged me." I grinned back.

After a few more rules, which only served to remind me how big I was going to bomb this, Truck and I headed back to the middle of the dock.

When we stopped and turned back, getting into a running stance, he looked over and winked. "Last chance to admit failure."

"In your dreams, pansy." I grinned and took off with him swearing behind me.

I had no idea what I was doing. When I got to the end of the dock, I pushed off as hard as I could with my feet and tried to twist my body into a somersault I hadn't done since I was little, and then somehow hit the water on my back.

The air rushed out of me. Pain seared through my body like ice picks shooting across my entire backside, and then I was sinking. No air in my lungs, body not even responding.

I heard my name. Heard who called it. Knew it was Eli. But didn't really register it until the water around me was moving and arms were surrounding my waist, pulling me from under the water, pulling us both to the surface.

I was drawn up against him. Skin to skin. Heat from his body filtering into mine that had started to shiver even though it wasn't cold. I was still trying to breathe. No air there yet.

"Ava?"

I couldn't speak, could barely move. I tried, but my body was still objecting to my brain.

Mac and Truck pulled me out of the water, laying me on the dock, and then Eli was there again, his eyes scanning mine. I blinked. He let out a breath I don't think he even realized he was holding.

"Is she okay?" It was the lady.

"She just had the air knocked out of her," Eli said just as the air came rushing back, hurting like nothing had hurt since I'd broken my toe kicking my bedroom door after Dad had told me he was making me change schools.

"Slow, steady breaths," Eli said, brushing my hair off my forehead, meeting my eyes with his own, staring like I usually stared.

Eventually, I felt almost normal. The pain in my lungs had almost subsided, but I did feel like I'd run a marathon.

I smiled at him, and he smiled back. That smile that changed his face from hard planes to blurred happiness. Like when you're on the tilt-a-whirl, and the world is passing by in a hazy swirl, but you're still smiling.

I was the first to look away. I moved my head toward the lady who'd come to judge us and said, "So, I won, right?"

She laughed, and she was joined by everyone there.

I sat up, and Eli steadied me when I seemed to waver.

"Take it easy. Take some more breaths."

He was rubbing my back, and that wasn't helping my breathing, his skin making mine tingle again, but with a pleasantness that was intoxicating.

I pulled away and slowly got to my feet. Eli hovered close, and I ignored it.

"Truck didn't win, did he? I mean, after all I just went through, I believe I should be declared the winner."

The lady laughed again. "Honey, if you were dumb enough to challenge him knowing you couldn't do the stunt, you'll just have to lick your wounds when I conclude that you lost by a landslide."

We all smiled, and Truck did a victory dance.

The couple left with a look that said we'd been the most excitement they'd had in a long time. I walked to the end of the dock and picked up my belongings. Eli was by my side, and he took it all from me.

"Where are you going?" he asked.

"Shower. I think I've had enough for the day," I told him truthfully. I was still sore. Shaky. I was done.

He didn't let go of my things and just threw back over his shoulder to the guys, "Going back to the house, asswipes. Want me to order pizza?"

"Do dogs bark at the moon?" Truck asked.

"I don't know, do they? I thought that was wolves," Mac replied, and they were shoving at each other as I turned away.

Eli was quiet on our way back. He got the door for me, and I couldn't help a weak smile at him as I passed by, the hairs on my arm reacting as his bare chest grazed against my skin. He watched me, eyes dark and stormy.

He even followed me to the bedroom but then just put my stuff down and left me to shower in peace. I wasn't sure I'd ever have peace when he was there. I wasn't sure I wanted it. It reminded me of how desperately I needed to leave.

Chapter Seven

Eli

WILD CHILD

Performed by Kenny Chesney & Grace Potter

I ordered the pizza while Ava showered. Truck and Mac showed up just afterwards. They seemed surprised that I was standing in the kitchen even though I'd said I'd order pizza.

"Dude, why are you out here?" Mac asked.

"Opposed to?" I replied, knowing exactly where his mind was heading.

"In the shower, with our little daredevil."

I shook my head and reached into the fridge for a beer that I was in desperate need of. "Not going to happen."

"She wants it to," Mac said, pulling my beer from my hand before I'd even had a chance to open it. I eyed him with disgust but just pulled another from the fridge.

"Not. Going. To. Happen," I said, shooting glares at them both over the bottle as I took a swig.

Mac shook his head in disappointment, but I think Truck got the risk of it all better. We were already tempting fate enough by staying there with her. I wasn't going to shoot my life goals in the foot on purpose by adding to the reasons Abrams would have us kicked out of the academy.

By the time the pizza had come, Ava had joined us.

She was in yoga pants and a T-shirt that just barely covered her ass but slipped from her shoulders whenever she moved, showing her bra strap like all her tops seemed to do. I itched to touch the exposed skin. I knew the guys would have been all over her if I wasn't there to stop them, one or both of them taking turns to hit on her until she caved. But I had a feeling that Ava would never cave to them. I don't think she'd cave to me either, even with the attraction that seemed to fill the air between us.

After we ate pizza—inside this time—with her on the coffee table and us at the kitchen table, she pulled out a bunch of board games from a closet. Scrabble, Monopoly, Life, and Clue all littered the floor around her.

"You planning on babysitting some eight-year-old that we don't know?" Mac asked.

"I don't feel like going out," she said with a shrug.

"Are you still hurting?" I asked.

"Nah," she responded. She'd hit the water with such ferocity, I was sure she felt bruised and battered, but I didn't force it.

She took us all in, a smile appearing on her face, and said in a voice full of sass, "In the great words of Mikhail Bulgakov, 'I challenge you to a duel!'"

"Our daredevil hasn't gotten enough yet?" Mac asked.

"You know what happened to Michael J. Fox when he couldn't resist a dare in the *Back to the Future* movies, right?" Truck added on.

"I get to travel backwards and forwards in time? That's okay by me. Doubly good if it's backwards, and I actually get to meet my mom," Ava said.

It hit me hard. The smile she sent to Truck as well as the fact that she hadn't known her mom. Like I'd barely started to get to know my dad.

"You didn't know your mom?" Truck asked the question that I wanted to ask.

She shrugged. "Nope. She died when I was only six months old."

That seemed to stun us all.

"What happened?" Truck asked again.

"Plane crash. Took her and my grandparents— her parents—out at the same time."

That reached into even Mac's tough heart and pulled on the strings, because he joined her on the floor, lying on his side and stretching out his long legs till they almost touched her. I watched his feet and could feel the frown appear on my face that I tried to shake off.

"What's the challenge, D.D.?"

She gave him a curious look.

"Daredevil. D.D.," he explained. Mac was in charge of all the nicknames at the academy, assigning one to every freshman that came in.

I grabbed us all more beers from the fridge and joined them on the floor, Truck following me. Ava grabbed one of the beers from my hand, and I didn't stop her like I should have.

"I bet that I can beat you at all four of these games."

"I don't know, Eli's pretty good with words," Truck told her, eyeing the Scrabble box.

"Mr. Silent Grumpy? Does he even know words?" she teased.

"We'll save the words for last then," I growled at her, but I was smiling on the inside.

True to her word, she beat the pants off of us at the first three games. To be fair, I didn't know the last time any of us had played these games. Just like I didn't recall there ever being a strategy to winning them. I'd remembered them being games of luck based on the roll of the dice. But Ava beat us, telling us that we sucked at strategy.

We were all groaning while she imitated Truck's victory dance on the coffee table. She'd only seen it once but had every move down pat. Except, her moving that way was pure sex, whereas Truck had looked like a giant idiot.

"You better stop before Eli starts throwing dollar bills your way," Mac laughed as he got up to get more beers.

I was buzzed. More than I had been in a long time, because I normally didn't like being out of control. Didn't like the way my body responded when my brain had been dulled.

Ava turned to look at me, her dual-colored eyes flashing with mischief, the corners of her lips quirking up. "I could use the cash."

She pulled at the bottom of her T-shirt as if to lift it over her head. "Don't even think about it," I said and instinctively reached out a hand to pull the shirt back down. Our hands tangled together in a dance that had chills breaking out along the back of my neck.

"You're such an old man," she harassed. I was glad that she hadn't called me Dad. Dad, I hated. Old man I could live with. It was something I'd been called before. Back at home, in Connecticut, after Dad had passed, I'd spent my days helping Mom at the bookstore, acting much older than I was.

"Dude, you have to win now. She celebrated early. It had to jinx her." Truck stood and joined Mac at the door to the deck.

"Where the hell you two going?" I complained.

"You know we don't got a shot at a goddamn word game," Mac shrugged. "It's all on you, oh Captain, my Captain."

I cringed.

"What's the deal with the captain stuff?" Ava asked once the boys had gone outside. "You're not a captain. None of the butts make captain."

"Technically, I'm a zip instead of a butt."

The academy terms for the cadets were old news to me, and I shouldn't be surprised that she knew them so well with her dad at the academy, but it wasn't often I found someone who could speak our lingo.

"So, you're a captain?" she asked.

I shook my head. I was higher ranked than that, but I wasn't getting into it with her. It wasn't why they called me Captain, anyway. That had started our freshman year.

"If you don't tell me, I'm sure Mac Truck would be happy to."

She had set the Scrabble board up, and I'd picked the highest scoring letter from the bag, so I got to start.

I pulled my letters and assembled them in the little tray.

"It's a poetry thing."

Her hand stilled in the bag.

"Wait. Did you just say poetry?" I could hear the laughter in her voice and could see how hard she was trying to keep a straight face.

I liked that I'd surprised her, because she was always surprising the hell out of me.

"Walt Whitman's 'O Captain, My Captain,'" I told her and returned to fiddling with my letters and trying to find a word that would give me the biggest head start I could muster.

"Do the boys expect you to die at the end of your illustrious career at A&M?"

I guess it didn't surprise me that she knew the poem. Knew the death that came at the end of it. It was why there was so much meaning in their nickname. Me. My dad. The *Dead Poets Society*. But, somehow, that all seemed too much to disclose to this female who I needed to keep at a distance.

"Har-har," I said. I laid down my letters and scored thirty-seven points. Not my best. Not my worst. I was rusty, having to shake off a few of the old cobwebs in my brain.

"Eli, are you some academic prodigy they didn't tell me about?"

"Hell no. I have to work damn hard to pull my grades."

"What's your G.P.A.?"

"It's your turn, Ava. We going to bullshit about my college career or you going to try to whip my ass?"

Her eyes sparkled. "Can't we do both?" Then, she leaned in and whispered, "You can't tease about ass whippings and leave me hanging."

I swallowed hard. "Put your words on the board, and we'll talk about whose ass gets whipped when it's over."

That made her smile disappear. The tease was gone, and I could see the pulse in her neck throbbing against the stray curls escaping her bun. I heard her breath hitch.

I loved it.

I was so screwed.

It was hours later when I had to concede defeat. Conceding wasn't anything I was good at. I usually played to win when I played anything. Instead of repeating her dance on the coffee table, Ava leaned in, and in her deep, throaty voice whispered, "Looks like I'm the one doing the whipping after all."

I just stared into those eyes, desire and smugness and humor bouncing through them as they sparkled in the light from the kitchen.

"Good luck with that." I eyed her back, my own breath caught in my chest so that the words were gritty and harsh, but she didn't seem to care.

Her eyes flicked to my lips, and I found mine following in the same way hers had gone as I looked at her full, pink ones that were waiting to be kissed. I ached to lean across the damn board and do just that. Kiss her.

Instead, I pulled back, dumping the wooden tiles from the board into the velvet bag. Ava eyed my hands that I swore were not shaking even though I felt like my whole body was trembling. I had control. I was in control.

Enlistment contract. Enlistment contract. Enlistment contract, I chanted to myself.

Ava stood, heading toward the hallway and the room she'd taken from me. "Goodnight, oh Captain, my Captain."

I breathed a sigh of relief as the bedroom door shut behind her. Because if she hadn't left, I didn't know how long I would have lasted before she'd have broken through every last ounce of control I had.

♪ ♪ ♪

The next morning, I was up early again. Mac and Truck came out to help soon after. We painted longer than we had any day prior. I wanted to say it was because we hadn't been disrupted by a half-naked Ava, but the truth was, she hadn't come out while we were working the day before either. Instead, I'd gone in at lunch time to check on her.

Putting in extra time now meant we'd finished almost three sides of the house. It looked like we were going to finish with at least a couple days to spare.

It was late, almost four, by the time the dumbasses went in to shower, leaving me, as always, to clean up. Ava still hadn't put in an appearance. I could see her car parked out front, so she hadn't taken off without saying goodbye. This thought made my entire stomach clench up.

It would be a good thing when she left, I tried to convince myself.

Yet, I still found myself making my way inside to find her. I told myself that it was just to see if she wanted to come with us to the Mexican restaurant we'd seen in town, but I knew the truth. I just ached to see her again. Ached almost as much as I had when we'd done theoretical SEAL training sophomore year.

I went down the hall to the master bedroom. The door was open, and I caught sight of Ava going through my things. I leaned on the doorframe and watched. She was pulling clothes out and then folding them back in. She hadn't realized I was there. Or at least, I didn't think she had.

Her lithe frame bent and uncoiled as she moved almost methodically through the dresser. If I didn't know better, I'd say she was a spy or undercover P.I. looking for something. She wasn't going to find it. There was nothing in my life besides the academy and the Coast Guard.

I should have been pissed that she was going through my stuff, violating my privacy and my trust. Instead, I was fascinated. What had prompted this sudden desire to dig through my life? Just the fact that she was touching it all, putting her scent on it, made me want to go behind her and pick up everything that she had handled so I could smell it.

I brushed the stubble on my head that was still longer than I ever let it grow during a school year and tried to get my bearings. She was doing me in. Temptation and threat rolled into one.

She pulled my uniform cap out of the drawer. It was my new cap, or bider, with the black and gold braids and no dent that declared my senior status. It meant I was almost done. One last cruise on the TS Kennedy, then my final year as a Sea Aggie before I could enlist and hopefully get accepted as a commissioned officer in the Coast Guard.

Ava turned to me, putting my bider on her head, as if she'd known I was there all along.

"Is this how you wear this thing?" she asked.

My whole body responded to that. Her in my cap.

"Yes." It was a rumble. From deep within my chest.

She smirked at me. She wasn't embarrassed at having been caught. She didn't stop pilfering through my things, either. Instead, she came up with my uniform shirt. The dark green matched her pond colored eye.

As I watched, she pulled her T-shirt over her head to reveal a pink lace bra that did little to hide everything underneath it. It was like her bikini tops but sheer. Giving me a glimpse of her brown areolas and pebbled nipples. That made my body respond uncomfortably, but I didn't move from my position on the doorframe with my hands carefully tucked under my armpits.

She pulled my shirt on and buttoned only a handful of buttons as I continued to watch. She was so goddamn beautiful. And confident. It was hard to imagine that she was only nineteen. That she hadn't even been to college yet. That she hadn't already spent years at college finding herself and becoming this strong, independent woman before me.

She looked up at me, her eyes and dark lashes loaded with emotions. Lust. Longing. Wariness. I knew, after a handful of days with her, that the wariness wasn't directed at me, but it was always startling to see it there when, really, she was almost always full of sass.

I couldn't move. If I did, I'd devour her. There would be nothing left of me or her or us. Just a puddle of spent desire. That couldn't happen, because our lives weren't ever going to touch again. Our lives were ships going in different directions.

Ava didn't seem to have the same reservations. Hadn't I already learned that? She could be controlled when she wanted to be, but there was very little that pushed her to allow that control. She was always going after what she wanted. In that moment, I could tell she wanted me. She moved toward me in my Midnights, a pink lace bra, and her miniscule jean shorts.

Her mass of messy, dark hair was pulled partially up, leaving some curls straggling down her back below my cap. Some curls twirled about her face, and my fingers itched to embed themselves in them.

When she got to me, her one blue-green eye had darkened so that it was almost the same color as her dark hazel one. I couldn't stop looking at them, drowning in them.

"Eli," she breathed out my name as she stopped inches from where I was propped up.

I didn't respond, I just looked at her rosy lips, dark lashes, and full cheeks stained with sun and color that suited her.

"Do you want me?" she asked, and for the barest of seconds, I saw the insecurity skirt across her face and eyes. The high schooler on the verge of new adventures.

That pushed me into doing the worst possible thing. Touching her. I ran a finger along her cheek. My rough hands, stained with the paint that I'd been using for the last few days on the outside of her dad's summer home, caressing the soft skin. She leaned into my palm, eyes closing part way. My other hand found the opposite cheek. Her skin was so perfect, so unscathed. But I instinctively knew it didn't match the part inside her that felt marked. I knew that feeling.

"You know I do," I finally responded gutturally, truthfully.

"Then kiss me," she demanded, eyes open again, searching my eyes for an answer I couldn't give.

I let my finger land on the corner of her lips like I'd been wanting to do since the day I'd met her. Instead of easing my desire, it only increased it. It made me wonder what those lips would taste like. Would they be full of the sea and citrus that she always seemed to drown me in?

God it hurt. To not kiss her. To not give in to everything my body was aching for. But I wouldn't. I tapped her lips with my index finger and then drew away, turning my back to her and walking down the hall, my mind reminding my body of what I'd been working for since I was ten and I'd lost my father.

"We're going for tacos," I called back. "If you want to come, you better put on your own clothes and join us in five." I didn't look back. I couldn't. I knew I'd just see disappointment on her face. The disappointment my heart was calling to me.

"Asshole," I heard her breathe out as I got to the guys' bathroom at the end of the hall.

That was okay. If she thought I was an asshole, it would keep her away. It would allow me to keep the barrier up that needed to be there. We didn't have a choice.

Chapter Eight

Ava

KISS YOU TONIGHT
Performed by David Nail

I watched Eli walk down the hall. My body throbbing for the kiss that I knew he'd been so close to giving me. My brain throbbing with the sheer arrogance of him. To touch me and leave me. To bring me so close to feeling the lips I'd been aching to taste.

But it wasn't him I'd called the asshole. It was me. For tempting us both. I knew as much as he did that he and I didn't belong. I knew the risks, to both of us, if we gave in to the feeling that our bodies were demanding. I also knew that I had never felt this way before.

I was slightly terrified that I'd never feel this way again. Understanding those stupid words that Jennifer Grey whispered to Patrick Swayze in *Dirty Dancing* for the first time in my life. Understanding Jenna's romance books and movies a little better. Understanding the girls in high school. Understanding Jenna.

Because what if Eli was the only one who could make me feel this way? No other guy had yet. No guy had drowned me in just his gaze and commandeered my heart and my body to accept his hand and his touch.

I shook my head out of my thoughts and pulled off his shirt, inhaling the scent of him as I did so. Masculine and salty. Like the sea.

I pulled on my T-shirt that I'd thrown aside, grabbed my phone and my purse, and headed down the hall and out the door. Mac Truck were already in the back of the truck, legs bent at all weird angles as I got in.

Eli thundered down the stairs and got into the driver's seat. We didn't say anything. Mac Truck seemed to sense the air between us. Full and heady, and yet unfulfilled. Everyone was quiet as we drove downtown.

When we got to the taco truck, it was crowded, but we were able to order and find seats at one of the picnic tables. We'd just sat down when a voice drew my head around.

"Ava! I thought you'd left already." It was Lacey, and she was right. I had planned on leaving after I'd played at the bar. Now, a day and a half later, I was still there. It was saving me money—money I needed to save—but the real reason was the stupid cadet sitting across from me, watching me and listening for my response.

"Decided I could save a few more dollars by staying a bit longer," I told her with a shrug. "But I'll probably head out tomorrow or the next day."

That still had a lot to do with Mr. Grumpy sitting there glowering at me. The fact that I was leaving before my originally planned end of the week departure.

"If we'd known, we would have booked you another night," Lacey said.

"Well, that wouldn't be fair to Ben. He was gracious enough to give me the mic for two nights already."

Lacey took in the three behemoths sitting at the table with me, landing on Eli—the one to pull me from her bar. And she could read, as easily as I could, that they were Dad's cadets. A little frown furrowed in between her eyebrows.

"You're still leaving, right?" She lowered her voice a little. Lacey was three times my age and had listened to me bemoan my life more than enough summers to know that I wanted Nashville and Juilliard more than anything else. More than a sexy cadet.

I nodded. "Yes. God, yes."

"Okay. Well…please let us know when you get to Nashville, okay?" She started to hug me and then stopped, knowing that hugs and me were often awkward.

"Will do," I told her.

She gave the guys and me one more look and then left just as our order was called. Eli and Mac went to pick it up while Truck and I saved our seats. I could feel Truck eyeing me.

"Just say it, Truck. I don't want your brain to explode from you thinking too hard."

He didn't smile when I'd expected him to. "What's the deal with you and Eli?"

I was surprised that he even asked. I shrugged. "Nothing more than is going on with you and me."

He just stared. We both knew it was a lie.

"What do you want me to say? I'm leaving, and he's one of my dad's cadets."

"Can I just say something?"

"God, please do before I crumble under your stare."

"Eli. He doesn't… He's never…"

"Wait. Are you telling me he's a virgin?"

Truck laughed so hard I thought he was going to blow a nostril. "Hell no."

"What then?"

"Let's just say, in the three years I've known him, I've never, ever seen him react to a girl the way he reacts to you."

"Like an asshole commanding an army?"

"Like a man who doesn't know if he can keep his hands to himself a moment longer."

We both stared at each other before Eli and Mac joined us.

"Who died?" Mac asked.

"What?" I asked.

"Yo mama. After I taught her how long a real man should last in her bed," Truck said.

Eli groaned. "Please. Don't start the yo mama jokes again. You actually made a Fish cry last year."

"But to be fair, that Fish cried over everything." Mac shrugged, completely undisturbed by the joke about his mama.

We ate as Mac and Truck continued to rib each other back and forth. Eli was quiet, eyes darting to me and away. After we'd finished, the food settled into my stomach in a lump. I didn't know why, except that it had something to do with my dreams, and leaving, and my dad, and the cadets…and Eli.

"Mac, I feel the need. The need for speed."

"You guys are like a whole slew of eighties movie knock offs," I laughed at them. "And please tell me that you don't literally mean speed."

Truck grinned. "Nope. But I do need a wingman at a bar with the ladies."

"It's your turn to be the wingman," Mac said.

"Either way. We both get drinks and ladies."

I rolled my eyes at them. "Well, don't expect me to be your wingwoman." I stood and tossed my trash in the nearby garbage can. "I can catch a CarShare back to the house."

"No need. I'm not up for playing wingman either," Eli said. "These two bozos can catch their own CarShare at the end of the night."

"Are you sure? You seem like a night of revelry is just what you need," I said.

"Revelry?" Eli smirked.

"It's what lost you the game last night," I told him.

"I lost because you cheat," he said. He knew I hadn't cheated.

"You two old people go back and have a rematch while we go out and entertain ourselves," Mac said.

He and Truck took off down the street toward Andy and Lacey's bar. At least they were going to the right bar. I was pretty sure if they'd headed toward the Bay Grill, they would have been shot down.

The silence between Eli and me continued on the way back to the house, as opposed to two nights ago when he couldn't stop asking me questions.

When we got inside, he went to the refrigerator and took out two beers. I went and got the Scrabble game. I put it on the kitchen table before joining the board there. He hesitated and then joined me on the table top. My hands froze on the wooden tiles, my heart pounding to a tune that I knew I'd have to write down later as I stared at him.

"What?" he asked.

"You're on the table," I breathed out.

"Had to see what it was all about," he responded with a shrug.

I continued to stare at him. His eyes didn't turn away from me, but drank me in as they almost always did. I'd never had anyone join me. Never. In the stares. On the table. I'd been on my own. Even Jenna thought I was freakish about them both.

"It's about perspective," I breathed out. "Ursus Wehrli said that he liked to turn things upside down to get a different perspective. I figure, climbing up gives you a different view as well."

"Huh," was his noncommittal response, as if he was still assessing it himself. He seemed huge sitting on the table. He was tall anyway, but on the table top, he looked like a giant.

I just continued my stare. Heart pounding.

"You gonna give me the bag or what?"

I gave him the bag, hands shaking, and he noticed it with a slight furrow to his eyebrows, not understanding why I would be shaking. Not understanding the dream that had become a reality.

Even though it was a dream I couldn't afford, because I had bigger dreams to tackle.

He leaned over to put the tile bag in the box and slammed his head into the chandelier, and it broke the trance. He swore, I laughed, and we were right back to where we'd been all along. Two people whose bodies talked to each other but wouldn't be anything more.

"You do that a lot," he said after we'd both played our first words.

"Do what?"

"The quote thing."

Jenna was probably the only other living soul who'd ever commented on my quote fetish. "Words are beautiful," I told him quietly.

"That's probably why you're going to kick my ass again," he said, and I smiled.

I did beat him…but I had to use my phone to cheat my way through because he came close to beating me on his own. He didn't know that I'd used it, though, so it was a small victory. One I enjoyed because he groused about it.

"I feel like a walk on the beach. Want to come?" I asked.

"More perspective?"

I shrugged. "Sunsets on the ocean always have a way of making you feel like there's more in store for your future."

"Who said that?"

"Um…me."

He considered me in that way he'd been doing all evening that made me feel really seen. Visible. Like when I was onstage. It made my heart beat extra fast.

We made our way down to the sand, barefoot, heading south along the shore. The mugginess almost as heavy as the air between us.

"What's in Nashville?" he asked finally. He had been listening to the conversation with Lacey. I realized that Eli really listened all the time. To words. To bodies. To life.

"I have a job and classes already set up."

"How'd you get a job without being there?"

"Andy. He's got a brother that owns a coffee shop. It has open mic nights on Wednesdays, and employees get preference."

"Do you have a place to stay already?"

"Are you always this practical?"

He stopped, and I stopped with him. He didn't look at me, though; he looked out at the sea. Melancholy in a way that didn't fit him. He'd been serious and commanding, but sad had never really rippled off of him until now.

"After my dad died, I had to grow up fairly quickly. Mom did her best, but she was struggling too, and even with the death benefits, things could get tight. Mom had always had a minimum wage job at a bookstore, mostly to get out of the house, but after he died, it was our main income. We kind of took care of each other. So practical was kind of built into me."

My heart stopped and started as I watched him, watch the sea, compassion and understanding filling me. Except I hadn't been forced to grow up too fast. Instead, my dad had practically refused to let me grow up at all.

"Did your dad die in the Coast Guard?" I almost didn't need to ask. It was so obvious now that he said his dad had died.

He nodded.

"Got shot boarding a drug boat."

I could still hear the loss in his voice. The anger. The sadness. But it didn't match his expression, which was blank.

"How old were you?"

"Ten."

I'd seen compassion in his eyes last night when Mac had asked about my mom, but now I knew that it had been empathy and not sympathy. He felt the loss as much as I did.

He turned and looked down at me, eyes dark from the sun's disappearing path and from his emotions. "At least I got to know him a little."

I shrugged. It was a reference to my mom. I turned and started back the way we'd come, and his long legs easily caught up to me.

"The thing that sucks most is not being able to talk to anyone about her. She has some cousins still alive, but Dad didn't stay in touch with any of them. I think he burned out his welcome with the family."

"How do you know that? You were a baby."

"I know my dad. I see how he is with anyone in a power position. I've seen the pictures. Whenever my grandfather is in them, my dad is right next to him, beaming as if he's just met the pope."

"Who was your granddad?"

"A senator. From North Carolina."

"Is that supposed to be a big deal?"

I looked up at him in surprise and saw that rare Eli smile on his face. He was teasing me, bringing us back from our serious moments.

"Well, it's not as big as being "The Boy Who Lived," but it's pretty big around these parts."

He frowned.

"Have you even read *Harry Potter*?" I asked.

"Sure, but it was a while ago."

"Like how long ago?"

"Ten years?"

"Do you even read at all?"

"I just told you my mom worked at a bookstore. How can you even ask that question?" he asked.

"That doesn't mean you have to read. What's your favorite book?"

"*Case Closed, Volume Six*," he responded immediately. My turn to stop.

"Wait, like a comic book?" I was trying not to laugh, but I could see this was not going to go over well. He wasn't going to take my making fun of his favorite book lightly.

"It's manga," he sighed. "And if you tell the guys, I will have to murder you in your sleep."

I lost it, laughing so hard that I had to double over to catch my breath, and the next thing I knew, I was in his arms, and he was charging toward the water. The waves hit me, splashing on my skin and clothes. Once we got deep enough, he dropped me.

I hit the water, and the coolness took my breath for a moment, reminding my body of the loss of air from yesterday and the sore muscles that I had because of it. I was still smiling.

I sunk to the bottom, holding my breath and waiting. Eventually, I felt his arms reach down and pull me to the surface.

My smile widened when I saw the worry on his face. My smile turned his worry into a growl, and he pushed me under again.

I came up splashing this time, soaking him from head to toe as much as I was soaked. My clothes were clinging to me just as his T-shirt was clinging to him, outlining his cuts and contours as the sun set behind us, turning the sky pink and purple.

I thought to myself, *There will never be another moment like this. Full of wants and desires and loss and freedom and hope. So much hope*.

Before I could even think about it, I leaped into his arms, where he caught me as if I'd always been doing just that. I wrapped my legs around his waist and my arms around his neck and planted my salty lips against his.

His lips opened in surprise but were still stiff and unyielding, all the reasons why we shouldn't still floating on the air between us. I just didn't care. I wanted this moment. This kiss. I slipped my tongue into his mouth and was rewarded with a groan.

His arms tightened around me. Giving in. Returning my kiss with ferocity. The energy that had throbbed between us becoming this one huge torrential wave that was igniting into a hurricane force.

He tasted of salt and beer and salsa. He tasted like a place I'd never known I needed. His tongue took control of mine, demanding more, demanding all of me. Taking things I'd never known I could give. Soul. Heart. Life. His kiss returned things, too. His soul. His heart. My body burned with desire, as if there would never be enough time for us to assuage the need in us.

I don't know how long we stood there, wet, bodies twined together, tongues dancing in the twilight, and hearts meeting somewhere in between. Finally, he started to slow the pace of our dance and then removed his lips from mine.

He buried his face in my neck, breathing me in like I seemed to breathe him in.

"You're beautiful, Ava."

His low, gritty voice could barely be heard over the crash of the waves. I heard the "but" in his voice without him having said it. I turned my face slightly so that I could place a kiss on his head that was still nestled against my skin.

"Don't freak out, Mr. Grumpy. It was just a kiss." I tried to lighten the mood. But the truth was, we both knew that it hadn't been just a kiss. It was souls speaking. It was lives blending. And it was going to tear us both apart when we said goodbye after knowing each other a mere three days.

He squeezed me so tight that I thought I'd lose everything that was me and simply become part of him. Then, he let me go, and I slid down him, feet landing in the ocean once more, body wavering so that he had to catch me at the waist to steady me again. As he had since I'd met him.

I realized that I needed that. Someone to steady my torrents. To stop me from going over the rail. I'd never had it. I'd just had my dad forcing me to live the life he wanted and never preparing me for the life I wanted.

Our eyes found each other's again. We stared for what might have been a hundred and eighty seconds or maybe more. Finally, I caved, reaching down and swooping up a handful of water, splashing him once more before I took off toward the shore and the beach house. And he let me go.

Chapter Nine

Eli

LITTLE MORE SUMMERTIME
Performed by Jason Aldean

I watched Ava walk down the beach toward the house, and I purposefully waited until she'd hit the shell path before I made my way out of the water to the sand. My body was awake in every possible, painful way. Just with a kiss.

A kiss that had seemed to take every sane thought from my head and replaced it only with desire. Desire to know every piece of her, inside and out. A kiss that had been unlike any other kiss I had ever shared with a woman in my life. There'd always been desire, but not the passion and out-of-control feeling that I'd had with Ava. Never. I'd always been in control.

Now, I was hard, uncomfortable, and regretful at the same time. I shouldn't have kissed her back. I shouldn't have let her think there could ever be more than that kiss. Even that had been too much.

You mean too little, my body said. My mind answered back its own chant: *enlistment contract, enlistment contract, enlistment contract.*

I groaned and headed for the house.

When I got there, she'd already started the shower. I grabbed dry clothes from the drawer and hesitated by the bathroom door, my hand reaching for the handle, knowing what waited on the other side. More kissing. More skin. More Ava. More life. More freedom.

My hand shook at the thought of tasting her lips again, of tasting more of her skin, of hearing that husky voice say my name as I touched all of her.

My phone rang.

The water turned off.

"Eli?" Ava called out.

"Just getting clothes. I'm going to shower in the guys' bath."

Silence. A battle she was fighting herself on the other side of the door. Maybe just like me. Hands shaking. Desire coursing through her.

My phone again.

It was Mom.

I turned and left, heading into the guys' bathroom, before answering it.

"Hey, Mom," I said, fighting for control of all my emotions and desire.

"Hi. You okay?"

I ran my hand over my head. No.

"Yeah, just got back from a run on the beach. What's up?"

"Can't I just call to hear your voice?"

"Of course you can, but you never do at nine o'clock on a Thursday. Why aren't you at Leena's Bunko night?"

"She's in Kansas. Her mom's dying. Only has a few more days."

"I'm so sorry to hear that. Will you let her know for me?"

"That's actually why I'm calling. I think I'm going to go out there to help her get through those last days. Help her with the funeral and going through all her mom's things. I'm going to be there for a few weeks."

"That's good. I'm glad you're going." Leena had been a lifeline to us when Dad died. She'd been my babysitter and second mom. She'd made sure my mom didn't come to a full stop. Leena was part of our family, and now she was losing part of hers. In many ways, I wanted to be there, too.

"Anyway, I might not be back by the time you get into port in Massachusetts."

My stomach clenched. I was looking forward to seeing her at the end of the cruise. Both of them. The plan had been for her to drive up from New London to get me when we docked in Buzzard's Bay. I'd wanted to stay with her for a few days before catching a flight back to Texas.

"It's okay. I'll just see if I can change my flight."

"I miss you," she said. I knew it was true. Just like I knew that she was going to help Leena for legitimate reasons, but I also knew that she hated seeing me in my uniform. Hated that I was following in Dad's footsteps. That she didn't want to see me walk off a ship.

"We'll figure out a way to see each other before Christmas," I told her.

She was quiet. "I love you, Doodles."

"I love you too, Mom."

Then we hung up. We did love each other, and we told each other almost everything. Just not the things that might make the other person sad. We'd gotten so good at making sure each of us survived the loss we both still felt in our lives to this day that we'd drifted into a place of perpetual "goodness."

I showered and made my way out to the main room, expecting Ava to be sitting on the coffee table. Except she wasn't. I walked back to the master bedroom. The lights were off, and I could see the shape of her, on her side, in the bed. I stood there, staring at it. Wanting to join her. Wanting to feel again that vibrancy—that life—that I'd felt when I'd kissed her. That I hadn't felt in so long that I'd forgotten what it felt like. To feel free with nothing tethering you to the dock.

I took a step toward the bed, and the sheet stopped moving its regular rhythm, as if she was holding her breath. Then I thought of my mom, and everything she'd lost because of the Coast Guard, and how it would be unfair to bring someone into that life. I thought of how close I was to making my own dreams come true, and I turned and left, shutting the door quietly behind me.

I sank down on the couch. My mom thought I was just joining because of Dad, as a way to honor the man I'd lost, and that was true. She'd also thought that because we lived in New London, where life revolved around the Coast Guard and the Coast Guard Academy, I hadn't experienced anything else. It's why she made me promise not to go to college there, even though I could have gotten a full ride.

She wasn't thrilled when I accepted the A&M offer, but she was happy that I'd at least gotten out of Connecticut. She'd been hoping that I'd see something that would drag me away from my quest. The truth was, I wasn't just doing this because of Dad. I'd always felt a calling to the sea—to the water. And also, to service. To do for others.

It was what I'd wanted with every breath of me since before Dad had died. It was just stronger after he'd gone. Another layer of meaning added to the desire.

I laid my head on the back of the couch and closed my eyes. I was exhausted. I felt more tired than if I'd been on the boat for eight weeks.

I felt like I'd disappointed two women tonight, even though the disappointment my mom felt had been running between us for almost four years. Ava's disappointment in me was fresh. A wound that I knew I'd regret years from now no matter which way I had let the situation go.

If I'd joined her in that bed and then she'd left, or I'd left, I would have regretted that. To have that intimacy, to touch her soul and then leave… that would have hung over me for years. But somehow, not joining her, not melding our souls, was equally painful.

When I finally dozed off, the turmoil in my brain turned into fitful dreams of my dad, and the ocean, and something I couldn't reach in order to save him.

I woke to my phone ringing and that dream still in the air. I hadn't had a dream about my dad since I was in high school. Not in a long time. They usually came when I was making big decisions. I wasn't sure how sleeping or not sleeping with a girl could be a big decision, but as soon as I thought it, I knew it was a lie. Ava was a huge decision. Life altering.

I couldn't go down that path. I wouldn't.

I answered the phone without looking. "Hello?"

"Cadet Wyatt?"

I sat up. It was Professor Abrams. Ava's dad. Shit.

"Yes, sir."

"One question. Did my daughter, Ava, show up there?"

I hesitated way too long, and it cost me.

"Goddamn it," he hissed into the phone. "Why didn't you contact me?"

"I wasn't aware you didn't know, sir." The lie fell from my lips before I could stop myself. Protecting my own ass. Protecting Ava's. I wasn't sure.

"Because I'd really send my teenage daughter to a beach house with three stupid-ass male recruits. What kind of father do you think I am?"

An asshole of one, my brain said as I bit my tongue. I didn't know everything that had gone down between Ava and him. Only that she felt the need to run away. That there was fear and anger and hurt in her eyes when she thought of him.

He didn't seem to care that I hadn't responded. "I'm on my way. I'll be there in less than four hours. You tell her that if she ever wants to see one penny of her trust fund, she better be there when I get there."

I grunted in surprise at his tone, his anger, and his words. Still unsure how to reply, I said nothing.

"You got that, Cadet?"

"Yes, sir."

He hung up.

"Shit."

I was on my feet and into the bedroom with Ava before I could even think. My bursting through the door jerked Ava out of her slumber. She sat up, eyes wide.

"What?"

"Your dad."

Panic hit her eyes. I'd never seen such terror on her joyful face. "He's here?"

"No. But he's on his way. He said less than four hours."

Fear radiated from her. I wondered again if he'd done something to her—physically. Panic invaded my soul at the thought. After a moment of stunned silence, she jumped out of the bed, her bare legs and her butt cheeks greeting me. Her graceful sway drawing me toward her as she started stuffing her belongings into the suitcase she'd left open on the floor.

I stilled her hands with my own, worry coursing through me. I had to ask. Had to ask what he'd done to cause this strong, carefree woman to panic. My thoughts were not pleasant ones. Abuse could come in so many forms. "Ava. He didn't… He doesn't…"

The words evaded me.

She shook her head, looking down at my hands and then back to my eyes. "No."

But it was quiet. I wasn't sure if I believed her. And I'd never not believed her. She was nineteen. She was old enough to be on her own. I didn't get it. I didn't get the fear.

"You've run away. You're afraid. Why?"

She pulled away from me, going back to stuffing her case. "He's controlled my whole life. Every detail of my day. Every moment had to be accounted for. He'd check my phone. My GPS. If I was ever anywhere he hadn't said I could be, I'd be grounded for weeks at a time. He'd take away my phone, my keys, my guitar. The only time I ever got to breathe away from him was when I was with Jenna."

"Okay," I said, still not fully understanding. It certainly wasn't the trust and independence I'd had with my mom. It didn't sound pleasant, but lots of people had overcontrolling parents.

She shook her head. "No one gets it."

"Explain it to me."

"My whole life… he's told me I'm nothing. That if he lets me, I'll make all the bad decisions my mother made."

"He can't stop you."

"He already did."

"What do you mean?"

"It doesn't matter."

She went into the bathroom to grab her things, throwing it all into her bag. She found a pair of her tiny shorts and drew her legs into them, buttoning without a thought of me standing there watching her.

"Toss me my bra," she said, and I looked down to where her pink bra was laying on the nightstand. I picked it up with so many emotions surging through me. Desire. Longing. Regret. Fear. Indecision. I handed it to her and then turned my back, so that I wouldn't see her put it on. If I did, I wasn't sure I'd be able to let her go.

"He said something," I told her, facing the door.

"What?" Her voice was shaky.

"He said if you wanted to see a penny of your trust fund, you'd be here when he got here."

"Asshole," she said.

"Is that how you were planning on paying for Nashville? For college?"

When I heard her suitcase zipping, I turned back around. Her hair was up in a messy bun again, her eyes still flashing different light and different emotions.

"Can he do that? Keep your money from you? Is it from your mom?"

"It was my grandparents'. My mom was an only child. I'm an only child, so the money comes to me."

"Then he can't take it away, right?"

"He's the executor of the estate until I'm twenty. He's been able to do whatever the hell he wanted with it since I was six months old."

"That's pretty fucked up."

"That's my dad."

She pulled her handbag over her shoulder and reached for her suitcase, but I took it from her, our hands tangling and that energy surging through us once more. Knowledge. Understanding. Desire.

She headed out of the bedroom, looked around, grabbed her portfolio from the kitchen counter, and then stared as if making sure she had everything.

"Ava, he can't do anything to you besides the money. I won't let him."

She laughed; it was bitter, harsh. So not the Ava that I'd come to know over the last few days that I realized that this man had wounded her. Deeply. If not physically, then emotionally.

"I'm tired of hearing that I'm a waste of space. I'm tired of him telling me I'm not good enough. I'm tired of him forcing himself between me and my dreams. I'm just done with it."

I wanted to tell her how much I disagreed with all those things she'd said he'd called her, but she was already headed out the door and down the steps.

I followed with her suitcase, with my own panic filling me. She was leaving. She was going. Was I ever going to feel like this again? This powerful urge to not let her go, to keep her to myself, to merge our lives into one… it all flooded me.

When she opened the trunk, I didn't put her suitcase in at first. She looked at me. "Eli?"

"Don't go," I said before I could even think twice about it having slipped from my mouth.

"What?"

"Don't go." I said it stronger. This time as a decision. I didn't want her to go. I wanted to see her again, in Galveston, when I got back from the ship. I wanted to be able to take her on a date, handing her flowers that matched her eyes. I just wanted more. Like her song. More time with her.

She reached up and touched my face with a gentle touch, her hand rubbing the stubble that had almost grown into a beard as I refused to shave on my time off.

"Thank you," she said quietly.

"What the hell for?"

"For wanting me." She said it so quietly that it was hard to hear. How could anyone not want her? This beautiful gazelle before me. But she was already running from the lion that had startled her into action.

She pulled the suitcase from me, put it in the trunk, and slammed it shut. She turned toward me then, and I wrapped my arms around her. She hesitated, as if unsure what to do with the hug, but then placed her arms around me, too. I willed her to feel what I felt, which was that we belonged together. Somehow. It didn't seem insane like it should have. She was mine. I was hers.

"If I'd stayed, would you have taken me on a date?" she asked, muffled against my chest.

"More than one," I told her truthfully, and even though I couldn't see her face, I knew she smiled at that.

"If we ever see each other again, I still owe you an ass whipping."

I chuckled, but I really felt like I was having my heart torn out. A heart I didn't know I'd given away.

"Promise?"

"A date and an ass whipping. It's all yours."

She pulled away, her fear of her dad driving her from me. Her fear of being held to a future that wasn't hers. I understood that. I only had one future in my mind, and I didn't want to give it up either. Not for anything. Not even for her. I wouldn't be chasing after her to Nashville.

That hurt. Tore at me in an unexpected way. Like the tear I'd felt when they'd told my mom my dad had died while I'd listened in the hallway.

Ava pulled open the driver's door and climbed in. I reached into the window, touching a curl.

"You have my number."

She nodded.

"Please tell me when you've made it to Nashville."

She nodded again.

"Please use it…if you need…anything." I choked on the words.

She smiled up at me, her smile hiding her own sadness. "Don't cry, oh Captain, my Captain, because Mac Truck will never let you live it down."

She was right. Did I care?

The engine was on, and she was putting the car in reverse before she stopped and looked up at me with only sadness. "I'm sorry," she said.

"Don't be."

"But he's going to take it out on you."

I hadn't been thinking of her dad. I'd only been thinking that she was sorry to be leaving me. I didn't want her to be sorry over anything. I wanted her to be brave and strong and independent like the girl that I'd seen jumping off the coffee table with her guitar as she screamed lyrics to the unseen world.

"It'll pass."

"If he causes you problems, will you let me know?" I nodded, but we both knew I wouldn't.

She backed up and then stopped again, leaning her head out. "Eli?"

"Yes?"

"I just wanted you to know that I think I could have loved you."

Then she left. With my heart no longer part of my body. Instead, I thought it had chosen to ride along with her. It would never be mine again. I'd lost it once to my dad, and now to a girl I'd known for three and a half days.

And I knew I would never be the same.

♪ ♪ ♪

We were outside, spraying paint on the last side of the house, when the Mercedes pulled into the drive. Professor Abrams got out of the car, slamming the door and making his way toward us. I shut the sprayer off, watching as he shoved his hands into his pockets and stared at us.

I couldn't read his eyes behind the dark sunglasses, but the line of his jaw was tight. "Where is she?"

He'd realized her car wasn't in the drive.

"She left, sir," I said.

"And you just let her?" The rebuke in his tone was clear. He didn't wait for an answer. He turned on a heel and mounted the steps as if to see for himself that she wasn't inside. I followed. Mac and Truck were right behind me.

He was standing in the main room, hands still in his pockets, keys jangling as if he was controlling himself by mangling them instead. The Scrabble board was still on the kitchen table. The kitchen was clean, but our food was spread out around it. We would have taken care of it all before we left. We might be doing that now if he kicked us out.

"Where did she go?" he demanded. He'd placed the sunglasses on his head, and now I could see his dark eyes. Lashed like Ava's—which surprised me— but where hers showed light and joy, his were cold and hard.

"To follow her dreams." I tried not to let my voice get choked up on those words. Tried to remain as emotionless as he was.

He didn't like my answer. His eyes narrowed as he took me in from head to toe. He didn't yell when he spoke, but you could still hear the condemnation in his words. "Are you judging me, Cadet?"

"No, sir," I responded. But I was. She was running because he wouldn't let her be who she was. I wouldn't see her again because of him. My feelings for him were all judgment. He knew it even as I lied.

He looked around and saw the beer carton where we'd been stashing the empty bottles for recycling. He stepped over to them, picked one up, and then turned on us. "Were you drinking with my underage daughter?"

None of us said a word. None of us could. We wouldn't lie, but we wouldn't throw ourselves under the bus either.

He was so controlled. Anger was radiating from him, but you couldn't tell from his face or the words he spoke. I couldn't imagine what it would have been like for Ava, growing up with a man who hid himself behind a mask of disdain. How she could have grown up under this man's thumb and still have so much vibrancy and light was almost implausible. It made her that much stronger…that much more admirable.

He left the bottle on the counter and then headed for the bedrooms, checking every one to make sure she wasn't hidden in them. He ended in the master. I hadn't thought to remove my things from the room. I hadn't thought he'd scour the place looking for her.

"Sleeping with her, too?" he asked, and I caught just a hint of barely veiled disgust there.

"No, sir," I said, thanking God that I could respond honestly to that one. "I was on the couch, sir."

I could tell that he doubted me, but he didn't go fishing for condoms in the wastebasket.

"Did you tell her what I said about her trust fund?" The tick in his cheek gave him away, the frustration there, brewing.

I nodded.

"Goddamn it," he said, keys jingling furiously.

I couldn't comprehend his anger or his actions. Ava was nineteen. Why was he so upset that she was gone? Why would he try to stop her from trying to make something of herself? It seemed more than control. It seemed more than a dad that didn't believe in the course his child had laid out for herself. It seemed almost desperate, which confused me.

He pushed past me into the main room where Mac and Truck still stood, hands behind their backs, at attention even though he wasn't one of our military leaders. We didn't owe him any sign of respect. I certainly didn't want to show him any. He was getting more out of me than he deserved.

"Finish the house, then get the hell out," he said, taking us all in. "If I like what you've done, I may not request multiple demerits for this appalling behavior." He waved his hand at the beer bottle and then toward the bedroom.

Mac stepped forward, and I put out a hand to stop him. We weren't going to win any points by fighting for our cause. He'd already made up his mind.

The fact that he said "multiple demerits" made my stomach sink. He was going to apply for demerits no matter what. The extent of it would be based on our work at the house and how clean we kept our noses from there.

"Yes, sir," I said again. I wanted to tell him to go to hell. I wanted to hand him the paintbrush that I still held in my hand and tell him to shove it up his ass. I wanted to run after Ava and bring her back to me.

Thankfully, none of us had any demerits at the moment. One wouldn't be the end of us. It would result in suspension of privileges and could impact our rank. More than one would jeopardize a lot more than our status at the college. It could end our time there. He knew that. We all knew that. So, he knew we didn't have a choice but to do what he said.

He looked us all over again, contempt evident. But knowing that he had us by our balls seemed to ease his anger. At least the anger he'd directed at us. I didn't know what he'd do to Ava if he found her.

"If you hear from her, I expect to be notified," he said.

I'd wanted to hear from her. I'd wanted to know that she made it safe to Nashville. I'd wanted to know how things turned out for her, but now there was no way that I could return any communication she made. I couldn't risk it. For her or for me.

She was running toward her dream, and I'd have to fight to keep the dream I'd had my whole life alive. We'd have to do that on the separate paths that we'd always been on until chance put us together for not quite four days. From this point on, I'd keep a level head. Focus on remaining in control. Focus on the hard work that was the only thing that would save my friends and me from the hurricane that had been Ava.

Chapter Ten

Ava

BREATHE

Performed by Taylor Swift

I saw Eli in my rearview mirror. Standing there. Watching me drive away. I was tempted to turn around. To go back to him. To stay as he'd asked me to stay.

But I didn't. My own dream too strong. My own fear too strong.

Instead, he disappeared and was replaced by a day that promised a storm. The one I'd felt in my soul the day I'd arrived at the beach house. The guys wouldn't be painting for long today. If my father even let them stay after today. My stomach twisted in guilt and then regret.

I knew what it was like to be on the bad side of my father. He wouldn't yell. He wouldn't scream. He would be calm, and the calm would hurt worse.

The thing was that I could actually see, like flashes of movie previews, images of Eli and I dating. Laughing at the movies. Hand in hand on campus. Him in the audience of a club I was singing at, waiting to hold out his hand and take me off the stage as he had from the bar at the Salty Dog. Kissing me as we'd kissed in the waves on the beach. Like we'd never known anything else and would never know anything but that again.

I knew with every fiber of my being that we would be good for each other. That our broken halves would make a perfect whole. That his lack of a dad and my lack of a mom would somehow allow us to fill that gap for each other. Not as parents, but as partners. Scrabble letters remixed.

A song in the making. Scrabble Tiles.

I was sad, deep in my heart, because the possibility of us was there and yet not. There was a whole host of things blocking that path. Choices. People. Dreams…that for both of us still had to work themselves out.

I could only wish for him everything that I'd never wanted for myself. Love. Companionship. Someone that was happy to see you at the end of every day.

I blinked back the tears in my eyes. Tears that I'd never let fall because I'd never been allowed to cry without being punished for it. But I felt them, inside, for a boy I'd barely known. A man that would never be part of my life.

I hit my Bluetooth button and said, "Call Girlie."

"Ava?" Jenna asked groggily.

"Hey," I said, the emotions clogging my throat as I continued to battle the tears.

"What's wrong?" She'd known me long enough to hear the emotion in my voice from that one word.

"I'm on my way to Nashville. I left Rockport." I said, desperately still fighting for control of my emotions.

I hadn't even cried when I'd gotten off the phone with Juilliard. I'd wanted to. Instead, I'd forced the tears into anger. Anger at losing a dream before I'd had a chance to make it a reality. Like now. Lost dreams. I was still going to make Juilliard happen. I had a new plan. That ripped dream was going to be repaired by my own hard work and determination.

This ripped dream…the one with a boy named Eli. That was never going to be repaired.

"What happened?" Jenna asked quietly.

"My dad called Eli."

"Eli. Is he the tall, dark, moody one?"

I nodded and realized she couldn't see it.

"Yes."

"And he told Ethan the truth? That you were there?"

"Of course. He couldn't lie. My dad would have slaughtered him when he returned to school in the fall."

"Your dad is going to slaughter him anyway," Jenna said seriously.

And I couldn't force back the tears then. They fell, and I sniffled so loud that she heard. I pulled the car over to the side of the highway. I was taking Highway 59 instead of the highway my dad would be driving. It would take me longer, but it would ensure he wouldn't see my car.

"God, Chick-a-dee. You never cry. What really happened?"

"Nothing."

"If it was nothing, you wouldn't be crying. You'd be singing and screaming out the window on your way to Tennessee." She knew me too well.

"I think I gave my heart away. Or at least…there was the possibility that I could have."

She was quiet for a long time. "It was going to have to happen sometime."

"But why now? When I'm leaving? When I only had the chance to know him for a few days?" I said as I got hold of myself and blew my nose on a stack of napkins from the glove box.

"Maybe you needed this to help you with what comes next. It's hard to write about love and lost love when you've never experienced it."

"I lost my mom," I told her.

"That's different. You didn't love her. You loved the idea of her. Of having a mom."

She was right. I was lucky to have a best friend who could always say the things I needed to hear when I needed to hear them most. I was going to miss seeing her daily. Texting, video calls, and phone calls wouldn't feel the same.

"How did you get so smart?" I asked, my smile slowly coming back into my voice.

"I was graced with wisdom by the fairy godmothers," she teased.

"I hate what he'll do to them," I whispered my thoughts out loud.

"What can he do?"

"Demerits at a minimum."

"That's just lost privileges. They'll survive."

Lost privileges could be as painful as bruises. I knew. I thought back to the time, my junior year, when I was supposed to be at the coffee shop, working, and had gone down the street to play at a club. I'd left my phone at the shop on purpose because Dad tracked it with the Find My iPhone app. Dad had come in for a coffee—really to check up on me— and I wasn't there.

When I'd gotten home, he'd taken my phone and my guitar and locked them away. I hadn't gotten my guitar back for six months. The phone he'd given me back after a week as a concession, because he wanted to track my every step. He told me if I ever left my phone somewhere I wasn't again, or if I didn't answer his call on the second ring, I could kiss away any future I thought I had.

"I should have left last year," I said quietly. "When I turned eighteen."

"You thought he was paying for college if you stayed. You thought you were sacrificing one more year for your dream of Juilliard."

I laughed bitterly. "How was I so naïve?"

"You can't blame yourself for wanting to believe in him."

"The only thing I should have believed was his actual words. He hated that Mom was on that plane with my grandparents because of her dream. He said she was reaching for things that could never be. He wouldn't let me do the same. He told me that over and over again. Why did I think this would be different?"

When I was younger and stupider, I'd asked Dad what her dream had been. It had made him turn purple in a way he rarely showed emotion. Not only because I'd dared to challenge him by asking the question when he was telling me I was a ridiculous dreamer like her, but because I'd dared to ask about her at all.

It wasn't until I was older and had access to the internet that I'd been able to scrounge up articles on my grandparents, and mom, and the crash. One of the articles had talked about not only my grandfather's career in the senate, but how my mom was developing a political news website. Back then, it would have been something fairly novel: a fact-based political blog. Supposedly, she'd been going to D.C. with my grandparents to meet with the Washington Post as a potential investor in her fledgling business.

It had made me realize that my mom hadn't been stupid. Maybe a dreamer. Maybe motivated to create something. But she couldn't have been dumb.

It had made me dislike my father even more. For making me feel like she was some flower who'd had to be carefully protected from doing ridiculous things. For making me feel that I, too, was ridiculous for having ambitions.

Jenna was silent, unable to disagree with me.

No more. I wouldn't be subject to his contempt any longer. I just hated, with every fiber of my being, that my freedom had been at someone else's cost. The fact that Eli and Mac Truck could be hurt by my actions riddled me with guilt.

"I gotta get back on the road," I told her, determined to put as many miles between Dad and me as I could. Determined to put the tears behind me just as I put the house in Rockport filled with muscled men behind me.

"Okay. Keep me updated on your drive?"

"Of course."

"Take care of you."

"Take care of you."

We hung up, and I looked at myself in the rearview mirror, unaccustomed to the tears that I'd shed. Tears I hadn't been allowed, just as I hadn't been allowed a chance to make my dreams come true. But I was going to make those dreams happen anyway. Jenna was right; this was just an experience I had needed. It was just one stanza, though. It wasn't the whole song. It was just a few lines in the more important adventure that was still to come.

Falling

CRAVING YOU
Performed by Thomas Rhett

Chapter Eleven

Eli

I ran up the steps of the apartment two at a time, partially because I knew I was late but partially because I was freezing my nuts off. New York City in March was not always a happy place. The weather was sporadic and inconsistent. I should have been used to it after being back on the East Coast for almost four years now, but I wasn't.

I still longed for the heat of Texas on many days. It felt like Galveston—and my time there—was a mirage amongst my lifetime of memories. Texas had been on my mind lately. Ever since I'd gotten a glimpse of dark brown curls in a messy bun walking out of a SoHo coffee shop. They reminded me of Ava's hair that summer in Rockport.

Truck would literally stuff me in a closet if I told him that—or even mentioned that name to him. He had no love lost for Ava. For me, she was the closest thing I associated with love. Or at least the possibility of love. I loved my mom. I loved my almost mom, Leena. Hell, I even loved Mac Truck like you loved brothers. But I hadn't ever loved another female even close to that almost-love that I'd felt in the not quite four days I'd known Ava Abrams.

As soon as I put the key in the lock, I heard a voice on the other side of the door. Mac's voice.

"'Bout goddamn time!"

When I opened the door, he was already there, engulfing me in a hug. I'd missed him more than I'd known, because hearing his voice filled me with an ache in my gut. I'd been in New York for four years, and Truck had been there three, but our wingman had been on his own in D.C. ever since we'd left Texas. And it had been a year since we'd gotten to catch up.

He was dressed in his Navy whites and smelled like he'd piled a whole bottle of aftershave on his body, but his smile was wide as ever.

"Jesus, what did you do, break a bottle of cologne on your head?" I asked, pounding his back and then stepping away to choke clear of the fumes.

"The ladies love it," he said. His smile grew as I continued to cough and frown at him while dumping my gear on the nearest available chair and heading for the kitchen and the fridge stocked with beer for his visit.

"Still a grumpy ass old man, I see," Mac teased. I was taken back to the fact that Ava was the one to start calling me all of those things. Shit. It had been almost four years, and she still hadn't let go of her hold on all of us. For many reasons—some not so great.

"Still an asswipe waiting to get his dick wet," I tossed back, but I was smiling, too. I brought him a beer with mine. "Where's Truck?"

"Getting his uniform on." He moved closer to me and asked quietly, "How's he doing?"

It was the same question we always asked each other. Truck wasn't the same. Not after that summer. He was hardened. Cold. His laughter less frequent.

"He's the same."

Mac nodded then looked down at my workout gear. "We'll wait while you get changed, too."

I nodded, because I did need a shower, but there was no way in hell I was putting on my uniform. Mac was insane if he thought I was going out in it. Not in New York. Not with him in his Navy whites. There was a difference. Coast Guard members weren't treated the same way as Navy guys. It was almost like the difference between a police officer and a crossing guard. It didn't matter how much you told people that the USCG was the fifth arm of the military. It didn't matter that you told them you had as much, if not more, training than some other branches of the military. You were a member of the Coast Guard. It was like saying auxiliary or reserves.

I'd known that when I signed on the dotted line. My dad had griped about it enough when I was little for me to remember it. But growing up in New London, where the USCG academy and DCO facilities were at, it had shielded me from the full extent of it. New London loved its Coasties. New York City saw you like a dock worker.

Not that there was anything wrong with being a dock worker. Those people made more money than me and had set schedules. They were good people. I ought to know. I worked with a lot of them day in and day out.

But the truth was, disparaged or not, I got a thrill every time we boarded a boat and stopped drugs from entering the country. I loved helping people when they needed it. I loved being part of a unit and having enlisted people under my command—leading. It was everything I'd wanted.

I was damned proud that I'd made it happen.

I loved it, and yet, I'd felt restless these days. I'd worked so hard to make this dream happen that I wasn't sure what to do now that I had. What was next? A series of promotions? A boat of my own someday? I had this blank slate of my life in front of me that I was struggling to fill. It was a strange kind of loss. To have the loss of a dream, not because it hadn't happened, but because it had.

Truck came out of the bathroom that we shared in the tiny walk up that we'd rented near the station. It took more than our housing allowance, but it was close enough that we were never late to work and could be onboard a ship in less than thirty minutes.

"You're an ass for letting him talk you into that," I said as I walked by him in his dress blues, a jacket in his arms.

Truck rolled his eyes, no smile. "I know, but I don't get to play wingman to him very often anymore."

I grabbed clothes, showered, and joined them in less than ten minutes. My hair was normally still stubble, whereas Mac Truck had let theirs grow to a military-allowed ear length. I just didn't have the patience for it after so many years of shaving it to almost nothing. At the moment, it had grown to what I considered an unacceptable length. It needed a cut.

When I came out in jeans and a plain T-shirt, Mac groaned. "Come on, man. We're going out on the town in New York City. Let's at least act like we're something big for a night."

"Says the man working in D.C. Aren't you really a big wig?" I tossed back and Mac glowed. He loved working at the Pentagon. His computer training, and his dad coming to his aid, had gotten him a post that Truck hadn't been able to claim. Not after Ava. Not after her shit-for-brains dad. Working at the Pentagon also put Mac closer to the politics, and he loved that. If only Professor Abrams had added him to his collection, maybe that last year as a Sea Aggie would have gone differently for all of us.

"Go change, dude," Mac insisted, but I ignored him.

I opened the CarShare app on my phone and ordered us a car. "Come on. Driver's going to be here in five."

I swallowed the rest of my beer, shrugged my way into a thick jacket, grabbed my USCG beanie out of the jacket's pocket, and pulled it on before heading out. The other two, in just their stupid uniform jackets, shivered as soon as we hit the stairs.

"Goddamn, it's cold," Truck griped as we waited for the car that was coming. It wasn't just because of the cold. Truck griped all the time. The guy who used to laugh everything off had still not shaken what had gone down four years before.

"It's your own fault. You caved to the Mac-pressure," I insisted.

"I'm going to change," Truck said.

"Too late," I replied as the CarShare stopped at our feet. We got in, and the driver headed toward a bar we liked near Midtown that would give Mac the whole NYC feel. It wasn't the bar we liked best—that was near our apartment—but it worked for when we were showing off the city to our pals.

I liked New York. Liked that you could lose yourself in the anonymity of it all. Be just another person, living just a normal life. I liked the diversity and possibilities that were always at your feet. As a single guy, it was fine, but I couldn't imagine being married with a family in the city. I saw families here every day, but it didn't seem like a way to grow up.

Not that I was envisioning myself with a wife and kids. The military life was hard on a family. I knew that from experience. Yet, a part of me objected to that. We'd had a good life, my parents and I. We'd been happy.

Truck was itching for a new assignment out of New York. He wasn't used to city life, having grown up in a small town in Northern California. I wasn't sure I wanted him on his own these days. He was a somber bastard as it was without Mac or me around to lighten him up.

But we were both up for promotions, and that probably would come with reassignments, whether I wanted Truck on his own or not. They were promotions we'd earned. I just didn't have a desire to go anywhere else. I liked being close enough to my mom and Leena that I could see them on the weekends. Not that they needed me. They were strong and independent and had each other if they needed anything. But as they started to get older, would they need me then?

"You should have put on your uniform," Mac said, not letting it go like he'd always ridden everything into the ground.

"Let it go, Macauley," I said.

"Jesus, I thought you were the only sourpuss of the bunch these days," Mac said to Truck. "What's wrong with Captain Grumpy?"

I wasn't grumpy. The name Ava had given me tore at me as it always did when they said it. I was just…in a funk. I had to get my head out of my ass and think about my next assignment. Then I'd be okay. New goals. New plans.

"He's been that way for a few weeks. Storm a brewing, I think." Truck shrugged. As if he could talk. As if he wasn't like this all the goddamn time.

I tried to shake off my attitude. It wasn't my normal mode of operation. I didn't usually wallow. Hell, I hadn't even wallowed when Professor Abrams had done his best to get us all thrown out of the academy.

Shit. Back to the Abramses.

"I need to get drunk," I said with a sigh.

They both looked at me in shock, stunned, mouths hanging opened. I laughed, pretty sure I'd never said those words aloud to either of them in the eight years we'd known each other.

"Well, hell, you've come to the right person for that," Mac grinned, and I thought Truck almost smiled. That was something. "I can certainly make sure that happens."

Drunk wouldn't solve my problems. Losing myself in a woman's arms wouldn't either, but for some reason, I just needed all of that tonight. A moment of forgetfulness.

We pulled up outside the bar, and I added the driver's tip on my phone before joining the guys as they entered the building. It was loud for a Thursday night. Then again, New York City was pretty much always loud. A pre-season baseball game was playing, and the Yankee fans were all screaming at the TVs. We made our way to the bar and ordered beers with shot appetizers that Mac thought would send me on my way to the drunk I was seeking. It probably would, because, even with my build and metabolism, I didn't drink much.

Mac Truck were already drawing eyes from the ladies in the room, but the bar held way more male eyes than females. They were drawing some male eyes too, but I knew neither of them swung that way.

After a couple drinks, and not really being interested in the females that were available, Mac demanded we go somewhere else. I blurrily brought up my Google Maps app and found some more bars in the area.

We started a long-forgotten college habit of bar hopping.

As we left the third bar for the fourth on the list, Truck grunted. "Hell, if we don't stay put long enough, we aren't going to get laid at all."

Mac slung an arm around his shoulder. "Dude, we'll find someone for you to take home yet."

"I don't want to bring her home with you assholes. I want to go to her place where we can make some noise."

"She might have roommates," Mac teased.

"Maybe they'll want to play, too." Truck shoved Mac off of him. He shoved his hands into his pockets, his permanent glower on his face.

"Maybe they'll be as ugly as yo mother," Mac said.

I groaned. "Not the yo mama jokes. Please. Anything but that."

Not even that pulled Truck into the ribbing Mac deserved.

As we hit the door of the last bar, we caught sight of a board that read "Open Mic Night" with the times listed. The music streamed out to greet us. It was sultry, soul music that was being sung by a female, and we all stopped dead. It wasn't Ava's voice, but it still brought us all back to Rockport and her onstage at the Salty Dog.

"Maybe not?" Mac hesitated, flicking his eyes at Truck.

"There'll be more ladies here," Truck insisted and went in. Mac and I exchanged a startled look.

As soon as we entered, we could tell the crowd was different from any of the other bars we'd hit so far—more moody, artistic types than working class. I wasn't sure if this was the place for Mac Truck to get laid either, but at the point in my drunk that I was at, I didn't really care.

We found a table in a corner, ordered another round of beers and shots, and turned to the stage where a blonde, all in black, was finishing up. She was good. Her voice dragged you to her, but she'd never get into my soul like one singer had.

The crowd broke into a loud round of applause and whistles that had the singer smiling like she'd won an AMA award. The MC came on, a guy in his thirties that was eyeing the blonde as she exited the stage like he was hoping for more than a goodnight kiss from her.

"Next up is one of our regulars. Give a round of applause for Brady O'Neil."

The crowd whistled as a tall, muscled guy with shaggy blond hair came onstage. He didn't have anything but his guitar and his attitude with him. He smiled his dark eyes into the audience, and we could feel the collective sigh that went through it.

I chuckled because Mac Truck weren't going to get anywhere with this crowd either. They were all about the sexy wannabes singing.

"What's so funny?" Truck grumbled.

"Just the fact that you've struck out again. Your uniforms aren't helping you at all. You would have been better off in torn jeans and a band T-shirt," I said.

"If we aren't getting laid, then we are certainly going to join you in your drunk," Mac said and flagged down the waitress again for more drinks when we hadn't finished the round in front of us.

The singer had the whole crowd on their feet, except a handful of tables like ours. They were singing along with him, a song about longing and wanting more. It sounded familiar to me. It tickled at the back of my brain and raised the hair on my arms in a way nothing had since Ava had been in my presence.

"Is this a cover?" I asked, slurring the words slightly. Shit, I really was drunk.

"Not for any song I know," Truck said, looking at Mac who had always been our music expert.

"Don't think so." Mac shrugged.

The guy finished the first song and headed into a second that tugged as hard at my memories as the first had. Then he stopped, talking into the mic. "You all know that I love my songwriter more than I love just about any person on this earth. Well, after months of begging," —some woman in the back yelled that she wouldn't make him beg, and he winked before continuing— "I've finally talked her into singing this next one with me, so give her some encouragement to make sure she stays."

The crowd hooped and hollered. I turned away from the stage to say something to Truck, but the stunned expression on his face and the wave of energy I felt coming from the front of the room drew my eyes back.

There she was. Ava. Weeks of seeing and thinking about her, and she'd finally appeared, apparating into the room like Harry and his friends that she'd mentioned so often. The room burst into color around me. Colors that I hadn't realized were missing from my life. Color everywhere, filling my vision and my heart and my soul with an ache that had me standing.

When I really focused my vision around the colors to look at her, I saw that she was both leaner and rounder at the same time. Stunning. Gorgeous. But without the hyper energy that had exuded from her in Rockport. This Ava was quieter, moving with a purpose that was still sexy as hell, but somehow subdued.

She took the extra mic from the Brady guy and smiled out into the audience. My breath completely stopped at that smile. The corner indenting slightly more than the other on her muddy green-eyed side and causing more flashes of sunlight to hit me.

"Goddamn," Truck whispered harshly.

Mac was as speechless as I was.

"This one you all know; it's called 'Scrabble Tiles,'" Brady announced, and the crowd erupted again in cheers of joy.

Brady started singing, more to Ava than the crowd. The way he moved around her and to her and with her spoke volumes about their relationship. About the intimacy that he was accustomed to with her, and I found my entire body going into defensive mode. Like when I boarded a ship that we knew held a drug haul. Adrenalin pumping, heart beating so that everything sounded as if it was underwater, dimmed and yet heightened.

The song was about how life can be shifted around like the words on a Scrabble board. Letters that should go together having to be broken apart in order to make the most of them. How the easy words weren't always the path to winning; that those are often the ones that hurt you the most. It was about walking away, dumping the tiles, and starting over so that you can accomplish things you never thought possible.

It was about her. Leaving me.

It was about the game we'd played atop a kitchen table in a beach house.

When she took over for him in the duet, when she started singing, all the wounds that I thought had been covered and healed broke open and bled.

And she didn't even know I was there, bleeding out on the floor of a bar that she was singing at. Singing with that husky voice that haunted me in my dreams, but somehow was so much older. Less childish enthusiasm and more old soul wisdom.

Brady wrapped her in his arms, and they cooed together, staring into each other's eyes. She accepted it. Accepted the arm and the stares, and even returned them, but I swore there was something missing in that look that she gave him. She didn't love him.

She wasn't looking at him as she'd once looked at me right before she kissed me in the ocean, and I'd kissed her back. Before I'd let her walk away. Fucking idiot.

Maybe that's what I wanted to see: her not loving him. Maybe it wasn't the truth, but I had to tell myself that in order to prevent myself from storming the stage in my drunken stupor, ripping his arms from around her so that I could bury her in mine instead.

I could feel Mac Truck's eyes on me, but just like once upon a time in a bar called the Salty Dog, there was nothing that could rip my stare from her. I wanted to walk up to the stage, hold out a hand, and demand that she jump into my arms like she had then. I wanted her to announce to the world that Mr. Grumpy was there to take her away.

When the song ended, the crowd went wild like it had a lifetime ago. Our table in the corner was silent, Truck's anger radiating from him while Mac was all nonchalance. And me? What emotion was wafting off of me? Longing. For something I couldn't have.

Brady didn't let her go. He kissed the top of her head, and she beamed at the crowd, because the stage was where Ava had always loved to be. Yet, she wasn't jumping from the stage to the bar top—and not only because the bar was on the other side of the room. There was something tamer about her now. I both hated it and loved it. I hated whatever had caused her to lose that sense of unrestricted exuberance. But I also loved that there was a new energy flowing from her that I hadn't yet named. Hadn't yet discovered. There were new layers to pull away, explore.

I felt my feet moving before I'd actually thought about doing it, my body going to her before my brain cells could catch up. I heard Truck's whispered, "Fucking hell!" and I heard Mac's, "Eli!" warning, but it didn't stop my body.

Ava and the blond were leaving the stage. They were at the curtain that separated backstage from the rest of the bar.

Maybe my movement caught her attention. Maybe the wave of particles that had hit me when she'd come onstage hit her as well, because, for whatever reason, she stopped at the curtain. It caused Brady to take a stutter step as she released his hand and turned to me.

I increased my pace to step closer to her before she could disappear, and our eyes caught across the space that was left between us. I was still moving; she was turned to stone.

When I got to the edge of the stage, a bouncer stopped me.

"Where you going, buddy?" His gruff voice barely registered to me.

I didn't have to answer because Ava had already joined me. The stage wasn't very tall, maybe twelve inches, but it was enough that she was looking down at me just as she had whenever she had stood atop a couch, a stage, a rail, or a rock.

Her smile had faded from her face and had been replaced with a stunned look that echoed the feeling that I had swimming through me.

"You're here," she breathed out, the raspy tone washing over me like a drug.

I nodded. I couldn't find my voice. This made her lips quirk.

"Still silent and broody, Mr. Grumpy?"

God. That tone. The tease. That look. She was wearing skinny jeans, ripped at the knees, showing her skin that was no longer tan from sunshine, and a sheer top with some tank underneath it that accentuated her curves. The top was the color of Caribbean seas and brought out the hints of blue and green in her multi-colored eyes. Her hair was cut, sharp angles that landed about her chin, swinging around like the curtain behind her.

All I could think was how badly I ached to touch her. To run my hands under the shirt. To feel her skin with my rough hands. To pull those straightened angles of hair into my fists so that I could force her head up to allow me better access to her lips.

I was insane. Drunk on way more than the alcohol that I'd let fill me.

"I've come to collect what you owe me." I finally found my voice and was surprised it wasn't shaking. That it wasn't full of doubt and longing. That it sounded just as calm as it did when I ordered the ensigns about deck.

Her eyes widened, her smile deepened, and she laughed. And I was lost all over again.

Chapter Twelve

Ava

GET TO YOU

Performed by Michael Ray

My heart thudded so loud that I could barely hear the crowd or Chance announcing the next act as his way of prodding us from the stage. Once I'd reached him, there wasn't really a way for me to move. Eli had always had that effect on me, commandeering my body into doing things.

He looked the same in that he was all military muscles, self-control, and intense eyes. But he also looked older, having aged in that way that men seemed to do as they moved through their twenties. Little left of the college boy I'd met on the beach. He hadn't had much boy in him even then, and now it was non-existent.

He was all man.

Muscled. Gorgeous. With a dark-haired evening shadow on his face. His whiskey-colored eyes, that I still saw vividly in my dreams, were calling to me just as they once had.

The pull on my bones and my skin and my heart was the same as well. I'd doubted those feelings so many times since then, thinking that there was no way my body had truly reacted to his the way I remembered. I had told myself that I had just been a stupid teenaged girl full of thoughts of freedom and escape and hormones. I told myself that his effect on me had been situational. Momentary. Fleeting.

But it wasn't. I was feeling all of those things all over again, my body aching to leap into his arms just as it had from the bar of the Salty Dog.

He was there to collect on a promise I'd made him so long ago that I was surprised he'd remembered it. I couldn't help but laugh at that. It was just like Eli… to have a demand be the first thing from his lips.

I felt Brady's arms wrap around my waist. My body screamed at me to push him away, but I didn't. Mostly because I was still stunned by Eli's appearance in a New York City bar.

"Babe?" Brady grunted.

I didn't take it personally, but I could see that Eli did—the arms wrapped around my waist and the affectionate *babe*. I wanted to laugh again, because Brady called every female in his acquaintance *babe*. Even some of the guys. It was his way of saying *Hi* or *What's up?* or *Come on*. It was his favorite word. It also allowed him to not have to remember names, especially the female names, from his long list of conquests.

Eli's eyes squinted so hard that I thought his forehead might explode. I didn't know how to react to that—his apparent jealousy at Brady's hands on me— when there'd been nothing between Eli and me but years of silence.

Irritation flashed through me, at him having gone all this time without contacting me and then still acting like he could demand anything of me. That irritation made me do the thing I never did. It made me ease back into Brady's chest even as I was smiling down at Eli.

"Brady, I'd like you to meet Mr. Grumpy."

"Seriously?" Brady reached out one of the hands that had been around my waist toward Eli. "Nice to meet you."

Eli looked down at Brady's hand, but his hands didn't budge from where they were shoved into his jeans, as if he was keeping them there on purpose. To prevent himself from doing something stupid. To not lose control.

What would Eli be like if he completely lost control? A memory of our heated kiss in the ocean filled me, my body responding as it leaned away from Brady and toward Eli without my consent. That night on the beach had been a start to his losing control. But it hadn't been complete. He'd still pulled away and let me walk down the shore without him.

The next act came onstage, brushing into Brady, irritated at the fact that we hadn't left. It was Brady that spoke, and not Eli or me.

"Hey, come on back, we have to get offstage," Brady said as he pulled me toward the curtain.

The bouncer took a step away from where he'd been standing, breathing down Eli's neck.

As I was being dragged through the flimsy material separating the back of the bar from the front, I saw Eli leap gracefully onto the stage and follow us. Without a word. His eyes never leaving my body. Glancing toward the hand that I had entangled with Brady's and back to my face.

It was Brady who let go of my hand and not the other way around. It wasn't because he was intimidated by Eli's gaze. It was because he was reaching for the water bottles we'd left with our bags in the rack that the performers always used.

Brady took a long swig, offered me his bottle, and I shook my head. I had my own. I wasn't sure why he offered me his. Scratch that. I did. It was like Brady was playing along with me now that I'd told him who Eli was. Because Brady knew I'd never be one of his girls. It was what had gotten us this far in our partnership. It was really part of the reason he and I had lasted this long. As friends. We both knew it.

"So, you're Scrabble Guy, huh?" Brady asked, once again being the first to talk.

"Yes," Eli said, his tone strong and sure even though he'd never heard the song until tonight. But if he'd listened to the words, there was no way it couldn't have been about him.

There was a fuss onstage, and then the curtains parted to allow Mac through. I hadn't seen Mac in as many years as Eli, and he had changed too. More man, less college clown. He wore a white Navy uniform that made me smile. Mac on the town. I wondered where his wingman was. I didn't have to wonder long.

"Eli, Truck walked out. Called a CarShare. He's pissed as hell that you're back here with her," Mac hissed.

That did stun me—that Truck would be pissed at anything. He had been the friendliest, most easygoing of the bunch back in Rockport. He'd been the one to accept me first. The one to treat me like a little sister. I frowned. Why would he be pissed that Eli was visiting with me? Why could Mac barely look at me?

"I'm coming." Eli's response was curt, but he hadn't taken his eyes from me. To me, he said, "I'd like to meet. To talk."

His eyes flicked to Brady for two whole seconds and then back to my face. I took in Mac's coiled stance, still looking away from me, and the serious look that was always on Eli's face and nodded.

"Sure. I'll be at Café La Mode tomorrow around ten. Will that work for you?"

He nodded and turned toward Mac, who didn't say hi or goodbye or anything. They both skimmed their way through the curtain, but Eli looked back one more time, eyes going to Brady lounging beside me and then to me, before he disappeared.

I let out a heavy breath.

"Well, that was certainly entertaining," Brady chuckled, shoving his stuff into his bag.

I turned and gathered my belongings as well.

"What do you mean?"

"Alpha boy and his squad. What the hell did you do to them?"

"Nothing. Absolutely nothing."

"Nobody harbors that much animosity because of nothing," Brady replied.

We headed out the back door and down the street, the cold air making me shiver in my scarf and fleece jacket. This was the only thing I really disliked about New York City. The cold. Not that it hadn't gotten cold in Texas, but it had always felt different—less bitter, more temporary. I tucked my hands into the pockets of my jacket and picked up the pace to keep up with Brady's long legs.

He never realized that he was leaving people in the dust. That was Brady for you. Self-involved. Self-focused. Not quite selfish, but close. He had his eye on the ball. The dream. And he wasn't going to let anything or anyone get in his way. He wouldn't quite step on people to get there, but he wasn't going to move out of the way for them either. Full tilt toward the goal. I'd been that way once.

Not willing to give up anything for my dream.

Now, I easily acknowledged that he sang my songs better than I did. We were putting together an album as part of our jury examination for graduation with hopes of peddling it out to radio stations, YouTubers, and agents. If he got picked up, I'd get song credits. That was a bigger deal than me actually singing the songs these days.

"He was pretty sexy. I see why you've been harboring these unresolved feelings for him for years."

"I haven't."

Brady shoved my shoulder with his.

"Babe, we've been friends since you showed up pissing all over Jaden's Pitch Fest. I know you."

He did. He knew me pretty well. He may be a self-focused sex addict, but he was my best friend at Juilliard. The only person in the whole world that knew me better was Jenna.

"I guess we all know now what you've been saving yourself for," he continued to tease. "But can you please give it up to him so that you'll lose your cranky attitude?"

"I'm not cranky," I said.

"You didn't use to be."

"What's that supposed to mean?" I gave him a side look. We were almost back to the dorms.

He shrugged. "When you first got here, you were all light and energy and words. And now…you're still words, but your lightness is gone."

"I've just had a lot going on. We're graduating in a couple months, and we have jury exams coming up," I told him.

"Try again, babe."

"Stop it. I'm not your babe." I took out my irritation on him.

He just laughed. "You let Military Man think you were."

I knew that he wasn't going to let me live that down. I smiled at him and shrugged sheepishly. It was true. I had. And Eli had hated it. That gave me a weird sense of pleasure. His reaction meant that he had been thinking about me the last four years, too, even though he hadn't called. I guess, to be fair to him, I hadn't called him either.

He'd said to call if I needed him. I had needed him, but he couldn't have done anything when my dad came after me. It would have just caused him more—

"Shit." I stopped in my tracks.

"What?"

"My dad."

"What about the asshole?"

"That's why they're pissed at me. My dad. He must have done something to them after I left. When they got back to school."

"What could he really do?" Brady asked.

I laughed bitterly. "You saw what he tried to do to me. What do you think he would do to the three cadets who had me in their sights and let me drive away?"

Brady, who rarely looked serious unless it was part of his act onstage, turned solemn. "What do you think he did?"

"I guess I'll have to meet Eli tomorrow to find out."

"Like you weren't going to meet him anyway." Brady grinned at me as he used his keycard to swipe us into the lobby. I didn't answer as we made our way through the doors and into the elevators.

We shared a dorm apartment. Two single rooms with a shared kitchen and living space. It cost a fortune to have the singles, and I was paying for more than my half in order to keep Brady with me. He couldn't have afforded the single, but it was one of the good things that I'd been able to do since inheriting the money that had been my grandparents' and would have been my mom's if she hadn't died.

Back when I'd left Texas, Dad had had my money, and I'd never thought I'd be able to do this for someone else. I'd barely thought I'd be able to find a way to afford Juilliard on my own. Now, I was helping one of my best friends, and it felt right. Brady didn't know that I was paying for it, though. He thought he'd earned a scholarship. I didn't want him thinking he owed me anything.

Dad would never have done that. He'd used the money for himself and only himself, bribing people to do things for him. It made me wonder if that was what he'd done to Eli and Mac Truck—bribed people to go against them.

It made my heart hurt. That Dad could have done something so bad to turn easygoing Truck into an angry man. That Mac wouldn't even look at me. Only Eli had. At least he hadn't looked angry—maybe surprised, but not angry.

My stomach flipped over at the thought of seeing him again the next day. After so long. By ourselves. And that made sleep pretty much impossible.

♫ ♫ ♫

I fidgeted with my scarf and my notebook while I waited for Eli. I wasn't drinking the mocha latte that I'd ordered. Mostly because I was afraid it would only add to the jitters in my hands and the butterflies in my stomach.

I'd woken up, in the dark of the night, from a few brief moments of sleep, to words pouring through me. I'd filled pages of my notebook. Brady would love it. We'd have a couple new songs to add to the album if we wanted. They were good. They were perfect for Brady.

My heart didn't object as much as it once would have at the thought of Brady, instead of me, bringing my words alive. Back when I'd met a cadet that twisted my world around, it would have seemed impossible. I would never have considered it. Now, I knew my singing days were in the past, along with the naivety of my teen years.

The door of the coffee shop opened, and Eli entered, a blue beanie on his head, hands shoved into the pockets of a leather jacket lined with fleece. He was drop dead gorgeous, drawing eyes from around the room. He was a movie hero. Or anti-hero. Either way, his dark good looks were beautiful and striking.

My heart broke for everything we could have been and weren't. For the once upon a time that hadn't happened for us.

He saw me the moment he walked in the door, his intense eyes not moving from mine. I used to stare like that—extra long—until the other person looked away. Nowadays, I found that I avoided eyes. I'd given up on finding what I was looking for.

Eli had known me from that time when I refused to look away. Now, I looked down and fidgeted with my pen while he approached. I fought with an unfamiliar desire to hug him. As if, by holding him, I could recover something of my old self that he remembered. But hugs and I went notoriously awry, and this wasn't the moment to start.

He sat down without ordering a coffee, pulling the chair closer and easing into it. I looked up and then down and away. This seemed to catch his attention more than anything. He leaned forward, removing the beanie and shoving it into his pocket before placing his arms on the table, hands only inches away from where mine played with my pen.

He watched me flip the pen. "I wasn't sure you'd come," he said.

That caused me to look up in surprise. "Why?"

"The boyfriend." Eli's voice was full of that gritty gruffness that had always gone down my spine like a feathery touch, causing goosebumps and tingling flesh. It did the same now.

I looked away again. "Brady doesn't care that I'm here."

It was a half-truth. He didn't care in the way Eli meant. In fact, he'd actually pushed me out the door and told me not to come back until I'd been completely satisfied in every possible way. He also wasn't my boyfriend.

"He's an idiot then," Eli said.

I bristled. "Maybe he trusts me more than you do."

Eli chuckled, but it wasn't with humor. It was filled with something else. A warning. A promise. "I trust you." He said the words, but I didn't understand what the undertone meant. Trusted me to what?

I swallowed and changed the subject. "Why don't Mac and Truck?"

Eli sighed. For the first time, he looked away. "I need a coffee. Are you good?"

I nodded and let him avoid the conversation. I watched him in line, not speaking with anyone, the women giving him second glances over their phones or their coffees, the male barista flirting with him in a way that Eli didn't even notice. He got his coffee and returned to the table, removing his jacket, showing off muscled arms in a thermal Henley that fit to every curve.

My body ached, my heart continued to ache, and now my head ached—from thinking and feeling too much.

I didn't give him a chance to talk. I spoke first. "It was my dad, wasn't it?"

He sipped his coffee and put it down, nodding.

"What'd he do?"

"Mac and I had already taken his class, so he couldn't screw with our grades. He petitioned the school for demerits against us for providing alcohol to an underage person."

"I'm so sorry. If I'd known—"

"If you'd known, you would have done what? Sent a note to the school board saying we hadn't let you drink with us?"

He was right. I had drunk with them. I had been underage. I'd put them in a shit position and ran. Remorse filled me.

"I'm so sorry." It was quiet. I wasn't sure he heard it.

He lifted a hand to my chin and forced me to look up at him, his eyes searching mine, concern flooding his face.

"What happened to you?"

There was so much heartache in his voice that it made my own heart ache once more but in a brand-new way.

"Nothing happened to me. What happened when Truck was in his class?"

He didn't remove his hand. Instead, a finger ran along my cheek, and I couldn't help but lean into it—body still in his command. That caused his whole face to light up. The simple action of my leaning into his fingers. I lifted my hand up and pushed his away. He returned to his somberness.

"Your dad failed him."

"Wh-what?"

"Said he hadn't turned in any of the papers. It got ugly, because we'd all been keeping track of everything together, just in case it went that way. Truck had pictures of turning things in as he'd done it. It went to a review committee."

"And?"

"He didn't fail, but they made him take the class again. He didn't get to graduate with us. Had to wait a semester. It ended up impacting his admission to the Navy."

"Crap."

Eli ran a hand over the stubble on the top of his head. "Mac's dad is in the Navy, and his grandfather is in Washington. The demerit didn't stop him after he graduated. I was applying to the Coast Guard, and I had my dad's reputation behind me. I had people at the DCO school that were pulling for me. Truck didn't have anyone."

"I think I'm going to be sick," I told him, hand to my stomach, thinking about how much I'd screwed up Truck's life by just showing up in Rockport. No. Not showing up, but by being a stubborn ass and not leaving.

"After he retook the class with a different professor and graduated, he applied to the Coast Guard. With some help from me and the people I know, they accepted him. But he's almost a year behind me now in promotions. In his career."

"I don't blame him for hating me."

I started shoving stuff into my bag. Pen, notebook, phone. I pushed my coat on. Eli was already standing, but I couldn't stay. I needed to go. Needed to process what he'd told me. About how a stupid teenage girl had ruined someone's career with carelessness.

"He doesn't hate you," Eli said. I just gave him a look. A look that he didn't counter. A look that said he was lying.

"Thank you for meeting me." I debated putting out my hand for him to shake, but then I thought twice about our skin touching. Instead, I moved toward the door. He followed. I kept going. I needed to get away. From him. From me. From thoughts that hurt.

Chapter Thirteen

Eli

BLUE AIN'T YOUR COLOR
Performed by Keith Urban

She ran, and I followed, my heart trying not to escape my chest at the thought of her disappearing again for another four years. At the thought of my life going back to the monotony of the daily grind. At the thought of not feeling ever again. Of not seeing colors again.

"Don't." I caught up to her outside, putting a hand on her jacket. She shook me off and kept going. I followed. "Stop. Please."

The please sounded so ridiculously forlorn. I wanted to take it back. To hide how much I really did need to see her. How much I needed to follow a path that I'd let my old dreams divert me from the last time she'd gone away.

As soon as I'd gotten back to the apartment last night with a silent Truck and a moody Mac, I'd been full of self-realization. I knew, with a sudden certainty, exactly what I needed. I'd realized my Coast Guard dream—I still loved the thrill of the missions—but all of that paled in comparison to the adrenaline-pumping feeling of life that I'd felt when I'd kissed

Ava on a sunset beach. When she'd looked at me and smiled with a face that lit up the sky more than the sky itself.

I wanted more. Just like her song. I wanted more life waiting for me after the mission. Something to look forward to coming home to—no, *someone* to come home to. Another purpose. Something personal. Something mine.

I wanted Ava in my life.

I wanted to know what had happened to her big dreams and her vivacity. To the things that had made her seem like the entire world was going to be laying at her feet. If I was feeling at a loss after my dreams had come true, I couldn't imagine what she must feel if she thought her dreams would never come true.

She stopped and turned toward me and, once more, wouldn't meet my eyes when that was all she'd ever done that summer in Rockport—stare at everyone until she'd memorized and captured our souls.

"I…" She fidgeted, looked up at me briefly, and then skittered her eyes away again. "I just need to process this."

"I wanted to know back then, when he was making life hell for us…I was worried…what had he done to you?" I hoped that this wasn't the reason she was a small reflection of the thundering life force she had been. I was hoping something worse hadn't happened to a young girl on her own in Nashville and New York City.

"Nothing. Nothing like he did to you."

"You said you'd call if you needed me."

"You said you'd call if he made life hell for you."

"You couldn't have done anything about it," I told her with a shrug.

"Neither could you," she told me, for the first time meeting my eyes and keeping them. "Yet I still hoped you'd call."

I had. I'd started to dial the number on my phone that was logged under "The One That Got Away" a hundred times at least. I hadn't given her that name. Truck had. I'd just had her name under Ava. After I'd moped around for a few days with her stuck in my head and heart, Mac had taken the phone and named her Daredevil. Truck had shaken his head, taken the phone from him, and changed her name to what it was now. At that time, I'd known it for the truth it was.

She was the one that got away. I'd let her go. I'd given her up for my dream. For her dream.

But I had tried to call her. It was just that every time I'd started to dial her number, I'd always stopped. Every time I'd started a text, I'd erased it. Truth was, I hadn't known what to say to her. Come back to Texas? It wouldn't have worked. Both our dreams had been too big. Too much a part of us. If either of us had given up those dreams at that time, it would have ended in bitterness and regret.

"I wanted to." I shrugged without an excuse. There was none that could really be an adequate response.

She didn't offer up whether or not she'd wanted to call me. I tried not to let it stab me in the gut. Instead, she looked at me with a frown between her brows.

"Why are you here?" she asked.

"I'm stationed here," I replied. She smirked just a little. Not enough to make the corner of her lip indent further than the other, but almost a full smile.

"Not in New York, Coastie. Why did you ask to see me?"

I loved the Coastie that fell from her lips. That she knew that we were called that. Not many people did. Only those really tied to the USCG. I rubbed my hand over the stubble that was growing on my chin and needed to be shaved. What could I say that wouldn't sound crazy? *I think you are the only thing in my life that will ever make me really feel alive* seemed over-the-top dramatic. Seemed crazy. Psychotic.

"You looked stunning last night," was all I could answer. Her eyes skittered away again, hiding from me like she never had. "You sounded…"

"Stale."

"Like life."

Her cheeks flushed, and I itched to touch the color there.

"Why was the boyfriend singing your songs and not you?"

The crowd around us was increasing as people hustled toward the subway station with a train arriving soon. We were standing in the middle of the sidewalk, being brushed on all sides. I stepped toward the building beside us, taking her with me, my hand returning to her elbow and remaining there, feeling the thread of life that burned between us through the fabric of her coat.

"He does a better job," she answered. I could tell she believed it. That she actually thought that the charismatic blond had more talent than her.

"No one could sing your words better than you. How could you even think that?"

For the first time, I got a full smile. The one that pulled the corner of her lip and echoed in her eyes. She chuckled. "Believe me, three years at Juilliard will definitely give you an appropriate sense of your talent versus others. Brady has more talent in his arm than I do in my whole body."

"I didn't believe in brainwashing, even when they talked about interrogation techniques in training, but it sounds like Juilliard has done a good job of it. Maybe they should sell their methods to the military."

She was still smiling, and I felt like I'd just done a full marathon in four hours because of it.

"Where are you going now?" I asked, desperate to see her again.

"To class," she said, a smile still there.

"Class…right. It's Friday."

"How can you not know what day of the week it is?" The humor in her eyes was still there, and I wanted to keep it there. Not the closed-down version of her that had been sitting in the coffee shop in a chair instead of on top of the table.

"I work all kinds of shifts. Sometimes it's hard to keep the days straight," I told her with an embarrassed shrug. "I'd like to see you again."

Her smile wavered, slowly fading. "Four years…why after four years?"

Again, I didn't have a reasonable answer.

"Why not?" was all I could come up with.

"Mr. Grumpy suddenly decides to be spontaneous?"

It was worth everything to see her smirk.

I waited while she thought. When she sighed, that citrus scent that was embedded in my olfactory memories washed over me, and I knew that she was going to agree.

"Brady and I will be at the Pink Poodle on Tuesday."

I didn't like the Brady and I combination, but I also couldn't help a smirk. "The Pink Poodle?" It sounded like a strip club.

"It's a hair salon that rents space out as an open mic spot."

"Will Brady be happy to see me?"

She rolled her eyes. "He isn't going to start a fight over me, if that's what you're worried about."

I couldn't help the scoff that escaped me. Because really? Me be worried about Singer Boy? She smirked again.

"He has his own muscles, Hot Shot," she tossed out.

I stepped closer so that she was forced to look up at me. "But I have something he doesn't."

"Yeah?"

"Training."

She pushed away from me, stalking toward the subway stairs with an energy that did remind me of the girl who sat on rails and rocks and tabletops.

"What time on Tuesday?" I hollered after her.

"Use your training to figure it out." And she was gone. Down the stairs. I could have chased her—part of me wanted to chase her—but I didn't.

I looked around, the world that had turned bright with colors dull again. But I headed for the apartment, knowing that Mac Truck were waiting for me. Pissed. Wanting answers that I wasn't sure I could give.

♫ ♫ ♫

The TV was on when I walked in—another Yankee game. Truck had always preferred baseball while Mac had been all about football. It wasn't even noon, and they both had beers in hand—hair of the dog.

I wasn't hungover. I should have been after the amount I'd drank last night, but seeing Ava had sobered me up more than ice down the spine.

They both raised furrowed brows at me.

I had pizza in my hand, and that won me some points. I set it down on the kitchen counter, and they both followed, grabbed plates, filled them up, and returned to the TV.

We'd always been a silent group. Military training and quiet mess halls. We were used to it. But this quiet wasn't really quiet at all. This quiet was screaming annoyance. No…not annoyance…anger.

I grabbed my own plate, filled it up, and joined them.

"She didn't know," I told them to the unasked question.

"You say that as if it's justification. She knew he'd react the way he did, and yet she stayed with us in the first place," Truck slammed out with a mouthful of food.

"It was my fault she stayed," I told them again, like I had a million times when Abrams had started cracking down on us.

"It wasn't. You didn't know him. She did." Truck was always the first one to defend me and throw her under the bus, even when he was pissed at me.

I lost my appetite and put my plate on the coffee table. "When are you going to stop blaming her and blame the real asshole—Abrams? Do you think he didn't punish her as much as he punished us?"

"Me!" Truck said, standing suddenly, pizza and beer flying. "Me! I'm the only one who got fucking screwed in this goddamn scenario. If I was going to get screwed, it would have been at least worth it to have screwed her first."

That pissed me off, and I was in front of him in two strides, shoving him in the chest. "What?"

Mac stood, getting between us. "You know he didn't mean it like that, Wyatt."

"Did you even fucking see her last night?" I demanded. Truck shoved Mac away, grabbing for the mess of beer and pizza.

"Why the hell would I stay and look at the person who was responsible for destroying my life?"

"Abrams was the one who tried to ruin you, not her. Don't blame her. She's hardly a shadow of the girl we met. I'd pretty much say he ruined her life way more than he ruined yours." I winced even as I heard myself say it. Truck's life had been pretty fucked up.

"Bullshit. She's here, singing her fucking songs, prancing around onstage. She doesn't seem to have had even one dream squashed."

"Then you didn't really see her."

"But you did?" Truck demanded. "Captain Dickwad always sees the truth before any of us. Must be nice to have twenty-twenty vision, asshole."

"Jesus Christ," Mac pounded out. "Both of you, back to your corners."

I couldn't eat. I took my plate into the kitchen and threw it into the fridge, eyeing the beers. I didn't grab one because I had to be on duty tomorrow. I didn't want to be hungover. Couldn't afford to be hungover. Truck couldn't either, but there was no way I could remind him of that now with the air between us so sour.

I leaned against the wall between the kitchen and the living area, watching Truck drink.

"She was heartbroken when I told her what happened."

"Why the hell would you even tell her? Why would you go see her at all?" Truck asked, glaring at me.

This was the real question, right? I couldn't tell Truck the answer any more than I had been able to tell Ava herself. Because my life was gray without her. It lacked color. It lacked that very word, *life*.

I needed a new dream. I needed her.

"Just come talk to her," I said quietly, wanting my best friend to see the woman who was stealing my heart the same way I did. Not as some fucking meteor that had burst in and caused wreckage, but as a star that had fallen and needed help getting back into the sky where it belonged.

"No fuckin' way," he growled.

"Just once. Just so she can apologize. She wants to. To both of you," I told them.

"Words are easy," Truck said.

"You're being an ass," Mac told him, taking my side when he rarely took my side. Both of us sided with Truck more than each other. It had always been Mac's and my way. Especially after that summer, once Truck had gotten the worst of it and turned inside himself.

"What?" Truck was as surprised as I was.

"Shit happened. She couldn't have known that her dad would take it out on you. He got even more pissed when his demerits didn't get the action he wanted. You were just the stupid ass who waited until senior year to take his goddamn class to begin with. Circumstance screwed you. He screwed you. But she never screwed you. You saw her. You knew her. She wouldn't have hurt any of us on purpose. She was running for her own life. Think about what it must have been like living with Professor Dick for nineteen years." Mac died off and slammed his way into the kitchen to get himself another beer. He was going to be in New York with us till Wednesday. He was going to be stuck in the middle of this.

I was grateful he was there, playing referee when it was usually my job to do that. To be the calm in the storm and not the instigator.

Truck took a swig of his beer before realizing the bottle was empty. Mac came back and handed him another one.

"Look. You've had four years to sulk. To throw tantrums. You deserved it. You were handed one hell of a shitty deal. But you're here, doing something you love, getting to hang out with Captain Prude every day. You're in New York where there are approximately a million single, beautiful ladies to hit on, and you are back on track. Maybe it's time to let the anger go and move on."

I looked at Truck to see his reaction. Truck looked at me, and we shared a smirk at Mac being all grown up and giving Truck a lecture. It was so opposite of what we knew of him. We both started laughing. Hard. It was good. Mac didn't appreciate it.

"You're both asswipes."

"Studying up on your politics for a run for office, Mac?" I said between full belly laughs that felt good after all the intensity of my morning. Ava. Truck. Worry.

"What if I am?" he asked, sitting down in the chair he'd vacated.

"You're too young to run for office," Truck said with a smirk that was so good to see when it was so rare these days.

"Technically, that's not true, depending on the office I want, but you're right. I need to burn some more wild oats, find a wife, kick out a kid or two, and look way more settled and responsible. But someday."

"We need to get you stationed away from fucking D.C. before you go all sleaze on us," Truck said, shaking his head in disgust.

"Go all sleaze? Hasn't he always been sleaze?" I asked.

"Go fuck yourselves," Mac said, but he was smiling too.

I was grateful, again, to have these two men in my life. Men who had become family. Whose families were my family. Who both considered my mom a second mom—Truck more than Mac. It was good. To have family I belonged to. I also knew now that I was missing something in my life. I wanted to go after that something with the same dedicated focus I'd had when I had gone after the dream of becoming part of the Coast Guard. I just wasn't sure that Ava would let me.

Chapter Fourteen

Ava

LOVE IS LOOKING FOR YOU
Performed by Miranda Lambert

Alone in our dorm room, I knew I only had a small window of time before Brady came back and harassed me about Eli. Brady would want to know whether I was going to see him again.

I was. Because there was no way that Eli wasn't showing up at the Pink Poodle on Tuesday. I knew enough about him to know that he did what he said he would—except for calling me when my dad had screwed them all over.

I was riddled with guilt for what my dad had done to them. The worst of it to Truck. The nicest, most easygoing guy you could ever meet. It made me want to cry tears that I rarely cried, even after years away from my father.

I hadn't cried when he'd tried to take my entire inheritance from me. Even when he'd said the same shitty words he'd been saying to me for years outside the courtroom where he'd lost and I'd won. My dad was never a good loser. Hated losing. He'd made his own bed, though, and I wasn't opposed to him wallowing in it for a long time.

He was lucky that he had a house to wallow in. I could have taken it all. Everything had been in my name, in the trust's name. Every last dime he'd spent since my mom died had been done with the trust's money. By the time he'd realized I was never going to be the subdued, obedient daughter he had fought to make me, he'd only been able to save some of it.

I hadn't wanted his house in Galveston. Or his car. Or the money he'd stuffed offshore.

I did want the house in Rockport.

In so many ways, it felt like that moment of time that Eli and I had had in Rockport was a bubble of fiction. It was a fleeting memory. But that memory… it had been one of the best memories of my entire life. There had been moments with Jenna that were like that… beautiful too. It was just that Jenna wasn't a memory. She was in my life every day, for real.

I picked up my phone and hit the call button.

"Ava?" Jenna answered with surprise. We usually texted during the week, saving our calls for Saturdays when we both had more time.

"Girlie," I sighed and laid back on my bed.

"What's wrong?"

"I said one word; how can you know anything's wrong?"

"First, you're calling me at my lunch time when you know I'm always with Colby at lunch. Second, you never call during the week. And third, it was mostly in your tone."

"I saw him."

"You're going to have to be more—holy shit! Eli, him?"

I wasn't surprised that she caught on so quickly. In the four years since Rockport, Jenna and I had gone around and around about Eli multiple times. At first, it was because she wanted me to text him or call him. Later, it was because she knew that I compared every other guy who came into my life to him, and she said it wasn't healthy.

"Yep," I responded.

"What's he doing in New York?"

"I guess he's stationed here."

"And you just happened to bump into him?"

I told her about the bar, and the coffee shop, and Truck. She said all the right things that a friend is supposed to say and then she got quiet.

"So?" I asked.

"I don't understand why there is a so," Jenna said with laughter in her voice.

"I don't know if I can do this again."

"What again? There was never anything to start. So, you kissed him once upon a time. So, you've only been saving yourself for him for years. So, he's the only guy that ever made you go all girl crazy. So, just do it already!"

"You're no better than Brady. This isn't about sex or not having sex."

"Oh, I'm pretty sure that Brady thinks it's all about sex," she snickered. Every time she'd come to see me, Brady had tried to make it with her, even though she was engaged to Colby and their wedding was scheduled for July.

She read my silence.

"What is it that really scares you most? The thought of actually allowing someone to love you, or the thought of loving someone and not knowing if they'll stay?"

"I spent four days with him four years ago. He kissed me once in the ocean at sunset when I was a stupid teenager. No one is talking love."

"You talk a good talk, but you know that if you'd stayed, your heart would have been a goner. You said it yourself. Now, you're so protective of that little body part that I worry you'll forget how to use it, and you'll die a virgin, all alone, surrounded by ferrets or something."

"Ferrets, really?"

"Well, cat lady seems way too stereotypical for you," she said. When I just huffed a response, she continued. "Chick-a-dee, go for it. Meet him. See where it goes. If all you do is sleep with the guy, then you have one more experience for the story of your life."

"Why are you *always* using that line on me?"

"Because it works on you."

"I hate you."

"You wish you hated me. I gotta run, but take care of you."

"Take care of you."

I made it to the kitchen before Brady came banging his way in. He tossed his stuff on the coffee table, causing everything to go flying in a way that he'd been doing for years but that I'd never been able to get him to stop.

"The song went brilliantly. I think we're just a couple short of a full album, but it's too many for an EP," he said, turning to me with his normal, brilliant

Brady smile that always knocked the girls for a loop but just made me smile back.

"I think we might have enough for a full album."

"Nah," he said and then caught my glance toward my notebook. He dove for it, flipping the pages till he got to the new ones. He read, hand pushing his floppy bangs out of his way, and then raced toward me, picking me up and swinging me around like I was ten years old.

"Shit. These are really good."

I shrugged.

"Man, when you hit gold, you hit gold. Tell Eli that he can come screw you here any time he wants. I'll even be a gentleman and leave."

I snorted. "You a gentleman? And you know it's not like that with us."

"With you and me or with you and him?"

"Either. Both."

"Tease."

"Slut."

"I really am," Brady smiled. He picked up his guitar and started playing some of the notes I'd casually marked, the words being more important to me than the rhythm.

He lost himself for a good thirty minutes in them. I watched, amazed as always at the way he could just see a few notes, a few words, and turn them into passion and emotion. Like he could live inside everyone else's head and read their thoughts and feelings.

He finally stopped and turned to me, putting the guitar aside.

"You're pretty over the moon for this guy," he commented.

"You're incredible," I told him at the same time.

He grinned. "You know I am, but don't change the subject."

I didn't want to repeat my conversation with Jenna all over again with Brady. "Maybe. Maybe not. We'll see."

"Ooh. That means there's a follow-up date," he said.

"Coffee wasn't a date."

"It's the closest thing to a date that you've had in a year."

"There was Logan."

"Logan? Logan does *not* count."

I laughed. Logan was nice, a waiter at a bar we often frequented. Essentially, there had been nothing there, though. He'd tried to get in my pants backstage when he first asked me out, and I'd promptly put him in his place, and he'd promptly lost my number.

"He's going to show up at the Pink Poodle," I said.

"Nice. We'll definitely have to play one of the new songs for him then." Brady went back to my notebook and the songs that I'd jotted down there. It was his usual focus, even more than the girls that came and went.

I wasn't sure how I felt about Eli hearing one of my new songs, but I also wasn't sure how I felt about Eli at all. That wasn't really true either. I knew I felt too damn much for a guy that I barely knew. That was my real dilemma. Too many feelings in too little time.

♫ ♫ ♫

By the time Tuesday hit, I was a basket case. I'd heard from Eli once. On Sunday. A simple confirmation of the time the open mic night started at the Poodle. I'd responded with a simple, "Your training has served you well," and a Yoda GIF.

He responded with a wink emoji.

A wink.

Eli didn't seem like the wink emoji kind of guy. He seemed like a guy who didn't use emojis at all. Like emojis were too much effort.

I dressed in my normal apparel for open mic nights: dark, ripped jeans, a floaty top, my cowboy boots. I momentarily regretted cutting my hair three months ago, because I remembered how Eli had always stared at it, especially when it was down and flying around me. How he'd tangled his hands in it when he'd kissed me. But I also liked the jagged angles of my new look. It made me feel more grown up and less teenager.

More new me. More realistic me. More practical me.

Brady could feel my nervousness radiating from me while we set up at the Poodle. We usually helped Georgie, the owner, by moving a temporary stage in between the hairdressing stations. We set up the equipment and made sure the covered walkway between the Poodle and the coffee shop next door was arranged. People could flit back and forth and get drinks. It wasn't a bar scene, but it was still an open mic night. It usually pulled a surprising number of industry people. Maybe because it wasn't a bar. Maybe because they got to see the musicians and the songs in an alcohol-free zone. Either way, we liked being there, and we'd been helping Georgie set up ever since we'd started singing at it a year ago.

Tonight, Georgie's hair was purple and full of curls on the top with the sides shaved. It was hard to keep up with her styles. Sometimes, she'd switch out contacts to match the color, and tonight, the lilac made her eyes a little ghostly.

Because we were her favorites and helped out for free, she usually put us as the third set to go on. It was like Goldilocks, the perfect place to be—not early, not late. You didn't have to be the first up to bat when no one had showed up yet, but you were on before the industry people gave up and left.

I wasn't looking for the industry folks as I scanned the crowd while we waited for our turn. I was looking for an almost shaved head standing out above the crowd and its accompanying muscled chest that would encourage a natural barrier between him and the other guests. Intimidating and sexy, but not sexy enough for women to cross his invisible line.

What I hadn't expected, when I did find him, was for Mac Truck to be with him—not after everything he'd told me. I'd thought they'd never want to be in the same room with me again. Instead of being nervous, I now wanted to throw up, and I never wanted to throw up onstage, even with the little amount of time I spent on it these days.

Georgie announced Brady, and he sang his normal one-two combination, and then he asked me to come up and join him for "Scrabble Tiles" again. I did, and tonight I could see Eli while I sang like I hadn't last week. His eyes never removed themselves from my body, especially when Brady and I sang like lovestruck fools. It was all part of the gig. The act. I wasn't sure if Eli knew that.

We moved from "Scrabble Tiles" into one of my new songs. It was called "Second Chances." It was about a girl running into a boy at the boardwalk, kissing him under the Fourth of July fireworks, and then not seeing him again until chance brought them together on a subway train.

It wasn't quite Eli and me, but it was enough for him to hear the truth. To hear that the girl's beating heart and longing were part of my own feelings toward him.

When we were done, the applause was loud and hearty. I looked to Eli's group, and Mac Truck seemed like they were ready to leave, but Eli was all stone, as hard to read now as he had been back then.

When we stepped offstage to allow the next group to come on, we were approached by a tall blond in a suit that didn't seem to be his comfort zone. He had cowboy boots on, but he looked like he should have been on a surfboard in California somewhere, his shaggy blond hair an echo of Brady's.

He stuck out his hand to me first and then Brady.

"I'm Blake Abbott. I'm an entertainment lawyer from Nashville."

Brady and I shared a look that said, *Don't get too excited.* We'd heard this before. Even though it was exhilarating, truth was, an entertainment lawyer wasn't an agent or a producer. Those were the best kinds of walkups. We'd had a couple of those in the last year, but nothing that had panned out. Nothing that hadn't seemed more scam than actual production offer.

"Ava Abrams, Brady O'Neil," I told him as we returned his handshake.

"You write your own stuff?" It was said as a partial question because Brady had announced me as his favorite songwriter when he'd pulled me onstage again.

We both nodded.

"Look, I'm only here for another day, because I have to get home before Cam—my wife—kicks my butt for being gone too long, but I'd like to have you talk to a producer I know. Can I call you and set something up?"

I was excited for Brady but trying not to show it. I could tell Brady was thrilled too, because his hand shook a little as he fished his wallet out. He pulled out one of the business cards he'd had made up as soon as he started singing.

The Blake guy took a look at it and then back up at us. "This doesn't have Ava's name on it?"

Brady tossed me a smirk and a look that said, *See*?

"I'm just the songwriter. Brady's the singer. If he gets a deal, I'll get credit that way," I said with a nonchalant shrug.

"Those songs you sang together, they were damn good," Blake responded with a confused look.

"Damn good is different from sensational," I told him. Brady dropped an arm around my shoulder.

"If it's a deal breaker, Ava will join in. She's way more talented than she gives herself credit for," Brady assured him. I scowled at him. I wasn't part of the deal. No way. I was done being the person onstage. I'd given up that dream for reality. I wasn't the most talented person in the room, and I wasn't going to let the music industry control my every move.

Blake ran a hand through his shaggy hair in a way that reminded me of Eli. As if he could read my thoughts, Eli appeared behind the blond in the suit, his eyes flicking between me and all the men surrounding me.

"Ava?" Eli said my name in that way that caused my whole skin to break out in goosebumps, that commandeered my body to turn toward him.

Brady and the blond, Blake, made room to include him in our little circle.

Blake looked him over as if eyeing the competition, but he caught sight of the USCG logo that was on Eli's T-shirt and relaxed. Blake turned back to Brady and me. "I'm serious about this. You're both really good. The songs are good. The looks are good. And Brady's voice will have the ladies throwing themselves at the stage. I've worked with a lot of people and got them agents and deals. I'm interested in you. Both of you. Do you know Watery Reflection?"

We both nodded because, hello, who hadn't heard of the soulful voice of Derek Waters and his band?

"The guy's basically my brother-in-law, and we have lots of connections. So, don't blow me off when I call," Blake said with a look that said he was trying to be stern but just turned into one huge grin.

"We won't. And thank you," Brady said, shaking the guy's hand again. Blake stuck his hand out for mine as well, and I shook it again before he left, fading into the crowd.

Brady and I exchanged a smile and a high five. "Let's not get our hopes up, but shit, that was awesome."

I nodded. I was excited for him and at the thought that this might kick-start the career he'd earned.

Brady stuck his hand out to Eli. "Eli."

Eli eyed it for a moment as if he didn't want to take it, but he did. They held each other's hands for a little too long, eyeing each other in that stupid way that guys do.

"Okay, lover boys, you can let go now. Unless you want to take it to a room?" I threw out.

Brady laughed and let go, but Eli just tucked his hand back into the pockets of his jeans that clung to every tight muscle on his body.

"I'm gonna go help Georgie. You good?" Brady asked, looking down into my face.

I couldn't help but shove his shoulder and then push him away. "Go, asswipe, before I have to do something to your guitar while you sleep."

He put his hand to his heart as he stepped away. "After I just got us a record deal? You wouldn't."

"Got *you* a record deal," I snarked back.

He walked away but not before tossing over his shoulder, "We'll talk about it back at the apartment."

When I turned back to Eli, his eyes were smoldering. That look that I'd named way back in Rockport because of Jenna's sexy romance novels. I wondered what it would be like if he was smoldering at me in a quiet room with just the two of us. Would the smolder burst into flames? Would I? More importantly, would I ever survive the fire?

Chapter Fifteen

Eli

I'd walked away from Mac Truck as soon as the tall blond in the suit joined Ava and Brady near the stage. I could feel Truck's eyes boring into the back of my head with a glare that would have burst it apart if he'd had laser vision.

When I approached, the guy was talking about getting them a production deal. It didn't surprise me, and yet it also made my heart skip about ten beats. Would this mean that Ava was on her way? That she would have the dream she'd wished for actually become a reality? Although, I'd also heard her put herself down as she propped Brady up. Either way, her life was going to be much more about a blond singer who held her like he'd never let her go than an enforcement officer in the USCG.

When Brady stuck his hand out for me to shake, I reluctantly took it, confused that he didn't seem threatened by me at all. In fact, he just teased her and left her with me.

She looked up at me, and she seemed nervous. Another emotion that I'd never associated with Ava back in Rockport. I had to keep reminding myself that four years was a long time. It changed people. Truck was a perfect example. He'd gone from a happy, laidback kid to a grouchy, sour man.

"Does that happen a lot?" I finally found my voice.

"That Blake guy? No. Brady's had a couple nibbles but nothing that panned out. But Watery Reflection…that's huge." Excitement lit her eyes as she spoke.

I didn't know what to say. What I wanted to do was pull her from the room and take her someplace where it would just be her and me and the rest of the world didn't matter.

The pleasure in her eyes faded as she connected with something behind me. "I'm surprised they even came," she said quietly.

I half turned to where Mac and Truck were still standing at the back of the room. Mac was drinking his coffee, checking out the people, as always. Truck was still glowering.

Before I could think to stop her, she was pushing her way through the crowd toward them, and I could barely keep up. Truck saw us coming, his frown deepening.

When Ava got close, it seemed like she flew the last few steps until she'd surrounded him in a hug, the impulsive Ava that I knew from Texas taking back over the reserved Ava that she'd been since I'd first seen her in New York.

I loved Truck, and I loved that she was hugging him, but I also hated it. I'd barely been able to touch her, let alone be held in her arms. It made me want to demand my own hug.

Truck's scowl turned to surprise as he looked over her shoulder at me. I heard her say, "I'm so sorry. I'm so sorry I screwed up your life."

It made my stomach clench and drop to my knees for the hundredth time since I'd entered the stupid Pink Poodle. I saw Truck's arms, that had been tight with fists clenched at his sides, move to wrap around her. He hugged her back. Then, he said the thing that Mac and I had been telling him but that he'd never agreed to before.

"It was your asshole father, not you." His voice was gruff with emotion.

They hugged each other, squeezing harder before she withdrew, bringing a hand to his face. I swear the big schmuck was crying. She wiped at his cheeks, her expression full of sorrow.

"I should have left the day I got there," she said, voice full of pain and regret.

"It wouldn't have mattered how long you stayed. He was angry. He would have found someone to land it on, no matter what," Truck said gruffly.

"I'm sorry it was you," Ava told him, the honesty in her voice so sincere that it would be impossible for anyone to stay mad at her, and Truck didn't.

"I'm pretty sure he took it out on you, too," he responded.

She nodded but didn't elaborate. She turned to Mac, starting to lift her arms to hug him too, but then awkwardly stopping for no reason that I could understand. Instead, she just said, "I really am sorry, Mac."

"I landed just fine. We all did. Truck just got a later flight, that's all," Mac assured her with his big smile that usually won him a few bras and panties.

Ava didn't seem to notice. She pulled herself away from him and turned so that she could look at me. "Pizza?"

She was including all of us.

"Won't the boyfriend mind?" I asked.

She didn't respond as a tall woman in black and white approached with the bag that I'd seen Ava with the other day at the coffee shop. It looked like the same bag she'd had four years ago, except it was softer, more scuffed and worn. The woman was easily five foot eleven, and the curls that topped her head almost like spikes made her seem taller. The curls had purple tips, and when she got close enough to us, I was surprised to see her eyes almost the same color as the hair.

"Brady said you needed these," she told Ava.

"Thanks, Georgie," Ava replied, taking the bag and a coat from her.

Georgie took us all in. Three giant men that didn't seem to dwarf her at all. "You going to introduce me to your friends?" she asked Ava with a smile in her voice.

Ava rolled her eyes. "Georgie, this is Eli and Mac Truck. Guys, Georgie."

Georgie laughed, a tinkle that seemed small for her overall height and the personality that was pouring from her. "Mac Truck, huh?"

"It's Macauley," Mac said, sticking out a hand. I had to bite back my own laugh. I'd never, in the entire time I'd known Mac, heard him introduce himself to anyone by his full name. He hated it. With a passion.

The way he was taking in Georgie made me wonder if he'd been hit with a wave of girl power like the one that Ava had been hitting me with ever since we'd first met.

Georgie took the hand Mac offered, flipping it over to look at the palm.

"Says here I should stay the hell away from you, Mac—Macauley." She glanced up at him with laughter in her eyes. "Should I?"

Mac grinned at her and then surprised her by turning her own hand over. "Says here that you will never be the same again now that you've met me."

She laughed back at him, pulled her hand away, and looked to Ava. "You okay? Seems like an awful lot of testosterone for one woman to have to deal with."

Ava smiled at her. "Nah, they're a bunch of cubs. Not a devouring lion in sight."

Truck and Mac took objection to that. I just continued to take it all in, Ava being just a little more like the Ava we'd known. I wondered if she'd needed the forgiveness from Truck as much as he had needed to hear the apology.

"Call me if you need me," Georgie said as she walked away, looking back over her shoulder to wink at Mac.

Mac seemed like he wanted to follow her.

Truck slammed a playful fist into Mac's shoulder. "Dude, did you just go all Macauley on us?"

Mac shook his head. "What the fuck just happened?"

Ava laughed, a full laugh that always made me feel like we'd won the prize in the Cracker Jack box. "I believe you were just Georgie-fied. Come on, I'll treat you all to some real New York pizza."

She headed toward the front doors, and I followed. Truck did too, but Mac seemed to hesitate, searching the crowd for purple hair and purple eyes. When he couldn't find what he was looking for, he joined us.

Ava shrugged into the jacket Georgie had handed her and led the way down the street. "It's not far; do you mind walking?"

We all just shook our heads and let Ava lead us through a tangle of streets and alleys till we ended up outside an Italian restaurant. It was busy but not so crowded that we wouldn't find a seat.

"Ava!" the hostess said with a smile. "It's been a while."

"Hey, Kay," Ava said. "Been busy. Not long till we're done. Brady and I have been writing and recording like crazy, so it's been hard to poke our heads out for anything else."

Kay looked behind Ava as if searching out Brady. "He's not here," Ava said, laughter in her voice. "But these three hooligans are. Can we have a table for four?"

"Sure, let me go get something set up." Kay looked disheartened as she left us to prep a table.

"She's always disappointed when Brady isn't with me," Ava said.

The conversation with the waitress had me slightly hopeful. Maybe Brady wasn't her boyfriend? She didn't seem to care that the hostess was drooling all over him, and she hadn't brought him along with us to pizza. Yet, the way they moved together onstage—the way he wrapped himself around her as if owning her—it seemed like so much more than friendship.

The hostess seated us at a booth in a far corner. Ava ordered beer and pizza without once conferring with us on what we wanted, but none of us stopped her, like we'd never stopped Ava from doing anything she wanted when she'd whirled into our lives and then back out four years ago.

"So, Mac, where are you stationed?" Ava asked.

"D.C. At the Pentagon." Mac said with pride.

"No way, they're actually trusting you with our country's secrets?" she teased.

"I'm completely trustworthy." He smiled, taking a swig of his beer.

"My dad must be kicking himself in the ass that he didn't include you in his collection," Ava said, grimacing at the mention of her dad.

"We were never interested in being collected, especially by a dickwad like him," Truck growled.

Ava nodded, the smile gone at the mention of her dad. "I'm glad you weren't."

The pizza came, and we bullshitted about the Coast Guard and the Navy, and Ava told us some stories about her crazy artistic friends at Juilliard. It was meaningless conversation, but after the mention of her father, Ava had lost some of the lightness she'd earned by her moment with Truck at the Pink Poodle.

When the check came, the waitress handed it to Ava as if it was something she did all the time. We all pulled for our wallets, but Ava stopped us. "No way. This one is on me. I feel like I owe you meals for the rest of our lives."

"Ava," I groused, reaching for the check, but she just shoved her credit card at the woman, who took it and walked away. I continued my protest. "You don't owe us anything."

She ignored me—another thing that Ava had been good at. We gathered our things and headed out the door. The noise of NYC assaulted us just as the cold did. The night air had dropped to somewhere close to freezing, our breaths heavy in the streetlights.

Mac Truck exchanged a look that I couldn't quite read. It was Mac who spoke first. "I gotta catch an early train tomorrow, so I'm heading back. Truck?"

Truck nodded.

Mac wrapped me in a hug—tight, hard, like we weren't going to see each other again. In our jobs, you never knew if that was going to be true. "If I don't see you tomorrow, I'll see you in June?"

I nodded and hugged him back before stepping away and shoving a fist into his shoulder. "Don't blow us up, asswipe."

Mac laughed. "I'll do my best not to hit the shiny red button."

Mac and Truck took turns hugging Ava, and she seemed uncomfortable for the first time since the Pink Poodle, as if hugs weren't part of her normal life. I still hadn't been able to hug her, though, and it was now making my hands and body itch. I wasn't sure how long I'd be able to go before I scratched it.

Truck said quietly, "Thank you."

Ava looked at him in surprise. "What?"

"Thank you for reminding me of who I was really mad at." He let her go and looked at me. "Make sure she gets home safe, oh Captain, my Captain."

It had been a long time since Truck had called me that. Mac had continued, but Truck had been sullen and unhappy. My heart tugged. If nothing else came out of seeing Ava again, the fact that she'd kicked Truck into a direction that was his old self was a gift. I swallowed hard and nodded.

When they took off down to the corner of the street to wait for a CarShare, I turned back to Ava. "Which way is home?"

She fidgeted with the strap of her bag and pointed in the opposite direction of Mac Truck. She started walking, and I followed. I was overwhelmed with a feeling that this was what I'd always wanted to do. Follow. Wherever she led.

We were quiet while we walked. Eventually, she stopped outside a building, and when I looked up, I could see the words Juilliard shining down on us.

"This is me. Dorms."

I was a little surprised that she was still living in the dorms as a senior, even though, as a cadet, that was where I'd spent all four years of college. The dorms weren't the home I was hoping for her—a quiet living room, a place to ease next to her on a couch. To touch her. To figure out what was going on inside the haunted looks she gave.

I looked down into her face, searching for something that showed she wanted me as much as I wanted her. That she'd missed the thought of me as much as I'd missed the thought of her. I stared for a long time. Like she used to stare. I saw emotions in her eyes: uncertainty, more regret, and other feelings I couldn't name.

"Thank you," I said quietly, adding my thanks to Truck's. Her eyes flashed with sorrow before she turned away.

"I don't think any of you should be thanking me." She pulled a keycard attached to a lanyard out of her bag.

"You don't understand what it's been like. Truck…he hasn't been himself since it all went down, but with one hug and a few words, you've sent him back on the path to finding himself."

She snorted in disbelief. I grabbed her arm and pulled her so that she was looking at me. So that I could stare down into her face and continue my examination, looking for the scars that I knew she was wearing, but that I couldn't see.

"You freed him tonight…of so much anger…with a hug. A hug that I was so jealous he got." The words came out of me before I could stop them, surprise registering in her eyes.

"You-you want to hug me?"

"Do you even have to ask?" I was pretty sure my desire for her rippled off of me. "But I'm afraid if I do, I won't be able to stop with a hug."

She didn't move. It was almost as if she didn't breathe at all. "If that shiny guy that you're dating and singing with is ever dumb enough to let you go, I'll be the first one to call him crazy. I'll be the first one in line, demanding that you keep that promise you gave me."

Her breath stuttered. "Promise?"

"You promised me a date."

"Four years ago. You can hardly hold me to that now."

"I can. I will. A promise is a promise."

I was deadly serious, no laughter in my voice, but she still smiled.

"You that desperate to get your ass whipped? I'm sure there are plenty of places in New York you could get that, if it's your thing."

Four years ago, it had been part of the promise: a date and an ass whipping. It made me happy that she remembered all of our conversations just as I did.

"I don't need a place. I just need you."

That had the smile fading some, and I needed to kick my own ass for making it fade, afraid that my words had been too much.

"Eli," she breathed out, the night air taking her breath and turning it white as it came toward me, caressing me in her sweetness before evaporating. "He isn't my boyfriend."

Shock had me letting go of her arm. My stunned expression turned her smile back on. Full blown. Old Ava full of sass and harassment.

"He really is stupid," I said. My own grin took over my face as something that I was pretty sure was joy filled my entire being. Joy that she wasn't his. That she could be mine—if I didn't blow it. If I didn't make some lame mistake that caused her to run away.

"I didn't say he hadn't tried to make the moves on me." She grinned.

"I'm sure he has," I replied, closing the tiny distance that was between us, not wanting to think about the things Brady had tried so that he could get her in his life…in his bed.

"We're just partners. I write, he sings. We're friends."

"I'm out to sea the next few days. I won't be off until Sunday. It isn't a typical date night, but I'm hoping you'll say yes." My hands were at her waist that was hidden by the puffy coat she wore and that I ached to remove so that I could feel her bones, and her skin, and the quiver that I saw more than felt go through her body.

"Yes," she whispered.

I pulled her to me, arms surrounding her tightly so that I could have my own damn hug, her scent filling me, taking me back to the warm sun and humidity of Rockport. Taking me back to a sunset where I'd given in and kissed her back.

It took a few seconds before I felt her arms go around my waist, but then she was hugging me equally tight.

Just like I'd told her I would, I didn't want to stop with a hug. I wanted to tilt her head up and kiss those damn pink lips until they were red and scuffed from mine. I wanted to kiss every part of her, but it would have to wait, because I wasn't kissing her like that on the street in the freezing cold. Nor would I be kissing her like that in a dorm room with girls waiting on the other side of the door.

"Sunday. Seven?" I said with her still in my arms.

"Sunday. Seven," she agreed.

"Ava?"

"Yeah?"

"I really liked your song."

"Which one?"

"All of them."

She laughed, muffled by my coat and our hug.

I let her go reluctantly. I pulled the keycard from her hand, swiped it against the keypad, opened the door for her, and handed the card back. She took it and looked up at me, happiness and confusion written in her eyes.

"Go before I can't stop myself," I growled out.

"Maybe I don't want you to," she said breathlessly.

I groaned. "Don't say that."

She stared at me then leaned up and kissed my cheek near the corner of my lips. If I'd turned, I could have had her lips on mine, but I didn't. I just stared into her beautiful face instead.

"Sunday it is," she said with a gentle smile and then walked away.

I let the door shut with a clang behind her, locking me out, preventing me from doing anything more.

She looked back through the glass at me, a smile on her face, and she waved.

I nodded, shoved my hands into my pockets, and watched until she entered an elevator bank. Then I turned and walked away, heart zinging.

I called for a car, and once I'd climbed into the back seat, I pulled my phone out of my pocket and brought up the contact that said "The One That Got Away." For the first time in four years, I was tempted to change it. Change it to "Hope" or "Life" or "Everything," but I didn't want to jinx us. I didn't want life and unrealized dreams to get in our way again.

Instead, I hit "message."

ME: Where's your favorite place in New York?

THE ONE THAT GOT AWAY: Battery Park, why?

ME: I have a date to plan.

THE ONE THAT GOT AWAY: You planning on taking me to see the Statue of Liberty?

ME: Is that what you want?

THE ONE THAT GOT AWAY: I want you.

I groaned, my entire body reacting to that statement.

ME: Good.

THE ONE THAT GOT AWAY: Cocky much?

I smiled. I couldn't help it, but my cock was definitely reacting to her comments even though that wasn't what she meant. Male bodies can't help but react to words like that from women they desire.

ME: It's only fair.

THE ONE THAT GOT AWAY: That you're cocky?

ME: Stop talking about cocks. And no, it's only fair that you want me because I've never stopped wanting you.

THE ONE THAT GOT AWAY: I'm not sure I believe you.

ME: I can think of a lot of ways I can prove it.

THE ONE THAT GOT AWAY: Promises, promises.

Hell. I was going to have a really hard time getting out of the back seat of the CarShare. I was going to have a hard time getting into the apartment and was going to require a cold shower before I could get any sleep tonight.

ME: Sunday. 7 pm.

THE ONE THAT GOT AWAY: Sunday.

ME: Goodnight, Ava.

THE ONE THAT GOT AWAY: Goodnight, oh Captain, my Captain.

I groaned again. Four days was going to feel like an eternity, but I was smiling. For the first time in probably four years. A real smile. Just like Truck had.

Ava had saved us both tonight.

Now it was my turn…to make sure she was saved, too.

Chapter Sixteen

Ava

I COULD USE A LOVE SONG
Performed by Maren Morris

When I got up to the room, Brady was fiddling with his guitar on the couch. He looked up and then around me, expecting a large body to emerge in the doorway. He seemed slightly disappointed when there was none.

"What did you do?" he asked, voice laced with accusatory humor.

"Me?"

"He's not here. Did you send him scurrying away like all the others?"

I chuckled, removing my coat and throwing my bag on the mess of papers on the coffee table. I sank down beside him on the couch.

"No. We have a date set up for Sunday."

"You've waited years to jump the guy, and you sent him away for a date?"

"He sent me away for a date."

He put the guitar down on the other side of the couch and pulled me up next to him.

"He's a stupid ass."

I laughed. "He said the same about you."

"Me? Why the hell am I a stupid ass?"

"Evidently, because you aren't my boyfriend."

"Did you tell him how hard I tried that first year? And isn't he glad I'm not your boyfriend?"

"Oh, he's glad all right."

"Like hot kiss glad?"

"You're as bad as Jenna. Besides, I don't kiss and tell; you know that. I'm not like you."

Brady sighed. "Do you know how long it's been since I've had a kiss to talk about?"

"You just slept with that black-haired dynamo from the bar last weekend!"

"But that wasn't talk worthy," Brady said with a smile.

I hit him in the abs. "You're cruel. And you wonder why I never let you in my pants. I can't imagine the nasty things you'd have said about me."

"We both know that there would have been fireworks, trumpets, and heavenly serenades. No nasty talk."

"You're so full of shit," I tossed at him.

"I'm glad we never hooked up," Brady said, leaning his head onto mine.

"Yeah, why's that?"

"Because then I wouldn't be able to sing all your amazing songs. We wouldn't even be able to be in the same room without you being all jealous and bitchy."

"Your ego has no limits." I pushed him off of me and stood as my phone dinged.

I looked down at a text from Eli.

"Lover boy?" Brady asked. I looked up, a smile on my face, and nodded. "If he hurts you, I'm going to hire Torrance from the Italian place to use his brass knuckles on him."

"You wouldn't rough him up yourself, huh?"

He rose to stand beside me, holding up his hands. "And ruin these guitar-playing babies, no way. Especially not with a contract finally coming our way."

I was lost in a sea of texts from Eli.

Brady patted me on the head. "Night, babe."

I didn't even reply, still lost in Eli. The fact that he was texting me. The fact that I'd agreed to go on a date with him. That he was here. Wanting me.

♪ ♪ ♪

After our little stream of text messages on Tuesday, I'd hoped to hear from Eli again, but I didn't. I knew he was on duty, out to sea. He probably didn't even have a signal most days. I wondered what it was like for him when he was on the boat. I wondered if he was in danger. That made my stomach flip. How did people do it? With their loved ones going into harm's way every day? That made me think of his mom.

I wondered what she must feel with him out on the water like her husband had been. Like the husband who had come home in a body bag. It wasn't a thought I could stomach for long, so I pushed it aside.

Instead, I threw myself into the songs that were filling me and focused on my classes and our time in the studio.

On Thursday, Brady got a call from Blake Abbott that was followed shortly afterwards by a call from Nick Jackson, a producer through one of Sony's many offshoots. Brady put it on speaker, and we were both silently dancing and smiling like idiots while we were talking to him. I'm sure he could hear it in the breathlessness of our voices.

We told him about the album we were finishing up. He said to send him a copy when we were done and gave us his personal email address so it wouldn't get lost in the deluge of unsolicited crap they received.

"Blake said something about it being a duo?" Nick questioned.

"No. It's really just Brady. I'm just the songwriter."

"Blake said he really dug your voice. Deep. Husky," Nick said on the other end. I felt a stab in my gut at that, the old longing resurging before I carefully pushed it aside. I knew that Brady's best chance was solo.

"She'll be a part of it, if that's what you want," Brady spoke, and I hit him in the stomach. He grimaced, but I also loved that Brady wasn't stepping over me to get where he wanted. I hadn't really given him enough credit. I thought he'd abandon ship without even looking back.

"I'd really rather you find someone else to sing any of the duets with him, but it's my voice on the album as of now," I replied honestly.

"You know, I don't think I've ever had someone tell me they don't want to be part of a recording gig," Nick said, a chuckle following his comments. I liked him. Even though we couldn't see him. He seemed down to earth. Reliable. Knowledgeable.

"I just know my limits, and I don't want to hold Brady back. You can find someone fantastic to sing with him."

"Send me the album, and we'll go from there," he said.

We hung up, and Brady and I screamed, danced, held on to each other. "This is really going to happen for you," I said, muffled in his flannel shirt that he only wore when we were in the studio or our dorm room.

"It could happen for you too, if you weren't so stubborn," he said, squeezing me so hard I choked. I pushed him away.

"I don't want it." It was true and not true.

"That's not what you said when you arrived at Juilliard."

I shrugged. "You get older, you get wiser, you get real."

"I hate that you think you aren't good enough. You have the best female voice in our whole class."

"You realize you just said *female* and *our* whole class in the same sentence?" I asked, grimacing and going into the kitchen to find the beers we had in the refrigerator.

"Only because no one can argue that Shayla has the best voice anyone has heard—ever—even if she's not in our class," Brady said, following me. "And, well, you are in the same class with me."

I skipped over his ego comment and dove for the comment about Shayla instead. "If you hadn't screwed Shayla and then left her, she would be recording with you, and then you'd have a platinum album on your hands instead of just a regular old chart-topping one." I handed him the beer.

We uncapped them, clanked them together in silent cheers, and drank. "She would have outsung even me," Brady said. "Plus, she was a shag who was worth talking about."

I laughed. "What? You trying to be a British country singer now?"

He smiled at me and then turned serious. "Really, Ava, I'd like you to do this with me. We work well together. Your voice is killer. Just like Blake told Nick."

It was a solace to my old self that Brady thought I was good enough to be on his album for real. To be a part of a band. A duo. Whatever. The girl who had left Rockport, Texas for Nashville, Tennessee would have jumped all over that. Would have been swinging from the chandeliers at the thought.

Now, I knew better. I knew what superstar talent sounded like. I heard it every day at Juilliard, and it wasn't me. I still loved to sing. Loved being onstage now and then, but I was getting more joy out of writing and hearing Brady bring my words to life than bringing them to life myself. Even still, some days I was more accepting of that dream dying than others.

"Your dad is an asshole twenty times over," he said.

"He's not the reason, Brady."

"He is."

I sighed. He might have been one of the reasons I'd questioned myself the first year at Juilliard. And he might have been the reason I was opposed to anyone ever having any control over what I did with my life, but he wasn't the reason I was dragging my feet now.

"I feel like I'm getting the best of both worlds this way," I told Brady honestly.

I could tell he still didn't believe me. That was because Brady was all about getting to stardom. He craved the chaos. He craved the fame and notoriety. He was also good with it. He was built to be a star. I hadn't been; I just hadn't known that at nineteen.

♫ ♫ ♫

Brady and I spent most of the next few days in the studio with our production team. We made enormous amounts of changes, arguing over which of the new songs should be added. Our advisor, Gareth, popped in often, hardly ever offering a word of advice but just listening to the dialogue, the music, and the songs.

On Friday morning, Gareth pulled me out of the studio as the team was wrapping up for the day. "Brady tells me you're sending the record to a producer at Sony."

I nodded.

"He also tells me that you don't want to be one of the artists; you just want songwriting credits," Gareth said, his heavy, salt-and-pepper eyebrows drawing together more than they usually did.

I nodded again.

"I think that's a mistake," he told me honestly.

"You're not the only one who's said that."

"I want you to really think about it before you send the album off. Take some time. Get out of the studio. Go explore the city. Do something for you. Envision what you want for your life once you're done here in May. Don't miss out on a life-changing event because of insecurities," Gareth lectured.

"I'm not doing it because I lack confidence," I responded, my hackles up a little.

"Are you sure?" He didn't believe me.

I didn't respond. I'd battled disbelief my whole life. I knew that continuing to force my case wasn't going to change his opinion. Just like my dad had never changed his opinion of me being nothing, even when he'd heard my music. Even when my high school music teacher had praised me in front of him. When I didn't respond, Gareth frowned more and said, "Just think about it."

Then he left.

I spent Saturday thinking about what he said and came up with the same answer. There was so much of the music industry life, that I'd realized with time and exposure, that I didn't want because it meant giving up too much of myself. And truthfully, Brady didn't need me onstage with him. He was spectacular all on his own. For any songs that really required a duet, they could find someone already in the music world to sing with him. It would only help Brady and the album. But if Brady wanted my songs, I'd continue to write them for him as long as I could.

On Sunday, I woke with a flutter of wings in my stomach. I was going to get to see Eli. That made me happier than the thought of a record deal with Brady.

The New York weather had finally decided to think about spring instead of winter. It was still cool but no longer icy, so when I looked into my closet for our date, my hands slipped to a dress.

Eli had never seen me in a dress—bathing suit, shorts, and now, buried in clothes for winter, but never a dress. A dress was good for a first date. It was also good for hands to wander after a first date. I pulled a shirtdress off its hanger. It was my favorite shade of purple with tiny paisley prints in teal and green that made me think of the ocean and Rockport.

I'd had Rockport on my brain a lot since seeing Eli. It made me miss the house there, even though I'd be seeing it after graduation. My plan was to go bury myself in the ocean and the breeze and write. It was the only plan I had.

I slipped on my cowboy boots with the dress and looped a long, thin belt twice around my waist. I put on earrings that I hardly ever wore, ones that dangled and flipped around my chin with the angles of my hair. Then I spent a long time on my makeup in a way that I hadn't in forever. Finally, I spent five minutes tossing about the pros and cons of lip gloss.

At six forty-five, my phone lit up with a FaceTime call from Jenna. I answered it, looking into my friend's brilliant blue eyes with a smile.

"I want to see the whole thing," she demanded.

"Hello to you, too, Girlie," I laughed. I propped my phone on the dresser and stepped away so that she could get a view of the whole me.

"You actually wore a dress!" she squealed in happiness. I went back to the phone.

"What made you think I wouldn't?"

"You, being all closed-off you."

She was right in that my normal go-to for first dates was not a dress. My normal go-to was enough clothes that it would prevent any hands from getting anywhere fast. But with Eli, I was thinking that even this might not be fast enough once he started kissing me.

I sat down on the bed. "I'm nervous."

"Why?"

"You know why."

She was quiet. "It's just a first date, Ava. It doesn't have to be everything in one night."

"I know."

"Just breathe and take it one minute at a time."

"'Kay," I responded, but my heart was already beating so fast I wasn't sure it was going to last the night.

"Call me when you get back, and take care of you."

"Will do. Take care of you." I hung up.

I pulled my essentials from my big slouch bag and placed them in my smaller handbag. Then, I grabbed my leather jacket and headed for the living room.

Brady looked up from the computer on his lap and whistled. "Damn, babe, breaking my heart here."

I rolled my eyes and sat down next to him.

On the screen was the home page for Nick Jackson's production company. "What are you doing?"

"Trolling. Making sure he's legit, that we want to get ourselves tangled up with him."

"That's smart."

"You say that like it's a surprise, like I'm not usually smart," he said.

"Well…" I teased back. He shoved my shoulder with his.

"What time is lover boy supposed to be here?"

"Any minute."

"Good, troll with me then," he said as he started reading from the page before moving over to a Facebook page and scrolling through that.

At fifteen minutes after seven, Brady said what my heart was starting to fear. "Are you sure it was supposed to be seven?"

I just nodded. There hadn't been any way I had misunderstood. The truth was, I knew in my heart that Eli wouldn't be late for any normal reason.

"You gonna text him?" Brady asked.

I shook my head. I wasn't going to be that crazy, needy first date. He was probably just stuck in traffic. Although, I was surprised I hadn't heard anything from him. Eli wasn't the type to be late and not let you know. He was a military man. You showed up when you said you were going to show up.

At seven thirty, my stomach had officially turned from knots of excitement to knots of worry. Still nothing.

"Text him," Brady said. "Or better yet, call him and let me chew his ass out."

I pulled my phone from my handbag and, with shaking fingers, typed out a text.

ME: Hey. Everything okay?

Brady and I both stared at the phone, waiting for a response. Five minutes later, nothing, and my stomach had dropped to the bottom of my feet, dread filling me.

ME: Please tell me that you just forgot and that you're okay.

Five more minutes passed. Nothing.

"That's it. I'm hiring Torrance to beat him to a pulp and dump his ass in a dark alley in the Bronx," Brady growled.

"I'm really worried," I told him, heart flipping and fear taking over like I hadn't been afraid since Eli had told me my dad was on his way to the beach house.

"Call one of his bozo friends." Brady was irritated. Not with me. With Eli.

"I don't know their numbers. I don't know any numbers," I told him truthfully. I didn't have Mac's or Truck's number—had never thought to get them. Never imagined I'd need them. I didn't even know what unit he was serving in with the Coast Guard. I supposed I could call some general line, but without being a family member, I doubted I'd get any information. I didn't know what to do.

"Shit," was Brady's response that echoed what I was feeling inside.

There was nothing I could do. Nothing but wait to see if I got a text back. Wait and see if the man that I'd thought I'd never see again would call or if I was, once again, going to lose him to a world that had different plans for us.

Chapter Seventeen

Eli

JUST A KISS

Performed by Lady A

I felt like my whole leg was being ripped from my body. The pain and accompanying nausea hit me so hard that it dragged me from the blackness until bright lights hit my eyes, making me close them again quickly. I threw an arm over my face while trying to get my brain to focus, to stop the dizzy swirl that was the world I'd briefly seen.

Where the hell was I? What happened?

Slowly, my brain started filtering in the answers. An image of a stupid harbor seal, stuck in a net, hit me first. It was tangled, drowning. My stupid ass jumping into the ocean with a couple of my crewmates, determined to save its life.

I remembered getting slammed against the boat by the seal's panicked movements. My knee. My fucking knee. It had been shattered. I'd known as soon as the pain had gone through me. We'd gotten the fucking seal out of the net and off to its family. Then, my crew had pulled me on board while I tried not to scream every curse word that existed as pain crawled over my knee and my body.

The crew had given me a shot of something from the first aid kit. The world had gotten fuzzy, and everything had been waves of nausea and blackness. I vaguely remembered being put on a gurney, driven to the hospital, and loaded into the surgical ward. That was the last thing I remembered.

I gradually moved my arm away from my face, blinking into the lights. It was day. Sun filtered in the windows of the hospital room, joining the fluorescent lights above me. Fucking pain shot up my leg as I moved to find the remote that would allow me to raise the bed into a sitting position.

"Hey, asswipe, what're you doing?" Truck's voice drew my eyes to him coming through the door of the room.

"Sitting the fuck up. What time is it?" I growled.

"About one," Truck said, sitting down in the chair beside me.

"Thank God," I uttered. "Hand me my phone."

"I don't have your phone," he said.

"I have six hours until my date with Ava. I'm not going to have her think I stood her up; go get my phone," I demanded.

Truck's face fell. "Shit."

"Don't shit, just go get my phone."

"Dude. It's Monday."

My heart fell to the pit of my already nauseated stomach and then pounded in panic. I'd missed our fucking date. She was going to hate me. She'd think I'd forgotten. She'd think the worst.

"I totally forgot. We were just worried about you." Truck was already up out of his chair, spilling the coffee from his cup in his hurry.

I looked down at my leg for the first time, wrapped in a cast from mid-thigh to mid-calf. My stomach clenched for a different reason. All the things a shattered knee could mean for me hitting me for the first time. Truth slipping in and out of my brain. Nausea for a whole new set of reasons. My curse word was quiet, fading into nothing like my career. "Shit…"

Truck looked at me, saw my eyes scanning the knee, and sympathy came off him in droves. It was the sympathy that got to me the most. Stupid. I'd been fucking stupid, and it was likely to cost me everything.

After barely getting what I'd wanted.

"They said—" Truck took a step back toward me, but I cut him off.

"Go get my phone. Everything else can wait."

My comment surprised him, but he took off in the opposite direction. I couldn't deal with the enormity of the broken knee right now. Strangely, the pain in my heart over Ava thinking I'd stood her up hurt worse than the pain in my knee or the pain in my stomach over my career.

When Truck left, I took my emotions out on the nearest thing, which was the bed rail. I hit it with such force that it jarred my whole body, including the fucking knee. I was tempted to swear loudly and vehemently, but instead, I just bit the inside of my cheek.

Frustration bloomed in me. I'd been stupid for two reasons. Stupid over the seal, and stupid because I hadn't memorized Ava's number instead of relying on ridiculous technology. If I'd memorized it, I could pick up the phone on the side table and call her right now instead of waiting impatiently. It was killing me to not know what she was thinking.

I doubted that she'd think I purposefully skipped out on our date. No way. It was obvious as hell I wanted to see her again. That I wanted her. But would she be worried? In that way that my mom worried? Crap. My mom. I needed to call my mom.

A nurse entered the room. "Your friend said you were awake. How's the pain?"

"Pain. What can you tell me about this?" I threw a hand at the cast, the stab to my gut returning.

"I'll let the doctor know you're awake and ready to chat. I can bring you some more ibuprofen unless you think you need something stronger?" she responded as she took my blood pressure. It was probably high. I was stressed to the hilt about multiple things all at once.

"Ibuprofen is fine," I told her. No way I wanted anything more clouding my brain and making me fall asleep when I had people to call. People to reassure that I was okay.

She left, and the doctor came in her place. She was smart, young, and pretty—if I was into noticing pretty. At the moment I only had one woman on my brain. A sexy, dark-haired one with eyes that didn't match.

"Broke your patella bone, your kneecap. We removed some of the smaller pieces, and wired and screwed up the rest. Cast will be there for about two to three weeks at a minimum. You can start rehab after that," she told me.

"How long will I be out?"

"Off duty? Probably eight to twelve weeks."

I took that in. Eight weeks. It was the longest downtime I'd had since I was in elementary school. Since before my dad.

"Honestly?" Her voice interrupted my thoughts.

"Yeah?"

"They might not put you back out in the field," she told me, watching my face to gauge my reaction.

Pain coursed through me again. Through my heart and soul this time. To hear someone else confirm the thoughts that had been in my head. To have visions of my Coast Guard career flying away like clouds after a storm. It was too much to think about without going crazy. The thought of everything I'd strived for being gone because of one careless moment.

I had to push it aside for now. It would be up to my recovery and a medical review board. I'd do my part to make sure that I was fit, that my physical strength surpassed every goddamn one of their standards. It was the best I could do. Push my body to the brink, like I always had, and hope that it was enough to save me from the fate the doctor and I both suspected waited for me.

Once the doctor was assured that I wasn't going to take my own life at the news she'd given me, she left. The nurse came back and gave me the over-the-counter pain meds, and then she disappeared, too, with a promise of scrounging up food. I wasn't sure I wanted any yet. My stomach was still lurching in uncomfortable ways.

While I waited, I picked up the phone and dialed the number I did know by heart: my mom's.

"Eli!" Mom greeted happily, and I hated myself for having to take that happiness and squash it.

"I'm okay," I started with, because I knew she'd flip out if I started with anything else.

Unfortunately, this didn't necessarily help her either. She was quiet for a moment. "What happened?"

"I fucked up."

"Don't cuss." You could hear the worry in her voice. I felt like a selfish bastard adding stress to her life. Getting the visit about her husband had been horrific. I knew. I'd been there, in the hallway, while she'd sobbed at the news. Getting calls about your son wasn't any easier. It was the thing I was always trying to protect her from as best as I could given the career choice I'd made.

I told her about the seal and my knee. I didn't have to tell her that it might mean the end of my career. She understood. She'd been a military wife, and she knew how little it took for someone to be discharged. I didn't think she'd be exactly happy about it, but I also knew that my not being in the line of fire would add a layer of relief to her life.

"I'm sorry…so sorry," she said gently.

"It's on me. I know better than to get in between the boat and a seal. It was a rookie mistake."

There was nothing she could respond to that. It was true. I'd screwed up. One fucking moment. It was all it took. Hadn't they drilled that into us enough? Sure, they'd meant one moment and a gun could end you, but this was equally painful. A mistake with a harbor seal still ending my life. My career life. The pain in my chest wasn't something the ibuprofen could fix.

"Maybe I'll be able to take a trip home," I told her as a way of apologizing for causing her distress.

Instead of jumping all over it, she hesitated, which didn't wound me but made me wonder what the heck was going on with her. "If you don't, it's okay. Make sure you get the physical therapy you need. Don't skimp. I don't want my son limping along beside me when I'm eighty."

I chuckled because she wanted me to. "You're a long way from eighty, Mom."

She sighed. "Some days I feel a hundred."

"I'm sorry," I said, remorse hitting me again.

"It's not you, Doodles."

She'd whipped out the Doodles, which she hardly ever called me anymore unless she was feeling sentimental, and that had me feeling guilty all over again.

We hung up with I love yous in the air. I did love my mom. My dad may have been a hero to me, but she wasn't any less of one. She'd raised me on her own from the time I was ten. She'd never given in to the loss and shut down. She'd supported me even when I'd gone down the same path as my dad, and she'd hated it. She was a quiet super hero, working behind the scenes to make sure everyone's lives ran smoothly.

By the time Truck got back with my phone, I'd had plenty of time to beat myself up over being a bad son, a bad officer, and a bad date. Thus, I wasn't in a great mood when he rushed in.

"Thank God they hadn't put out to sea yet," he said, phone in hand.

"Took you fucking long enough; you probably could have rowed out to meet them," I groused.

He lifted the phone, keeping it just out of my grasp, and I hissed my frustration, trying to reach for it.

"Thank you, Truck, for hurrying to get my phone for me when I've been an asshole all morning," he said in a patronizing tone that told me he was just going to continue to give me shit if I didn't get my act together—and fast.

"Thank you. I'm sorry I'm being an asswipe. Now hand me my fucking phone."

"Do you really want to call her when you're being a royal dickwad?"

"Yes, goddamn it," I said, leaning toward him and groaning as the movement caused pain to radiate down my leg once more.

"Maybe I should call her instead." He smirked, phone still out of reach.

"I may be stuck in this bed right now, but I can guarantee you, I'll be out of it soon, and I'll still kick your ass, cast and all." I was losing my patience, but Truck just laughed. That had me stalling in my anger. Until we'd seen Ava the other night, I don't think I'd seen Truck laugh so easily in four years.

Ava was a miracle worker. I wanted her to be my miracle worker. It felt like I was in sudden need of miracles.

When he noticed that I'd calmed down, he handed me the phone, and I grunted a thanks. Once I had it, I was suddenly at a loss. Did I text her or call her?

"Wussing out? Are you sure you don't want me to call her for you?" Truck offered again with a smile.

"No, I want you to go get me a burger and fries while I take this call in private."

"Will they let you have all that?"

"I don't really care what they say," I told him. He nodded and took off.

My hand shook when I hit the call button. It rang and rang. I was worrying that it was going to go to voicemail because she never wanted to talk to me again when she finally picked up.

"Eli?" Her voice was breathless, concern floating through the phone.

"I'm sorry," I told her. It was the first thing that came to mind. It felt so insufficient.

Silence.

"Ava?"

"Are you sorry you didn't make it to our date, or sorry like you never want to see me again?" I could tell from her tone that she had shut down. Her face would be that silent, emotionless one that I'd seen so often since finding her in New York.

"I want to see you again." It was a growl. "I'm sorry that I stood you up. It wasn't my intention."

More silence. "I've been worried about you. I had no one to call…"

"I'm an ass. I'm sorry you didn't have a number. I'll give you those. As many as you want. I just woke up this afternoon, and you were the first thing on my mind."

"Are…are you okay?" Hesitation in her voice again.

I looked down at the cast and was surprised that I didn't feel anything but relief at hearing her voice, at knowing that she'd picked up and that she wasn't hanging up on me.

"Now that I've heard your voice, I'm fine."

"What happened?"

"A harbor seal happened."

She chuckled, like I'd meant her to. "What's that supposed to mean?"

"I made a rookie mistake. Got in between a seal trapped in a net and the boat. It panicked. Smashed me into the stern."

"Oh my God. How…how bad did you get hurt?"

"Broken patella. Some bruises. Nothing life threatening. It happened yesterday at the end of our shift, and I've been out of it pretty much since the surgery. Then, my stupid-ass-so-called friend didn't have my phone with him."

Her breath caught on the other end. "Where are you?"

"Staten Island Hospital," I said.

"Can I come see you?"

Did I want her to see me in a hospital gown? With bruises covering my face and my body that I hadn't seen yet but could feel? With a cast on my left leg that would make me immobile for weeks?

All I could think was yes. I wanted to see her. I didn't care how fucked up I was. I just needed to see her. To know that I hadn't screwed things up beyond repair with at least this one thing in my life.

"I'd like to see you, but if you can't make it out here, I'll come to you as soon as I get released."

"I'm on my way."

"Now?"

She laughed. "Yes, now."

My heart leaped. My chest pounded. For good reasons. Ava was coming to me.

"Ava," I said.

"Yes?"

"Hurry."

She laughed and hung up on me. I was still smiling by the time Truck got back with a bag of fast food. I forgave him for all his failings, devoured the food, and waited for "The One That Got Away" to show up and make my world right again.

♪ ♪ ♪

It seemed like "now" was another long forever, but it also gave me time to brush my stinky teeth and make sure that I didn't smell as bad as the damn harbor seal had smelled before Ava showed up. Truck was unusually cooperative. I had a sinking feeling it was because he thought my career had just washed out to sea with the last cutter.

All thoughts about guilt over my mom, the potential loss of my career, and the pain in my leg drifted away when I saw Ava framed in the doorway of the hospital room. Her short hair swung about her chin as she paused to take me in. She clutched the hem of the brown leather jacket she wore as she moved toward me, squeezing and releasing as if she was nervous, upset, or both.

When she got close enough, she did that half-run thing she'd done with Truck the other night and gave me a loose hug. And it struck me again that it was almost as if she didn't know how to hug. I wanted to pull her tighter to show her how hugs were supposed to feel, but the bed and the cast got in my way. I still had her in my arms, and she didn't pull back for quite some time.

When she did remove herself from my arms, there were unshed tears in her eyes, like there had been when she'd hugged Truck and begged for forgiveness. Except now, I could see that there was fear and relief in her eyes as well. I was swamped with my own conflicting emotions—relief, happiness, and anguish. I was pissed that I'd caused her to worry, but I had to admit a certain sense of joy that she cared enough to do just that—worry.

"You look like shit," she told me with a weak smile, sitting down on the bed with me, the soft, patterned leggings she was wearing rubbing against the hospital gown and the nothing I had on underneath it—tantalizing me.

"I don't feel like shit," I told her with a smile.

"That's only because you haven't seen yourself in a mirror," Truck joshed.

I ignored him and focused on Ava, on the weak smile on her lips. "I'm sorry that I made you worry."

"Worried-schmurried. I forgot about our date until you called," she teased.

"Liar."

We were grinning at each other like people who had lost every shred of sanity. Truck stood at the foot of the bed, and I could feel his eyes on us, but I didn't bother looking his way.

The long purple shirt that Ava had on hid some of her curves but brought out the color in her eyes. Eyes that were bright and sparkling. It felt almost like the years since I'd seen her had wandered away. She was smiling and shining. It was hard not to be drawn to that. I wanted to see her this way all the time.

"Well, I can see I am no longer needed here," Truck said. "I'm going to go catch some z's. I'll call you later to see if you need anything."

Then he was gone.

"Where's your phone?" I demanded.

She pulled it out of the bag that was at my feet. "Why?"

"I'm typing in a few numbers."

She didn't object; she just unlocked it and handed it to me. I plugged in the three numbers I did know by heart: my mom's, Mac's, and Truck's. Then, I handed it back to her, along with my own.

"Your turn," I told her.

"What?"

"Numbers of people I need to hunt down if you disappear on me."

"I don't plan on disappearing," she said, but she took the phone and typed in a number for Jenna and Brady.

"Do you have any family that I should have in here besides the asshole?"

She shook her head. "These are the two people on the planet who would notice if I vanished for more than a day."

I vaguely remembered Jenna's name from our time together at the beach house. But it was Brady's number that caused my smile to wilt a little. She'd said they were just friends, but I could tell they had a bond—a bond that her and I hadn't developed yet.

She put my phone down next to me, and I put my own hand on top of hers, capturing her thumb with my own. "I'm sorry about our date. I'm sorry about this."

"Can I just say that it's kind of sexy that you got hurt saving an animal," she replied, the huskiness of her voice lowering another notch and making a part of me awaken that had been asleep with the pain coursing through me.

"Idiotic, really. I know better."

"Were you supposed to just let it die?"

"No, but I know better than to be between it and the boat."

She didn't respond for a moment. "I thought…I don't know what I thought."

I brought her hand to my lips, placed a kiss on the inside of the palm, and was rewarded with her sighing.

"Our date will still happen."

She looked down at our hands that were now on my chest where I'd placed them. "Do you think that maybe life is telling us that we shouldn't?" she asked.

"Shouldn't what?"

"Date."

"Because I got smashed by a seal?" I was rewarded with a smirk.

"It just seems…that when we meet, there's always drama around it."

"Again, I don't think the seal had any intention of derailing our date. I'm pretty sure it was just thinking of its own survival," I replied. I wasn't going to let those kinds of thoughts take hold.

She was silent, thoughtful.

"Ava," I said her name so that she'd meet my eyes, and she did. "When you see me—when you're near me—tell me what you feel."

"I think—"

I cut her off. "Not what you think. What you feel. What does your body tell you without your brain getting in the way?"

She tried to pull away, but I held on to her hand tighter, wrapping mine around her wrist and lifting my other hand to her chin so that I could gently push it up, locking our gazes again.

"I don't know," she said.

"That's lie number two of the day," I told her. Her eyes drifted sideways and then back to mine. "Do you want me to go first?"

Her head barely inclined, but I took it as a yes.

"When you're in the same room with me, I feel like my body is being called to yours. Like the waves are called when the moon is drawing the tides. Like the pull you have on me is ancient and old. As if we've been doing this dance for longer than man has been on Earth. I feel like the only place I was ever meant to be...is next to you."

I felt her pulse increase under my fingers, the thumping pattern matching my own.

"You can't say stuff like that when we hardly know each other at all," she whispered, as if what I'd said was both the best thing she'd ever heard and the most impossible.

I nodded, because it was true that we hardly knew each other. If you looked at the total sum of hours we'd ever spent in each other's company, it wouldn't fill a week. It was a blip in the number of hours of our lives, and yet, they felt like the most important hours I'd ever had.

"Tell me it doesn't feel the same, and I'll stop saying stuff like that, but even then, I can't promise to walk away without trying. Trying to see what the waves are telling us."

She watched me in that old way she used to, but she didn't answer how she felt. Instead, she asked a question. "Do you know why I used to stare for so long?"

I wanted to hear her say that her body felt the same way as mine, but I let it go and just shook my head in response to her question because I didn't know the reason she'd stared so long.

"One of my favorite authors, Jessica Park… she wrote a book called *180 Seconds*." I frowned, trying to remember if I knew the book from the bookstore I'd helped my mom with growing up in New London; it didn't ring any bells. "In the book, they do this social experiment where you stare into someone's eyes for three minutes. And the main character says that it's like the person is taking in pieces of you, just as you are taking in pieces of them. That they can find value in each other just by sharing that simple, unguarded moment. From the moment I read that book, I was searching for someone who could meet my gaze and see me for who I was with no walls—no barriers—and who I could see back…the them inside. And when I found that person, we would promise not to drop each other. To not let the other drown in whatever had happened to them. To keep them safe. I wanted to find all of that through a simple stare."

I watched her as she watched me. Unguarded. Letting her see whatever it was she thought she needed to see in my eyes as I searched her own, the seconds pounding away. I wasn't sure it had been one-hundred and eighty before she spoke, but it had certainly been a lot.

"I never did. I never felt a connection…until you."

Those words took every breath I had and knocked them out of me, just like the seal knocked them out of me. Just like she'd had the air knocked out of her when she'd done a crazy stunt off a dock one summer long ago.

My hand went to her cheek, and despite the pain that pulled itself through my lower half, I sat up and took her lips with mine. The soft pinkness bent and flowed beneath me. It molded itself to my own softness until they shifted and pushed back, demanding a return.

Just like the moon called the tides, she had called me home. To her. I hoped that in calling me to her, she'd allow me to save her as I promised myself I would. And I hoped that I'd get my own little miracle that I now needed.

Chapter Eighteen

Ava

Eli was kissing me. I felt the kiss not just on my lips, but I swore I felt it in the very fabric of me. The molecules and the DNA that made up my body. The body that was no longer mine. Instead, it was as if somehow our negative and positive ions were finding their rightful positions next to each other. Part of each other. That we were one.

His hand moved from my cheek to the back of my head, as if, by that motion alone, he could somehow bring us even closer together. His tongue whispered against my lips, and I let him in where he found new parts of me to explore.

I responded by placing my hand behind his neck and pulling him closer, finding solace and peace within a kiss that was always meant to be. It was no wonder that other boys' kisses always turned me off, shut me down. I had experienced this kiss once before, and my body knew the truth. There was only one man who should ever kiss me.

A throat clearing near the doorway brought our lips apart, but our eyes still found each other, our hands still held our heads together. He rested his forehead on mine, and a glorious smile lit his face—the one that I'd said changed him back when I was nineteen and clueless. I was obviously still clueless because I hadn't realized that this was all I needed.

"I was just checking in before I left. Do you need any more ibuprofen?" the voice behind me said—a nurse, obviously.

"I have everything I need right here," Eli responded, his words a kiss to my heart that I promised to keep forever. His voice was so low, so thick with emotions and desire that I was sure the nurse would be blushing all the way home, but I didn't care. I only cared that Eli was there. In my hands. In my soul. In my life.

"Oh. Okay." We could hear the whisper of her scrubs and the squeak of her shoes as she left the room.

His smile widened, and it was impossible to not smile back. "Did I answer your question?" I teased.

"I'm not exactly sure. We might have to try that again."

He didn't wait for my answer; his lips were already back on mine, exploring, touching, tongue slipping back between my lips. The ache in me to be one grew, surrounding my heart, filling my chest, expanding until my entire body wanted to melt into his. And when I tried to do just that, leaning forward into him, he let out a sharp groan that had nothing to do with the beauty of our kiss, and I pulled away.

"I hurt you," I said, looking down his body to the cast, unable to ignore the bulge that had appeared under the thin sheet and the hospital gown that was partially over his body.

"You didn't, the break did," he said wryly. A faint hue of color filled his cheeks when I looked back at him. "I'd apologize for my body's reaction to you, but…"

He shrugged as his words faded away, that glorious, almost bashful, smile still on his face. The one that I was almost a hundred percent certain no one had seen but me.

"Just because you can't see it, doesn't mean my body doesn't feel the same way," I told him with my own flush at the bravery of my words.

I was just happy that I could keep the grin on his face. His hand traced my cheeks, following the bloom I knew I wore that matched his.

"You're beautiful," he told me.

It wasn't that no one had ever told me that before. Somehow, I'd never really believed it, though. It was like it had always been said as a means to an end, or from my friend who couldn't see clearly because of her affection for me. Eli said it like it was a simple fact. To him, I was beautiful.

We sat like that, close, touching, sharing words that weren't spoken, until the afternoon started to fade and the room crept into darkness. At one point, he fell asleep, his body weary. I watched him in awe that this gorgeous man had somehow found his way back into my world.

My eyes drifted to his leg, and I wondered what it would mean for him. A broken knee in the military. They discharged people for less than that, right? Let alone a screwed-together knee that would forever be a handicap, healed or not. It didn't sound promising. It made me hurt for him in a way I'd never had to hurt for Eli before.

When he woke with a new groan, I pushed the call button before he could stop me. The nurse came and went, promising more pain meds.

"What did the doctors say?" I asked with my fingers finding their way back into his.

He shrugged, and I could tell he was darting around the truth. "I'll be out for a while, at least."

"I'm sorry," I told him, because I was.

"We seem to use that word a lot with each other. There's nothing for you to be sorry about," he told me.

I nodded. "I just don't want it to stop you from having everything you've worked so hard for."

He took that in, eyes going to his cast, mind thinking thoughts that I couldn't read for the first time since I'd come into the room.

"Tell me something," he said.

I nodded.

"What stopped you from pursuing your dream?"

I looked up at him in surprise. "What do you mean?"

"Don't. Don't do that with me. We both know what I mean."

He was right. I did know what he meant, but I was still surprised, when I shouldn't be, that he'd seen what I'd done with my life. How I'd turned it into something different from what I'd told him I wanted when I'd first met him.

"It's hard to put into words."

"Try. For me."

My brow furrowed as I tried to think of a way to explain it that wouldn't sound like I was giving up. So that he'd see that I wasn't tucking my tail between my legs in failure.

"There's this quote by Mary Webb that goes, 'Saddle your dreams before you ride 'em,'" I told him, and I could see that I'd confused him more than helped. I tried again. "I think I had this dream that I hadn't really envisioned or thought through. I hadn't tamed it into my own, and once I did, it wasn't the same horse."

"I still don't think I understand," he told me.

"When I went to Nashville, I thought I wanted to be a country singer, and I worked on that dream really hard. Put myself through junior college, played at a lot of open mic nights, and applied again for Juilliard."

"Again?"

The fact that he didn't know why it was "again" was proof that we hardly knew each other, regardless of what our bodies told us. "The first time I applied to Juilliard in my senior year, my dad called a friend— one of his collections— and they had the application pulled."

I could see the storm in Eli's eyes at the thought that my dad had done that to me.

"That's why you ran away?"

"Partly. He didn't even tell me he did it. I had to call Juilliard to figure out why I hadn't gotten my rejection letter like the rest of the kids. When I found out, I swore I wasn't going to stay, and I didn't. You know how that turned out."

I gave him a weak smile, and he ran his hand up and down my arm, as if he could go back in time and take away the pain. Thing was, pain and my dad were synonymous. I wouldn't say I had come to terms with it, but I was closer than when Eli had first met me at the beach house.

"When Juilliard accepted me, I was over the moon."

"I know that feeling. It was how I felt when I signed on with the Coast Guard finally," he told me.

"I hadn't had contact with my dad since I'd left Galveston. It was like he had known that I was going to still pursue Juilliard, and he waited patiently for me to do just that."

"But…you got in?" He was puzzled.

"Yes. That wasn't what he was waiting for this time. This time, he was waiting to serve me papers."

"Papers?"

"To take away the trust fund that my grandparents had left me like he'd threatened you he would. It was money that was supposed to be mine when I turned twenty and would pay for Juilliard. He knew I couldn't afford to do it otherwise."

"He couldn't do that after so many years had gone by since they'd died, could he?"

"He gave it a good old-fashioned try. Mostly to hide the fact that he'd slowly been bleeding the trust dry," I told him.

I could see Eli's anger increasing, and we'd gotten far away from my dreams and why I wasn't chasing the one he thought I should be chasing.

"I found a lawyer, and we went to court. That was the last time I saw him, outside the courtroom, after he'd lost. He told me that I was, 'A waste of humanity, a talentless and reckless nobody who would always be a nobody.'" I was proud that my voice didn't shake when I said the words aloud to Eli.

"You are the furthest thing from any of that," Eli sputtered out, almost as if he was going to rise to his feet and start a fight with my dad when he wasn't even in the room.

I laughed, and that stunned him enough to relax. "You'd think I'd be upset, right? I wasn't. It was the same thing he'd told me for nineteen years. And I knew the truth. The truth was, I had enough talent to get into Juilliard. He couldn't take that away from me."

"Ava. You are so talented. The stage and you…when you're on it, it's like it comes to life. That inanimate object rises up and joins you—becomes a part of you."

I held my breath, letting his words soak into me. "You find such lovely words to say to me. How do you do that?"

He looked embarrassed again but didn't respond to my question. I moved on with my story, willing him to see what I wanted to believe myself.

"When I got to Juilliard, I was overwhelmed with the talent there. The pure genius of the kids." I shook my head, still in awe. "It's incredible. Indescribable. And at first, I felt like I wasn't good enough to be there—because of my dad, and his words, and just the volume of talent surrounding me. My advisor told me that a lot of students feel that way, but that I truly wouldn't be there if I didn't have the talent Juilliard expected, and I chose to believe him instead of my dad."

"I'm still not understanding the saddle analogy," Eli told me, bringing me back.

I grinned. "The dream I had that I was trying to ride…it wasn't really mine once I really looked inside and found the things that made me happiest. I love music. I love words. I love putting those things together and sharing them with the world. I don't want to let others control how and when I do that. So sometimes, I can do that onstage, but sometimes, I can give them to someone else who'll take my words and make art out of them."

"Like Brady?" he asked.

"Yes. Maybe someday, others, too. I want to give my words away so they become the aurora borealis."

"The aurora borealis?"

"You know, a magical display that seems like more than a mere natural phenomenon. Something life changing."

He took me in, seeing me as I was, assessing if I was being honest or if he should call bullshit on me for the third time in a day. I was being honest. As honest as I could be at that moment. I believed what I told him.

"You're already the aurora borealis to me." He pulled my head to his and kissed me on the lips. Sweetly, gently, as if trying to deliver a sermon that I must hear and take to heart. "You've changed my life."

I wasn't sure how that had happened, or what he thought changing his life looked like, but I didn't get to ask him because the doctor came in with the hospital administrator folks to release him.

I was surprised.

"You're letting him go?"

"Nothing more we can do for him here."

Eli called Truck to come get him and then asked if I wanted to go back with them to their apartment. I did. I wasn't ready to walk away from him yet. My fear from the night before that I'd never hear his voice again was still echoing around the kisses and words we'd shared. So, I went with them. My heart, rather than Eli, not giving me a choice this time.

♫ ♫ ♫

I woke with a start, my face against a warm body with a heavy arm draped over my shoulders. The sound of a TV, almost muted, was in the background, and it took me quite a few more seconds than it should have to get my bearings.

I was at Eli's apartment. In Eli's bed.

We'd come back to their all-male apartment full of leather and electronics, and Truck had gone to get Chinese food. After trying to get comfortable on their loveseat and in one of the armchairs, Eli had given up and headed down the hall.

I had followed, not nervous—because I knew there wasn't really any way we were getting naked tonight—but still unsure about being in his room. I hesitated at the door, and he noticed.

"I promise to keep all my hands and toes to myself tonight." He was gray and tired, the bruise on his cheek standing out more, and his voice sounded tired too now, when it hadn't at the hospital.

"Do I want to know what you use your toes for?" I teased, and he chuckled.

"I'm sure I can come up with something creative." He lay down with a huge groan and a sigh. "Just not tonight."

"Do you need more pain meds?"

"Not yet."

He eased himself over on the double-sized bed that still dwarfed the small room and patted the spot beside him. I rolled into the bed, my body pressed up next to his.

"This is so much better." He sighed again.

"I really should go. You're just going to fall asleep, and I have an early session in the studio."

"What are you recording?" Eli asked, trying to hide a yawn.

"You're being stubborn. I can come back tomorrow…That is…" I trailed off, having just invited myself to his house.

"Tomorrow. The day after. Every day. You are always wanted here. Welcome here. I still don't want you to go." I lay there, feeling the hum of his body matching the hum in mine, the energy from our kisses still wafting between us.

"I'll stay until you fall asleep, but only because I'm sure that's going to be in like five minutes." I smirked at him.

He nodded and then proceeded to be stubborn, flipping channels on the TV and settling on some Japanese cartoon.

"What the heck is this?"

"Anime?"

I sat up and looked down at him. A flush had crept over his cheeks again. "Like Japanese anime. Girls with big lashes and people with squeaky voices," I said in disbelief.

He snorted. "That's so judgmental of you. They have good story lines."

"Um. Okay."

He waved a hand over to a bookshelf that was under the TV and that I hadn't paid much attention to. I pulled myself away from him and the bed and went to the shelf.

It was chock-full of graphic novels and comic books. I vaguely recalled a discussion with him as we'd walked on the beach in Rockport about a manga book being his favorite book of all time. Even then, it hadn't seemed to quite fit him. I didn't know what to make of Coast Guard Eli, all-man Eli, all-testosterone-and-no-nerd Eli having a bookshelf full of the nerdiest, cutest bookaphile things. I picked through a few before returning them to the shelf.

"I see this is not a new fetish. At least you're not a twenty-something loner using anime as porn."

He chuckled, a deep, slow chuckle, as if he was trying desperately to keep his eyes open and only half listening to me. The sexiness of it all called me back to him.

When I tucked myself up close again, he wrapped an arm around me. A wave of different emotions coursed through me, but the one that resonated most was that I felt like I belonged—for the first time in a very, very long time. Because even at Juilliard, surrounded by people chasing after creative pursuits just like mine, I'd always felt one step removed from them all.

"Your eyes were what drew me first. You have anime-worthy eyes." His words were slurred, almost like he was already half dreaming.

I didn't respond. I just let myself do the thing I normally didn't, which was to wrap my own arms around his middle, thinking back to that first moment when I'd turned around on the coffee table of the beach house and saw three enormous men standing in the room. The shock I'd felt, and the draw to Eli's eyes that had made me feel seen in a way I'd never been seen.

I sighed, closing my own eyes, thinking I'd just soak up the feeling of being with him for a few more seconds before I left.

I must have fallen asleep in that warm embrace, because now it was early morning. The room was no longer completely dark as the sun fought to banish the night. The weak morning light was easing its way in from behind the slats of the blinds.

I pulled myself slowly, carefully away from his warmth. He mumbled something in his sleep, but then nothing. His body was tired, trying to heal.

I stood by the side of the bed for a long moment, eyeing the shape of his chest beneath the T-shirt he'd never taken off. The muscled contours of his arms. The quiet, peacefulness of his face as he slept.

I was still reluctant to leave, even with Juilliard and the work I needed to do with Brady calling to me. I forced myself away and went in search of my bag in the living room. I tore a page from my latest notebook. I never really went anywhere without one. Some people used their phones; I still loved the feel of the paper and the ink as I wrote. It was a tactile thing as much as a heart and mind thing for me. Music was alive. My words should be too, not caught in just a technological maze of zeros and ones.

I wrote: "He slumbers…the stuff that dreams are made on, and our little life…will hopefully always be surrounded by sleep. These dreams. These moments."

A twisted reference to Prospero and The Tempest, but also the only way to tell him that I wanted many more of these moments with him.

At the bottom, I wrote: "I'll be back later, and hopefully you won't wake regretting it."

I signed my name and then shouldered my bag. Truck's bedroom door was shut; the apartment was silent. I left, quietly shutting the door and ordering a CarShare at the same time.

The street was foggy, cold but without the bitterness of the weeks before. There was a hint of a change in the air that spoke to my soul, as if the fog was really going to clear from my life for the very first time. It terrified me as much as it filled me with hope. I knew that Jenna was right. The thought of actually allowing someone to love me was almost as terrifying as the thought of loving someone and not knowing if they'd stay. If they'd stick around for all the pieces of me that weren't beautiful, that were torn and ragged.

When I closed the dorm room door as quietly as I had Eli's apartment door, I wasn't greeted with silence. Instead, Brady threw a shoe at me—a huge, man-sized cowboy boot to be exact—that hardly missed my head.

"What the hell was that for?" I asked, dropping my bag and heading to where he lounged, as he always did, on the couch with his guitar beside him on the floor. It seemed like he'd been up all night.

"You could have at least called. I've been worried, babe," Brady grouched.

"Wait. What?" I looked down at him, arms on my hips and a frown on my face.

"I've. Been. Worried," he enunciated slowly.

I laughed. "Brady, you have my number. Why didn't you just call?"

"In the middle of hot and heavy sex? And be like a dad checking up on his errant teenage daughter? No thanks."

In surprise, I realized that he was actually upset.

"There was no hot and heavy sex. His whole left leg is in a cast from a shattered kneecap."

I pushed his legs off so that I could sit with him. I'd left one man to curl up next to another, but it didn't feel anywhere near the same. Brady felt like the brother I'd never had.

"Don't come all curling up to me with your smell of another guy and expect me to forgive you with that sweet smile," Brady responded, but I could see his worry and grouchiness was turning back to his normal Brady lightness a little at a time.

I whiffed myself. "I don't smell like Eli."

That did cause him to smile. "I knew it! Spill the beans, babe."

"No beans to spill." I smiled up at him. "He was exhausted and hurting. I fell asleep after he fell asleep. End of story."

"You keep causing me to lose respect for this guy. He had you in his bed and didn't make a move?"

I laughed so hard I snorted. "Brady, he literally just came out of surgery."

"I can guarantee no surgery will ever prevent me from making it with a hot woman in my bed."

"Even if you've just had a vasectomy?"

He slapped a hand over my mouth. "Curse those words!"

I laughed behind his hand and licked his palm so that he'd remove it. He grimaced, wiping my spit on my leggings. "You'd be able to have as much sex as you wanted without risking a pregnancy."

"Who said I never wanted to get someone knocked up?"

My mouth fell open.

His turn to laugh. "Someday I'm gonna be Tim McGraw and have my own Faith Hill, and we'll have kids that we name Tennessee and Londyn."

"Oh. My. God. You're a girl! Who knew that the sex addict, Brady O'Neill, was actually a girl inside that body of his?"

"Sexy body." He pushed me away and stood, stretching, his T-shirt riding up to show his own muscled stomach that had never, ever turned me on the way that Eli's non-bare one this morning had. "Eyeing me? Didn't get enough from your military man?"

I rolled my eyes. "In your dreams, sexaholic. I'm gonna go shower before we hit the studio."

"'K. I'll have coffee ready." He moved to the kitchen while I went to the bathroom.

My heart was really full this morning. I had two of the best friends a person could ask for. People that made me part of their lives when my dad hadn't, and now I had Eli, in whatever shape or form that came to be.

Some days, reality was better than a dream.

♫ ♫ ♫

In the middle of the afternoon, I got a text from Eli.

MR. GRUMPY: I woke and you weren't here.

ME: I told you I had to be at the studio early. Did you find my note?

MR. GRUMPY: Yes. I'm waiting for our new moment. You also said you'd be back, and yet you aren't.

*ME: **eye roll emoji. I'm finishing up a couple things for class. But I can leave in a few minutes. Shall I bring pizza?*

MR. GRUMPY: Truck will try to steal you away if you bring pizza, I'm not sure it's worth the risk.

ME: Pizza it is.

MR. GRUMPY: You want to be stolen away?

ME: If you're willing to give me up over pizza, you deserve to lose me.

MR. GRUMPY: I am brandishing my dueling swords even as we speak.

ME: That will be interesting with you in a cast.

MR. GRUMPY: It is as you wish it to be.

ME: How many pain meds have you taken today?

MR. GRUMPY: None. I was trying to make a Princess Bride *reference, but it fell flat.*

ME: I'll have to teach you the art of quoting.

MR. GRUMPY: You can teach me whatever you want, just get here already.

I couldn't deny that. I wanted to be there already, just so that I could feel the hum of his body next to mine. When I arrived at the apartment, Eli greeted me with a kiss that made me feel like he truly had missed me—more than a day's worth of missing, more like four years of missing.

My heart flipped over.

After filling plates with pizza, we sat back down with Eli and me on the loveseat and his leg up on a side table. Truck hit play on the movie they'd paused. They were watching this movie called *Days of Thunder* that I'd never seen. As the movie continued, I saw that it was about someone having to give up the thing they loved most. It seemed, somehow, both inappropriate and on point given Eli's own predicament.

When Eli went to the bathroom, I said as much to Truck.

"Preparation, Ava. Preparation is everything," Truck responded. Semper paratus—always ready. I understood what he meant.

"Do you really think it's over? His whole career?" My stomach lurched at the thought of Eli losing the thing he loved most in the whole world. The thing that made him think of his dad. The thing he'd wanted since he was a kid. If it hurt me, I couldn't imagine what it was doing to him.

Truck looked down at his empty plate and then looked back up with weariness and sadness in his eyes. "Yes."

"Do you really think they'll be that strict?"

"They won't enlist you if you have a knee injury like that. It isn't any different once you're in. But back when I thought my career was over before it began, Eli and Mac wouldn't let me give up. So, I'm trying to prepare him for the worst but not squash his hope, you know what I mean?"

I nodded.

"Hope can work miracles," he said quietly.

I believed that, too. Hope was a huge motivator, but I also felt like the truth was better than giving someone false hope, even if I didn't think you needed to watch a whole movie rubbing it in your face. "You know what Buddha says?"

Truck's confused expression was priceless. I smiled.

"He says, 'Three things cannot be long hidden: the sun, the moon, and the truth.'"

Truck took that in. "Maybe, but I'm not going to be the asshole that delivers the cold, hard facts to him. Let the hope keep pushing him like he always pushes himself."

That made me sad and happy. That Eli had people in his life that wanted things for him so much that they wouldn't dare to tell him to stop trying. That they wouldn't let him give up. I was also glad that I was here, though, because I'd had one dream end. I knew what that felt like, and I had a feeling Eli would need someone at his side that knew that feeling firsthand if his ended, too. Maybe my dream had ended on my own terms, but it had still been painful.

After the movie was over and Eli started to fall asleep again because he had taken pain meds, I kissed him gently and said I'd see him again soon.

"Tomorrow," he said groggily.

"Maybe."

He pulled my fingers into his. "Tomorrow," he said again.

"We'll see."

But we both knew that I wanted to come back. He could see it in my smile. I could see it in his.

When I got back to the dorm, Brady was waiting up for me once more. Or maybe he was just sitting up late, working, as he always did, on his music. On our music.

"You really are acting like a parent with a teenage daughter." I couldn't resist the tease, landing beside him on the couch.

"About time someone acted like a real father in your life."

I rolled my eyes.

"How was Eli?" Brady asked with an undertone that was all innuendo that I ignored.

"Brokenhearted and trying not to show it."

"Is his leg really a game ender for him?"

"I guess so. Yet nobody wants to say it to him. I mean, no one is saying he has a chance at keeping his commission, but no one is saying he won't either."

"That's good. He's got a lot of healing to do. Why kick a man while he's down? Let him have the possibility hanging out there to get him through the dark days and all that," Brady said, agreeing with Truck while I struggled with it.

"But…don't you think the truth is better? Like ripping the Band-aid off. Help you deal with it right away? Get it over with instead of continuing to dream about something that isn't ever going to happen?" I asked.

"I feel like we aren't talking about Eli anymore."

"What?"

Brady sat up, taking my hand and pulling it to his heart in a way that had felt sexy when Eli did it in the hospital but just seemed over-the-top dramatic when Brady did it.

"Ava, you're at Juilliard. One of the toughest schools in the world to get into for choral music. You are talented enough."

I sighed. I knew I was talented enough to be here, but I also knew there was way more talent than me ready to sing the words I wrote. Brady had proven that to me from the first day he'd snuck one of my songs to sing. It had changed my world.

I'd entered the quad, and there he was, with a pile of Juilliard students listening to him with all their hearts, and it had been my song. At that moment, I'd known: he was going to bring my songs to life in a way I never could.

"Is that really why you won't sign the deal with me? Because you still think you aren't good enough? Gareth thinks that's the case," Brady continued.

I pulled my hands from his. "Gareth needs to mind his own business."

"Ava. Seriously. Why won't you do this with me?"

"Remember Ashton?" I asked.

"Um, hello, who could not remember him? He went on to win *The Voice*!"

"Do you remember what he told us when we saw him the next year, after he'd spoken at graduation, and we all went out to the bar?"

Brady shook his head. Brady had probably been drunk or involved in some girl's skin while I'd been all eyes and ears, listening to Ashton's experiences. "He told us—or me, I can't remember. Anyway, he said that his whole life was controlled, from the time he woke up until the time he shut his eyes, by managers, publicists, agents, and the studios. He said his social media accounts had blown up so much that he had a personal assistant that was responding to all of it, acting as if it was him and saying shit that he'd never really say."

"I'm missing your point here. This is a good thing, right?"

"Maybe for you. I don't want anyone controlling my life like that again. I had that for nineteen years. I want to make my own choices about every single thing in my daily life—big or small. I don't want to be on someone else's schedule, with my life and words being dictated for me."

"It would still be your choice. You don't have to do what 'your people' say," he said.

"Do you really believe that?"

He tilted his head, thinking, before he spoke again. "Maybe not in the beginning, with your first deal. Maybe then, you have to listen to what the people around you say. But once you've gotten a couple records under your belt, and you've built a successful platform, you get more say."

"That's a lot of maybes."

"If we were in it together, we'd be able to support each other against the throng of people telling us otherwise."

"What if they told you the best thing was to lose me?"

He was shaking his head again. "You're saying that because you don't believe in yourself."

"Maybe you believe in me too much."

We were both quiet, letting our words settle in. His words were kicking my nineteen-year-old self in the gut, trying to bring back to life the dream I'd just said was dead. The dream I'd carefully wrapped in tissue paper and put away because I honestly thought it wasn't mine anymore.

"We haven't finished the album. We haven't sent it to Nick. We have time, and I'd really, truly like you to consider doing this with me—being a duo. Our chemistry is killer because we trust each other. I'm afraid that if I lose you, I'll lose some of what makes me good enough," Brady said honestly, his normal ego in check as he said it.

His words both lifted me up and depleted me. I loved that he thought I was talented and that my being with him made him better, but it also made me sad. Sad that he thought he couldn't do it without me when I very much knew he could.

"You're a gazillion times better than me at this whole professional singer thing," I said.

"Just think about it. Please." He still wasn't doing his normal bragging Brady thing, so I knew he was more serious than ever about what he said.

I nodded.

"Thank God."

"I didn't say yes," I told him with a frown.

"At least you're considering it instead of being your stubborn ass self."

"You want me to do something gross to your guitar?

"Babe, you'd never."

"Don't push your luck."

That night, I lay, staring out the window at the New York City lights that always made it feel like daytime in my room, and thought about Eli, and me, and our dreams that we'd wanted back in Rockport. How they'd happened and not happened. How they'd been pulled apart. How Eli's were crumbling around him still, and how mine were trying to build themselves back up. I didn't know where either of us would land. I did know that it felt right, somehow—almost predestined—that this time we weren't walking away from each other while we were trying to figure them out.

Chapter Nineteen

Eli

I RUN TO YOU

Performed by Lady A

The day after I got out of the hospital, I woke up and Ava was gone. Even though she'd told me she was leaving, I found my heart giving way a little. Then I'd found her note, and the cracks had slowly sewn themselves together again.

I'd wished that she could sew my knee and my career back together so easily. By late afternoon, I couldn't stand my own thoughts and Truck's sympathy, so I sent her a text begging her to come back. It was begging. I knew it for what it was, but she answered my beg, and I was grateful.

Truck had put on *Days of Thunder* before she arrived. Another old classic from his grandparent's collection. Although, I didn't miss his point in choosing that particular film. He might as well have chosen all the "fallen star" movies. It was his way of telling me what he thought about my career without saying it out loud.

Ava was a welcome distraction. She didn't stay long enough for me to really lose myself in her. I wasn't able to forget everything. It was probably a good thing. I didn't want to use her like someone would use alcohol and drugs to dull their senses and their memory. I wanted to lose myself in her for all the good reasons. Because we belonged together, not because I was drowning. I wouldn't pull her under with me. I wanted to buoy her up. She was just starting to show little bits of the old Ava. I didn't want that to disappear again.

The next afternoon, our commander showed up at my apartment. Truck was on duty. It was just me, wallowing in layers of pain. It wasn't normal for a commander to take much interest in some low-level officer, but Stan had been keeping an eye on me since I was little, especially when I'd shown interest in becoming a member of the Coast Guard, too. I was pretty sure he was the reason Sector New York had been my first assignment.

Stan told me what I already knew. I wasn't allowed back on duty until I'd passed the physical exams all over again and had my case presented before the medical review board.

"Your dad was a good friend," Stan said. "I'm going to do everything I can for you." What he didn't say spoke volumes. What neither of us would say aloud. What no one but the doctor had said. It wasn't likely I'd be on active duty ever again.

The ache in me at the thought of giving up what I'd worked so hard for filled me to the breaking point. A breaking point that none of my physical training had ever pushed me to before. This…this felt almost as painful as losing my dad.

"I have a friend. He runs a civilian company that we work with all the time. They help train and run emergency preparedness operations for local, state, and federal agencies. Phil is a good guy. He's hired a lot of ex-military on his staff," Stan continued.

"You're telling me I'm done." I said it calmly while the torture in my heart increased until I thought it would burst out of my chest. I'd only served four years. Four fucking years. I was due to reup. Due for a promotion. Due to be reassigned.

I didn't have a goddamn clue what I'd do without the Coast Guard. It was all I'd wanted. Years of going with my dad whenever they'd let me on board the ship. Years of dressing up as a Coast Guard for Halloween. Years of working out at the academy in New London whenever they'd let me on the field.

It was all I'd ever wanted. It was all that I had left of my dad.

I clenched the arm of the chair and looked away from Stan, swallowing hard, trying to rein in my emotions in front of this man whom I respected.

"I'm not in a position to tell you anything, Lieutenant. That will be up to your doctors and the review board."

"But you're telling me to be ready for it."

"It's our motto, son."

I nodded. Semper paratus. My heart squeezed again, threatening to cut off air, tears threatening to leak. I couldn't do it. I couldn't face the fact that the Coast Guard was falling away from me. I didn't know how.

When he left, I took my crutch, walked to the bathroom, and stared at the bruised face that looked back at me. I'd fucked up. So badly that it was going to be the end of me.

I was struggling for more than one reason. I'd never fucked up like this. It wasn't in me. I worked hard, kept my nose clean, took the safety precautions. None of those things had helped my dad either. He'd still ended up with a bullet through him. I should be thankful that it was a harbor seal and not something worse that had attacked me. Yet, I couldn't find any relief in that at the moment. Only pain.

My phone buzzed.

THE ONE THAT GOT AWAY: I'm going to be late in the studio, but I could bring dinner again? Chinese? Or Mexican?

I didn't respond right away. I was trying to reel myself in from the cliff. Ava had brought color back into my life. I'd had momentary visions of her being the one waiting for me when I got off the boat each time I was done with a shift. I'd had visions of her filling the part of my life that wasn't the Coast Guard. I just hadn't thought that the piece without the Coast Guard would be my entire life. I didn't want it to be my entire life. It was who I was.

I heard Truck coming in. I gave myself one last pitiful look before limping my way out to the sofa. Truck was still in his uniform. It ripped more holes in my heart after Stan's words. It also made me realize that the months Truck had had to wait to retake his class and reapply to the military had probably been harder than I'd ever thought. Like everything he'd worked for would never come true. For me, it was like my life that I'd wanted was being slowly washed away.

"Ava wants to know if we want her to bring Chinese or Mexican?"

"Hell yes," he said, sitting down in the chair.

I laughed. I needed the laughter. "Which one?"

"I don't care. Food."

ME: Truck says bring food, any kind of food. But I don't want you buying dinner every night. I'll pay you back when you get here.

THE ONE THAT GOT AWAY: Don't be all alpha male. I've got dinner.

ME: We haven't even been on a date yet. I can pay for dinner.

THE ONE THAT GOT AWAY: When we go out on a date, I'll let you pay.

The tension around my heart lessened. No matter what happened, I had good people in my life. I had Mac Truck. I had my mom and Leena. Now, there was the chance of having Ava. It wasn't enough to make the ache disappear, but it was enough to get me through that night. I just had to take it a day at a time while I figured out how to swim without legs.

♫ ♫ ♫

I shifted on the table, the little saw that the doctor was wielding next to my skin making me just a little nervous. She looked up at me with a smile.

"Don't move. You'll be fine. I promise I've never killed anyone with my saw yet."

It had been almost three weeks since I'd had surgery. Early March had turned into early April.

Those weeks had drifted by with me seeing Ava almost every day. I'd needed the distraction of her to keep me from going insane. Many days, I made my way uptown and watched her in the studio at Juilliard where I focused on listening to her songs and her voice instead of my broken bones.

When Ava and Brady were in the studio together, I saw glimpses of the Ava I'd seen onstage in Rockport, music flowing through her as if it was just an extension of the air she breathed. She was incredibly talented, but she was right that Brady was talented, too. He had a force to him that was addicting to watch.

It had given me a moment of heartburn when I'd found out they shared a dorm room, but it was easy to see that what they had was nothing like what Ava and I had. Brady and Ava's relationship was almost sibling in nature. The relaxed back and forth that flew between them as they worked out the kinks in a song eased the stress level of everyone in the room. And that stress level was high due to the jury exams that were only weeks away.

Ava and I still hadn't been on an official date. My screwed-up leg and her schedule made it seem impossible. The rare times that we were alone together, we spent with slow kisses and caresses, our bodies learning the curves and contours of each other as the hum inside us increased. It was as if we were slow dancing our way into whatever we were becoming.

As the doctor pulled the plaster away, replacing it with a brace and a cane, I was making new plans. Some of the plans were for the real date that Ava deserved. Some of them were for my rehab. It was going to be a long haul, but I'd do what I'd always done: push my body until I'd made it into what it needed to be. It was the only shot I had at getting my career back.

On the journey back to our apartment, my leg hurt like hell as I put more weight on it than I had in over two weeks—that pain being the first sign of what was to come. I made it into the shower before succumbing to the emotional pain that had come from seeing the leg without the cast.

As the water ran across my back, I stared down at the mess of cuts across my skin with my gut wrenching. The scabs and scars were somehow more real than the cast had been. The cast had felt temporary. The marks on my skin made everything more permanent.

Doubts raged through me as I stepped out of the shower. Staring at myself in the mirror, it was hard to recognize the person I saw. The bruise on my cheek was all but gone, only a hint of it left beneath my skin that was always tan from being out on the sea. But my hair had grown out, longer than I'd worn it in years, as if already telling me I didn't need a crew cut anymore. I looked tired. Older. Worn.

I shook myself out of the funk, refusing to believe that it was over. I'd get a fucking haircut. I'd get my body back in shape. I'd still be on deck and at sea before I knew it.

There was a barber down the street that I'd been using. It was Friday. I could get my hair cut, and, while I sat in the barber chair, I'd figure out a new first date for Ava and me. I'd continue to focus on her instead of the shitstorm that was my leg and my life.

I dressed in jeans for the first time in weeks, replaced the brace, and then pulled on a thermal

Henley. Then, I grabbed my wallet and keys, heading out just as my phone rang.

I looked down, ready to ignore whoever it was unless it was Ava. I saw Leena's name and the side of her face like she had the phone pressed up to her ear. I rarely heard from my mother's best friend—my second mom—unless she was with my mom, talking at me from the background when they put me on speaker at the bookstore or at one of their houses.

I was pretty sure Leena didn't realize she was FaceTiming me. I held in a laugh as I answered. "Hey."

"Hi, Eli, it's me, Leena."

I couldn't help the chuckle that I let out. "Yeah, I kind of figured it was you since I can see the side of your face."

"What? How?" She pulled the phone away from her, squinting at it.

"You do realize you FaceTimed me?" I was still trying hard not to laugh, and once she realized she could see me, she rolled her eyes.

"Now how the heck did I do that?"

"Well—"

She cut me off. "No, don't tell me. I'll never remember, anyway." I just smiled at her, and she moved on, face turning serious again. My smile faded some.

"You got your cast off today?" she asked, playing for time.

I nodded. "Yep, look, free man." I moved my phone so she could see the brace.

"You'll get to start physical therapy now?"

"Yep."

We were both quiet for a moment. "What's wrong, Leena?"

"That obvious?"

"You never call me. You text and harass me like I'm still one of your students, but calling on your own doesn't really happen. I usually only hear your voice with Mom's."

"That's sort of why I'm calling," she said slowly.

My gut twisted into a tight ball, and before I could ask what was wrong again, she kept going, in a rush, like she was saying it before she lost her nerve.

"Look, she's going to be angry, but with you not on active duty right now because of your leg, I didn't think there was any reason not to tell you."

"Tell me what?"

"She's been battling breast cancer." She blurted it out, grimacing at the phone, before stopping completely, breathing hard like she'd run a race.

The air was knocked out of me, the knot that pretty much lived in my stomach these days enlarging until it engulfed my lungs and my throat, causing it to slowly constrict like a collapsing tunnel. My mom had cancer. No. Leena must be wrong. Mom would have told me.

"Look," Leena said again, her favorite word on display. "She's going to be okay. They caught it early. It's stage one with only microscopic amounts having spread to the lymph nodes. There's like a ninety-nine percent cure rate or something like that. She's had the cancer removed, and she's pretty far through the treatments. She's still sick, though, and still going through chemo as an adjunctive therapy. If you have the time, I know seeing you would help her."

When my breath returned, it came with a wave of anger. That mom and Leena would keep this from me. That the universe would mess with my mom when I already lost my dad. When it would mess with all of us when my life was already crumbling around me.

"Why the hell didn't she tell me?"

"You know your mom. She doesn't want to be a burden. Doesn't want you to have things in your head that will distract you on your job."

"She hates my job."

"But the thought of you being distracted on the job…"

She didn't have to finish her statement. I got it. She didn't want me to end up with a bullet through me like Dad because my head wasn't in the right place.

"Jesus Christ. I haven't been at work for three weeks. Three! Someone could have fucking told me."

She was silent, eyes almost closed, evading the camera on the phone. I didn't usually cuss around my mom and Leena. They never let me get away with it, and it was somehow disrespectful to the women who raised me. However, I was a little short on words to better describe how I was feeling.

She took a deep breath and then said, in a wavering voice, "So, you're coming?"

"Of course. I'll have to notify my command, but I'm on leave, anyway. They won't really care."

"She's going to hate me," Leena said forlornly, and my anger faded just ever so slightly at the sight of a gray-haired Leena looking so tired and sad all of a sudden.

"She could never hate you," I tried to comfort her.

"She'll be mad."

We both knew this was the truth. Mom hated it when we did something for her own good behind her back. Like the time I'd arranged to have a new used car sent to her because her old one kept dying. I'd recruited Leena to help me, and Mom hadn't talked to us for a week. But…she'd kept the car.

"Just means Sunday brunch will be quieter than normal," I told her, trying to make her smile, but she didn't. She was still thoughtful. "I would have come sooner, Leena."

"We both know you would have tried. Who knows if they would have given you leave? Anyway, she didn't want that." Leena shook her head as if convincing herself as much as me.

"Sometimes what you want and what you need aren't the same." And even as I said the words, it hit me how applicable they were for my own life, too. My want to be in the Coast Guard—to have that be my life—it was different from what I needed. What I needed was my family: Mom and Leena, Mac and Truck, and now Ava. Nothing else really mattered beyond that.

I took a moment to acknowledge that I'd included Ava in that. That I could see her as part of my life even if there was no Coast Guard.

"Don't tell her I'm coming. She can be pissed at both of us at the same time," I told her.

Leena nodded, looking like she might cry.

"Love you, kiddo." She said kiddo like the Japanese did, like kee-toe. It still meant kid. It was what she'd called me since she'd found out about my love of manga and comic books. Since I was ten, and my dad died, and she'd practically moved in to our house to help us while Mom and I got used to a life without him.

"Love you, too. I'll let you know when I'm on my way."

She nodded her head and then clicked the off button. I sank down into the armchair, causing my knee to scream at the angle, and I quickly stuck it out in front of me.

I let the knowledge settle over me. My mom had breast cancer. My mom had been battling breast cancer and was too nervous to tell me for fear that I'd end up dead from the distraction. None of that was okay—not even the slightest bit. Nothing about her choices or my choices were.

Screw getting a haircut. I wanted to be with someone who could reassure me that, somehow, we'd make it through. Me. Mom. All of us. Truck was out on the cutter for a three-day op, but Ava wasn't. Ava was a CarShare ride away.

Before I could process anything else, I was out the door, calling the car, and waiting on the street corner for it to pick me up, shivering as a cold breeze picked up. I hadn't grabbed a jacket, just walked out the door with my wet hair and a Henley, but it didn't matter.

Once I was out of the car and on the steps of Juilliard, I hesitated, unsure about bringing my mood and anguish to Ava. I didn't have a chance to move away, though, because she saw me as she was passing through the lobby. It was chance—pure chance—but her eyes spotted me as we always seemed to spot each other regardless of the volume of people and objects between us.

She came out the glass door, a smile on her face. "Look at you, cast-less." As she got closer to me, her smile faded, reading my turmoil on my face.

"What's wrong?"

"My mom has breast cancer," I told her.

"Oh, Eli." She wrapped her arms around me before I could even blink, squeezing me tightly, her smell and her energy infusing me as they always did. "What do the doctors say?"

She was still buried in my chest, arms tucked around my body, while I wobbled on my cane, and she seemed to hold me up—a six foot three wavering idiot.

"Leena, my mom's best friend, called. She said that it's stage one. Extremely likely they got it all."

"She's already gone through treatment?" Ava lifted her eyes up to mine, and I saw the same surprise there that I know must have been in mine talking to Leena.

"They didn't tell me," I said it quietly. "Mom was afraid I'd let it get in my head on the job…"

My throat closed up, a sob getting stuck there that I wouldn't let out. I refused to be a blithering idiot on the steps of her college. Ava slipped her hand into mine and pulled me gently in the direction of the building that housed her dorm, but I didn't know if I could handle being in a room right now. Closed. Without air.

"I need air," I told her, not letting her hand go but also not letting myself be led toward the building.

She looked up into my face and must have seen the panic and fear and anger that resided there. "Let me grab my coat and my purse."

She brought my hand up to her lips and kissed the back of it before letting it go and taking off into the building. While I waited for her, I leaned against the wall and tried not to cuss my entire existence. Tried not to berate myself for the single-minded purpose I'd had to follow in my father's footsteps no matter the price to anyone. I was good at the job. I was built for this life, but for the first time ever, I wondered if it was worth the sacrifices the people I loved had paid for it. I didn't want the people I cared about to not tell me things because they were afraid of how it would affect me…how it could affect whether I made a life-ending mistake.

When Ava came back to me, my expression must have read the self-flagellation that was raging through me, because she gave me a questioning look. I just pushed myself away from the wall and joined her.

"Can you do the subway?" she asked.

I nodded and let her lead me to the nearest subway station. When we finally emerged from the depths of the subway, we were at Battery Park—Ava's favorite place in the city. The place I'd wanted to take her on our first date.

We walked through the park until we got to the edge of the bay with the Statue of Liberty rising before us. My leg was killing me. I'd overdone it for the first day without a cast, but at the moment, I didn't care. The breeze was ice cold coming off the water, and I still didn't have a jacket. I shivered, and Ava wrapped her arms around me as we both stared out at Lady Liberty.

My brain wandered back to my mom and the questions I hadn't asked Leena, like whether she'd had a mastectomy or not. If she'd had to lose a part of who she was, yet again. This time a physical piece. We were both losing parts of what made us who we were. Life was so damn cruel sometimes.

"Talk to me," Ava said finally, pulling me from thoughts I didn't want.

"I'm wondering how it can be fair for so much to hit one family."

"Did you know that the statue gets struck by lightning several times each year?" Ava asked, seemingly so random, just like her talk of saddling dreams had seemed random.

I shook my head. "No, but it doesn't surprise me. Copper is a conductive metal."

"You're missing my point," she said with a quirk to her lip that caused my finger to go to the one side dipping in more. She moved to kiss my finger. "My point is…she gets hit all the time—by lightning, no less—and yet, she's still there: Liberty Enlightening the World."

"Are you trying to tell me that my mom can handle it? You don't even know my mom."

Ava shrugged. "I know you. She has to be strong to have raised someone as stubborn and dog-faced as you."

I smirked. "I'm dog-faced?"

"Maybe more wolf."

I moved my fingers under her chin so that she couldn't look away. "Wolf. Dog. I'm not sure if I should be offended or pleased that you're telling me I'm animalistic."

My other hand tugged at the waves of hair at the back of her head. My eyes scoured her face, memorizing it again for maybe the hundredth time since we'd found each other once more.

Then, I bent so that my lips could capture hers. It always stunned me, the feeling that hit me when we touched, but especially when our lips touched. The breathless feeling of being drawn into something more than myself. No matter how much I got, I was always craving more. More touch. More of her. I wasn't sure what would happen when I had her all. Would my craving be sated, or would I just continue to desire her like an alcoholic needs his hundred proof?

She removed her lips from mine and looked up with eyes filled with desire. "Eli?"

"Hmm," I said, lost in her and our lips and our touch.

"Do you still need air?"

I frowned, not following her.

"If not, perhaps you could take me home?" Her husky voice was even huskier, filled with a promise that I couldn't resist any longer. Ava and I were meant to be one.

Chapter Twenty

Ava

HEAVEN
Performed by Kane Brown

Eli swallowed hard at my words, searched in his pocket, and came up with his phone. He opened the CarShare app and ordered a car. By the time we got back out to the front of the park, his limp was more pronounced, and he was leaning on his cane heavily. But there was an energy to him that hadn't been there when he'd arrived at Juilliard.

When he'd shown up at the school, he'd been withdrawn. Like he was beating himself up. Like life was beating him up. I didn't want to see that on Eli. He'd always been strong, confident, and determined. I hated that he was being asked to deal with so much at once and that it had him questioning everything in his life.

I was glad to take him away from that, even momentarily. As we left Battery Park, the thought of being with him, melding our bodies together, completely and utterly, in the way they'd been craving since we'd first kissed, filled me with anticipation and heat.

Once we were in the car, on the way to his apartment, my nerves started to get to me. I wasn't some sixteen-year-old girl losing her virginity and not really understanding what that meant. I was too old for that. I was too old for naivety. Yet, I couldn't help being a little nervous. I'd fooled around with guys. Fooled around a lot with Eli.

My nervousness wasn't stemming from the thought of him seeing me, or me seeing him, naked for the first time, and it wasn't because I was having sex for the first time at twenty-three. I was just nervous that it would disappoint him in some way. It was stupid. Our time together had not been disappointing. I knew I'd never disappointed him yet. But I was, if not uneducated then at least unpracticed, in the final steps that we hadn't danced yet.

We got out of the car in front of his apartment. He paused to give a tip to the driver via the app and then pulled my hand back into his. We maneuvered the stairs with his cane, a bad leg, and hands that were tied together.

He opened the door and threw his stuff on the counter, and then he pulled me back into his arms.

"Where are you at?" Eli asked, and I realized that I'd gone into my head longer than I should have. He rubbed my palm, sending shivers of anticipation back through my body.

"I need to tell you something," I said.

He heard the falter in my voice and jumped to the only conclusion he could have: that I'd changed my mind. That was the furthest thing from the truth. I wanted him. All of him. I wanted to know what it was like to have him fill my body as he already filled my soul.

"Ava, we don't have to do anything. You don't—"

"I've never had sex." I cut him off before I lost my nerve and before he got too far away from the thought of going the final step with me.

His brow furrowed as if he wasn't sure he'd heard what I'd said. Realization dawned, and instead of a smile or a joke at what I'd told him, the smolder returned to his gaze.

"Never?" His voice was full of emotions and longing that I couldn't understand. I shook my head, and he asked, "Why?"

"Does it matter?"

"Yes."

"Why?" I asked.

"I believe I asked first, but okay. I want to know why because I don't want to be the person you break some promise you made to yourself with just because you think that this has to be the next step for us."

I was shaking my head even before he finished his words. "It isn't like that."

"Then explain it to me," he said, like he had about my dreams and singing. Like he wanted to know everything, the truth inside me, and not just what he thought he saw. He wanted the honesty of it. The realness of it.

"Truthfully, at first it was because, in high school, when all my friends were losing their virginity, I saw what it did to them. It made them all goopy, and mushy, and hardly able to do anything without the boy they'd lost it to. I didn't want to lose my dreams to sex with some guy who would keep me in Texas and not at Juilliard."

He nodded. "I get that. First loves and first sex can really get tangled up in your head when you're young."

"Wait. Is that what happened to you?"

He half-smiled. "Don't get distracted, Ava. Tell me."

The way he said my name always sounded like its own term of endearment. Like he didn't need to call me "babe" or "honey" or "sweetie" because he could just say my name with that same emotion behind it. It was enough to tangle my heart and my head just like I *was* an inexperienced teenager.

"Then…after you…" God it was going to sound so stupid. He frowned again as if trying to place the jump from my being a teenager to now and the us that we were becoming, when, in fact, it had nothing to do with now, but four years behind us instead. "After we kissed that day in Rockport, nothing else has felt the same. And I guess…I was waiting for someone to light me up the way you had that day before I let them have all of me."

"Ava." That tone again, this time laced with something that sounded like reverence.

Then he was kissing me, devouring my lips like he had on the beach, and in the hospital, and on so many days since then. This time, there was something new in the kisses. As if we'd added a promise to them. A promise I wasn't even sure I understood but didn't mind making.

He picked me up by the waist, and my legs went around his middle, feeling every part of him that wanted every part of me. But he only took one step before he had to set me down with a frustrated groan, lifting his broken knee.

I couldn't help but smile. "Don't hurt yourself trying to be some stud muffin."

He chest rattled with a deep laugh.

"Dog, wolf, and now stud muffin?"

He took my hand and tugged me down the hall to his bedroom. I jumped onto the mattress, turning to look down at him.

"Eli?"

"Yes?"

"Will you light me up?"

He swallowed, eyes turning a deep color, back to smoldering. "If you'll let me."

I kissed him then, full of longing to be a part of him, for him to be a part of me. And our kisses turned to frantic movements, shedding clothes and his brace. I momentarily got sidetracked by the scars on his knee, but he drew me back to his face with a kiss and a hand anchored into my hair so that I would stay where his lips could travel from my lips to my neck and back again.

I was gasping, panting, and he was exploring with his other hand the parts of me that he was more than adept at exploring. I wasn't embarrassed any longer that I hadn't done this before. I just wanted him. All of him. And I pulled him with me as I went down on the bed, his body engulfing my own in warmth and heat and desire.

He reached for a bedside table, pulling out a condom packet. I watched with wide eyes as he rolled the condom onto the length of him—the length that I'd felt but not yet experienced. Then he was back over me, his right side countering the weight he couldn't put on his left leg, with a look in his eye that made me feel like I was the only girl he'd ever rolled a condom on for, even when I knew that I wasn't.

He kissed my neck, and my breasts, and down to my stomach, and then to the place that was slowly melting as it waited for him, and then he trailed kisses all the way back up, and when his lips got to my neck, he entered me. All of him joining with all of me. It did hurt, but then his caress, and kisses, and the slow rocking of our bodies had me losing myself again in the completeness I felt in his arms.

The rhythm of him in me, our hearts beating furiously, our kisses leaving marks not unlike tattoos on each other's skin built until I felt the pressure and pleasure gathering such that I was gasping and moving my mouth away from his in order to get air. He continued to trail kisses on my neck as I threw my head back.

And I shattered into a million pieces.

Then he shattered, too, as he called my name in a way that sounded like a prayer and a demand all rolled into one.

We lay there with pieces surrounding us, hearts still pounding, bodies momentarily sated. I wondered if we'd ever be able to figure out which pieces belonged to whom, or if we would, somehow, find ourselves with pieces that belonged to the other tied up inside of us when we moved apart again.

"Thank you," he said, tenderness, and devotion, and a word I didn't want to name yet in his voice.

"For what?"

"For waiting for me to be the one to fill you. Not just with…you know…my stupid penis. But for letting me be the one to fill your life."

God, his words. They were like his own band of lyrics that he wrote just for me. I smiled up at him. "I don't think your penis is stupid. Not at all."

He grinned back at me, that shy, glorious smile that I knew was my own. The thing he hadn't given to anyone else, just like there'd been the piece of me I hadn't given to anyone else. We'd each given each other a first of sorts.

"My penis thanks you very much, but you're going to have to stop saying penis now," he teased.

The playfulness of it took me away from the quiet sentimentality that had built up inside me. I sort of got my friends now. The ones who'd lost themselves in a boy because of sex. If they'd felt anything close to what I'd felt with Eli, it would be near impossible to not want this again. Over and over. To spend days wrapped up in just us.

"Shower?" he asked.

I nodded as he pulled himself from me, and I tried to collect the unseen pieces that had fallen around us. He held my hand and drew me toward his shared bathroom, naked.

"Wait. When does Truck get back?"

He lifted his eyebrows. "Truck is out to sea for three more days."

That made me very happy.

♩ ♩ ♩

Eli and I spent Friday night lost in each other's skin, our souls reaching out to each other. When he got out of bed Saturday morning, it was to find me curled up in an armchair in the main room, my notebook in my hand, words running across the page.

He hobbled over to me, picked me up, and then sat in the chair with me on his lap. "I woke, and you weren't there," he said quietly.

It wasn't said accusatorially, or demandingly, or even despondently. Just matter-of-factly, like he said most things in his life. Yet, it was still clear that he hadn't liked it. Like the first day out of the hospital, when I'd left, and he'd texted me the same thing. That I wasn't at his side.

"I wouldn't leave without telling you."

"Promise?"

"Promise," I said. His words made me think about how he probably hadn't been able to truly say goodbye to his dad.

I turned back to my page, more words crawling across it. He rested his chin on my shoulder, peering into the notebook at some of my words.

"Were you inspired?"

The tease in his voice had me looking back into his face. Eli wasn't usually full of lighthearted humor. He ribbed Mac Truck relentlessly, and he'd even teased me, but it was usually still with some seriousness to his soul. Even more so since his accident…after finding out about his mom's cancer. But this morning, he looked younger, happier, more at peace.

"It was an inspiring night," I told him with my own smile.

"I agree."

He was kissing my neck and the spot behind my ear that about left me breathless whenever he did it. Then it was the back of my neck and my shoulders that showed over the top of his Henley that I'd thrown on with my panties. His hand slid under the shirt and up to my breasts waiting for him.

I moaned.

"How do you do that?"

"Do what?" His voice was gruff and muffled in my skin as he continued to move over it at a tranquil pace that was turning my insides back to fire.

"Make my body yours."

He stopped his kisses, looking up into my eyes that were watching him. "It's not mine, Ava. I would never demand that. Your body is always your own. You can always tell me no. Just because we've had sex once, just because you've allowed me to touch you and kiss you, it doesn't mean that I have the right to that whenever I want. Your body is yours. I will graciously accept it whenever you permit me to have it, and I promise to honor it each time you give it to me."

I threw my notebook on the floor, turning in the chair so that I was straddling him. "Eli?" He waited expectantly for me to continue. "Today…Today my body is all yours."

He accepted my body. He took it and cherished it until the morning turned into the afternoon, and the afternoon turned into the fall of night. We continued to find each other's pieces, sometimes returning them and sometimes keeping them. One thing was for certain: we were never going to be the same again.

♫ ♫ ♫

When I woke Sunday morning, I smelled bacon and maple syrup before I realized Eli's side of the bed was empty. I found my own clothes, showered quickly, and then joined him in the kitchen. His cane laid against the counter as he maneuvered around the small space without it.

"I'm pretty sure you overdid it this weekend." I wrapped my arms around him, reveling in the fact that I was hugging him, holding him. I placed a kiss near his Coast Guard tattoo. He wore a pair of sweats and nothing else. He was like the very best of Jenna's romance novels in real life.

After four years, I was finally able to read the words around the Coast Guard tattoo on his back. The Semper Paratus motto—Always Ready—and the whole Coast Guard emblem was surrounded by a version of a Khalil Gibran quote: "Life and death are one, even as the river and the sea."

It snuck into my heart that Eli had his own love of words, his own love of quotes. We were mismatched souls. Or matched souls? I didn't know. Just like I didn't know if his quote meant he was always ready for life and death, or if he saw the way his dad's death had been part of the cycle of life. It was enough to know that he found meaning in words like I did.

"Nah. Pushing is the only way you get results," he replied.

He turned in my arms and kissed me warmly, making me continue to feel special. Adored. When I tried to deepen the kiss, he pulled back. "No way. You are not distracting me from breakfast. I'm starving. We hardly ate yesterday."

I pouted, he laughed, and I couldn't help but smile back. I wanted him like this. Full of smiles and laughter. Away from the pain of his life at the moment.

"Sit down." He motioned to the stools at the counter. The guys didn't have a kitchen table. I'm sure they ate in front of the TV more than anywhere else.

Once he'd placed two very full plates on the counter, he joined me. "I'm going to drive to New London on Tuesday," he said as we ate.

We'd talked about this yesterday, in between moments in each other's skin. He wanted to wait for Truck to get back so he could tell Truck in person. Truck was almost as attached to Eli's mom as Eli was. I'd known he was going to go after that, but I couldn't help the patter of my heart at the thought of him actually leaving the city.

I nodded, trying not to let the bite of pancake that I'd taken get stuck in my throat. "That's good," I whispered out.

He looked at me and could see the doubts filling me, even as I tried to hide them. He stopped eating, putting down his fork and turning toward me in order to take my hand into his. "I've been thinking."

"Wait. Does the Coast Guard let their people think on their own?" I teased.

He smirked. "Ha ha. You have spring break starting Friday, right?"

I nodded. "Really, Thursday because my professor won't be in that day."

"Come join me in New London once you're out."

Thoughts flitted through my head. I'd be by myself in the city over break if I stayed. Brady was going home to upstate New York and his family. I could fly to Texas to see Jenna, but she was working and involved with wedding preparations. I didn't really have anywhere else to be.

It was just that…New London was his home. With his mom who was battling cancer and his mom's best friend who was like a second mom. I wasn't sure I was ready to meet moms. I wasn't sure I was ready for that part of his life to become part of my own.

"Your mom's sick. She doesn't need a houseguest."

"My girlfriend isn't a houseguest."

I looked into his eyes, examining his reaction to his own words. We hadn't labeled us. Hadn't said we were dating. Hadn't said we were exclusive. I wasn't obtuse. I knew that was where Eli's head was at. I knew that was where my head was at, because I sure as hell didn't want to see him with another woman, but we still hadn't said we were in a relationship.

"Your girlfriend, huh?" My lips quirked, and he leaned in and kissed the corner of my mouth.

"You taste like syrup." His voice was husky with longing. I didn't know how either of us could still feel that longing after an entire weekend together, but it was still there. The same craving I'd felt before we'd taken the last step. No. It wasn't the same; it was stronger, more demanding, if anything.

"Ditto," I breathed into his lips. Somehow, we both forgot breakfast, and the fact that I was fully dressed and ready to return to campus, as the desire made itself known again, requiring all of our attention.

Reviving

COME A LITTLE CLOSER
Performed by Dierks Bentley

Chapter Twenty-one

Eli

BLESS THE BROKEN ROAD
Performed by Rascal Flatts

Sunday night, Ava went back to Juilliard, and I was left to toss and turn in my bed alone. My mind reeled with thoughts of my mom, thoughts of my job, and thoughts of Ava. The fact that my sheets smelled of her and the lives we'd joined together a step further only added to my unrest.

The fact that, by some strange twist of life events, Ava hadn't had sex before me made me appreciate the piece of herself that she'd given to me even more. I wasn't old-fashioned. I didn't expect a woman to be a virgin until she got married. It would have been incredibly hypocritical of me if I had, seeing as I'd lost my virginity at sixteen.

But I loved that I'd been able to be her first.

I loved Ava.

It was as simple as that. Our conversations may have been limited. Our time together may have been limited. But the time we had spent together had been full to the brim of moments that were seared onto my heart and soul.

Since joining the Coast Guard, my future had become my present. The goals I'd set had become a reality. Now, I was being forced to consider what came after in a way I hadn't ever thought I'd have to do. The one thing I knew for certain was that, whether or not I got to keep my commission, I couldn't look forward and not see Ava entwined in that future.

I waited, tired and impatient, for Truck to get home on Monday. Truck had barely gotten in the door and set his stuff down before I let loose with the news about Mom.

"Cancer…shit," was his first response. My response had been the same, so I couldn't blame him. "And she didn't tell you? Us? That's pretty screwed up."

Truck was as close to his own mom as I was to mine. Both of us were raised by single moms who worried about their sons and the career path that put them at risk. It was probably why he'd been completely comfortable spending time with my mom and Leena when he'd been at the DCO school. They'd sort of adopted him as a second son, and now I could see the same hurt on his face that I'd felt because Mom hadn't told us.

"You know Mom. She feels like anything she says to me that isn't one hundred percent positive will somehow mess with my head and end up with me on a stretcher. Little did she know, I'd be stupid enough to end up there on my own."

Truck was silent. What was there to say, really? Eventually, he cleared his throat and said, "I'm going to try to make it out there while you're on leave. To see her."

I nodded. "She'll be happier to see you than me. Especially once I've worn away her anger at Leena telling me."

I gave him our normal hug goodbye. I was planning on being up at the asscrack of dawn, so I wouldn't see him.

As I walked down the hall, he called out, "It's good to see you without the cast, Eli."

I waved the cane in acknowledgment.

I was on the road by three in the morning. I didn't want to deal with the New York traffic in commute hours. I'd timed the trip so that I'd be there after Mom's alarm had gone off, but before she left for the bookstore—if she was even going into the bookstore.

When I drove up to the house I'd grown up in, parking behind Mom's Chevy, my brain and emotions were dragged across the coals for a new reason. There was a "For Sale" sign in the yard. The first emotion that hit me was anger—yet another thing Mom had done without telling me. I didn't have any right to stop her from selling our home, but the fact that she'd do it without even mentioning it cut me to the quick. It was the home that she and Dad had filled with love and memories. For me. For them.

After the anger worked its way into my heart, a new emotion joined it: fear. Fear that she really was worse than Leena said. That she was selling the house so that I didn't need to later. Or so that she'd have money to cover the medical bills.

I looked at the house I'd grown up in, trying to see it as an outsider. A simple cottage from the forties. Someone had painted it recently. It was still white, but the shutters were now black instead of the dark red they'd been for as long as I could remember. My heart clenched at the thought of not coming back to it…of not coming back to Mom.

My leg groaned at me as I stepped out of the truck, stiff from the long drive and the position it had been stuck in. The physical pain was just another reminder of all the things going wrong in my life besides Mom and a "For Sale" sign.

I let myself in quietly. The living room was still dark, but the smell of coffee came from the kitchen. I could hear muted sounds coming from her bathroom with her bedroom door open. I was sure it was a podcast. She was addicted to them these days.

There was a stack of unassembled boxes against the wall by the entrance to the kitchen. The books, that had constantly been scattered everywhere growing up, had constantly been scattered everywhere growing up, seemed organized into piles that I'd never seen her do.

Our house had always been well-worn. Well-loved, I guess. The furniture squished down from use and was covered in so many blankets and pillows you could hardly see the cushions, anyway. The blankets and pillows were a hodgepodge of things that my mom fell in love with or others gave her as gifts.

A lot of the pictures that had always filled the walls and the tables were scattered and stacked in random places, the pictures of our lives being removed. It was painful. It made the anger flare inside me again that she could do all of this without saying one word.

As something to do, I made my way to the kitchen and made Mom's coffee, adding the cream and sugar just like she took it. I heard Mom talking to the one cat that she had left living with her, Snickers. A cream-colored tabby with strange dark and light brown markings that had given her her name.

"I know, impatient one. I'm going to feed you now." Her voice was its normal soft lilt. It normally soothed me. Not today.

As she came around the corner, she froze, a hand going to her heart because I'd startled her. All my anger turned back to fear once I'd seen her. My throat closed around the emotions that were threatening to overflow from me. She looked tiny. Frail. I'd never thought of my mom as frail. She'd never been a heavy woman, too busy—too into yoga and walks on the beach—to ever gain too much weight. Now, there was no escaping the word.

Her hair was short, buzzed close on the sides and barely longer on the top. It was colored a red that suited her, but that I'd never seen her wear before. It had always been dirty-blonde. The haircut had to be due to the chemo, or radiation, or both.

Her gray eyes widened and then squeezed shut at the sight of me.

"No hug for your son? I even made your coffee." I tried to keep the utter terror out of my voice. Terror at seeing her look so not like herself. Terror that had masked the anger, but it still burned in me, too.

"I'm going to kill her," was what she said in return, but then she was hugging me, and I hugged her back as tight as I dared, afraid to hurt her, or break her, or just make her cry.

"I love you, Mom," I said, kissing the top of her head and not letting go, because, even hurt and afraid, it was the emotion I felt most.

She wrapped her arms around me and put her face on my chest. "I love you too, but you shouldn't be here."

That just pissed me off again. So when she pushed away and took the coffee cup that I had sitting on the counter for her, I let her go without a word. I tried to get control of all the emotions pouring through me before I spoke.

She sat at the old oak table in the kitchen alcove with its built-in bench. I followed her with my own coffee, sitting in one of the chairs across from her. "I think I should have been here months ago."

"Why? What would you have done?" she asked.

"Taken care of you. Helped you," I said, trying to keep the frustration and hurt out of my voice but not being able to help the waver that came anyway.

She looked up at me, her own eyes full of tears. "They probably wouldn't have given you leave. Then, you'd just have been worried…and you know I don't like to be coddled."

"Mom…you have cancer. I think some coddling is in order." Snickers jumped up on me, meowing pitifully because Mom had gotten sidetracked from feeding her. I got up, carrying the cat with me, and filled up the food dish by the sliding glass door to our backyard.

The light was starting to break over the fence, and I could see the wild herb and flower garden of Mom's that had felt fairylike when I was growing up. It was even more wild. Unkept. She'd not had the energy to take care of it.

"I'm okay, Eli. I promise," she said quietly.

"If you're okay, why are you selling the house?" I demanded.

She looked into her coffee cup and stood. "I don't have time for this right now. I have to be at the bookstore."

"Goddamn it, Mom. Stop avoiding me."

"Don't swear."

I stared at her, correcting my language like I was some adolescent. Maybe that was the problem. She couldn't ever see me as the adult I was.

"Then just tell me the truth. Are you really okay?"

"I will be."

"That isn't the same thing."

I'd done lots of Google searches on stage one cancer. I knew the odds were good because they'd caught it early. I also knew that it had been a rough go. The pain and nausea had probably been unbearable. She'd probably spent more days throwing up food than eating it. But I bet she hadn't stopped going into the store. I bet she'd kept moving.

She moved past me into the kitchen, looking for her travel cup. She poured the coffee in it and added more. After, she stopped and hugged me again, saying, "I've missed you."

The loneliness in her voice got me, melted my anger a little, forced back the words that I wanted to say. They'd wait. It must have been hard, going through the cancer with just Leena. If I'd been there, she could have had at least two of us going through it with her.

She was also right, however. It would have been unlikely that the Coast Guard would have granted me leave just to take care of her. For the first time, I wanted to bless the stupid harbor seal instead of gut it. Being hurt meant I was there.

"I missed you too," I told her, squeezing her again, feeling the fragility of her bones. "But for the record, I haven't forgiven you yet."

"I'll see you tonight?" she asked as she moved toward the door.

"Give me a second to put my bag in my room and use the facilities, and I'll drive you in."

"I can drive myself, Doodles." She was trying to soften me up by using my nickname. It wasn't going to work, not right now.

"Can't drive yourself unless you want to back into my truck to do it. Give me thirty seconds."

I grabbed my cane on my way past where I'd left it propped against the side of the fridge. I could feel her eyeing my limp and the brace that was over my jeans.

"You going to be okay, too?" she asked me.

I nodded. "It was just a break. I don't have cancer." I was going to keep needling her until she acknowledged that she should have told me.

"Have you been before the medical review board yet?" She was a Coast Guard's wife. A military wife. She knew how these things went. She knew that I may not have cancer, but that, in many ways, my life was ending.

"Not yet. I had to come see my mom…who has *cancer*, instead." It wasn't true. I wouldn't be before the board until I finished my PT.

I was halfway down the hallway, but I still heard her mutter, "I'm going to kill Leena."

It lightened my heart just a little. At least her attitude was the same, even if she didn't look the same.

♩ ♩ ♩

We spent the day at the bookstore, with me helping her unbox new inventory. Mom had a new girl helping her at the store. Some woman about my age named Jersey who was so pale and quiet she almost blended in with the whitewashed bookshelves. Jersey brought in pastries, said a hello I could barely hear, and faded into the fabric of the store.

By around three, Mom looked worn out. Exhausted. Like she needed to be wrapped up in bed. But she sat behind the counter, on a stool that had never been there before, going through receipts.

I eyed her from my place stocking the comics. Jersey flitted past like a ghost, and I almost didn't catch her words as she spoke. "She's never here this late anymore."

Then she drifted away again.

I texted Leena.

ME: We're still at the bookstore. The girl here says Mom doesn't stay this late?

LEENA: What? You're still there? I'm on my way.

As soon as Leena entered, I could tell in a way I hadn't been able to tell on the FaceTime call that mom's illness had taken a toll on her, too. Her hair was grayer, and her face held more lines. She looked tired, but she smiled when she saw me, hugged me tight, and whispered, "I'm so glad you're here, kiddo."

Her Japanese accent on my nickname warmed my heart. I hugged her back and said, "Thank you for telling me."

My mom had seen Leena come in as soon as the bell on the door jangled, but she'd studiously gone back to the receipts and not said a word to her.

Leena stepped away from me and went up to the counter. "We're going to the Crab Shack, right?"

She said it to my mom, but Mom continued to ignore her. The Crab Shack was our tradition. Every time I came home, we went there on the first night. It had always been a place we celebrated at while I was growing up. It was nothing fancy, mostly picnic tables outside with a few tiny tables shoved into the well-worn building, but it was good food. It was our food. It meant home.

Jersey came over and exchanged a look with Leena that let me know they'd been handling Mom together while I'd been gone. One more person who'd been able to look after her besides me. I loved it and hated it. It made me hurt.

"Let's go, Mom," I said.

"I'm still finishing up." Mom was being stubborn. Something I recognized. It was in me, too. That stubbornness. I'd gotten it from her.

"I can do it," Jersey said in her whisper voice.

Mom looked at her in surprise, as if she hadn't expected Jersey to gang up on her like that.

"Mom, it's tradition," I told her.

"Fine." She got up and went to the back to get her purse.

She didn't say a word to either of us as we drove to the restaurant. She didn't even say anything when we got there. She just went to grab a picnic table while Leena and I ordered. She didn't need to tell us what she wanted. We knew. It was tradition.

My phone buzzed while Leena and I were standing waiting for our order. It was Ava. That morning, I'd texted her to let her know that I'd made it home, but I hadn't texted again as I'd had my head wrapped in Mom, and the house, and all the things she wasn't saying.

MY LIGHT: Does your mom know I'm coming? Is she okay with it?

ME: We haven't talked about it yet. She's barely speaking to me at the moment.

MY LIGHT: Maybe I shouldn't come.

ME: They'll be thrilled that I'm bringing a girl home. It'll give them an excuse to buy me extra boxes of condoms this Christmas.

MY LIGHT: I...I don't even know how to respond to that.

I chortled and looked up to find Leena watching me.

"You're smiling," she said, like it was a surprise, like I never smiled. Which wasn't true, but I knew the goofy smile that I usually wore around Ava these days was probably one she hadn't seen in quite some time.

"I smile," I groused, but it wasn't a real grouse.

"Well, there was that one time you came home after dropping off Becky Anderson."

I groaned. "Don't start."

At sixteen years old, I'd been unable to keep the smile from my face after Becky and I had had sex for the first time. Mom and Leena had taken one look at me and known exactly what had gone down. From that point on, they'd started giving me condoms as birthday and Christmas presents. All different kinds of condoms. It was just wrong to have your mom and her friend buying condoms for you. But they'd also made their point: keep it covered.

"Who is she?" Leena asked.

"You'll see for yourself on Thursday. She's coming up for spring break."

"A college girl?" Leena frowned. "She's too young for you."

In Rockport, when Ava had been nineteen and I'd been twenty-two, our age difference had been the main thing on my mind. Her age, her underage drinking, her dad's reaction to her being underage. But since seeing her in New York, I'd never really stopped to think about it once.

I didn't get a chance to respond to Leena's jab before they called my name. Leena and I grabbed the trays and headed out to where Mom sat watching the waves. It had dropped to somewhere close to cold, and she was bundled up in a jacket, a beanie, and mittens. The beanie was just like the one on my own head with the Coast Guard emblem on it. I wondered if Mom's was actually Dad's, and that made my throat close up again for the hundredth time that day.

My phone buzzed again.

MY LIGHT: Seriously. I don't want to come if I'm going to be in the way.

ME: If you stay in New York, you'll make me drive six hours round trip to come get you and bring you back.

MY LIGHT: Don't go all alpha male on me, oh Captain, my Captain.

ME: Then just show up like you promised. I need you here.

She didn't respond, and I was afraid that maybe I'd overstepped some unspoken boundary that she'd raised and I hadn't noticed.

ME: I'm at the Crab Shack with Leena and Mom, so I'll call you later?

MY LIGHT: You're at dinner?! Don't text during dinner with your mom. It's rude.

ME: Are you lecturing me on table etiquette now? This is the exact reason why my mom and Leena will love you.

MY LIGHT: Go. We'll talk later.

"Seems like Eli has a new girlfriend," Leena told my mom.

This had Mom gasping and turning to Leena to say the first words she'd said to her since she'd entered the bookstore. "What? How do you know?"

"Look at his face. Just like when he came home from dropping Becky—"

I put a hand up to stop the story from going further, but I was still smiling when I texted one last reply to Ava.

ME: I'll call you later. But I'm also buying the train ticket for you now, so you can't back out.

I slid the phone into the pocket of my coat and turned back to the ladies at the table and our food.

"She's coming on Thursday. You'll both get to meet her."

Mom looked like a fish, mouth hanging open as if I'd just told her that the ocean had dried up.

"You're bringing a girl home?" Mom asked, a smile breaking out on her tired face. One of the first smiles I'd seen all day. It made her look more like the Mom I knew and less like the Mom that had withered away.

I shrugged. "Technically, she's taking the train and coming to me, but sure."

I bit into my lobster roll, trying to stay nonchalant, doing my own bit of egging them on. They deserved it.

"Who is she?" Mom asked.

"Her name's Ava. And she's finishing her senior year at Juilliard."

"She's an artist!" Leena gushed, and any concern she'd had about our age gap went out the window, because Leena loved art. She was a retired English teacher, but she'd also taught the art classes at the high school. Now, she spent time at the Y, sharing her love of painting there.

"She's a singer and a musician. She writes all of her own songs."

Mom's smile turned into a frown, and she was thinking. I could tell she was putting the pieces slowly together.

"Ava. This is Ava from Rockport, Ava?"

"No!" Leena gasped.

I shrugged.

"What does Travis think of this?" Mom asked, concern lacing her voice. Mom and Leena never called Truck by his nickname. Not the entire time he was in training here at the DCO school, nor any of the times he'd come home with me since then.

"Truthfully?"

"No, she wants you to lie to us." Leena scoffed.

I ignored her. "Ava brought Truck back to his senses."

"What does that mean?" Mom questioned.

"Once he'd seen her, and they'd talked, it was like Truck was his old self again. Like he let go of all the anger that had been welled up inside of him. Truck is the best I've seen him in years."

Mom and Leena watched me as I talked, the smile on my face when I spoke of Ava giving me away to them just like it had when I'd come home from leaving Becky Anderson at her house in high school.

"I'm going to have to run to the drug store," Leena teased.

I had one more thing to thank Ava for. That she could make these two grumpy women talk to each other again and make them both smile when they'd just lived through months of hell without telling me.

"She's nervous about coming. Thinks she'll be a burden, considering…" I hated myself for making their smiles falter at the mention of the cancer.

"You tell her that we are more excited about having her here than having you here," Leena said.

"Hey, now!" I complained, but I knew she was teasing, and my protest was only half-hearted.

"I can almost forgive Leena now," Mom said, looking at me while her best friend nudged her in the side.

"You know I did the right thing," Leena defended herself.

"She did," I agreed.

Mom ignored both of our digs and took a bite of her fish and chips, but I could swear that she seemed lighter somehow than she had this morning when I'd first seen her. That made my heart tighten in happiness but also regret that I hadn't been here sooner. Regardless, I was here now and not planning on going anywhere for a month at least.

Chapter Twenty-two

Ava

WRITTEN IN SAND
Performed by Old Dominion

Eli and I texted back and forth almost nonstop from the time I left his apartment on Sunday until it was time for me to leave the city. The first night he was in New London, he'd called, and there'd been so much hurt and anger in his voice that it had made me want to skip the rest of my classes and run to catch a train that very moment.

"She's selling the house," he told me when I asked how it was going. I could hear the loss in his voice. "And she hasn't told me why."

"I'm so sorry," I responded, not really knowing how else to soothe him. He'd had so many losses in such a short amount of time that it seemed impossibly unfair.

"She looks…like she could just fade away. With her selling the house, it's like…"

He couldn't finish.

"You said the outlook was good, right? That they'd gotten the cancer. Stage one has such positive results. She's going to be okay, Eli."

He took a long time before he answered, as if the emotions playing through him were too much. I waited, knowing he didn't want to show that much emotion, knowing he wanted to be in control of them before he spoke again.

"You're coming, right? You got the ticket I sent?" he asked.

I sighed. "You didn't need to buy me a ticket."

"This way you won't back out."

"Bribery?"

"I'm not above it. I need you here."

It was the second time he'd said that he needed me, and those words echoed around my heart long after we'd hung up. I didn't have any doubt that Eli could survive whatever life threw at him and his family. He was built to survive. Still, the fact that he had convinced himself of needing me made my weak heart patter a tune that I wasn't used to it singing.

That was why I hauled a bag and my guitar onto the train leaving Penn Station, heading to New London on Thursday morning. Then, I texted Jenna as my nerves started to jangle, and butterflies filled my stomach in a totally different way than Eli normally filled it.

ME: Morning.

GIRLIE: Morning back. You on the train?

ME: Yes.

GIRLIE: Don't be nervous.

ME: I'm not.

GIRLIE: Liar.

*ME: Okay. I'm hella nervous. Is that what you needed to hear? **puking GIF***

GIRLIE: They're going to love you.

ME: I'm only going because he said he needed me. I've never been needed.

GIRLIE: That's not true. I need you!

ME: No. You have Colby and your family. You don't really need me. It's always been the other way around. I needed you.

My phone rang. I looked down in surprise to see Jenna's picture. I answered. "Hey, what's up?"

"You scare me sometimes," Jenna said.

"Why?"

"You act like you're not important. That no one would miss you if you weren't here. You are so important to me, Ava. My life would never be the same if you weren't in it."

A lump filled my throat. I couldn't reply at first.

"Look, I know that your dad is a total ass, but you have people who care about you. I may not know Eli, but I can easily imagine why he would want you in his life. Why he would *need* you in his life."

I wouldn't cry. Tears and me didn't exist well ever since Dad had punished them out of me. Plus, I didn't want to show up in New London with mascara running down my face.

"Tell me you hear me."

"I hear you," I said.

"Tell me you believe me," she demanded.

"Okay."

"Say it."

"I believe you," I told her. It wasn't that I didn't. I did believe that she thought she needed me, but I also knew the truth. She could easily get through life without me.

"Before I forget, and because we are talking about the asshole, I have to tell you what happened the other day."

My gut clenched again.

"Did you see him?"

"My mom did. She said that somehow it came up that Colby and I were going to see you for your graduation, and how bad she felt that they couldn't make it themselves because of Dad's schedule in the House. He acted like he knew all about it and already had his own arrangements made to go."

I sat stunned for a moment before fury filled me. Fury I hadn't felt toward my dad in a long time. "He wouldn't dare."

"I think he was just bluffing so that it didn't look like he hadn't known anything about his own daughter, but I wanted to make sure you knew. Colby and I will be there, so if he does show up, we can tell him to shove off."

"He won't. It would be too much work for him to come. There's no reason for him to come."

"Again, Ava. You are worth it."

"But not in his eyes."

There was nothing she could say to that. I'd never been enough in the eyes of my dad. He'd told me repeatedly growing up how, just like my mother, I'd end up chasing things that I'd never succeed at. That I'd never amount to anything. It would probably never stop hurting. That he thought I was nothing. I'd keep working on it, but it would always be a wound that could easily be reopened.

"They're going to love you," Jenna said, reminding me of why we'd started this conversation to begin with. I didn't respond. Eventually, she sighed. "I'm sorry, I have to run. Colby and I are already late for a new client. But I need you to know how loved you are."

I was still fighting the tears today, but I wouldn't cry. Instead, I said goodbye the way we always said goodbye.

"Take care of you."

"Take care of you," she replied and hung up.

I tucked my phone away and stared out the window at the scenery as it flew by, thoughts of Eli and his mom and me and my dad running through my head. If I'd heard that my dad had cancer, I didn't think I'd care. I certainly wouldn't run home to look after him. I didn't think I'd be glad, but I wouldn't miss him. He hadn't given me anything to miss. Nothing but hurt and fear and anger. My anger so different from the anger Eli felt at the moment. His anger stemmed from love. My anger stemmed from the absence of love.

By the time the train stopped in New London, I was tired from feeling too much. Like I'd been dipped in the ocean, and it had thrown me out on the sand again. The butterflies were back, bouncing around my stomach at the thought of seeing him and of having to meet his family that he did care about.

I grabbed my carry-on suitcase, my guitar, and my handbag and headed for the terminal. Like always, our eyes connected immediately. If I'd never believed in "the force" from *Star Wars* before, I did after knowing Eli. We had a force that bonded us together. An unseen energy that always connected the minute we were in the same room.

He still hadn't gotten a haircut. It was the longest I'd ever seen on him, reaching toward his ears in a wave of hair so dark that it was almost black. He must not have shaved for a couple days either, because the scruff on his chin looked like it might almost be soft instead of rough against my fingers…against my lips. It aged him some. Made him look older than me by far more than our three years, but I also found it flaring the desire in my stomach.

He was using his cane still, but his stride was big as he moved toward me. Then, he was picking me up and squeezing me so tight that I thought I might lose my air and my insides. It felt glorious. It felt like it was the first time that anyone, other than Jenna, had actually been happy to see me, had missed me. I held on tight, letting myself believe in the importance of a hug like I once hadn't. My lips found the space on his neck right below his ear that had made him gasp last weekend. The same spot that he'd found on me. Matching spots. I felt his arms tighten even more.

"God, I missed you," he breathed in my ear, and my flesh prickled happily.

He still hadn't let me down, was still holding tight, and I didn't mind. But I suspected the weight of us both on his bad knee was going to be too much, so I pushed gently. He reluctantly let go, but as soon as my feet touched the ground, his lips found mine, crushing them in a kiss that felt like we'd been apart for four years again instead of four days. I responded with equal fervor.

I'd never come home to anything before. Not once. But I could imagine that this was what it felt like. Home. With someone who loved you. Eli hadn't said those words. I certainly was terrified of even thinking them to myself, but I was pretty sure that was what we shared. Love.

I pulled back and looked up again. We were both smiling this time. Not just him, with that full smile that I was lucky enough to witness, but me too.

"Is this all you have?" he asked, looking down at the suitcase I'd dropped and the guitar that was beside it.

"Should I have more?" I questioned. "Do we have plans that I don't know about?"

His eyes twinkled at me. He leaned in close and said, "The plans I have don't involve clothes."

My stomach curled happily, and my legs wobbled, but I frowned at him. "I don't think that's necessarily a good idea. We'll be at your mom's house. I'm not exactly sure what the etiquette is for having sex in your boyfriend's mom's house."

"Her room's not next to mine."

"So."

He grabbed my case and tried to wield it, and the cane, and my hand at the same time. It was cute and pathetic.

"Just give me the suitcase," I said, pulling it from his grasp.

"I'm only letting you because I'd rather have your hand than be a gentleman at the moment."

His truck was parked outside, and we threw my stuff into the backseat. He held my door, and I smiled at him. Before shutting it, he leaned in and kissed me again. The kiss was meant to be sweet and short, but it turned deep and frantic before either of us could help it, him leaning up against the truck seat, me leaning into him.

A voice cleared behind us. "Excuse me. Um. Can I get into my car now?"

We smiled at each other, and he turned to shut the door and apologized to the woman parked beside him who was waiting. She wouldn't meet his eyes. It made my smile widen. Public displays of affection and I weren't a thing. It wasn't something I'd ever allowed, but with Eli, it was hard to resist touching him.

He climbed in, started the truck, and then looked at me. "Do you want to go to the house first or the bookstore first?"

"Is there a right answer to this question?"

He chuckled. "Well, I know I want to go to the house, but I'm afraid that we will lose ourselves in each other for hours, and then I'll never hear the end of this story either."

"I don't follow," I said, confused.

"Mom and Leena both know that I'm picking you up. If we don't show up for hours, they'll know—"

"Bookstore! Definitely bookstore," I cut him off with a wave. "I'm not even sure you can convince me to have sex in a house with your mom in another room, let alone have them look at me knowing for sure that's what we've been doing. I'm already nervous enough about meeting them. I don't need to add a walk of shame to it."

He backed out and headed down the road. "Just for the record, there would be no shame in it. It's not like we're a one-night swag and bag."

"Did you just say swag and bag?" I choked out a laugh.

He nodded with a twist to his lips that wasn't quite a smile, but hinted at it. "You know, swag—swagger—and bag—as in the sheets."

"I knew what you were alluding to, oh Captain, my Captain. I've just never heard it called that before."

"That's because you haven't hung out with Mac enough."

"I can't believe he would call it that. Even Brady isn't that crass with his long list of conquests."

"Oh, Mac has a whole slew of phrases for it."

I shook my head. "I'll never understand boy humor."

The banter had eased the nerves in my stomach that were growing since he'd mentioned going to the bookstore to meet his mom and the lady who was pretty much a second mom. I flipped down the visor, tugged at the angles of my hair, wiped at the non-existent makeup marks under my eyes, and then flipped it up again.

When I turned back to him, his eyes were darting between the road and me. "What?" I asked.

"You're beautiful. They're going to love you. Hell, I think they already do."

I narrowed my eyes. "What exactly have you told them?"

"I didn't have to say much. They saw my smile and knew."

"Knew?"

Suddenly, he looked nervous, squeezing the steering wheel. When he spoke, his voice was deep. "Knew that you make me happy."

It wasn't what he was going to say. I didn't push it, though, because I wasn't ready for him to say the words. I wasn't ready for discussions of what came after we said the words. Discussions about what came after I graduated and he had his hearing. At the moment, I planned to return to the house in Rockport. It was the one place that was truly mine.

We pulled up in a lot next to a bookstore that took up the corner of an old brick building. There was a beautiful mural of a sunset on the side of it, and I could already see three cats lounging in the windows beside the books.

"Does your mom own the store?" I asked.

"No. She just manages this location. The owners have a much larger location outside town. It has a full petting zoo and barns full of books and cats."

"Wow. So, you worked here a lot growing up?" I was procrastinating, trying to calm the flutters that had worked themselves up inside me.

He nodded. "You don't need to be nervous, Ava."

I loved it when he said my name. The caress of it across his tongue. The endearment of it in his tone. No one had ever said my name and made it sound like love. Eli was good at that.

"'Kay," I told him, but I was unable to move, turned to stone. I didn't normally get nervous onstage. It was a rare thing, but I could imagine that this was what people who got stage fright felt like.

Eli got out of the truck, came around, and opened my door. He reached in to help me out. I eased down beside him and looked up.

"If they hate me, I'm blaming you."

His lips quirked again. He tucked my hand into his arm, and we made our way to the store. When he swung open the door, three people turned to greet us. There was a young girl with hair so fair it looked white, a gray-haired lady in jeggings and a flowy top, and a tiny, red-haired lady with Eli's eyes that had the frailness of someone who was sick.

His mom was in jeans and a sweater. The sweater was covered in cat faces, and her shoes, when I looked down, were Chucks that were covered with cats. She was a cat lady. It made me smile, and when I looked up at her face again, she was smiling back.

I'd barely taken two steps into the store when she was next to me, engulfing me in a hug that, even though she seemed skin and bone, was still tight and full of life—like her son's. I fought my normal reflex to pull away from a hug. I tried, the best I knew how, to return it with warmth.

"It's so nice to meet you," she said and then stepped back, and I swear, there were tears in her eyes.

I looked from her face to Eli's. He was frowning at her. "Jesus, Mom, you'll scare her away if you start crying."

She laughed, and it made her seem younger than she looked. She wiped at her eyes and then smiled at me again. "Don't mind me. It's the medicines they have me on. And don't mind him." She slapped Eli on the chest. "He's just afraid of everything we're going to tell you about him."

Eli groaned.

It felt so…normal. A guy bringing a girl home, and his family filling her with stories. It felt like a country song. It felt like something I'd never had. Normal. My throat constricted, but I continued to smile through the feeling.

The gray-haired lady reached out a hand. "I'm Leena. I'm glad to see you too, but I'll reserve the hug for when Eli isn't here to berate us for getting all emotional."

"He has no right to harass you. He was practically crying when he picked me up at the train station," I teased.

Both women laughed, and Eli shook his head, but he didn't deny it. My nerves that had been fluttering about recklessly suddenly settled. This was going to be okay. These women loved Eli. I was pretty sure I loved Eli. We already had that much in common. What could be more important than that?

"Eli, go pick up the food from Nate's. Ava and I are going to go sit on the patio and talk books, or music, or you—whichever she prefers in whatever order she prefers," his mom said.

He huffed. "Nate's delivers, Mom."

"But they charge four dollars."

"I'll pay the fricking four dollars."

"Don't cuss."

"Fricking isn't a cuss word."

I chuckled. "Eli, it's okay. Go get the food. I'll be fine."

I'm sure he doubted it, when not even five minutes before I'd been a nervous wreck in his truck, but it was the truth. My nerves were gone. I was surrounded by people who loved him. That wasn't intimidating anymore.

"Listen to the girl, kiddo." Leena grinned.

He gave me a questioning stare, and I just inclined my head toward the door with a smile. It was all going to be okay.

While Eli was gone, Eli's mom and Leena peppered me with questions—about growing up in Texas, about my time at Juilliard. It felt like I was being interviewed. I loved how protective they were of him.

They asked to hear some of my music, and I promised them that I'd share some with them later. Eli had my guitar in his truck, and, even without stage fright, I wasn't really ready to bust out singing to his family.

After Eli had come back and we'd had lunch on the patio just outside the bookstore, the three of them bickered back and forth about the leftovers and who was taking them and who was going to clean up. When I offered to clean up, all three of them turned to me with an emphatic, "No."

While they argued, I risked looking down at my phone that had been buzzing throughout the meal.

BRADY: I sent Nick Jackson the first song.

BRADY: I sent Nick Jackson the first song.

BRADY: I sent Nick Jackson the first song!!!!

BRADY: Are you ignoring me? Did you read any of my texts?! I SENT THE FUCKING FIRST SONG TO JACKSON!!!

ME: WHAT?!

BRADY: Finally. I was having a heart attack over here. And I'm full of good news.

ME: Why did you send it to him now?! We don't have the album ready. We told him we'd send it to him when we were done.

BRADY: I didn't want him to forget about us between now and graduation.

ME: It's only a couple weeks away.

BRADY: You know that's ages in show business. He could find someone else to fill the spot he's eyeing us for on his platform.

ME: You could have told me.

BRADY: Babe, STOP! LISTEN! He fucking loved it!

My heart flipped excitedly. I looked back up to the bookstore, and Eli and his mom were still fighting over the pizza boxes, but it was with a smile. Both the text conversation and the images in front of me felt dreamlike. Unreal. Not my life.

ME: Really?

BRADY: How can you doubt us so much?

ME: I don't doubt you.

BRADY: He reiterated how much he loved your voice.

ME: Liar.

BRADY: I'm wounded beyond repair. You know I wouldn't bust your balls over this.

ME: I don't have balls.

BRADY: Stop changing the subject.

ME: I didn't realize there was a subject.

BRADY: You. Considering our upcoming record deal.

ME: Your ego really does have no limits.

BRADY: Tell me you're still considering it.

Eli was coming back out on the patio. He had a stack of books in his hands. Really, they looked like comic books. I smiled at the thought of him loving something so contrary to the image he put out to the world. I felt that way too—contrary to the image people believed of me these days.

BRADY: AVA!!!!

I'd waited too long to respond. The truth was, I didn't know how to answer him. If I told him I was considering it, I'd just keep his hopes up. If I told him no, he'd never stop harassing me about it.

ME: I have to go. We'll chat about it later.
But I'm really happy he liked the song.

Then, I put the phone away and turned to my boyfriend. The one I was pretty damn sure I was in love with. The only man I'd ever fallen in love with. For now, I just wanted to concentrate on him and how he said he needed me.

Chapter Twenty-three

Eli

WORDS ARE MEDICINE
Performed by Tim McGraw

We spent a few hours after lunch at the bookstore. Ava looked through the comics I'd brought out on the patio and then took off inside to examine the graphic novel section like she was trying to learn something about me from them. My mom joined her, telling her that she'd never stocked any of it until I'd shown an interest. I watched them, enthralled with the way they seemed comfortable with each other already.

We left the store early again, leaving Jersey in charge. When we got home, Mom apologized to Ava for the mess. "Sorry. I've been sorting through all the stuff to give and keep with the move."

"You still haven't even told me why you're moving," I told her with a growl.

She gave me a look that said, *Not with company here.* I gave her a look that said, *You will have to tell me eventually.*

After putting Ava's stuff in my room, Ava and I headed out to the backyard while Mom rested on the couch with Snickers on her lap and a book in her hand. It was something my mom had done her whole life.

Another thing that felt normal and somehow grounded me even though everything was changing.

Yesterday, I'd started to clean the weeds out of the garden while cutting back the overgrowth. It had wiped me out physically, but I was determined to push myself hard. I'd arranged to see a physical therapist in New London while I was there, but I wasn't going to just wait around for her workouts. I also wasn't going to be stupid and not listen to my body. The slim chance I had of keeping my commission was dependent on a recovery that was quick and successful. I wasn't going to hurt that miniscule chance by doing damage cleaning out the yard.

Today, I didn't want to work in the garden, but I did want to lose myself in the quiet of it with Ava. She took it all in before sitting on a bench near the back fence. It had a view of almost the entire chaos of wildflowers, herbs, and plants that Mom had tucked into old wine drums and rusted out wheelbarrows. It was a beautiful yard.

"It's like a fairytale garden," she said.

I nodded in agreement.

"You must have loved growing up here."

My throat constricted. I had. I pulled her up tight against me as I sat on the bench with her, not wanting to let go of her now that she was finally there.

"I'm sorry that you're losing it," she told me. "Grief is in two parts. The first is loss. The second is the remaking of life."

"Who said that one?" I asked into her hair with a smile.

"Ann Roiphe."

"Don't know her."

"I'll have to make you watch *The Sandbox* then."

We sat there, quiet, satisfied to just be in each other's arms. At least, I was. I was hoping she was, too.

"You know that's why she's selling it, right?" Ava asked.

"What do you mean?"

"So much loss in this house. I'm sure it's full of love, too, and happy memories, but sometimes it's hard to escape the loss. You have to move out of it to see what's next."

We'd both had losses, Ava and I. Lives full of them. Mine were still lurking around the corner, waiting for me.

"Brady sent the first song to Nick Jackson," she told me. Her lost dream reappearing on her horizon once more.

"And?"

"He loved it. Brady says he wants the song. Wants us."

I squeezed her. "That's wonderful."

And I meant it. I wanted her to have every dream she'd ever imagined come true. She didn't seem thrilled about it. The Ava that I'd first met would have been jumping off the back of the fence in joy.

"Why aren't you more excited?"

"I'd kind of reconciled myself to not having any of this. I was happy at the thought of writing songs and letting others take them out into the world."

The aurora borealis of songs, she'd said before. But I also knew, painfully, how hard it was to give up the things you'd wanted for a lifetime, so I pushed her.

"What's your biggest fear if you said yes? If you took the deal and became a country music legend?"

"Legend?" She grinned.

"Don't get distracted." I kissed her on the head. "Just tell me. What's the worst that could happen?"

"The list is long."

She was stalling, like she always did when I was forcing her to tell me what was going on inside that beautiful head of hers. So, I started with the good things I could see. "You get to sing all the time. You make music with someone you trust. You make gobs of money and win a CMA. You have fans who adore you. Those don't seem like negatives."

She laughed. "CMA?"

I nodded, serious. "You know your songs are that good."

She nudged me with her elbow and then was quiet again before finally sharing the truth.

"A part of me—the little girl who was denied love and acceptance from her father—still wants the crowds chanting her name. I've never been afraid onstage because the worst thing that could happen would be the audience not liking me, and I already knew what that felt like. I'd lived it."

"Ava." I pulled her hand into mine, rubbing the palm. I hated the asshole who hadn't loved her as a child when that was all she'd needed—the simple act of being loved by someone.

"But that little girl only saw the good parts of it. The singing. The acceptance. She didn't see all the things behind the shiny curtain."

"I don't understand."

"A professional singer's life is set to this crazy schedule."

"You have a set schedule now with school, and studio time, and your open mic nights," I told her.

She nodded. "But I also get to say no and back out if I want to. You can't do that with a tour schedule, with fans expecting you to show up. You can't do that with a host of studio execs requiring you to go to every interview and recording session. You can't tell them no when they want to change your cover or the songs on the album."

"Those are definitely some of the downsides. But are they enough to give up the dream?" I asked. I was still fighting hard for my dream even though I knew the downsides, too. The perfect example was sitting in the house—not being able to be there for the people you loved when they needed you most. And while I hated that, I couldn't walk away yet. It made me a selfish bastard, because I wanted it all.

"I'd be giving up so much of my freedom. The freedom I said I'd never give away again," she said quietly. She'd been caught in a life with no freedom for nineteen years, and while I didn't know what that felt like, I could understand not wanting to give it up once you'd finally gotten it.

"You still have time. You don't need to make the decision today."

She nodded, but I could tell that it was going to weigh on her until she made the choice. I was glad that she was there with me in New London. Glad that she wasn't alone in her dorm room where the weight of it all would just cause her to sink. She was my light. I could be hers too. We'd find a way to guide each other home.

♫ ♫ ♫

I made cheesesteak sandwiches for dinner. It wasn't anything special, but it was something I could cook. Mom didn't eat much, and she still looked tired, but she joined us at the table when I took out our ancient Scrabble board.

"I'm not sure you want to play. Ava cheats," I said.

"Not hardly. You just can't stand that I kicked your butt when I was only nineteen."

"He should be used to it. I kick his butt all the time," Mom said.

"I bet he didn't get all squinty-eyed and growly at you, though, Mrs. Wyatt."

"Enough with the Mrs. Wyatt. I'm Mandy. Mrs. Wyatt is some old lady I don't know. And he always gets growly when he loses. That boy was all competition from the day he was born."

Ava smiled at her.

"He had to beat every single average at every age. First tooth, early. First steps, early. First words, way early. But if he didn't come in first, God help us all," Mom teased as she put her word down on the board.

Ava chuckled. "That explains it then."

"Explains what?" Mom asked.

"Why he gets squinty at me. I never just let him get his way."

Mom's laughter filled the room, and I took a moment to watch her smiling at Ava and Ava smiling back. The two women I loved most liked each other, and that filled me with pleasure.

Regardless of their ribbing me about wanting to win, they both kicked my butt, and I didn't give a damn. I loved seeing them duel it out. They each won a game. My mom, the book lady, losing to my girlfriend, the word lady.

After the second game, Mom yawned.

"I'm heading to bed. The meds make me sleepy." She rose from the table where we'd been playing and started toward the hallway. "They seriously conk me out. Like dead-to-the-world type of sleep. Like it-would-take-a-train-crashing-through-the-room-to-wake-me kind of sleep."

I caught on to what she was trying to insinuate, and I probably turned the same shade of red as the kitchen chair. "Jesus, Mom."

She smirked then looked at Ava who looked as stunned as I felt. She smiled at Ava. "Goodnight, sweetie. I'm really glad you're here with us."

She turned and walked away, calling back, "Have fun, you two." Her bedroom door closed with a resounding slam.

"This is why you don't bring women home," I said, running a hand over my face, through my too long hair, and then down the back of my head.

"Women? As in plural? As in more than one?"

I cut her words off with my finger to her lips. "Only one. And she was in high school."

"Was she really letting us know that it was okay…to um…you know…"Ava's voice faltered and wafted away.

"I guess the etiquette for having sex in your mom's house is that it requires approval?" I grinned at her.

"It's going to be pretty much impossible now, because she'll just know that's what we did. How could I look at her in the morning?"

I didn't really care how my mom looked at me in the morning. After all, I didn't think it could get much worse than it had after I'd come home from Becky at sixteen. However, I did know that it would be impossible for me to not touch Ava while she was there.

So, I pulled her to me on the bench seat. Her legs flopped around me because I'd caught her by surprise. I started kissing her before she could protest. The kind of kiss that had both our hearts pounding out a melody that only we could hear. The kind of kiss that promised of things that I knew my body could do to her. A kiss that had me tugging her down the hall to my own room and the small, but functional, full-sized bed that resided there.

Ava seemed to have forgotten her embarrassment as her hand wandered under my shirt, pulling at it so that she could caress the skin along my abs and my back with a gentle touch that had me groaning in her mouth. I covered her cheek and neck with kisses, and she pushed her body tighter into mine, desire coursing through both of us.

When I went to pull Ava down on the bed, I saw what waited for us there and couldn't help the laugh that erupted from my chest.

Ava looked puzzled but then caught my gaze and looked down to find the box of extra-large, ribbed condoms sitting there. Her mouth dropped open, and her skin turned a beautiful shade of pink, like a sunrise creeping over the horizon of the ocean.

I ran my fingers over her blush, the smile still on my face.

"Where? Did she?" Her voice was a wash of mortification.

"It's a joke," I told her. "Mom and Leena have been buying them for me as presents since I was a teenager. Since they suspected I'd started having sex."

"It's so…inappropriate!" Ava gasped, but she was trying not to laugh as well.

"Yeah, I guess they just didn't know how else to talk to me about it. I didn't have a dad to discuss it with. They made a joke out of it while still getting their point across."

"But…now that you're, what, twenty-six? Don't they think…I mean, don't they know…" Ava was so flustered. It was cute and sexy at the same time.

"Ava," I said her name, and her eyes flared. It happened a lot when I said her name. The look she gave me was like no one else in the world had ever called her by her name before. "I don't want to talk about my mom, or Leena, or the reason they buy me condoms. I would, however, very much like to use one of those and get reacquainted with your skin and your scent and your touch. If you'll have me."

She responded by pulling at my T-shirt until it was thrown on the floor and then pulling off her own blouse before joining me in removing our pants. That was all it took for us to forget everything else, including my mom down the hall, decisions that were waiting for us both, and lives that weren't settled. Instead, we simply lost ourselves in each other again.

♫ ♫ ♫

The next morning, I snuck out of bed while Ava was sound asleep. For a moment, I stared down at her with her dark hair sprawled about her face. I itched to move it and run a finger along her smooth skin, but I didn't want to wake her. I pulled on sweats and a Coast Guard T-shirt and quietly made my way to the kitchen to make breakfast.

Mom came in as I was in the middle of tossing the first round of chocolate chip pancakes onto a plate and placing them in the oven to keep warm. Mom secretly adored these pancakes, even though most people said they were just for kids. She kissed me on the cheek, filled her coffee, and sat at the counter.

"Before Ava gets up," she started, and I turned to her, expecting something about Ava. Maybe my face showed the defensiveness I felt, because Mom smiled. "I like her, but that isn't want I was going to talk about."

"She's pretty impossible not to like."

Mom laughed. "It's cute that you're so defensive. I'd ask where it's all going, but I don't think either of you have a clue yet."

"No?" It was my turn to smirk, as my brain had been filled with lots of ideas about Ava, but we had a lot of uncertainty ahead of us before we could truly make plans.

"Okay, so what did you want to talk about?" I asked as I went back to the pancakes.

"I wanted to apologize."

This stopped me completely. "What?"

"I should have told you I was selling the house."

I looked at her, flabbergasted. It wasn't that she shouldn't have told me about the house. She should have. But she should have told me about the cancer more.

"Leena and I are two old ladies rattling around in two separate houses, paying separate bills, trying to take care of everything on our own. This was a wake-up call for both of us. I can sell, take some of the money, and help her redo parts of that old Victorian she's inherited."

It hurt that she needed someone, but she wasn't reaching out to me. She was going to Leena, her best friend, instead.

"Why didn't you just tell me that?" I asked.

"I'm never sure what I can."

"What do you mean?"

She looked out at the garden, clutching her coffee cup tightly, fingers white. "If something happened to you…because you were thinking about me instead of focusing on your job…I couldn't…."

I choked on the emotions that hit me as much as the quiver in my mom's voice as it faded away. I realized she wasn't just apologizing for the house. She was apologizing for not telling me about the cancer, too. But it was also the reason I continued to feel like a selfish bastard these days. My career was the reason for her apprehension, the reason she couldn't count on me.

"Mom—"

"No. Don't. I don't want you staying here to take care of me. I want what every mother wants for her child—for you to follow your heart and make your life everything you dream it can be."

My heart twisted, because the Coast Guard had been my dream. Now, there was also a good chance that it was going to be taken away from me. Stan's words about a life that he might be able to connect me with had me, for the first time in my entire twenty-six years, wondering if there was something outside of the Coast Guard for me. I wasn't sure it would fit me quite right. But it might allow me to have things that I hadn't known were important before.

Mom was waiting for my response, and I just told her what I was thinking, like I should have done our whole life together instead of telling her the thing that would cause her less pain. Because I wanted her to start doing the same with me. I needed us both to just say the truth, no matter how much it hurt.

"I don't want you to ever feel like you can't tell me things, Mom. You have to trust that I've grown up enough to handle it. If you don't tell me the truth, I'll just worry more about what you're hiding from me."

"It's hard, as a parent, to accept that your baby has grown up. That they don't need you anymore."

"I'll always need you. Always. You're my mom."

I pulled her from the stool to hug her. To make sure she knew with my actions as well as my words that I meant it. My life wouldn't be the same if she wasn't in it.

Ava came into the kitchen at that moment, her hair up in a bun, my T-shirt on over a pair of leggings. She looked like my future. I swore that the whole room got brighter just because she'd entered it. More sun filling our lives. Ava filling our lives.

My mom reached out an arm to invite her into our hug, and Ava hesitated at first and then smiled, joining us. I got to hug the two women that I knew I loved most in the world. A girl who'd turned into a woman since I'd first seen her, and a woman who'd done her best to give me everything she could, even though we were both missing a part of us—Dad.

It felt like home. Mom might be going to sell the house I'd been raised in, but it didn't really matter. Home was always going to be wherever these two women were.

Chapter Twenty-four

Ava

THE STARS
Performed by Lady A

On Saturday, Truck showed up at the house bright and early, bringing donuts with him. The guys shared a hug that I admired. In the last few weeks, their hugs had made me realize that my own awkwardness with hugs came from inexperience—a hugless childhood. Eli's hugs were slowly increasing my comfort with them. When he hugged me, it felt like pieces of me coming back together. And when Mandy had included me in their hug on Friday morning, it had felt like yet another thing I'd been missing and suddenly found.

On hearing Truck's voice, Mandy came bounding into the room.

"Travis!" she said, beaming a smile at him.

"Mama, you've been bad." Truck waved a finger at her.

Mandy just swatted at him before giving him his own hug.

"You boys are ridiculous," she said, muffled in his embrace. When she let him go, she reached for the donut box, but Truck took it away.

"Nope. No donuts for you."

"Travis!" The scold in her voice made me smile.

"Apologize."

"For?"

"For?! You have to ask what for? Definitely no donuts for you."

Eli was watching the exchange with his best friend and his mom with a smile. I was watching Eli with my own smile. This. This was something I'd never had. Jenna's family and I had a good relationship. But it was always two teenage girls squirreling themselves away in a bedroom, avoiding parent conversations. They loved me, and I loved them, but we didn't tease and harass each other like this. There was never the sense of camaraderie that filled this kitchen.

"You'd keep donuts from a dying woman?" Mandy asked with a smile. Eli's and Truck's faces fell, and Truck's hand holding the donut box slipped. Mandy grabbed the box and started laughing.

"Ha! Got you." She brought the box to the table where I was sitting. To me, she said, "You have to fight fire with fire when you live with boys."

"That wasn't funny in the slightest, Mom," Eli said, coming around and squeezing into the bench with me.

"Yeah, what he said," Truck agreed, sitting down on the chair beside Mandy. "I still think I need an apology."

Mandy sighed heavily. "You keep one little secret and they never let you live it down."

"Not little," Eli grunted.

"Fine. I promise I'll never keep anything important from either of you again," Mandy responded.

"Mom!" Eli said.

"What?" she asked, all innocence.

"You just tried to give yourself an out."

"I did?"

"Yes, the word important did not escape any of our attention."

Mandy bit into her donut, still smiling.

♩ ♩ ♩

We spent the majority of the day like we had on Thursday and Friday: at the bookstore. Truck and Eli argued over comics and superheroes. It wasn't a conversation that I knew much about, but I enjoyed their good-humored argument. Mandy came up beside me and handed me a huge encyclopedia-sized book with comics on the cover. She said, "You might need this. You're playing catch up."

None of us had seen or heard Jersey enter the building, even with the bell on the door, so I startled when she spoke in her whispery voice next to me.

"Let me know if you need any help," she said. "Comics and I have a long history."

Eli turned to us, a smile on his face as he continued to rib Truck. "I need some help here, ladies. Tell Truck the truth; the Hulk will never be the best superhero."

Truck turned to us also, and his gaze stopped on Jersey.

"Too bad Wonder Woman is such a fad these days, because she is pretty incredible. But I kind of admire Jessica Jones more. She deals with a lot of difficult issues while still being strong. She's complex." Jersey's voice was probably the surest I'd heard it in two days, but it was still quiet, barely lilting its way through the room.

Truck crossed his arms over his expansive chest and took her in. I heard Jersey swallow hard next to me, and when I looked at her face, it had the most color I'd seen on it.

"You just picked women because you're female," Truck said.

"You just picked a man because you're male," Jersey said back.

Eli and I exchanged a look because, really, Jersey had hardly spoken at all since we'd known her. Eli said she barely breathed in the bookstore, flitting around like a ghost, and I'd thought it an appropriate analogy once I'd met her.

"Not true. Natasha Romanov is one of my top five," Truck argued back.

Jersey let out an exasperated sigh that I wasn't sure Truck heard. "Of course, she is."

"What's that supposed to mean?"

Truck stepped closer, taking in Jersey's pale hair that was even lighter than his and her pale skin that looked almost translucent. He eyed her curves in the dress she was wearing, and I knew he saw what we all saw: a very pretty girl.

"She's just a typical male pick. Deadly to men, so it's like a turn on or something," Jersey said with scorn.

Eli let out a chuckle. "I guess she told you. Okay, Jersey, you still agree with me, right? The Hulk is definitely not the greatest *male* superhero."

She nodded. Then, as if realizing how much she'd just spoken aloud, her skin went from the very slightest pale pink to almost paper white again. She ducked her head and moved toward the back office to put her things down.

Truck's eyes watched her as she went. He brushed a hand over his face after she'd gone. "Tell me you all saw her, too. She isn't a ghost?"

Mandy smacked him on the arm. "Be nice."

"Me?" Truck seemed shocked. He was still staring at the doorway where Jersey had disappeared.

It was something that Eli and I noticed and drew attention to the rest of the day—Truck perking up whenever Jersey was in the room. We teased him, and he'd brush it off, but he couldn't keep his eyes from her pale figure. The playfulness of it all continued to lighten the mood that had seemed heavy this week before he'd appeared.

For dinner, we went to the Crab Shack because they always ate there when the boys came into town. Tradition. My heart snagged at that. I didn't have any traditions, not even with Jenna. We loved each other and spent as much time as we could together, but there was no ritual that had become ours. Maybe because we'd never had the threat of death hanging over our goodbyes as this family did.

After dinner, we dropped Mandy off at the house, and Eli and Truck shared another tradition with me. We hit up a bar that was full of Coasties and locals.

"Well, I'll be damned, if it ain't Eli Wyatt and Truck!" the bartender called out when they walked in.

Eli and Truck shook hands with the man, and we all sat down at the bar.

"Who's this lovely creature?" the bartender asked.

"Rusty, this is Ava," Eli responded.

When I extended my hand, he brought it to his lips. "You are too lovely to be hanging out with these rookies."

I laughed and pulled away. "I'm pretty sure Eli and Truck have their own fan club wherever they go."

"Damn right," Truck said.

The conversation turned to catching up on people they knew. Not quite gossip, but something close. I noticed that everyone avoided the question of Eli's leg. Like avoiding talking about He-Who-Must-Not-Be-Named. Like they were all protecting him, shielding him as best they could before reality hit, just like Truck had been doing since the accident had happened.

"What can I get you, Miss Ava?" Rusty asked.

"I'd like a Salty Toad," I told him with a smile, but I knew he wouldn't know what it was. This bar felt like Andy and Lacey's. It made me ache for them in a way I hadn't in a long time. It gave me the urge to be behind the counter again. I was hoping Rusty would let me make the drink, so I could recapture a few moments of the calm I always felt when I was with them.

He scratched at the scruff on his chin. "Is that like a Bullfrog?"

I shook my head with a smile. "Nope. I don't like anything made with an energy drink."

"Well then, I'm not sure I know what you mean."

"Can I show you?" I asked.

"Well…" He hesitated, and I understood the hesitation. Not many bartenders would allow some random off the street behind their bar.

"I promise," I said, crossing my fingers over my heart, "I know what I'm doing."

He still wasn't buying into it.

"How about if I swear on the Coast Guard motto that I won't mess anything up? Plus, you'll get a new drink to add to your menu."

More reluctance. I could feel Eli and Truck watching me, but this battle was between Rusty and me.

"One drink," he finally said cautiously.

I smiled and went around the bar. When I looked up at Eli's face, wonder was written there. It was like I'd just done something so amazing that it was worthy of a prize. My heart stammered in excitement.

I assessed the area, quickly finding the drink mixer, the shot glasses, and the ingredients that I needed. All except one. "Caramel sauce?"

"Well…hmm…I do think I have some for the sundaes in the back." He left to go into the kitchen.

"Tell me, Miss Ava," Truck said, picking up Rusty's nickname. "Where did you acquire this bar expertise?"

"I've been working summers with Andy and Lacey at the Salty Dog."

Truck frowned as if trying to figure out where that was, but Eli got it. "You've been to Rockport every summer?" he asked.

I nodded. "The house there was the only thing that Dad bought that I kept."

Rusty was back. I finished pouring the ingredients into the mixer, shook it, and then poured it out into the waiting shot glasses.

"We usually serve this in a pint glass, but this way, you can all get a taste." I handed them out to the men who were still watching me as if they'd never seen me before.

"Normally, I don't drink while serving, but you've got me damn curious," Rusty said.

"Cheers," I said, bringing my own shot glass forward, and they all clanked their glasses with mine before swallowing the liquid.

I watched their faces. It tasted like a Milky Way bar to me. It was too sweet for most beer drinkers, but it was perfect for someone who didn't want to taste the alcohol as it went down. None of them grimaced, which was always a good sign when you made a drink, in my opinion.

"That's mighty tasty," Rusty said. "Who taught you to make that?"

"I created it," I told him.

"Well, 'round here, I think we'll just call that the Miss Ava," he said with a grin.

I couldn't help the huge smile that came over my face. I made another one and poured it into a pint glass for me before bringing it around to the counter and the stool that I'd been sitting at between Eli and Truck.

"Have I told you recently, Eli, that this one is a keeper?" Truck teased.

Eli pulled me to him, kissing me. We both tasted like caramel and vanilla vodka. "I thought you couldn't surprise me any more, and yet, you still do."

I let the happiness of the moment fill me, not wanting to lose it, not wanting to think of our futures and the things that were waiting around the corner for both of us. I wished that I could keep this feeling forever. The sense of contentment. The sense of belonging. This was what I wanted—peace.

♫ ♫ ♫

Sunday, Truck left to go back to New York for his shift. I could tell that it killed Eli that he wasn't going back yet—might never. It showed in the quietness that came over him the rest of the day, the humor and lightness that Truck had brought with him disappearing.

Mandy and I pulled him into a Scrabble game, but we both could tell that his mind was elsewhere. I saw her watching him with a concern that he didn't register.

The next morning, Eli dropped Mandy and me off at the bookstore on his way to his physical therapy appointment. I'd brought my guitar and my notes, and I made my way outside to the little patio area behind the store.

There'd been new songs bouncing in my head all weekend, and I finally had a few minutes to myself to explore them. So, I lost myself in the sunshine and sang about family. About belonging and loss. About how emotions could be a storm, and how family could guide you through to the rainbow waiting on the other side.

"It's lovely." Mandy's voice dragged me from myself and my music. I grimaced.

At Juilliard, people were practicing their craft everywhere. You never thought twice about strumming out notes and a song wherever you were. I hadn't really thought about what it might look like there, me crazily singing on the patio.

"It's a work in progress," I told her.

She took a seat at the table beside me.

"Can I ask you something?" Mandy asked.

"Of course."

"Do you love him?"

I hadn't had this conversation with Eli, so it seemed strange to have it with his mom. My body and Eli's body… He was right when he'd told me it felt like they'd been together for a long time, like we'd done this dance over the centuries and had just been drawn back together one more time. But our bodies weren't our lives, and we both had so many unknowns scattering around us. Did it matter if we loved each other? Would it be enough?

"You're taking a long time to answer that," she said gently.

"It isn't because I don't love him." It was the closest thing to the truth that I could think to say.

"Then what?"

"I'm afraid…"

"That he'll hurt you?"

I shook my head. "That I'll hurt him."

Her turn to be silent.

"I didn't really have a great example of love in my childhood. I'm a little broken in this regard," I told her.

"Ava." She said my name so sweetly that—like when Eli said it—it felt like its own endearment. "We've all been broken into a million little pieces and had to put ourselves back together. Not just because we were hurt by the ones who were supposed to love us the most, or the ones who left, or the hopes and dreams that skittered away from us. We've been broken and chipped at, daily, by the small things. Frowns instead of smiles. Lifted eyebrows instead of nodding chins."

She took a breath, her own voice shaky. "But being broken doesn't mean you can't love and be loved. Sometimes, you just need someone who loves you enough to help you see the full brilliance left inside after all the breaks."

My heart squeezed tight at her words.

"Thing is…" Mandy paused, her tone full of worry. "I think Eli is pretty attached to you, and I'm not sure he could handle another loss these days."

The thought of losing him curled unpleasantly in my gut. I wanted, with every vein in my heart, to be the one to show him his own brilliance if his world did fully fall apart. But I was also afraid that she was wrong about the breaks. I was scared that mine would shatter me, or Eli, or both of us.

I did the only thing I could do at the moment, which was try to lessen her worry by squeezing her hand and saying the thing I wanted to be true. "I'm not going anywhere anytime soon."

Her turn to nod.

It was all I could offer this brave woman who'd experienced her own set of losses and yet continued to fight every day. I wanted to be that brave. I wanted to look back someday and say that I hadn't walked away when I had the chance to stay.

"I'm sorry you lost your husband. I'm sorry you have cancer," I told her.

"Had cancer. I've beat that piece of crap in the ass."

"Mom!" Eli's startled voice came from the doorway.

I wondered how much he'd heard of our conversation.

Mandy laughed, and it reminded me of Eli's, just like the warmth in her voice always did when there was really no pitch or tone that was the same. It was in the quality of it. The fullness of it.

"Just because I tell you not to cuss doesn't mean it isn't appropriate at moments."

"You told me there were no appropriate moments," he said as he came up to the table, looking down at both of us.

"That's because you and your friends seem to think that cuss words are the only adjectives in the English language." He shook his head at her, but she just smiled at him and said, "I'm hungry. Who's up for enchiladas?"

"You're hungry?" Eli asked.

"Yep. You too tired after therapy to take us to Tito's?"

He did look tired, but I knew that Eli would never deny his mom anything, like he would never deny me anything. I hoped I could be strong enough to do the same thing—give him whatever he needed and maybe even the things he didn't realize he did.

♫ ♫ ♫

That night, as we lay in bed with me pulled up tight against his body, I said what was in my heart. "Eli?"

"Hm?"

"Your life. It's amazing."

"What?"

"This. Your mom and Leena and Truck. It's amazing."

His hand slowly ran up my arm, a finger landing on that tender spot behind my ear. Chills filled my skin. Chills that spoke of the things our bodies did when they were together.

He nodded, as if the emotions I'd evoked in him by my words were too much.

"I just think you should know," I continued, "that regardless of what happens with your knee and your career, this…everything you have here…it isn't going away."

I wanted to start to show him those rays of brilliance in him that his mom and I had talked about. I wanted him to see the beauty of the life he had.

"Thank you," he said quietly.

"Me? For what?"

"Reminding me of the best things in my life, and how they aren't tied to the job I have."

My heart soared just a little, and I hoped that Mandy was right. That somehow, we would help each other see all the light instead of all the breaks.

Chapter Twenty-Five

Eli

IN CASE YOU DIDN'T KNOW
Performed by Brett Young

Ava and I spent the week helping Mom pack up the house, going through pictures, some that she boxed and some she said I could take with me. Going through the volume of books that she would either resell, give away, or keep.

Mom and I had seemed to reach some kind of truce. I wasn't angry with her anymore. She seemed to have relaxed into letting me help when she'd never easily accepted it before. It was like Truck and I both showing up and confronting her about the choice she'd made to go it alone had made her realize that she didn't need to. At least, that's what I wanted to believe. I wanted to believe that, going forward, we wouldn't keep the darker stuff from each other.

Ava seemed to enjoy helping us pack because she caught glimpses of my past. Mom was constantly telling her stories about me that were supposed to be embarrassing but weren't. I loved Mom sharing my childhood with Ava, especially knowing that her life had been mom-less—really, parent-less.

"Wait. Eli played football?" Ava asked, holding out a photo album that she was perusing. I was about twelve, and I had on a football uniform with a football tucked under my arm. I chuckled.

"God, no. Why?" Mom came around the counter to look over Ava's shoulder, and she started laughing and turned to me. "Was that your Halloween costume?"

I grimaced. "Mom told me I couldn't go as a Coastie for another year. She refused to buy me a new costume unless I chose something else. And I'd grown, what, two inches that year? Maybe more."

"That boy was drinking a gallon of milk a day and shoveling in food. I almost let him join the academy just so they'd feed him," Mom said.

"How many years did you go as a Coast Guard?" Ava asked.

I flushed a little. I couldn't help it. "All of them."

Ava laughed and then nudged my mom. "Good for you, forcing him to be something else for a change."

The pain hit me, as it often did, when I realized that everything I'd ever wanted and had accomplished was probably going to be ripped away from me. What would I be now that I was being forced to change? I couldn't answer that yet—didn't want to answer it yet. But I was leaving Stan's offer stewing at the back of my brain until I absolutely had to use it.

Mom asked Ava, "What was your favorite Halloween costume?"

Ava's smile dipped a little. "Dad didn't believe in Halloween. Told me it was a ridiculous holiday started by misguided, uneducated people who created the idea of warding off ghosts and goblins as a way of explaining life. He refused to participate in it."

"Wait. You never trick-or-treated?" I asked, my career pain dissipating with thoughts of Ava's dysfunctional childhood.

"Nope. I really think he said that just because he knew I wanted to trick-or-treat more than anything. When I was in high school and they had a Halloween dance, Dad refused to let me attend. Jenna's mom tried to intervene on my behalf, but he just got pissed that I'd told her. Grounded me with no phone or internet for a week."

My anger at her asshole father continued to flare. What man would deny his child anything as simple as Halloween? As dressing up and trick-or-treating like a normal American kid? I guessed it was the same kind of man that had denied her love.

"This year, we are dressing up," I told her with force.

She grinned at me. "I think at twenty-six and twenty-three it might look a little odd to be trick-or-treating door-to-door."

"We don't have to trick-or-treat. We can either pass out our own candy or throw a huge party," I told her.

Ava just rolled her eyes at me, but I was determined to make it happen. One more reason that I was sticking around in her future. Someone needed to give her all the things she'd deserved and had never been given.

♫ ♫ ♫

On Ava's last night in New London, I took her out on a date. A real date. She complained when I told her my plan, because she'd only brought jeans and leggings to wear. I told her that I didn't care what she wore and that even the fanciest restaurant in New London wouldn't care either. But she seemed to care a lot.

"I'll take you downtown. There's this little boutique that has some really lovely things," Mom told her, coming into our half-hearted argument with her own commentary.

"I highly doubt that Ava's going to want to wear the crazy cat lady apparel," I teased her, because most of my mom's clothing had books or cats or both.

She slapped me on the back of the head. "Don't make fun of my clothing, and this isn't where Leena or I shop. It's one of the trendy, touristy places."

"So now you're going to have her wearing an 'I heart New London' T-shirt?" I asked. I was dragging my feet because it was Ava's and my last day together for what would probably be a month, and I didn't want her to be away from me for any length of time. Selfish but true. It was why I was taking her on a date—so it would just be the two of us.

"Doodles, you can live without her for an hour or two. Let her do this her way," Mom scolded, and Ava smirked. She'd been smirking every time Mom called me Doodles. It didn't happen often, but it had happened enough over the course of the week for Ava to have appreciated it.

They left me…to go shopping. I just groaned and spent the afternoon working in the garden until they came back. When they did, Ava rushed past me to get ready in Mom's room, and I went to shower. When I came out, Mom was on the couch with a book—her and Snicker's favorite spot.

"You look handsome," Mom said, glancing up at me.

I was just in jeans and a button-down, with a pair of Timberlands on my feet. It wasn't a suit and tie. It wasn't my Coast Guard evening wear, but it was date worthy.

"I need to get my hair cut," I told her, brushing my hand through the strands that I was still unaccustomed to having.

"I like it," my mom said. "It's a new you."

We both let that settle between us, the weight of it pressing on me as we both understood that a new me wasn't my choice. That it was being forced on me because of my dumbass mistake.

Mom's eyes strayed to movement behind me. Ava. I turned, and my heart stopped. She looked…alive. Full of color, and vibrancy, and almost that same energy that she'd had in Rockport. I'd slowly seen it coming back to life in her this week. With us. I'd even caught her sitting on top of the picnic table in the backyard one morning, coffee in her hand, notebook on her lap, hair in a messy bun. If I'd half-closed my eyes, I could have seen the Aransas Bay behind her.

Now, with a dress the color of the ocean foam, and sparkly heels that added to her height, she looked like the sea nymph I'd once thought her to be. Like she'd emerged from the tides just in time to call me in. The dress she'd bought was floaty and yet clung to her curves, and I fought the urge to pull the straps away and kiss her skin.

She had makeup on when she'd not worn any all week, and it didn't make her look any more beautiful, but it made her beautiful in a different way. She was always sexy, but this was a new sexy.

"You're stunning," I told her.

She smoothed her hand over the dress. "It was a lovely find. Your mom has a good eye."

I stepped over, lifted her hand to my lips, and kissed it. "It's not the dress, Ava. You. You're stunning."

She smiled up at me, happy. I liked that I made her happy.

"Well, have fun, you two. I'm going back to this novel about a Gothic heroine who is never going to find true love," Mom said behind us.

I didn't look at her. I just took Ava's hand, placed it on my arm, guided her out to the truck, and drove to the restaurant. It wasn't as nice of a restaurant as we could have gone to if we were in New York, but it was a nice place for New London. It had white linens, flickering candles, and bright flowers on the tables with a view of the ocean and the sun setting over it. It was enough to be a real date.

We ordered cocktails and appetizers and then sat, taking in each other and the view for a moment.

"Thank you for bringing me here," Ava said.

"I wish we'd done a real date sooner," I told her, regret in my voice.

"Life had different ideas," she responded. It was true, and life was still messing with the ideas that I had for us.

"I love that I'm going to be able to help my mom, but I hate that I'm going to be away from you," I told her honestly.

"When I get back, I'm going to be swamped. There's still so much to be done on the album and in my classes. It's probably good that you won't be in the city."

"Are you saying that I'd distract you?" I grinned.

"You know you would." She returned my smile and then turned to watch the ocean.

"Have you given more thought to singing with Brady?" I asked.

"Not really," she answered, but I knew that, just like the medical review board was hanging over me, this was hanging over her.

"What will you do if you turn it down?" It seemed crazy that I didn't already know her answer to that question. I'd been thinking of our future, us together, but hadn't really stopped to consider what that looked like. What would she be doing if I was out to sea? What would she be doing if I was having to chase after something new?

"I'd planned on going back to Rockport and writing songs until someone bought them. I'd probably continue to work with Andy and Lacey at the bar until they kicked me out."

I was quiet, and she noticed. "Spit it out, oh Captain, my Captain."

"It's just…there's no one there for you," I said.

"Andy and Lacey are there."

"But no family."

"Eli, I don't really have family anywhere. Not like you have here."

That about broke me. "You have Jenna," I said gruffly.

"I do have Jenna. But she's getting married, and she's focused on running her business with Colby. She has a life that isn't mine. A life in Galveston that I don't want."

We were interrupted with our food, and we ate in silence for a few moments. Not an uncomfortable silence, but one heavy with things we were both still trying to figure out. I finally pushed my plate away and said the one thing that I really wanted.

"You could stay with me."

I knew, even as I said it, that it wouldn't work, thinking of Ava having to squeeze into the tiny apartment that Truck and I shared that looked temporary because we hadn't done anything but shove furniture in it. Because it had been temporary to us. We'd known we'd be moving on to new assignments eventually.

Ava smiled weakly, her brain probably going to all the places that mine had. "No, I don't think living with you and Truck is the answer."

I couldn't really argue it. "Is it the thought of Truck and me, or just moving in with me in general?"

Her eyes searched mine, but we were interrupted with the waiter coming back again. He asked about dessert, and we both declined. I paid the bill, slipping my hand into hers as we left the restaurant so that I could pull her down the path to the pier. At the end, we stopped, watching the sky turn to black as the stars came out above us. She shivered, and I wrapped my arms around her.

"It isn't the thought of moving in with you," she finally answered me.

"Then what?"

"Remember when you asked me to stay…"

She was talking about our time in Rockport, when I'd stopped her car and asked her to stay. I nodded, burying my face in her neck both to keep her warm and to remind her of us. Of what our bodies knew.

"It wouldn't have worked, right?" she said breathlessly. "I mean, I'd have hated being in Galveston. I'd have been worried that I'd see my dad around every corner. I may not have applied again to Juilliard…"

I knew what she was getting at. I'd known the same thing that day in Rockport. It would have been impossible for her to stay, just as it would have been impossible for me to follow. If we had, it would have been filled with regrets.

"It's different now," I told her. We'd found each other again. I saw her as part of the future I was making. There wasn't going to be regret in that.

"It is different, and yet it's not, right? I mean, we still are two people trying to figure out our place in this world."

She was right. For all I knew, I'd be jobless and homeless in a few weeks. I might be coming home to live in New London with Mom and Leena in the Victorian they were going to restore.

"Rick Springfield said, 'If the timing's right and the gods are with you, something special happens.' We still haven't figured out our timing yet," she said.

"Timing or not, what we have is already special," I told her, because I believed it to be true, and I hoped that she did too.

She turned to face me, lacing her arms behind my neck. "You're right. We are."

"You figure out what you're doing, I'll figure out what I'm doing, and then we can figure out how to do that together." I kissed her, and she returned the kiss with what felt like longing and hope rolled into one.

She pulled her lips away and breathed out. "Okay."

"Okay, what?"

"Okay, we'll wait to figure it out."

That was going to have to be good enough for the moment. It was going to have to satisfy us both until we had answers to questions that weren't completely in our control. Neither of us was good at that—not having control, not having a plan.

But her words prodded at the possibilities that had been rolling around in my head. It made me think that, if I was willing to change, reimagine myself into something different, it just might bring our lives a little closer. That the doors that I felt closing on me might really lead to better doors ahead.

Chapter Twenty-Six

Ava

THIS KISS

Performed by Faith Hill

Leaving Eli at the train station and boarding the train back to New York was like being slapped with reality after you'd been in a dream. For a while, it had just been Eli and me and his family. And now, I was having to go back to the reality of my world that existed before Eli.

Eli and I had so many unknowns ahead of us. We both had huge chapters ending with blank slates on the next page. We'd said we weren't giving up on us, but it also seemed fragile, like the big decisions waiting could still pull us apart.

Leena and Mandy had hugged me goodbye at the bookstore, teary-eyed and emotional, as if they'd known me my whole life. It felt like family should. The hugs and the tears. Family should be sad that you were leaving, even if they were happy you were going off to chase the things that were important to you.

It made me miss my mom. A mom. Having a mom. Having a childhood filled with hugs.

When I got back to the city, Brady was already there. We spent a few hours sharing stories of our breaks. He'd spent the week in his hometown with ladies and music as the focus. I'd had Eli and his family as the focus.

"It looks good on you," Brady said, shoving my foot with his on the coffee table.

"What?"

"Love."

I flushed.

"Don't deny it," he teased.

"I can't," I told him, feeling strangely guilty that Eli and I still hadn't said the words to each other, and yet, I felt comfortable sharing them with others—his mom, Brady.

Maybe Eli and I just didn't need to say it. Maybe we just knew. Just like our bodies knew something more than our brains about how our worlds were tied together. Maybe we needed to trust the world to figure out the timing for us.

♫ ♫ ♫

The weeks of April slowly bled away. Eli and I talked to each other at least twice a day: first thing in the morning and last thing at night. Plus, we usually had a few conversations by text. On the rare occasion, I'd get to hear his voice in the middle of the day, but not often. We were both busy.

He was helping his mom get her stuff settled into Leena's house, and they were hiring contractors to do some remodels on it. He was helping at the bookstore and taking his mom to her doctor's appointments as the last phases of her treatment started to wind up. Cancer in remission. Another battle they'd fought and won together.

Family.

The word haunted me a lot these days. It found its way into my songs and my heart, like my subconscious was trying to noodle something out that my brain hadn't caught up to yet.

Jenna and I had a whole conversation about it.

"The last song you sent me made me sad," Jenna said.

"Why?" I asked.

"I realized that you don't think of my family as yours."

"I love your family." I told her the truth, because I did.

"They're your family, too," she said forcefully. "My parents would have taken you in if they'd been able to find a way to prove Ethan was abusive."

"He never abused me."

"Yes, he did," Jenna said fiercely. "Emotional abuse is still abuse, Chick-a-dee."

My mind kind of reeled at her words—the fact that she considered my father abusive. I'd known he was controlling and that he made me feel like I was nothing and would always be nothing, but I'd never really put a tag on it. I'd always considered him an asshole, for sure, but not abusive.

The fact that Jenna's family had seen it and wanted to take me in astonished me. I'd rarely talked with them about the things Dad did. Maybe Jenna had. Regardless, I'd never really thought of them as more than my best friend's parents—people I liked and who were nice to me. But I'd never considered them mine, a support network that was waiting for me.

It made me wonder if, like I'd told Eli's mom, I was truly broken when it came to love and relationships. I wondered if my breaks would just continue to crack, and if they would shatter the fragile thing that Eli and I had built.

♫ ♫ ♫

On May first, Eli called, waking me from sleep before the sun hadn't even started to lighten the sky. I panicked. "Eli?"

"Hey." His voice was gruff, tired. "I'm sorry to call so early. I'm on my way to the city."

My heart leaped. I was going to get to see him. Yet, he didn't sound so excited about coming back. He sounded…terrified.

"The review board?"

"Yes. It's at fifteen hundred hours."

I did the math in my head.

"I'll be in class," I told him.

"I know."

"Shall I come to your place after?" I asked.

"I'll come to you. I don't know how long it will take."

"Okay," I told him, but I wanted to reassure him. Wanted to tell him it was going to be fine. That they weren't going to discharge him. It wouldn't have been the truth, though, and I wouldn't lie. I was as terrified as he was.

"'Not everyone gets a true ending,'" I started.

He chuckled. "Are you giving me another quote?"

"Shh. Listen. 'Not everyone gets a true ending. There are two types of endings because most people give up at the part of the story where things are the worst…Only those who persevere can find their true ending.' You've worked really hard for your true ending," I said.

"Was that Ghandi?"

My turn to laugh. "No, Stephanie Garber in a fantasy novel."

He was quiet. I could hear his doubts, even though he wasn't speaking them. They were so often my own. What if my true ending would never come to be no matter how hard I work toward it? Or, in my case, what if I was giving up before I'd reached my true ending? I hated that he was full of those same doubts. Hated that, in a few hours, he might lose everything he'd worked for.

I just wanted to give him something that he could take with him. Something positive. Something to show the light through the cracks. The brilliance of him.

"Eli," I paused.

"Hmm?"

"I love you," I said. I hadn't told him before. I'd saved it, because I'd wanted to say it for the first time when I was face to face with him. I wanted to say it when I could see his eyes flash and his gorgeous smile. But at that moment, I knew he needed this. He needed love to go into the room with him.

"You can't say that to me while I'm driving," he said, but there was joy in his voice. Happiness filled me, knowing that I'd been able to give him that—joy at a time of fear.

"Don't crash; you'd have to start recovery all over again."

"Shit, that would really suck."

"Are you going to be full of cuss words now that your mom isn't hanging over your shoulder?"

"Maybe," he teased and then was quiet. "Ava."

"Yes?"

"Thank you. And…I love you, too. You know that, right?"

My heart filled so much that I thought it would break apart inside my chest. More cracks that could be shattered. More pieces of us that we were embedding into each other with no hope of getting them back. Still, I was glad. Glad that we loved each other. Glad that we'd said it. I nodded my response but then realized he couldn't see it.

"I do," I finally breathed out.

Silence again, him driving, my heart still pounding from the huge step we'd taken over a phone call. So not the way it should have been done, and yet perfect for what we'd needed from each other at the moment. For what Eli had needed at the moment.

"I can't wait to see you," I told him.

"It's going to be the best thing about this day," he said.

"If you get your commission back, that will be the best thing," I told him honestly.

"No. You're wrong. That will be great, exciting, an over-the-top relief. But seeing you… Seeing you after a month of not seeing you… I don't have enough words for that."

Eli's own brand of beautiful words filled my heart. I'd used many of them in my songs and told him that. He'd laughed at me, but when I said that I was putting his name down as one of the songwriters, he'd growled and said he'd deny it. I was still doing it, anyway. They were his words and my words mixed together. Strong and soft. Happy and sad. Joy and sorrow. Guard and lyricist.

"Good luck," I told him.

"Say it again," he said.

"Good luck?"

He chuckled into the phone, the sound making my toes curl in pleasure. "Not that."

I had to think for a nanosecond of time before I realized what he wanted. "I love you."

"Again."

The command that I couldn't disobey. "I love you."

"One more time," he asked.

I laughed. "I love you, oh Captain, my Captain."

He groaned. "Really making it hard to drive."

"I just obeyed my captain's command."

"Shit."

I laughed. "Please don't crash."

"I need to hang up, but I don't want to."

"Go. I'll see you after."

"Okay."

"Hey, Doodles," I said, and he snorted at the nickname coming from my lips. "I love you."

"Hey, Ava," he said. "I love you more."

Then he was gone.

They weren't original words. They weren't unique. People had said them a gazillion times a day for centuries upon centuries. I love you and I love you more. But they were new to us. They were original to this moment in time, and they could never be said for the first time again. I cherished them. I cherished the memory. It was mine.

No matter what happened. No matter whether everything worked out in our lives and we spent another seventy years saying them, or our lives drifted apart and we had to wait for another lifetime for us to come together again, the moment and the words were ours.

I realized something that made my heart patter and skip a beat. Something that sounded like Jenna speaking in my head. I realized that, sometimes, the perfect love story was simply to have loved. To have taken the risk. To have shared that experience with another human being who loved you back. If it broke, if it shattered, if it came apart, it wouldn't matter. No one could take away a love story that was yours.

♫ ♫ ♫

That afternoon, as I left class, Eli texted me that he was on his way. I texted back, asking how it went, but he just said he'd tell me when he saw me. I didn't know if that was good or bad. It made me want to vomit.

He was leaving the truck at his apartment and taking a CarShare into the city. I was anxious. I wanted to know what happened. I wanted to see him. I wanted to wrap my arms around him in a hug that I was learning to love, kiss him, and say, "I love you," to his face for the first time.

My concentration was so shot that I went to leave the dorm room with two different shoes on before

Brady caught it, laughing at me. "I've never seen you this nervous. Ever."

I gave him a one-fingered wave but changed to a matching pair and then left. I wanted to meet him on the steps. I wanted to see his face and know what had happened.

The tension grew as I waited.

Then he was there, striding toward me with hardly a limp and no brace, a bag on his shoulder. He was almost the Eli that I'd known from before the accident. He was still in his uniform, as if he'd been too impatient to change. I realized it was the first time I'd ever seen him in his uniform.

It was heart-stopping. Stupid. More mundane words for our day, but he was just so "perfectly perfect in every way" that it was hard to come up with not mundane words. He wore the uniform like it was just part of him, part of who he was. And that made my heart ache in a different way, because I hoped they hadn't taken who he was away from him.

His face was the normal blank slate as he moved toward me, but as he got closer, I could see emotion swimming in it. Emotions he was trying to contain, and yet I still couldn't read them because they seemed so mixed.

"What did they—"

He cut me off with a kiss, dropping his bag, and wrapping his arms around my body in the dress I'd slipped on. The kiss… Faith Hill's words surrounded me. This kiss. Bliss. Centrifugal motion. Unstoppable. Fairytales and reality mixed. Filling me as he always filled me with his scent and his life and his Jedi force.

We stood there on the steps of the school, kissing. Joining. Rejoining. Finding each other again after a month of being apart. I realized what he was trying to tell me with his lips. It didn't matter. It didn't matter what they'd said. This. This was what mattered.

We heard a whistle and, "Get a room," that finally drew us apart, my hand to his cheek, his hand to my neck. He was smiling. That goofy smile.

"Again?" he asked.

My smile met his. "I love you," I told him.

He smiled, groaned, and kissed me again. Slowly. In that way he did that always felt like he was trying to deliver a sermon to my heart of adoration and love. He loved me.

I pulled away. "My turn," I told him. He grinned.

"I love you," he responded, that deep tone tingling over my skin.

I reached my lips back to his and kissed him one more time before stepping back. I pushed my fingers into his and pulled him down so that we sat on the steps in the warm May sunshine that had filled the city.

"Tell me what happened," I told him.

He sighed, and I watched his face. He didn't look devastated, which eased the pain in my heart, but he didn't look overjoyed either. It was hard to understand.

"Do you want the good or the bad?"

"The beginning. To the end."

"I'm being discharged."

My heart broke for him. I squeezed his hand.

"Eli—"

He kept going, ignoring my pain at his pain. "Stan, my commander, was waiting outside the room after. It isn't the norm for a commander to show up, but he knew my dad, and he's kind of looked out for me."

I listened, watching him as he spoke, trying to place all his emotions so that I would know how to help him.

"He'd already told me, back in April, that if everything didn't go as planned, he had some ideas for me. It was his way of forewarning me, I guess. And he came today because I think he knew that I'd need him more today than when I'd first broken my knee."

He shrugged and smiled weakly. I reached up and kissed him, my compassion and sorrow bleeding into his, tugging at the loss I knew he felt. It was the first and last time that I'd see him in his uniform, and that twisted my insides to shreds. For him.

It also made me realize that I didn't see the Coast Guard part of Eli as being the main part of him. I'd never seen it as the biggest piece of him. It was a job. A job he loved, but it was just that. It wasn't who he was, so they couldn't have taken any of that from him, after all.

"You said there was good?" I asked him.

"My minor at A&M had to do with emergency planning. Stan knows a guy, Phil, who runs a private consulting firm that assists local, state, and federal agencies with emergency readiness. Phil works closely with the Coast Guard, which is how he knows Stan. Stan arranged for me to have an interview with him. It's tomorrow."

"That's wonderful!" I said.

"It's in California."

I realized, then, why the good was still the bad. On top of giving up the thing he loved most, he was having to go away again. He was leaving behind his mom, and Leena, and Truck. He was leaving me. "You're going away."

He nodded.

"Wow."

"If he offers me the job, I'll have to stay in California, at least for a while. There'll be training, and I'll have a lot to learn. The good thing is that he has offices all over the country, pretty much anywhere a Coast Guard station is at."

"You'd still get to work closely with the people you love," I said softly.

"Yes."

I was sad and hopeful for him. He'd lost the thing he'd wanted most in life, and yet he was trying to reassemble it into something that wasn't a complete redo. Something that allowed him to stay close to the thing he'd loved first.

I put my head on his shoulder, and we just sat there, on the steps, in the sunshine, tangled together. I tried to figure out what all of this meant for our love story. For the story that I'd said didn't matter how it ended as long as we'd loved, but now I was doubting my own words. I wanted more. I wanted a true ending.

I didn't want the story to end with just I love yous.

Back in New London, we'd said we weren't giving up on us. That we each had to figure out what was next, and then we'd figure out how "the next" would also include "us." I still hoped that we could do that. I hoped that more distance between us, more time apart, and the breaks inside us both wouldn't destroy the fragile relationship we'd started to put together.

Chapter Twenty-seven

Eli

DIE A HAPPY MAN
Performed by Thomas Rhett

I sat on the steps of the school with Ava wrapped in my arms, and let her love and compassion hold me up while I grieved. My gut was twisted in pain. I'd known in my heart what was coming, but now, being slapped with it in reality, it was like I'd lost it all over again.

The word "discharged" was still ringing in my ears. It was all the more bitter because it was my own failure that had caused it. I wished that weren't true. I wished I'd thought for two more seconds before jumping in the goddamn water with the seal, but I hadn't. And now, no matter my physical strength, I would always have a knee that was barely screwed together. And that knee would have interfered with my ability to perform my duties in the future. The review board had simply spoken the truth.

And that truth was tearing at me. I was familiar with loss, but it didn't make it any easier each time I encountered it. The anguish that existed not only for that moment, but for all the future moments that would never come to be.

The feel of Ava tucked up next to me reminded me that I had a reason to move forward. For her. For us. I'd handle this defeat as I handled all my defeats: by making a plan. By not letting the rips dismember me. Once upon a time, those next steps had been toward the Coast Guard, and now they were steps away.

I hadn't told Ava the full story, the things that were spinning in my head about the interview, and Phil's company, us, and Texas. I wasn't sure I could make it all happen, so I didn't want to get her hopes up. Having my hopes up was hard enough, because I wasn't sure I could handle yet another blow.

First things first, I had to see if Phil would hire me. Stan had thought it was basically a done deal, but I couldn't count on that. If Phil did take me on, I'd have to prove that I was good at this new job before I could make my own demands. Once I had, then I might—just might—be able to work on that true ending Ava had talked about this morning.

The thought of this morning and her "I love you" brought me away from the abyss of my grief a little further. It brought me to the other plans I'd made while, waiting for the review board's decision.

"I want to take you out," I told her. "I want to spend tonight with you. I don't want it to be in your dorm or my apartment. Pack a bag?"

She looked up into my eyes, and I hated what I saw there. That she was afraid that my leaving would end in goodbye. After I'd just said I loved her. After she'd just said she loved me. After we'd promised back in New London, that we wouldn't give up on us. It reminded me that Ava hadn't had anyone but Jenna stick by her for the long haul. That I had to prove to her that I was going to be there, too.

I stood up, pulling her with me. I looked down and kissed her gently, reassuringly, trying to convince her with my body that she seemed to listen to more than my words. We weren't done. This door closing was just that—a door. The house hadn't collapsed in on us.

I needed to believe that myself.

We went up to her room, and while she packed a bag, Brady assessed me again. He seemed to do it every time we were in the same room together. I liked that she had another person looking after her. I wasn't sure Ava understood that yet—how many people she did have, even if she didn't have her parents.

"I've never seen you in your uniform," he said.

"I haven't been on duty with the leg." I didn't tell him that I'd never wear it again. It hurt too much to say it. I couldn't. Not yet.

He nodded. "She's been a nervous wreck today. I've never seen her like that."

I'd sensed it, too. I didn't respond. What was I going to say?

He stepped away from the counter he was leaning on to move closer so he could speak quieter. "If you hurt her, I have friends. Friends that are quite used to leaving people in dark alleys in need of more surgery than you went through."

I wanted to laugh, but I didn't. "I'm pulling together all the strings I can so that I can make her dreams come true. Are you?"

That seemed to catch him off guard that I was throwing it back at him. "I'm doing my best. For both of us. But she keeps telling me she doesn't want it."

I nodded. Brady and I both knew that she said her goals had changed along the way, that she'd grown out of that old skin, like I'd suddenly been forced out of mine. I just didn't want her to give it up unless she was absolutely sure that old skin didn't fit anymore, because I knew how badly it hurt. I was living it at that very moment.

"Then we're both on the same page." It was all I could respond back.

Ava came from her room, bag slung over her shoulder. I took the bag from her and threw it over my own. She seemed ready to protest, but Brady's proximity to me distracted her. She looked between us to see what had gone down, but neither of us was ready to share.

"I'll see you in the morning," she told Brady.

"Sounds good. Have fun," he said to her. To me, he just nodded. I returned the motion and then took Ava's hand and led her from the dorm room.

When we got downstairs, I had a car already waiting for us. After we got in, Ava turned to me. "Where are we going?"

"Patience."

She shoved my shoulder gently. When the car stopped outside The Carlyle hotel and the doorman opened the door for us, Ava frowned. I grabbed both our bags from the trunk, took her hand again, and led her inside.

It was an expensive splurge, not something I was used to doing. I couldn't normally afford five-star hotels in New York City. It wasn't something I could do often, and without a job at the moment, it was something I really shouldn't be doing at all. But I was doing it. For us. For this night together.

"Eli." Ava pulled on me as we neared the registration desk. I looked down into her beautiful face, her eyes that I adored full of worry. "Why are we here? This is…it's too much."

I kissed her forehead. "Tonight, it's not."

I led her to the desk; we registered, got a key, and took the elevator up. It was a small room, just a queen bed. It wasn't their most expensive, but it was still nicer than most places I'd stayed. It was a place where I could make love to her later and know that I'd given her the best I could for one night.

I put the bags down and pulled her close. A hug. Wrapping her in my arms. She slid her hands under my uniform jacket at the back, her warmth spreading through me.

"I'm going to go change really quick, but then we have somewhere else to be."

"Wait. What?" she asked, confusion causing her face to wrinkle.

I brushed at the wrinkles. "Did you think that I was going to hole you up in the room and make love to you all night?"

"Um."

I smiled. "Later. We have time for that later."

I unbuttoned my jacket, and a sudden heaviness filled my heart as I did it…removing it for the last time. I left it on the bed before grabbing some clothes out of my bag and heading into the bathroom. Normally, I would have just changed in front of her, but I needed a minute to get a hold of myself as I discarded my old life for a new one that was just a hazy cloud on the horizon.

In the bathroom mirror, I took in the image of myself. My heart was pounding, and my body was aching. What I noticed was that my hair didn't fit the uniform anymore. Too long. Too not military. I should have had it cut, but a haircut wouldn't have saved me. I swallowed hard, fighting the sting in my eyes as I took the rest of my uniform off. I folded the pieces, placing them on the counter, the folds like the flag they'd gathered and given to my mom at my dad's funeral. So final.

The permanence of it all hit me. I stood in my underwear, hands on the counter, fighting for control. Fighting off the waves of emotions coursing through me, the waves threatening to pour from my eyes. I splashed water on my face to combat the storm.

I must have taken too long, because Ava knocked at the door. Maybe she could feel the heartache I was trying to shield her from through the walls. "Eli?"

"Yes." My response was garbled. Choked. She heard it. I knew she did.

"Can I come in?"

I hesitated but then reached over and pushed the handle down. She came in with my jacket in her hands. She was fingering my uniform ribbons, the ones I'd worked so hard to earn. She touched my bare arm and looked up at me, beautiful, with her hair swinging about her chin, the dress she wore showing off her curves and her bare arms.

She was my light. A light in my storm. She was still guiding me through, and I was battling to get to her, my sea nymph calling me home. My own personal aurora borealis.

Her eyes drew me just as they had the first time we'd met. This time, her eyes were full of tears. Her husky voice was full of sorrow when she spoke. "I'm so sorry that you lost this dream of yours."

I couldn't stop my own tears, but I closed my eyes, trying to battle against them. They slid from the corners, anyway, pain radiating from me. My pain for me and for the pain I was causing her.

"You don't want your mom hiding the bad from you, so don't hide the bad from me," she said quietly. I opened my eyes and watched as she set my jacket on top of the folded pile. Then she forced her way between me and the sink, wrapping her arms around me.

She looked up into my face, brushing at my tears, bringing the wetness to her lips. "The pain is mine to bear with you. Together."

I pulled her tight, burying my face in her hair and her neck, letting her hold me up while I said goodbye to the thing I'd loved for as long as I could remember. Let the tears roll over both of us.

Slowly, I fought and won control of the emotions. I reminded myself that I had something new I was working toward. It was bigger than the dream I'd ever had of the Coast Guard. It was a life that would let me keep Ava at my side—if she'd have me.

I pushed away the tears, kissed her lips gently, and said, "I love you."

She smiled at me. The smile was weak and unsure, not because she was unsure of our love, but because she was unsure of my mood. I matched her smile with my own. It was forced. She knew it was forced, but it was the only way that I could get through. I returned my focus to her and the plans I was making, not only for our future, but for our day.

"Let me get dressed before I decide that all my other arrangements for today can go to hell and I undress you instead," I told her.

She moved out of my arms, taking my jacket and my folded clothes with her as she left. I slipped into my jeans and my T-shirt—into my civilian clothes. The only thing that I would be now. A normal citizen. When I came out, she was shutting the door on the closet where she'd placed my uniform in my duffle.

Door closed. I couldn't go back. It hurt like nothing had hurt since I'd lost my dad. It hurt like I wasn't going to be able to breathe, but I'd make it through. With Ava and my family. With Mac and Truck. They'd all help me through. I was lucky. I had them all to hold me up when I couldn't hold myself.

I grabbed Ava's hand and led her out the door.

When we stepped outside the hotel, the typical noise of New York City greeted us, slightly quieter near the hotel where residences intermixed with the commercial. I'd already memorized the path from the hotel to our next stop while I was on my way to Juilliard. She seemed happy to walk with me, our hands and arms tangled together in such a way that it seemed that we took one step together for every step we took apart, slowly melding our lives like our bodies wanted, like I was hoping our futures would be.

We crossed the street in front of The Met, heading toward the huge steps, and she looked up at me with curious eyes. "I didn't really take you for a museum guy."

I wasn't. I couldn't remember the last time I'd been in a museum, but after we'd hung up this morning while I was driving, my brain had gone to Ava's penchant for quotes. For her ability to pull the right ones out of her head at all the right moments. That had made me think of an essay I'd done in my art history class back at A&M. It had been on maritime art, and the words that had been the driving force behind one particular painting were swimming in my head. It had me Googling the painting once I'd gotten to the station and had been sitting in the chairs waiting for my hearing. I'd been stunned to find the painting on loan to The Met. That had me making the plans for our day even before I'd seen Stan or heard the medical review board's decision.

At the entrance, I paid the fee for us to get in. Once we'd gotten our wristbands and had gone through security, I tugged her in the direction of the American Expeditions exhibit that was on display through June. We wandered into and around the exhibit, stopping here and there as something caught her attention or mine, until I spotted the painting on a back wall. We moved closer, and in the final steps, I turned so that I could block her vision of it, wrapping her in my arms and looking down into her eyes that reflected so many different versions of the water that I loved.

"Are you ready?" I asked her. Semper paratus…my heart heaved. I could still live by the motto even though I was no longer part of the unit. Being ready wasn't just for the Coast Guard.

She seemed to sense my reaction to my own words, because she teased, "Is this a test?"

I smiled and turned her so that her back was up against my chest, and so she could see the Frederic

Edwin Church painting that I'd written my essay on years ago. It was as if that prior version of myself had inherently known that I would need it at some point in my life. It had meant something to me back then. Now, it meant more. The title on the plaque below it swam before my eyes for a moment: *Aurora Borealis*.

I felt rather than heard her intake of breath as we both stared at the painting. The sky full of streaks of color over an ocean where a lone ship sailed into safe harbor.

I leaned so I could whisper into her ear the words that I'd memorized today so that I could give her one quote for the hundreds she'd given to others. "Church painted this after his friend, Hayes, had described the northern lights for him. Hayes said, 'The light grew by degrees more and more intense. From irregular bursts it settled into an almost steady sheet of brightness... at first tame and quiet, it became, in the end, startling in its brilliancy.' That's you. No longer tame and quiet, you are the brilliance filling my world. I'm the ship. You're the skies. And the only place I'll ever have safe harbor is with you spreading your light on me. This painting…it's us."

I felt her body convulse, a silent cry going through her. I squeezed tighter, turning her toward me again so I could see her face and the tears that spilled out from her closed lids and down her cheeks.

"Why are you crying?" I asked, wiping inadequately at the trails as my tears threatened to join hers.

"You. You're beautiful," she said.

"So beautiful that I make you cry?" I tried to tease, tried to lighten both of our moods.

She rested her forehead on my chest while she fought for control just like I had back at the hotel. I rubbed her back. "I'm afraid that we won't be able to figure it out—our lives and how they can fit together," she finally said quietly.

"I don't give up that easily on the things that I want. I don't think you do either."

I'd been forced to give up the Coast Guard. I wasn't going to be forced to give her up, too. I'd be damned before I let that happen.

"But…things change. People change. Look at both of us. Four years and we're completely different," she said quietly.

I nodded. We were different. I wasn't convinced that it was completely different. If it was completely, then I didn't think our bodies and minds would have still called to each other the same way they had when we'd met in a house on a sandy shore. I didn't have the words to convince her, though. I would just have to show her. It was going to take time. I'd just have to hope that she stuck with me for the duration.

We spent a few more minutes strolling through the museum, but I didn't have an interest in any more of it. She seemed to sense that, and she finally stopped me, dragging her feet to a halt.

"Eli," she said. I looked down at her in response. "Take me back to the hotel."

What could I say to that? Our bodies demanded their own relief, their own satisfaction, after weeks apart. I took her back like she requested. I removed her dress while she removed my T-shirt, and we were finally able to touch skin to skin once more. I was able to find that safe harbor in the woman I loved.

♫ ♫ ♫

The sun hadn't risen when I dropped her off at Juilliard. I had to pack and head to the airport for my flight across the country. I handed her a small package that I'd tucked into my duffle. It was wrapped in paper covered in cats because that was all my mom had had.

"What's this?" she asked.

"Your graduation gift—in case I can't make it back," I told her. She started to pull the ribbon, but I stopped her. "No. Keep it. Until graduation. That way, if I'm here, we can do it together, and if I'm not, it will be like I'm here, anyway."

Both our throats worked on the tears we were both trying not to shed. It was going to be a long time before my emotions weren't raw and unsettled.

I pulled the gift from her hands. "Maybe I should give it to Brady. Can I trust you to not open it?" I teased.

Her lips curled up, but the dent didn't appear on the side. "I'm completely trustworthy."

"With gifts? I don't know this about you. I kind of think you'll have a hard time keeping your hands off of it."

"You can demand daily pictures of it, if you like."

"You can always open it and then rewrap it. How will I know that you haven't?"

She dug in her purse, coming up with a Sharpie. "Hand it over, Doodles."

My heart clenched at the name, but I did her bidding. She drew a curved line with squiggles and hearts and shapes all over the sides. "There. It'll be almost impossible for me to match those back up if I do unwrap it. Satisfied?"

I kissed her as I pushed the present back into her hand.

"I love you," she whispered as she pulled away, trying to leave. I wasn't ready. I grabbed her hand to stop her.

"Again."

She smiled. "I love you."

I pulled her close, kissing her lips as if I was trying to memorize them, as if I could keep them with me. "I love you more."

I let her go, and she left. She stopped at the door and looked back at me as if she was trying to memorize me too, and then she went in. I moved, going toward the waiting CarShare and a journey that I was taking for both of us.

Chapter Twenty-eight

Ava

GIRL

Performed by Maren Morris

Eli got the job in California as we'd both suspected he would. Stan's recommendation and Eli's background making him a perfect fit for a company that worked on a daily basis with the Coast Guard.

The new job was a blessing, but it was also hard on Eli, being so close to, but not one of, the unit. Shifting into the civilian role that he'd never wanted. He called me a lot, trying to stay positive, but I heard the ache in him. He didn't hide it from me, because I'd asked him not to. He left it out there, but he also didn't dwell on it. It wasn't his way. He dealt with loss by moving forward, and I loved that about him, even if it meant he was now a continent away from me.

He liked to tease me about how much better his pay was now. That he'd be able to splurge on nights at The Carlyle more often. I let him tease, because it was a way for him to accept his new life—his new role—even if I didn't care an iota about the money. I only cared if he was happy.

In an attempt to help his mood, I took the gift he'd given to me everywhere, goading him about opening it, but also so that he could see that it was still with me where I wished he was. May slowly crept away with me sending him pictures of the present and me at the coffee shop, in the studio, and in class. I even sent one of the present and me on the rooftop where all of us went to celebrate having survived jury exams.

The week of graduation, I packed almost all my things and shipped them to Rockport. It was a strange feeling, sending things away from a life that I'd had for three years, sending them toward a life that was hazy and unclear. The few things I had left in the dorms, I'd take with me on the plane back to Texas with Jenna and Colby.

The day before we graduated, Brady and I sent the album to Nick Jackson. While we waited to hear back, I told Brady the decision I'd made. I didn't want to do the recording with him. I didn't want to be a part of the deal.

"Why?" he asked, although he didn't sound surprised.

"For all the reasons I told you. And more. It isn't my dream anymore."

I didn't tell him what my new dream was. I hadn't told anyone. It was something that had wiggled into my head, finally, through the songs I'd written. This dream had everything to do with family.

"What are you going to do?" he asked.

"Go back to Rockport. Probably work at the bar. Definitely write more songs for some guy I know who's going to take the world by storm."

"You could take the world by storm with me. Think of all the places we'd be able to travel to together. All the stadiums we'd perform in with everyone singing your songs, throwing bras at you." He was teasing and yet also serious.

"I hope I wouldn't get bras thrown at me."

"Babe, you'd totally have bras thrown at you."

I pushed his shoulder.

"I just think that I never understood, when I was dreaming of being a country star, what it would really mean. What it would really look like," I told him honestly. "I don't want that, Brady. I love singing onstage. I love interacting with a crowd. I just don't love it enough to give up every other thing in my life that means something to me."

"Eli."

"Not just Eli. But, yes, him too."

"Your dreams have changed…" His voice faded away as he nodded his understanding.

"I just wish I'd known it earlier."

"I'm glad you didn't. Then you wouldn't have come to Juilliard, I wouldn't have met you, and I wouldn't have platinum-charting songs at my disposal."

"Think of the money I could have saved on tuition," I joked.

"Psh. Money-schmuny. You're going to be raking it in with me singing your songs."

"Your ego knows no limits," I said, and it made me think about Andy from the Salty Dog and what he'd said, so many years ago, to me about somebody putting me in my place.

The truth was, I'd needed to put myself in my place. I'd needed to understand what I really valued in my life. It definitely wasn't giving away all my days to some schedule that someone made for me. Giving away my freedom. I'd done that for too long under my dad's command. I needed to be able to sail my own ship.

It wasn't even two hours later that Nick called us. He wanted Brady. He wanted the album. He wanted the songs. He had some ideas of things to change and was working on a duet partner for the couple songs that really needed it. Brady needed to sign papers. I needed to sign papers.

Brady and I danced around like fools, screaming and dancing on the sofa. It was happening. My songs were going to be out in the world. They were going to be touching people's lives. That made my heart surge with happiness. For Brady and for me.

It was a huge moment in my life, and I wanted to share it with the people I loved. Eli came first to my mind. I knew he was in meetings for an upcoming emergency simulation, but I texted him. Jenna and Colby were on their way to NYC. They were on the plane, airplane mode on, but I texted them, too. I knew they would all be happy for me. For us.

Brady and I and the folks who'd worked on the album went out to celebrate. I was dizzy with happiness, and Brady was smiling because everything he'd wanted was coming together at the same time he was graduating. Success. We'd done it.

When Jenna and Colby's plane landed, they joined us at the bar. Jenna hugged me closely, and I think I surprised her when I hugged her tightly back in a way I'd never done in all our years together. Tall, lanky Colby hesitated before hugging me, but I pulled him close, startling him. It felt good to hug people that I loved. And I started to feel like maybe my new dream wasn't that far off. That maybe I already had the starts of a family. That maybe it had been there all along. That maybe I did know what loving relationships should look like.

We bought champagne and followed it with shots. There was a euphoria in the air that was contagious. We were all smiling. My phone rang at about eight o'clock. Eli. I stepped away from the table and the noise. It was only five o'clock on the West Coast—way earlier than he normally called me—but I knew he'd gotten my text.

I was still smiling when I answered.

"Hey," he said. "I'm so happy for you. For Brady. But are you sure? Really sure that you don't want to do this with him?"

God, I missed him. I wished he was next to me, celebrating with me. I wished that our lives weren't still so far apart.

"Yes," I said with confidence in my voice. It was the first time in a couple months that I felt this confident about my decision. I wouldn't have regrets. I wasn't giving it up because of my father. I was giving it up for me and the things I wanted now.

"Why?" he asked.

"You ask that a lot."

"You avoid answering it a lot."

"It isn't me."

"You and the stage will always be one, Ava."

"Yes. Just like you and the sea." I heard his intake of breath even over the phone. The loss of the Coast Guard was still painful to him. What did it say that it wasn't hurting me at all to turn down the record deal? That I only felt happy and no sense of loss? It meant that I really had changed. That I really didn't need or want that as my life anymore. To him, I said, "We can still have those parts of us. It just doesn't have to be the center of our whole world."

He was quiet for a long time and then said, "So, you're going back to Rockport."

"Yes."

"I feel like I need the present to have some AI built into it," Eli said, drawing me back to the noise of the bar.

"Why?"

"You're out on the town, drinking. I need something to protect you."

"I'm not drunk, but even if I was, Jenna's here. I have protection."

"I bet you're smiling with that dent in your cheek."

"What dent?"

"When you smile, you have this little dent on one side. It's super sexy. The guys will be all over you, and I don't think Jenna or the present is big enough to ward them off."

"You mean a dimple? I don't have a dimple."

"It's not a dimple. Just one side of your smile is deeper than the other."

"No one has ever said that to me before."

"No one has memorized you like I have before."

I didn't know how to respond to that. "Aaaavvvvaaaa!" Brady called to me, demanding my attention back at the bar.

"I gotta go before Brady does something stupid," I told him.

"Ava?" he asked.

"Yes."

"Again."

My heart flipped. "I love you," I responded.

"I love you more."

That made my whole soul happy. That he was still asking me to say the words that we both felt. That no matter what, we still hadn't given up on the possibility of us.

When Brady and I got back to the dorm room after leaving Jenna and Colby at their hotel, I picked up the mail for the last time. Tomorrow, Brady would be leaving with his family, and I'd booked a room at the same hotel as Jenna. The dorms were no more for us—the dorm we'd lived in for two years together. That dragged at my heartstrings in a different way. Brady and I were good together. A small part of me was afraid that Brady and I would never have songs like we did now because we weren't going to be next to each other every day, building off each other.

There were video chats and Google share. We'd make it work, but it wouldn't be the same. My eyes suddenly welled at the thought, sad for the first time that day.

I handed Brady his mail, and he saw the tears I was holding back.

He hugged me, and I let him.

"I'm gonna miss you, but I'll be damned if I give up having your songs. You're not getting away from me that easily."

"They may want you to have different songs for your next album," I told him truthfully.

"No. They won't, Ava. Your songs are going to be the reason they make a fortune."

Having Brady believe in me with such ferocity—the same fierceness Jenna and Eli believed in me with—returned the joy to my day.

"I gotta hit the hay, sleep off some of this drunk before I stumble up the steps at graduation tomorrow and some douche films it and it's the first thing that is online after they announce the record," Brady said. His slur from earlier was gone, and I was pretty sure he wasn't drunk anymore, but I loved that he was still Brady, still thinking of his career and not letting anything get in the way.

"See you in the morning, egomaniac," I said as we both walked to our rooms.

"Sexaholic is better," he teased.

"You're both. It's why the ladies will be drooling after you."

"Sure you don't want to experience it at least one time before you let me go?" he teased, nodding his head toward his room.

I shut my door in his face, and he chuckled on the other side.

I changed, washed my face, and then sat on my bed with the few things that were addressed to me from the mailbox. There was one letter without a return address. I tore it open.

It was a letter written in the neat, tilted slant that was my father's. My breath left my body. My stupid, foolish heart leaped momentarily, hoping that he'd written as a step to repairing whatever we'd lost while I'd grown up.

Ava,

I heard you're graduating. I want to say congratulations, but you and I both know that it would be false. I never wanted you at that school. I never wanted you chasing foolish dreams like your mother did.

I heard that you have no plans for after graduation. Is this really what you wanted? To spend so much of your grandparents' money only to have it amount to nothing?

My anger surged. He'd spent more of their money before I'd taken control of the trust than I had at Juilliard. That he thought the time and money I'd spent had amounted to nothing had me wanting to call him and throw the record deal Brady and I had made in his face.

Except, it wasn't my deal—just the song rights. I crumpled up the letter, not wanting to read any more, letting the hurt that was my father course through me, and wanting to find solace from that hurt.

I reached for my phone and called Eli's number. It rang three times before going to his voicemail, his voice, even on the recording, easing my pain slightly. It reminded me that I had love and acceptance— something my father had never given me. I didn't need it from a man who'd been my father by DNA only. I didn't need it from someone who'd always seen the worst in me when I'd done nothing to deserve it.

I picked up the letter, pressing it flat and reading the rest.

I'm mailing this letter because I need you to know that you can't come home. I've moved on. I have a life now that isn't surrounded with taking care of you. I've met a woman who is everything you and your mother were not. Someone who's happy to be here by my side, supporting me.

Neither of us would welcome having to look after someone who threw away everything that was given to her to chase after a dream that will never come true.

I do wish that you find something in your life that will tether you to reality. That will allow you to, somehow, eek out a successful life.

Someday, I hope you see that what I did for you was my duty and that what you did in return was the complete opposite of that.

Sincerely,

Your father

His words burnt their way through my heart. I felt nothing but sadness for the woman he'd found. The woman who would never be enough, because I doubted my father knew how to be satisfied with anything in his life.

That he thought he'd done his duty by me made me want to scream. His duty would simply have been to love me, to guard my trust fund until I could use it for my dreams. Instead, he'd shown only disgust. Instead, he'd spent my future on his own life. After his lawsuit had failed, he'd made it clear that he felt the money belonged to him. That it was just an oversight on my grandparents' behalf that they hadn't changed their will to include their wife's husband.

That bitterness over the money was what had fueled his dislike of me. It may have been his loss of my mother as well. I hoped that he'd loved her. I hoped that she'd had that from him before he'd turned vicious and cruel, but I wasn't sure. I'd never be sure of the truth.

The only thing I could take from my father's letter was the fact that I had found something to tether me to reality—Eli. It was a reality that felt dreamlike in many ways, because it was full of all the love and joy that my father had never given me—had been incapable of giving me.

Tomorrow, I would have Jenna and Colby. I'd have Brady and his family. I'd get a call from Eli, and before long, I'd be able to see him. I had a new dream I was working on. One that was everything my life hadn't been with my father.

Chapter Twenty-nine

Eli

SWEETHEART

Performed by Thomas Rhett

When I got off the red-eye flight, I had one missed call from Ava. I'd talked to her when she was at the restaurant with Brady and Jenna, celebrating, before I'd rushed to the airport to catch the red-eye to New York. She'd called when I'd been in flight, but she hadn't left a message, and she hadn't texted. I didn't text her back. I concentrated on making it into the city from the airport in time for her morning graduation.

Ava had been set to give away all but two of her tickets for graduation before Brady had picked them up, telling her he needed them for extended family. She had given them to him without question, and he'd given them to me. I'd used them to make sure Ava had people filling the seats for her.

When I got through airport security, Mac and Truck were waiting for me. They were both dressed in jeans and button-downs, looking respectable. I was surprised that Mac wasn't in his uniform. He loved wearing it to any event he could get away with it at.

I wondered if he hadn't worn it because of me. Because I was still coping, on a daily basis, with not being part of the military anymore. Working with Phil and his team was a double-edged sword. I was still close to the things I loved and yet further away. A wall between them and me that would never fade away. Not a wall…a knee of metal and screws.

It hurt—the knee, the loss.

I was still filling the loss with hope for my future. A future with Ava that I would attempt to make a reality as soon as I finished training. As soon as I worked out with Phil my placement in his many offices around the states.

When I reached Mac Truck, we gave each other our customary hugs, be damned what the world around us thought. Then, we made our way out to where they'd parked my truck. I let Truck drive. I was exhausted from the red-eye and yet full of energy at the thought of seeing Ava, of surprising her.

I put on a fresh coat of deodorant and changed my shirt while we drove. It wasn't the best way to show up at a graduation, but I was there. I wasn't going to let her do this day on her own.

I knew Jenna from the pictures on Ava's phone, and I'd texted her to let her know about the surprise. When we got to the auditorium, I easily spotted her strawberry-blonde hair that trailed behind her like Ava's used to. She was sitting beside a tall, dark fellow that I assumed was her fiancé, Colby.

Instead of shaking my hand, Jenna hugged me.

"I'm so happy to finally meet you," she said.

She released me, and we all shook hands as I introduced Mac Truck, and she introduced Colby. Then, I heard my name and turned to see Mom and

Leena making their way toward us through the crowded seats. Mom's red hair was fuller and her smile brighter than when I'd left her almost a month ago. My chest expanded with relief. She wore a colorful dress full of cats. Mom at her best.

I hugged her tightly, and then we were both wrapped in Leena's arms as she hugged us too. Leena's gray hair was up in a bun that looked like an attempt to copy Ava's messy one, her flowy dress making her look more artist than teacher.

I introduced everyone one more time before we all sat down to wait for the graduates.

When I spotted her, she seemed to glow, her cap and gown unable to hide the shine that was Ava. Her face was smiling, but she also looked tired, almost as if she'd been crying, and my heart lurched at the thought of the missed call. Brady was behind her. He looked tired too, and I hoped that nothing had gone wrong with the record deal.

"What time did you all stop drinking?" I asked Jenna.

Jenna turned to me. "Early, really. Around ten, why?"

"She looks like she's been crying."

Jenna looked back toward her friend, and her hand went to her chest. "She does. And she never cries."

Ava's best friend and I shared a look of worry.

When Ava was close enough to us, we all shouted her name. She turned to the seats and saw us, freezing. It caused the line behind her to stutter and stop.

Her face lit up. A smile so huge and full of so much love that I wanted to run over and kiss her. To make sure that she never stopped being lit up. She waved. Brady prodded her in the back, and she said something to him that had them both smiling, and then they made it to their seats.

I knew I had the goofy smile on my face. The one I only wore for her. I knew Mom and Leena would be teasing me about condom boxes, and Mac Truck would just be teasing me, but I didn't care. Ava knew I was there. I'd made it. That was all that mattered.

My phone vibrated.

MY LIGHT: You're here!

ME: Yes. Is this proper graduation etiquette? To be texting during the speeches?

MY LIGHT: Your whole family is here!

I loved that she included Mac Truck in that statement.

MY LIGHT: Why? How?

ME: It's what family does. We show up.

Even over the distance, I could see her wipe her eyes as she read my text. I hated that I'd made her cry, but I could only hope that it was happy tears and know that I'd be able to hold her in just a few minutes.

It seemed like it took forever for them to finish the graduation ceremony, for them to hand out diplomas, and finally throw their hats in the air. It was forever until I got to find her in the crowd and sweep her off her feet with a hug first and then a kiss.

"I'm so proud of you," I whispered in her ear. She sniffled, holding back the tears that I knew she'd been crying. I didn't get to ask about them, because my mom pulled us apart.

"Let her go, Doodles. The rest of us want to hug her too," Mom said with a laugh.

I sort of let her go, but I still had my hand tangled with hers while everyone who'd come to see her hugged her too, and she let them.

"I can't believe you're all here. How did you all even get tickets?" Ava asked.

"That would be my extended family," Brady said, coming up behind her with a sea of his own family with him. An older man and woman, which must have been his parents, a young girl that I suspected was a sister, and then Georgie from the Pink Poodle. Today, her hair was jet black, and her eyes were such a dark blue that they were almost black, dark puddles that matched her black dress and black heels.

"Brady!" Ava said with an exasperated laugh.

"I asked him to make sure you didn't give them away."

She squeezed my hand.

"Ready to head over to the restaurant?" Brady asked, and we all agreed we were.

The restaurant was the Italian place that Ava had first taken Mac Truck and me to. The hostess, whose name eluded me, was still there, and her eyes lit up on seeing Brady. She congratulated Ava and Brady and then led us to a small room at the back that Brady had rented out. It was tight for the crowd that we had, but it worked.

Ava slid her gown off, and I almost lost all ability to think about anything but her. She had on a purple dress that clung to her lithe frame in a way that left little room for anything else. Like always, she took my breath away. Gorgeous beyond anything I'd ever encountered.

I slid my hands around her waist, pulling her body up to mine. I kissed her, and she responded with the same intensity she always did. I pulled my lips away with a quiet groan. "It's going to kill me to see you in that dress all day."

She smirked. "Then just imagine taking it off later."

I groaned again. "That's exactly the problem. Thanks for not helping at all."

She laughed and pulled away from me to join my mom at the table. Mac had somehow finagled his way into sitting beside Georgie. I watched in amazement as he stuttered a response to something she said.

Mac was never one to lose his cool around the ladies. He was normally smooth like honey. I made a note to harass him about it later and nudged Truck with a nod in Mac's direction so that he'd do the same. He gave me a large smile that I loved seeing on my friend's face. Ava, and the orbit that swung around her, had changed us all.

When the gifts started floating around the room, Ava pulled the present out from her bag, and I took it from her hand and put it back inside.

"Later," I told her, and she looked up at me with happy eyes and just nodded.

♫ ♫ ♫

We stayed at the restaurant until well into the afternoon, then slowly started to filter away. Mom and Leena were off to the train station to head back to New London. Jenna and Colby were off to the hotel. Their flight was early the next morning. Like mine. Like Ava's. She was heading out to Texas with them.

Truck waited by the door. He asked, "Are you heading back to the apartment?"

"Ava?" I asked her. I hadn't made plans past showing up at her graduation. All I knew was that I wasn't letting her get away from me before I'd seen her out of that purple dress.

"I'm staying at the same hotel as Jenna and Colby tonight, but I have to go back to the dorm room first to pick up my bag."

"Would you like an uninvited guest?" I asked, my voice deep with longing that I knew she could hear.

"Uninvited, invited. I'll take you whenever I can get you," she said. My body reacted. My smile widened.

Truck guffawed, and Ava slapped him on the arm. "Get your head out of the gutter, Travis."

He smiled. "Mac?" Truck called.

Mac was standing with Georgie, model tall and gorgeous in her own way that was so unlike Ava's. She could almost look Mac in the eye with her heels, which was saying a lot as Mac was an easy six foot four. Georgie laughed at something he said but then left him to say goodbye to Brady before making her way over to where Ava was at my side.

"Congratulations, girl," Georgie said. "I'm going to miss you two helping me at open mic night."

Ava kissed her cheek. "I'm going to miss you, too. If you ever need a vacation, you can come hang with me on the beach in Rockport."

"It's a deal," she said and then swayed away with Mac staring after her like he'd just lost a puppy.

"Eli's staying with Ava, so it's just you and me out tonight," Truck said to him.

"Sounds good. I have to catch the early train, anyway."

Ava and I exchanged hugs and goodbyes with them. As my two best friends started to walk away, I hollered after them, "Remember to stay away from the red button, asswipe."

Mac stuck up his middle finger at me, and I just laughed and then turned back to Ava. She was looking up at me with a grin that I couldn't help returning.

"I can't believe you're here," she said again. She'd said it several times.

"It would have taken a lot more than four thousand miles to keep me away."

We made our way back to her dorm room for the last time, her body swaying against mine in a way that made me want to stay like that forever. The sway soothed me like when I was on deck of a boat.

At the dorm room, I helped her pack the few things she'd left out, grabbing the things off the desk in her room. That's when I saw the crumpled paper. Crumpled paper and Ava went hand in hand. It was often the sign of a song that was eluding her. One that she'd eventually come back to.

"Do you want me to grab..." my voice trailed away as I saw "Father" written in a masculine hand at the bottom.

I'd scanned the letter by the time she made it back into the room from the bathroom. My heart was aching, because I knew why I'd had a missed call and why she'd looked like she'd been crying when I'd first seen her.

I turned to her as she came in and grabbed her by the waist, hauling her up against me. I buried my head in her neck, kissing her there before moving my lips across her cheeks and her nose and her mouth, before pulling away and staring into her eyes. When she tried to look away, I grabbed her chin and gently turned it back.

"He isn't worth your tears," I told her quietly.

She closed her eyes and then opened them again, meeting my fierce look with her own. "I know, but the tears actually felt good, like I was finally able to cry after he hadn't let me for years."

My brow creased in confusion at her words.

"What do you mean?"

"If I cried, he punished me more. So, the tears…they were kind of cathartic. They were a way of saying that he couldn't do anything to me anymore."

I kissed her because I didn't know what else to do. Kissed her to show her that she was loved. That she didn't need him. That she had people in her life who would let her be herself no matter what that looked like—tears, smiles, songs, and all.

Chapter Thirty

Ava

OH, WHAT A WORLD
Performed by Kacey Musgraves

My joy at seeing Eli and his family in the stands at graduation took all the hurt I'd felt at my father's letter, bundled it up, and sent it away. While the family in the stands wasn't mine by blood, they were there, making me theirs anyway, making my new dream come true already.

That joy carried me through the day. Eli's touch kept me grounded and yet floating at the same time. It made me realize how much I missed him. Life kept placing us so close that we touched and entwined, but then it pulled us back apart. I wanted to get to the part of our story where we found a path together. For the moment, I was going to have to be satisfied with seeing him, being held by him.

When he found my father's letter in my dorm room, it reminded me again of the pieces of the letter that had been true. I'd found success. My songs were being sung. And I'd found a tether in the real world. I'd found Eli.

When we got to my hotel room, we lost ourselves to everything but each other and the demand our bodies had to touch, to reclaim the pieces that had been torn away from our grasps by a divide the size of a continent.

When we'd finally found the pieces and put them back together, we lay, tangled in the bedsheets. Both smiling. Both happy. Both sated.

"Where's the present?" Eli asked.

"In my bag," I said.

He pulled away and walked, naked, over to my slouch bag that I'd had for as long as I'd known him and pulled the box from it. The present was a little mangled, paper and ribbons mushed from being taken everywhere, but the marks I'd made were still there, showing that I hadn't opened it.

"Okay. Open it," he said, coming back and putting the gift on my stomach.

"I don't really want to," I told him honestly.

He frowned. "Why?"

"It…it's just this part of you that I've been carrying around and…" I trailed off. As stupid as it seemed, the gift had made me feel not so alone. Now, I was going to be leaving everything, going back to Rockport by myself, and I wouldn't even have the stupid box to go with me.

"I know I haven't been here to hold you. To help you through these last few weeks. I know that I'm still not going to be with you when you go back to Rockport and I go back to California." His voice was quiet and somber. "But if you open the gift, you'll see that it'll be okay. It'll be like I'm here with you always. Like I'm holding you."

I wiped at a tear that had leaked from my eye, but I would no longer stop them from coming. Tears were a part of life. They were okay. With trembling fingers, I put a fingernail under the wrinkled corner of the box, and with a last moment of regret, tore it open.

All along, I'd known it was a jewelry box. It was the size of a jewelry box, after all. I wasn't worried that it was a ring. I didn't think Eli would have given it to me when he'd thought there was a chance he couldn't be with me in person. He wouldn't propose over the phone on graduation day. He wasn't impulsive like me. That was more something I would do—unable to wait, like I'd been unable to wait to tell him I loved him. Truth was, we weren't ready for a proposal. We still had too many unanswered questions in our lives.

When I opened the box, it was a necklace—platinum setting, an oval filled with abalone surrounded with tiny diamonds that were probably only crystals but still shone brightly. The abalone was a swirl of blues and pinks and greens, more vivid than most abalone you saw, unless the shell was wet and sparkling with the sunlight. It was exceptional even if it wasn't expensive.

"I know it isn't really worth much—" he started, but I cut him off.

"Aurora Borealis," I sighed.

He smiled, relieved that I'd caught on. How could I not? He'd taken me to see the painting on the day he'd given me the gift.

"It's so lovely," I told him honestly, tears now a hopeless trail down my face.

He wiped at my tears but didn't tell me not to cry. Then, he took the necklace from its box and moved behind me so he could clasp it around my neck. His fingers danced over the skin at my neck, across my shoulders, and down my arms. "Now, you can still take the present with you everywhere. Except, it'll be around your neck, and it can be like I'm with you, with my arms around you, even when I'm not."

I fingered the shell and knew that it would be staying there for a very long time, joining us when we couldn't be joined.

♫ ♫ ♫

The next morning, Eli and I rode with Jenna and Colby to the airport. His flight was leaving just after ours. We were heading in different directions again.

He waited with us at our gate, and I stayed with him until they called for the last passengers. I turned to him and kissed him, wanting him to feel that, just like Mac Truck hugging him goodbye, I was kissing him goodbye in case we never got a chance to do it again.

He held me and whispered in my hair, "Again."

"I love you," I responded.

"I love you more."

Then he released me, and I walked down the jetway. I looked back one last time, our parting always reminding me of the view of him in the rearview mirror of my Honda as I'd left Rockport, like I was losing something that I wanted so badly it hurt.

It never made sense anymore, because we'd both said we weren't giving up on us. We'd both continued to text and call, but maybe it was just too many endings all at once for me. My heart couldn't keep up.

When I got off the plane in Texas, the muggy air hit me. It was muggy in New York often, too, but this muggy felt different, laced with ocean and memories. Some welcome, some not.

I spent the night with Jenna and Colby in their tiny house in Galveston. It was their starter home, Jenna said. Still, it was filled with pictures of them, and me, and their families. It was full of color and light that Jenna loved. It felt like a home.

Jenna and I sat together on the porch swing after Colby had gone to bed. The comfort of friends who felt like sisters. My new dream of family had started right there, with her. I just hadn't realized that I'd already had some to begin with.

"What's going on with you and Eli?" Jenna asked as we pushed our feet off the wooden planks to keep the swing moving.

"I love him. He loves me."

"Okay, but what does that mean exactly?"

"It means that we're still trying to figure things out. He had his whole world pulled out from under him and is trying to remake that world."

"And you? You've suddenly got things all figured out?"

I smiled at her, and I surprised her by pulling her to me in a hug. I was getting so much better at it—hugging—but the people who'd known me longest knew that it was still an unfamiliar movement on my part. "I've kind of got this plan of just making a family."

"That's kind of hard to do without Eli…or at least someone, unless you're planning on visiting the sperm bank."

I laughed at her.

"Not that kind of family. I mean, sure, maybe someday, but that's not what I mean."

She looked at me like I was crazy, and I didn't blame her.

"I'd been sending you all those songs about family because my heart was trying to teach my brain a lesson. My heart had already learned it when I was with Eli and his family in New London. I'd learned that family was the most important thing in life. I want that sense of community and camaraderie that I felt there. I want to belong somewhere. To open a door and have people call out your name and come running. To hug you," my voice wavered on the word hug as I squeezed her again, "and to just be happy you're there."

"Well, then why are you going to Rockport? You have all of that here. With me," she said, pushing her shoulder into me but not letting me escape the hug that I'd started.

"It is. You are my family. I'm sorry I didn't really ever see it before. But I also don't want to stay in Galveston. So, for right now, I'll go to Rockport. I'll work with Andy and Lacey, who have also been my family. I'll send songs to Brady, who is part of my family, too. And hopefully, once Eli figures out what's going on with him, we can find a way for both our families to become one."

Jenna smiled at me. "That sounds like a really good plan."

I nodded because I thought it was, too.

♫ ♫ ♫

The next day, I drove to Rockport. I called Eli on the journey. I knew he was at work, but I missed him, and I wanted him to know that I wasn't giving up on us. That I was still hoping for that true ending we'd talked about so long ago on his drive to his review board hearing.

When he answered, he sounded excited for the first time in a long time. He was going into an overnight emergency simulation with a group of first responders. Phil was letting him run with things in a way he hadn't expected so soon.

It didn't surprise me that Phil was relying on him already. Eli was a natural leader. I'd known that the moment I met him and thought he was one of Dad's collections.

After he'd talked about what the next twenty-four hours was going to look like for him, I nervously tried to bring up what was in my head.

"I want to say something."

"Okay," he said, listening, as he always did, to me. As if he was hearing everything I said and didn't say at the same time—the spoken words and the emotions behind it.

"Back when we were in New London, you asked me to move in with you, and I told you it wasn't the right time."

"I know. And you were right; it wasn't. You'd be stuck in an apartment with Truck, and I love him, but I'm not sure I could handle the thought of you there with him while I was here," he teased.

I laughed. "Eli, you are missing my point."

"I am? I must be more exhausted than I thought after all the plane rides and time changes to get back to California."

"What I'm trying to tell you is that, once you've figured out all this stuff with Phil and the new job, I want us to be together."

"What about Rockport?" he asked.

"I love Rockport. I love the house there. But I don't love any of that as much as I love you."

He was quiet for a moment, taking it in.

"Say it again," he said quietly.

"I love you."

"Not that part."

"I'm confused."

"The part about not loving anything as much as me."

My heart twisted and soared, and a smile crossed my face. "Doodles, I don't love anything like I love you."

"Thank God," he said.

♫ ♫ ♫

When I got to the beach house, I stood outside, staring at the turquois color that Eli and Mac Truck had painted it four years before. Emotions swelled through me. Happiness to be here. Happiness that Eli and I were slowly moving toward something, but also a weird sort of melancholy.

So many endings and so many beginnings all at once.

I checked the rooms, as I always did, to ensure the rental agency had kept it up as I'd paid them to do, and then I went out on the deck. For the first time in so very long, I climbed up on top of the table and looked out at the sea, trying out my new perspective.

The sound of the waves washed over me, feeling like music to my heart.

I hadn't lied when I'd told Eli I loved the house. I did. In truth, I could see myself spending my days here, meandering on the beach, swimming, writing along the shore with the sound of the birds in the air. In that vision, I could also see that, when I opened the door, he was here, waiting for me. That may never happen. But I also knew that it was okay. That the most important thing was not where we were but that we would be together.

I stayed on the deck until I could watch the stars rise up in the sky. My breath caught at the clearness of them here after they'd been hidden away from me for so long in New York. I could almost imagine green and purple streaks shooting their way across the black silkiness. Aurora borealis.

As I had the thought, a shooting star darted across the darkness, and I made a wish that, somehow, my dream of family and of Eli would find its way home someday soon.

The next day, I drove into town to see Andy and Lacey and get my normal summer job back. They normally put me on the live music schedule with Ben and his band. I'd have a place to fill my days while waiting for Eli.

I was stunned to drive up and find a "For Sale'" sign in the window. They were selling. That made my whole heart flop to the pit of my stomach. For the first time, I truly understood what Eli must have felt like driving up to the same sign in the yard of his family home. It hurt. Not only because I hadn't known, but because I'd been making plans around these people and the bar. The people I'd thought of as family.

At midday, the bar wasn't exactly packed. There was a handful of locals and tourists, but it also didn't look like the business was hurting. I didn't understand why they were selling.

Lacey saw me first, her hair that she'd always dyed black was pulled up away from a face that showed a few more wrinkles, but, really, looked the way it always had. Open. Friendly. Relaxed.

"Ava!" she called, coming around the bar to greet me, and I surprised her by hugging her tight. She hollered toward the kitchen. "Andy, get out here. It's our Ava girl!"

My heart warmed at the "our Ava" because I knew that they were part of my family just like I'd told Jenna. Andy appeared from the kitchen, face already wide in an attempted smile as he hustled toward me. While Lacey had looked the same, Andy looked very different. One side of his face wasn't moving at quite the same speed as the other; his grin was crooked. Plus, he walked funny, with one arm lagging at his side.

"Ava!" he said, and where we normally just greeted each other with smiles, I hugged him too. What I'd picked up from Eli and his family, I was putting to good use with mine.

"You up and graduated on us now? You got a record deal yet?" Andy asked, stepping away but with that same lopsided smile on his face.

"Well, Brady got one, using my songs."

"Great Gatsby! That's awesome!" Lacey cried. "Sit, we'll pull out some champagne to celebrate."

I sat at the bar while Lacey rooted around in the fridge, coming up with a bottle of champagne and several glasses. Andy took a seat at the bar beside me.

"Congratulations, Ava," Andy said as we clinked our glasses together and sipped.

"You're selling the bar?" I asked after a moment.

Lacey nodded, but Andy looked unhappy about it. I waited for one of them to explain. It was Lacey that spoke. "The boys are set in their lives in Alaska and California. They aren't coming back to run this old place. Andy had a stroke in January. We've got him back up and going, but it made us both realize that we need to go enjoy ourselves before we can't."

Their boys were way older than me, with families and successful jobs of their own. I could understand them not wanting to drop everything to come back to Texas to run a bar in the middle of nowhere that did more business during the summer than any other time of year.

Running a bar took time and energy—a lot of it. It hit me. Out of the blue. Like the shooting star from last night. Like the wish I'd made was being answered. A niggle of hope filled me. I had money left. Enough to invest in something that could mean a future even if I never sold another song again.

I spoke in a rush before I could change my mind. "I don't know anything about the price of bars. I don't really know anything about running a bar, but I was coming here to get my normal summer job back. Maybe I could swing buying the place, and you could teach me how to run it?"

Even as I spoke, my mind was filled with images of Eli and his new job. If I bought a bar, it wouldn't be something I could walk away from. It would be something that tied me to Texas. I wouldn't be able to run off and join him wherever he landed, California or otherwise, like I'd told him last night that I would.

"Well, now…" Andy trailed off, exchanging a look with Lacey—a look I couldn't exactly read but I was pretty sure held plenty of doubt.

"Look, I'm not asking for a handout. I have the money from my trust fund."

"You should probably think about it," Lacey said. "Don't jump before you see."

I laughed, because having said I would buy the bar was so like the old me, jumping on top of things. But it felt good to let go of some of the things that had been weighing me down. To act from my heart. But she was right; I did need to think about it. I needed to talk to Eli about it.

"You're right. I should think about it," I responded. "In the meantime, how about I work here with you and learn the business side of it all? That way, I can see if it's really for me, and you get some help."

They exchanged another look, and then Andy stuck out his hand. "It's a deal, young lady."

I gladly shook it, suddenly feeling excited. I couldn't wait to talk to Eli to see what he thought, to see if he thought this could be a dream that we could make together. If maybe there was a chance that we could build a life together in Rockport.

Chapter Thirty-one

Eli

ONCE IN A LIFETIME
Performed by Keith Urban

It was close to midnight in Texas, which meant it was only ten in California by the time I heard from Ava. I'd started to worry. Ava had been on her own so long I knew better than to worry, but I couldn't help it. I loved her, thus I worried.

"Where've you been?" I asked when she FaceTimed me, hoping I didn't sound accusatory, hoping she heard the worry instead.

"I was at the Salty Dog with Andy and Lacey," she told me.

Images of her on bar tops came unbidden into my head. I didn't know if I should smile or scowl at the thought. "Were you dancing on the bar again?"

She smiled at me. "Not tonight."

I groaned. "Damn. That means I'm going to have to quit my job and come running over there to rescue you from standing on the bar all over again."

"I may have a job for you if you quit yours," she teased, and my whole body reacted. It felt like it had been months instead of days since I'd held her in my arms.

"Yeah?" I said while trying to get my body in check.

She nodded, and then I saw the sky behind her.

"Wait, are you out on the deck? Are you on the table?" I asked, smiling, loving the thought of her on the table, loving that she'd slowly become a mix of the old Ava and the new Ava.

She returned my smile and twisted her body so that I got a glimpse of the moon shining on the water behind her, diamonds dancing on the water top.

"This makes me happy." I couldn't keep the pleasure from my voice. I brought myself back to our conversation from before I'd realized where she was. "Sorry. I got sidetracked by this exciting revelation. What job would you have for me in Rockport?"

The innuendo in my words was unmissable, and she wagged a finger at me in front of the phone's camera. "Not that job. Well, I mean, you can do that job too, but—"

I groaned again, burying my head in my hands before looking back up and saying, "You're killing me."

"Get your mind out of the bedroom, Doodles, and listen to my news."

She'd taken to calling me Doodles since I'd lost my commission. I think she was afraid to call me oh Captain, my Captain. I sort of missed it. Like I missed my life in the Coast Guard—with the ache of bones that were healing, but not with the pain of the first crack. I had more ahead of me than behind.

"News?" I asked.

"What would you think about me buying the Salty Dog?"

I didn't know what to respond to first: the thought of her trying to buy a bar at twenty-three, or the fact that her owning one would mean a life tied to Rockport in a way that I wasn't sure I could make happen for us yet. I was trying to make it happen, but I hadn't told her about it because I was afraid to give her false hope.

I'd wanted to tell her my plan when she'd called the day before and told me that she didn't love Rockport as much as she loved me. But I was still so afraid of getting both of our hopes up. One of us having hopes get squashed was enough if I couldn't make it happen.

"You really want to own a bar?" I finally asked, pulling myself from my own doubts and fears.

She laughed lightly. It was the lightest laugh I'd heard from her in a very long time. It echoed over the deck and out into the night, joining the crash of the waves on the shore behind her. It was so much better than the melancholy that had been filling us both lately.

"To be fair, I didn't know that when I went down there tonight. I was just trying to get my normal summer job back," she explained.

"What made the leap from getting a job at a bar to buying one?"

"When I showed up and there was a 'For Sale' sign in the window, and Andy was barely moving from the stroke he'd had in January."

My heart sank for Andy. For his wife. But I was still trying to figure out why that had turned into buying the bar. "That's awful. I'm sorry for him. For them. I'm still not getting it, though."

"The timing. 'There is no such thing as an accident; it's fate misnamed,'" she quoted.

"Who gave you that one?" I asked as my heart continued to constrict with worry about us and our future. Her quote also made me think of all the times that Ava and I had met in ways that seemed accidental. It would be nice to believe it was fate and not just random chance.

"Napoleon Bonaparte," she replied.

"Didn't his entire empire crumble at the seams?"

She laughed. "Yes. I see your point. Do you think it's a mistake?"

I shook my head. "No. It's just a big step."

She nodded. "It is, and I don't know if it's the right step. I don't know if it's the right next chapter for me, but I also don't have to rush into it. I'm going to work at the bar over the summer to see if it's something I could feasibly do on my own. They've agreed not to sell it until after the season to give me a shot at it."

The tightness in my heart eased ever so slightly. I had time then. If I couldn't make it work, then we could go down another road before she made this huge decision that we couldn't undo.

"How would you get the down payment?" I asked.

"I still have quite a bit of money in my trust fund. Not enough to make stupid decisions, but enough to get me started in a new direction if I spend it right."

I tried to take it all in. That she had enough money in her trust fund to buy a bar. That she was seriously considering it. Somehow, in my heart, it felt right. It felt like maybe she and I were both working on writing words to a story that might really become ours.

I'd been waiting to talk to Phil about the office in Corpus Christi. The office that was just a handful of miles away from the house that Ava owned and loved. I'd been thinking about it since she'd told me she still owned the house. I'd been trying to make it a reality since I'd been discharged.

There were lots of hurdles in the way still, but I wanted to believe that we could make this new dream a joint dream if we didn't give up at the worst part.

"The remaking of life," I told her quietly.

"What?"

"The quote you said from the sandbox lady. After loss, comes the remaking of life."

I heard her intake of breath. "Yes."

"Then, I think it's a really good idea," I said.

"You do?"

I nodded, knowing she could see it over the tiny screens we both held, knowing she could see that I meant it.

"I thought you'd be…upset?" she said quietly.

She felt that way because I still hadn't told her what I was working on, and, for not the first time, I was tempted to spill my guts. To not hide the good or the bad or the hopes from her. But there was a piece of me that just couldn't bring another lost dream to her feet if I couldn't make it happen.

"We both have to figure out a few things before we make anything permanent, right?" I asked.

She nodded, and I could see the wariness in her eyes. The doubts.

"Ava, we're going to be okay."

"I love you," she said as if she needed to remind us both.

"I love you more," I told her. Then I prayed to the gods that they would put in a good word for us with the three fates who controlled destiny. I prayed that they'd help our lives to truly be aligned this time.

♫ ♫ ♫

It was July. The heat and humidity assaulted me as I stepped out of my truck and looked up at the house on the shore of Aransas Bay. It was just like when I'd arrived to paint the place with Mac Truck four years ago. Ava wasn't there, like she hadn't been there the day Mac Truck and I had arrived.

Ava was in Galveston. Jenna's bachelorette party had been the night before. I had two numbers in my phone for Ava, Brady's and Jenna's, and I'd had to use both of them over the last few weeks, arranging this surprise. Hoping that I could pull it off. Hoping that she'd be happy with it. Hoping that it meant our life together would finally be starting.

It had meant keeping things from Ava. I wasn't used to that—or good at it. Ava and I had talked several times a day while I was in California, and she was working at the bar. We'd still talked daily while she thought I was in California, but I was really in New York, packing up Truck's and my apartment, sending our things in different directions. Truck was off to Hawaii. I was off to Texas. Truck had gotten teary-eyed on me as we'd hugged goodbye. For the first time in a long time, our lives were going in different directions.

Then, I'd gotten into my truck and headed the almost two thousand miles to Texas. To her. To my light, my fate— whatever you wanted to call it. She was my own aurora borealis, and she didn't know I was coming.

Jenna had told me what the code was for the lockbox on the door. Ava had been renting out the place while she'd been in New York. Now, it was her home, but she still had the lockbox as if she might not be staying, because she'd told me that she loved me more than the house. But now I wanted her to stay.

Once I'd opened the door, I unloaded all the boxes from the back of my truck into the extra room. It was presumptuous of me to assume that I'd be staying here with her. I wanted to be presumptuous, though. I wanted her to see that I'd thought that way, that I'd felt this way, that I was serious about a life together.

According to Jenna, Ava was going straight to the bar once she got to Rockport, but I didn't want to risk her seeing my stuff. So, I left my things in the room I was hoping she hardly ever went into and then drove into town, my body and mind remembering the way when I hadn't been there in years.

When I arrived at the bar, I saw the "For Sale" sign had a "Deal Pending" covering it. My heart leaped with happiness for us both. That we were there, making a life for ourselves after all the things that had come and gone in our lives.

I'd had Ava reintroduce me to Andy and Lacey over FaceTime this month, making sure they knew my face, and I knew theirs. Ava hadn't understood why I was being so persistent, but she'd done it anyway, with a roll of her eyes and a tease about me being all alpha male.

I'd almost told her the truth right then, for the hundredth time, but I'd wanted to surprise her more. I'd wanted to see her face in person when I told her everything. I wanted to feel her reaction in my hands and in my heart.

When I walked in, the bar was about half full, people eating and drinking their summer afternoon away, keeping out of the humidity for a few moments. It was Lacey at the bar when I approached it.

"What can I get you?" she asked, not really registering me.

I reached out my hand. "Lacey, it's Eli. Good to meet you in person again."

Lacey's eyes widened, but she shook my hand. "It's good to see you. Ava didn't say anything about you coming. You know she's not here, right?"

I nodded. "I know; she's on her way back from Galveston. And she doesn't know I'm here."

I explained my plan to her. The one Jenna, Brady, and I had been working on ever since Phil had agreed to place me where I'd requested. Since I'd known for sure I could fill Ava and myself up with hope and not loss.

Lacey's face turned into a sea of smiles once I'd explained my intent. She came around the bar and hugged me. It felt like my mom's hugs. All energy and force and love.

"I'm so happy she has you," she said quietly.

I couldn't speak without breaking into foolish tears, so I just gave a curt nod.

"Let me call Ben and the band to see if they can make it in early to learn the new music." She left to make the call.

I turned and took in the room. I hadn't been there in four years, but it was burnt into my memories just like the house and the town had been. Just like Ava had been.

My only regret—my only moment of hesitation in this leap I was taking—was leaving my mom and Leena thousands of miles away as they got older. What if Mom's cancer came back? How would I help them?

I'd gone to see Mom before packing up the apartment in New York, and she'd been happy when I'd told her my plan. She'd looked so much healthier than she had even in May, the months putting weight on her, her hair longer than it had been. She and Leena were puttering about the ancient Victorian together. They were making plans for a two-week cruise through the Panama Canal.

She'd startled me by saying that she didn't need me hovering, but that she thought Ava did. She thought Ava needed someone by her side maybe more than anyone she'd seen in a long time.

And I'd agreed, which was why I was there, waiting for her to show up from Galveston.

When Ben and the band showed up, they were slapping me on the back and acting like we were old friends. They seemed happy to do something for Ava, as if she was part of their family. I left the band with the sheet music that Brady had me print out. They immediately set to work practicing it.

By seven o'clock, the bar was filling up. There were still empty tables, but the volume level had gone up several notches, and I felt nervous for one of the first times since starting this journey. Brady had been coaching me—told me I sucked to high heaven, but that Ava would probably get all soft in the knees anyway. That was enough for me. I wanted Ava soft in the knees. I wanted her to forget everything but the fact that our bodies already knew what our lives had been trying to figure out. That we were one. Not pieces left apart but Scrabble tiles that made up one word.

Jenna called. "She's about five minutes out. She's cranky as hell with me because I've called her like a hundred times."

"Does she suspect something?" I asked.

"No, I don't think so. I just kept badgering her with wedding stuff. If anything, she's thinking I've gone all Bridezilla on her."

I chuckled.

"Thanks for helping me with this."

"Eli?"

"Yep?"

"Thank you for giving her everything she's been missing."

I choked back more emotion and hung up. I was afraid that Ava would know I was here as soon as she walked in, the energy that always seemed to waft between us so palpable. So, I stepped out for a few minutes. Lacey would text me when Andy had taken her into the back office for some paperwork, and then I was going to come back.

I waved to Lacey as I left, the heat and humidity hitting me with its own force as I exited the building.

I made my way down the back alley to where I'd parked the truck.

The wait was killing me. I was so close to having her in my arms again. So close to being able to breathe her in like I'd breathed in the salty air that surrounded the town. Relief. Peace. Home.

When Lacey texted me the all clear, it was hard not to run back into the building. My heart was hammering. I wondered—for not the first time this afternoon—how anyone could go onstage without throwing up. Put me on a boat full of known drug dealers instead of a stage any day of the week. It felt safer, but that wasn't my life anymore. This was.

Lacey handed me the microphone as soon as I entered the bar. I'd planned on doing it from the stage this whole time, but then I had a better idea. Lacey's grin turned even wider as I pulled myself onto her bar top, my head barely clearing the ceiling when I stood. I gave Ben the signal, and he and the band started the notes of the song that Ava had written for us.

It took longer than I thought for her to come into the room from the back, with a frown on her beautiful face, her dual-colored eyes flashing as she took in Ben and the band.

My voice cracked on the first note, sounding ridiculously like my puberty-wracked body from long ago, before it smoothed out as I continued. "I felt the pieces of me fall around you."

Her eyes shifted immediately to me on the bar, and she froze. I wasn't sure if it was good or bad that she was frozen. So, I just kept singing. A wounded bird could sing better, but I did my best for the one I loved more than the ocean and the sea and the Coast Guard.

"And you felt yours slip away too. The pieces of us that were a shattered mess. All on the floor. I had to pick them up as I walked out the door. Hoping you'd see what we were meant to be. Hoping you'd keep the pieces of me that I'd left with you there."

She finally moved so that she was standing at the edge of the bar closest to the stage. I'd made my way down it, eyes locked on her. When I got to the end, she reached out a hand. A silent command. Like the one I'd given to her once upon a time when we'd first met.

I grinned, my voice losing the train of the song and of the words that I was supposed to be singing. Ben picked them up, his voice so much stronger than mine.

I reached for her hand, bending, and letting my feet find their way to the ground next to hers. She looked beautiful. Her hair was longer than when I'd first seen her in the bar in New York in March. It was curling about her face and shoulders now. She was wearing a summer dress that made her appear young and old at the same time. A mix of so many things.

When our hands touched, it was like it had always been. Energy. Waves. Connection.

"How are you here?" she asked with a smile. I reached out to touch her lips with my fingers, tracing them all the way to the corner that I loved as it sunk into her cheeks.

"Kiss me first, questions later," I said, and I took her lips before she could take mine, impatient like she had once been impatient. We lost the world for a few moments, the kiss bringing our bodies back together. Our souls together. Aligning our stars the way they were meant to be.

Ben was singing about pieces behind us. But we weren't pieces anymore. We were a whole. One thing. One entity. One life force made out of two independent bodies voluntarily joining together.

The crowd was cheering around us as Ben wrapped up the song, and we were still kissing. My phone was ringing. I knew it would be Jenna. Or Brady. Or both. But I wasn't ready to talk to them yet.

I pulled myself away from her lips. She seemed happy. The last tiny bits of doubt that had floated through my brain left. This was right.

"Phil gave me a new assignment," I told her, smiling.

Her eyes widened.

"I'll be working with the Coast Guard out of Corpus Christi," I said. Her eyes widened at the realization that my work would be a mere thirty miles away.

She flung her arms around my neck, pulling herself tight up against my body so that I could feel every single curve and line, so that I could feel the furious beat of her heart that I knew matched my own furious beat. "Eli!" she breathed into my neck.

I kissed her hair and her neck and found my way back to her lips. She responded with a kiss that seemed full of relief and longing and hope. Maybe the hope was in my own heart, but I wanted to believe it was in hers too.

Removing my lips from hers after over a month apart was difficult, but I did it. I looked down into her flushed, smiling face. "I was kind of hoping you'd be amiable to a permanent houseguest, seeing as the station is just down the road."

She was crying, I realized, tears streaking down her cheeks. And I wiped at them, feeling inadequate, as I always did, to catch her tears, but knowing how important it was for her to feel them, to let them loose in a way she hadn't been allowed to growing up.

"That terrible of an idea, huh?" I said quietly.

"Rotten luck, I've just rented out the extra room."

It wasn't true. I'd stacked my boxes in it just hours ago. "Good thing I didn't want space in the extra room."

"What, you think you're just going to take the master?"

"I remember you inviting me into that bed once upon a time. It's just taken me a while to accept."

She grinned. "You're a slow learner."

"They don't train us for how to deal with the aurora borealis in the Coast Guard." I smiled.

"I love you," she said.

"Again." I kissed her lips.

"I love you," she said between kisses.

"I love you more."

♫ ♫ ♫

I woke to the unfamiliar warm breeze flowing through the dark room, the scent and the humidity nothing like it had been in my time in California or my years in New York.

I spread my hand out toward where I'd left Ava. Her legs that had been entwined with mine were gone. The bed was empty. My body was calling to her already, searching for her in the dark.

I stood and pulled on my jeans before making my way through the house. The doors to the deck were open in the great room just as they'd been open in the bedroom, but here, I could see her.

She was sitting on the patio table, her back to me. Her face was turned toward the sky as it slowly woke, pink and magenta beginning to surface near the horizon, turning Ava into a mix of shadow and colors like the colors she continued to throw into my world. Her hair was blowing in the breeze.

I made my way out, drawn to her as I'd always been and loving that I was. I climbed up on the table, ignoring the wobble and protest it gave. I wrapped my body around hers the best I could, my legs overlapping hers, her back to my chest. She relaxed into me, turning her head slightly so that she could look up at me, a smile on her face.

"All my teenage years, I waited for someone who would join me on the tabletop. You've joined me several times now." Her voice was soft but full of emotions.

"I'd join you anywhere," I responded.

"Eli?"

"Hmm," I said as I nuzzled into her neck, kissing her and absorbing the scent that I adored, that I'd missed while I was without her.

"In the painting," she started. She didn't have to tell me which one; I knew. "You said I was the sky, and you were the boat."

I nodded, kissing her shoulder that was bare except for the tiny tank that she wore with a pair of panties that wouldn't be there long if I had anything to say about it.

"I don't want to be the sky," she said quietly.

I stopped my motions, listening to her closely, waiting for her words.

"I want to be on the boat. With you. Finding safe harbor."

My heart lurched, emotions filling me.

"Together then. We'll let the light guide us home."

"We're already there, don't you think?"

I nodded, resting my chin on her shoulder and watching as the sky turned a thousand shades of pink and orange and purple. Watching as the colors filled our world. Knowing that she was right. The light that had guided us home…it had guided us to each other. We were here. We were our own life-changing phenomenon. We'd taken what we were and filled it with color and brilliance. A magical display. Us.

Epilogue

Ava

THE REST OF OUR LIFE

Performed by Tim McGraw & Faith Hill

"This is ridiculous," I groused at Eli as I came out of our room. The room we'd been sharing for over three months now. The room that had become a haven for me of everything a home should be. Love. Hands. Hope. Someone there every night, making your world better.

We'd had lots of visitors over the last few months: Jenna and Colby, Mac Truck, and even Mandy and Leena had made the journey before heading out on their two-week cruise. The visitors had made it feel more like a home to me. People coming to see us. Together. Making our two families one.

Eli's job consulting in Corpus Christi kept him busy and gone a lot. My signing ownership papers for the bar, had meant I was gone a lot. But we always came back to the house we'd made a home. The place we belonged.

Now, I was wearing a stupid Harley Quinn costume, feeling like an idiot, while Eli was in a suit like Will Smith from *Men in Black*—only the second time in his life that he hadn't worn a Coast Guard uniform for Halloween. It didn't escape my notice that it was still, technically, a military uniform, but I hadn't called him on it. The Coast Guard was still a painful loss to him even if he did his best to move forward without it.

We were late. We should have been at the bar almost an hour ago, but I'd had second and third and fourth thoughts about my costume. Eli had come into the bedroom to help me with my jitters, but that had just ended with us with no clothes, skin on skin—which had only added to our lateness.

"You look cute," Eli said.

"Cute?!"

Eli laughed. "Are you mad at me for calling you cute?"

"If I get mad at you, that means I still care. Worry when I don't get mad," I said, trying to sound like Harley Quinn as I quoted her words from *Suicide Squad*.

He laughed again. His laughter had become a regular part of our life together. Something unexpected from the grumpy cadet that I'd first found in the beach house when it had belonged to my father. It was as if he'd been holding in the laughter, saving it for the right moments in his life, and I was thrilled that all those moments were mine. Us. Together.

We were in these stupid costumes because Eli had remembered our conversation with his mom way back in April when I'd said my father had never let me dress up for Halloween. He'd kept his promise. We weren't trick-or-treating, but he'd thrown himself into planning the Salty Dog's 1st Annual Halloween Party. There was a kid's fair in the bar's parking lot until nine o'clock where people could bring their children for safe treats. All the shops in town had participated with booths and special activities. After nine o'clock, the party was set to move inside for adults-only-themed activities.

The whole town was due to show up, and I felt very much like a child instead of the adult owner of a bar in an outfit that showed a lot of skin. Hence the time we'd spent in the bedroom instead of getting ready to leave.

"If I say you look sexy, we'll be back in the bedroom, and we're already late," Eli said, eyes drifting away from me instead of staying on me as they normally did.

"What's up with you?" I asked.

"I can't look at you. It's killing me," he groaned. "Maybe you should change. We can cut holes in a sheet. You can go as a ghost."

"I'm not hiding in a sheet."

He sighed and stuck out a hand for mine. My body responded to the silent command as always. I put my hand in his and let him lead me down the stairs to his truck.

When we got to the bar, the parking lot was already crawling with people and kids. We parked in the alley and joined the crowd. People called out greetings to us as we made our way through the booths. I loved that Eli and I had become a part of the community, like the one I'd felt when I'd been with him in New London. Home and family all rolled into one.

Andy and Lacey had finally turned the bar completely over to me in September. They were still around when I needed help, and they often covered for me when I needed time off. It kept them involved, and it helped me from feeling overwhelmed.

They'd planned on coming tonight, working the bar and allowing me moments to celebrate with Eli and my friends—to have a Halloween that was mine for the first time ever.

As the kids and families drifted off with the outside fair dwindling away, Eli and I moved inside. Ben and the band were dressed as zombies and already had typical Halloween music going—some light and stupid, some punk and rapid. The crowd was drinking neon, glowing shots that we'd designed specifically for tonight. It was fun. It was Halloween.

I moved behind the bar, placing my Harley Quinn bat near the register, and started serving drinks. Eli joined me. We worked well together, like Andy and Lacey had worked well together, our bodies and minds speaking a language only we knew.

My bat rolled off the counter, and I went to catch it, but it fell before I could reach it, hitting the corner of a tray of glasses as it went, the glasses going with it in a loud crash. Thankfully, most of the bar glasses were built to be tossed about, and none of them broke, but as I was stacking them back up, I noticed a teal-colored gift bag tucked into the recesses of the space behind the trays.

"What's this?" I asked, more to myself than anything, but somehow, Eli heard me over the band and the hum of the crowd.

"Wait," he said, panic invading his voice as it never did, but I'd already dug my hand into the bag and come out with a box.

A jewelry-shaped box.

He was at my side in an agile movement that belied the fact that he'd left behind his military life. I was already opening the box, though, not really registering him, or his panic, or his hands trying to pull it from me.

It was a ring.

A beautiful ring.

Platinum, with a host of different colored stones built together to be a mosaic of color. A magical display of color. And it hit me then. The ring. Eli's panic. And I turned to him with a smile on my face.

"Is this mine?"

"Not yet," he said with a huff that did very much remind me of Mr. Grumpy.

He pulled the box from my hand and closed the lid with a snap.

"Why on earth did you leave it at the bar if you didn't want me to see it?" I smiled up at him, happiness invading my soul. He hadn't moved away. He was so close to me that I could feel the flex of his thighs on my mesh-covered ones as he stepped from foot to foot.

"Frank just delivered it tonight. I haven't had a chance to put it anywhere else."

I wrapped my arms around his middle. "Oh Captain, my Captain, did you have something you were going to ask me?"

"Not on Halloween, with you dressed as Harley Quinn."

"You picked out the costume with me."

"But I wasn't going to propose in costumes."

"You're in a suit."

He sighed, resting his chin on the top of my head, pulling me closer.

"Eli."

"Hmm?"

"The cat's out of the bag, so to speak." I was smiling into his chest. I was ready. Ready to put his ring on my finger. Ready for us to put a name to everything we'd been through. Ready to make a statement to the world of what we already knew to be true. That we were each other's. We were a family.

He huffed one last time and then moved away from me, grabbing the mic we always left on the bar shelf before effortlessly jumping onto the bar. He looked down at me as he had back in July when he'd surprised me by showing up out of nowhere. When he'd surprised me by trying ever so badly to sing me the song that I'd written about us—one of the many songs I'd written about us—it had been the best song I'd ever heard, no matter that his deep voice had sounded like he was being strangled.

It had been gorgeous, reverberating down my spine and filling my soul. Because he'd sung it for me. Because he'd gone out of his way to learn the song, and had the band learn the song, and arranged it so that he could surprise me. It had filled my heart to what I thought would be its fullest point ever.

But I was wrong. Because tonight, with him on the bar once more, tapping the mic to get everyone's attention, I felt like my heart might have swollen an impossible notch more.

Eli's voice effectively shut Ben and the band off. They came to a screeching halt in the middle of "Monster Mash."

"Hey, everyone, sorry to interrupt, but you can blame it on Ava."

Everyone looked to me, and I was already smiling, knowing what was coming.

"This is not at all how I wanted this moment to go, but you know Ava. Everything is on her schedule."

The crowd chuckled. He stuck a hand out, and I followed it by pulling myself up onto the bar top with him.

"Four years ago, I was stunned into silence by a voice and a body that somehow seemed already familiar to me even though I'd never met her before," Eli continued, his eyes locking on mine. "When I met her for the second time, she told me that she wanted her words to be like the aurora borealis. A life-changing phenomenon for the world. Except, she didn't know that she'd already changed my entire world with one song."

He stopped for a minute as if he had to catch his breath, but instead, he'd been thinking. "Anyone who knows you knows you love your quotes. I believe that it was Eleanor Roosevelt that said, 'The future belongs to those who believe in the beauty of their dreams.' My only dream now is of a future with you. You're the beauty in my life. We'll create our own magical display." He pulled my hand and placed it on his chest where I could feel the batter of his heart against my skin. "Ava, will you marry me?"

I wanted to say something funny. I wanted to say something moving. I wanted to say something that would be remembered. However, in that moment, full of so many emotions that my body couldn't process them all, all I could do was nod and grin. Like I really was psycho Harley ready to bash a head in with a bat.

Eli saw the nod, and he saw the wave of emotion on my face, and his softened. He pulled me closer, the mic by both of our lips. "Just so the crowd knows…is that a yes?"

I nodded again and then found my voice. "Yes, oh Captain, my Captain. I'm all yours."

His lips found mine, and even as his lips commanded my body, he joined our hands again, slipping the ring onto my finger and once more allowing me to find safe harbor in a world of his making. Of our making. Under lights made by a disco ball and the crowd clapping and cheering. But it didn't matter. Eli was always right. We were our own magical display. We were us.

♫ ♫ ♫

Need more of the <u>Anchor Novel</u> gang? Keep reading to see how you can get more of Mac, Truck, and Brady, PLUS A LITTLE TEASER FROM EACH BOOK!

Or check them out here:

FORGED BY SACRIFICE, is Mac and Georgie's **roommates-to-lovers, opposites-attract, military romance**. See why Angela's Book Addiction says its, "Beautifully written, emotional, sexy, and full of depth with exciting twists and turns.!"

"I'd really like to kiss you," he said quietly.

I looked into his eyes that were the color of the sky and the sea all rolled into one. His face was so gorgeous, with its day-old stubble and square planes, that it was like looking at a piece of art you'd never expected to see up close in person.

"I'd really like you to kiss me too. But let's face it, it isn't a good idea," I answered back, unable to deny the attraction that existed between the two of us from the moment we'd met in my salon two years ago, regardless of the relationship I'd just left behind.

His head inclined in silent agreement. It wasn't a good idea. Disappointment curled through me even as I knew it was better this way.

His hand moved to caress my cheek. Gently. Soothing.

"Can I ask why you think it's a bad idea?" he inquired.

His voice had turned a notch deeper in blatant desire, making my heart pound against my chest in a heavy beat that denied my words. I ached to kiss him. To feel those almost too-perfect lips against my own. To feel the strength that poured from him, in muscle and character, reaching out to touch my soul.

"Ava and Eli," I said quietly. "Awkwardness later."

He nodded again, that new and unfamiliar feeling of disappointment reaching up into my throat at his action. My body didn't want him to nod, but my brain was still ruling my movements.

"One kiss," he muttered, a finger traveled to my lips, caressing the bottom one with a gentle touch like the one he'd used on the tomatoes the day before. Surprising. Sexy. My breath escaped in a gasp that sounded almost like a moan.

And then his lips were on mine, just like the touch,

gentle and yet full of heat, longing filling us both, desire escaping from us and mingling in an excursion that felt like heartbreak and loneliness and promises that would never be. The gentleness gave way to a fierceness that was as unexpected as the gentleness had been. His hand went to my lower back, pulling me toward him tighter so that our bodies and curves joined in a way that felt like opposite ends of magnets finally clicking together. Parallel forces drawn, as if by physics itself.

<u>FORGED BY SACRIFICE</u> is FREE in Kindle Unlimited

Truck and Jersey's fake-marriage, forced-proximity romance, **<u>AVENGED BY LOVE</u>**, is a small-town, standalone that one 5-star reviewer calls, "The greatest love story adventure."

The man shut the bar, clicked the button next to him, and we swooshed backward while he loaded the next car. Our seat continued to sway, and I gripped the bar.

Jersey laughed next to me, and I turned my head from the ground disappearing beneath us to her. To the beauty that was the pale vision next to me. "This is funny to you?"

"It's just...you're this big, bad Coast Guard, all protective He-man action. So, it's strange to see you afraid of a simple machine."

"We aren't birds. We don't have wings. If we fall, there will be nothing to save us."

"We're not going to fall. Don't look at the ground, look out." She tugged my chin up from the ground so I was looking out at the ocean, and I realized, for the first time, that the skies weren't blue, and the sun wasn't shining. I hadn't really noticed it when I was spending time with someone who was as bright as the sun. And Jersey was exactly that when she let herself come out from behind her shield.

The ocean was rough, and the wind whipping around us was more from the ominous clouds than the ride. The air was hot and humid, but it was also charged with energy, and I regretted ever stepping foot on the ride.

"What the hell are we doing on this thing in a storm?" I croaked.

She laughed again. "It's beautiful, right?"

The stormy seas were beautiful, like she'd said, especially with the clouds seeming to blur into the waves. But that beauty could turn deadly in a second. I knew it for a fact, because I lived on the sea for a good portion of my daily life.

She tucked her arm through mine. "I'll keep you safe."

And then it was my turn to laugh. This little tiny thing next to me, offering to keep me safe. As if she really did have her own superpowers. As if she was Cat Woman, or Black Widow, or that damned Glasswing she idolized and could deliver me from a fall, unscathed.

Except, I'd already fallen. Hard. For her. For my wife.

<u>AVENGED BY LOVE</u> is FREE in Kindle Unlimited

Need more Brady O'Neil in your life? His HEA story, **<u>BRANDED BY A SONG</u>**, is a single-mom, rock-star romance that reviewers said was a "Top Read of 2021," and that they "absolutely fell head over heels for Brady."

The feel of his gentle exploration as he kissed me almost broke me. The slow and steady pull on my sleepy nerve endings was tearing my veins apart. A kiss tasting like berries and wine and picnics in the filtered sunlight between shady tree branches. A kiss that caused a burst of lust to spread through me because of its tenderness. A simple kiss with just lips and tongues joining and no hands or bodies, as if he knew how painful the experience would be for me and was trying to soften the blow.

A simple kiss that was anything but simple.

It felt so damn good it was hard to imagine stopping. It felt perfect.

Which sent a wave of ice down my back.

Perfect.

How could it be perfect?

I stepped away, regret filling me. Regret because I was being cruel, and I didn't like to be cruel. I'd let him kiss me, knowing it could only be a kiss and nothing more. Knowing I couldn't give him what he deserved to be given when he touched someone like that. When he kissed someone so wholeheartedly, so openly, so devotedly.

He deserved a beginning. He deserved someone giving all of themself.

And I didn't have that to give anymore.

I'd already given it away.

<u>BRANDED BY A SONG</u> is FREE in Kindle Unlimited

Did you know that you can get the 1st **THREE ANCHOR NOVELS** as an eBook box set with a bonus novella? Don't miss any of these **slow-burn, sizzling, military romances** about true friends, real "family", and the dreams we reshape as we go through this wild ride called life. It includes: ***GUARDED DREAMS, FORGED BY SACRIFICE, AVENGED BY LOVE***, and ***THE HURRICANE*** — a bonus novella with the entire gang.

https://geni.us/anchorset

If you want to keep tabs on LJ' stories as she writes them and get exclusive content, giveaways, and more, then you might want to join her weekly newsletter, http://bit.ly/LJEmoGive. You can get all these FREE Flash

Fiction stories when you sign up: https://www.ljevansbooks.com/freeljbooks.

Want even more teasers? Want even more chances at giveaways? Join her Facebook Group, **LJ's Music and Stories**, to chat with LJ on a daily basis.

Message from the Author

Thanks again for reading *Guarded Dreams*. I hope you loved Eli and Ava's story of love that I wove for you here. I hope the strength and resiliency of the characters, along with my mix of lyrics and story, burned a memory into your soul that you will think of every time you hear one of the songs from now on.

We talk about music, books, and just what it takes to get us through this wild ride called life a lot in my Facebook reader's group, **LJ's Music & Stories**. If you do nothing else with the links here, I hope you join that group. I hope that we can help *YOU* through your life in some small way.

Regardless if you join or not, I'd love for you to tell me what you thought of Ava and Eli by reaching out to me personally. I'd be honored if you took the time to leave a review on BookBub, Amazon, and / or Goodreads, but even more than that, I hope you enjoyed it enough to tell a friend about it.

If you still can't get enough (ha!), you could also sign up for my newsletter (http://bit.ly/LJEmoGive) where I write lyric-inspired scenes and share them with you on a regular basis. Plus, you'll get the details on releases and be entered into a giveaway each month for a chance at a signed paperback by yours truly.

Finally, I just wanted to say that my wish for you is a healthy and happy journey. May you live life resiliently. With hope and love. I truly hope to hear from you!

Happy Reading!

LJ EVANS

♫ *where music & stories collide* ♫

www.ljevansbooks.com

FaceBook Group: LJ's Music & Stories

LJ Evans on Bookbub, Amazon, and Goodreads

@ljevansbooks on Facebook, Twitter, Instagram, and Pinterest

About the Book

I've done my best to not consciously misrepresent anything about the military, music, Juilliard, knee injuries, breast cancer, or any of the quotes Ava uses in this book. But I may have taken a few liberties for the sake of entertainment.

I researched the U.S. Coast Guard, their lifestyle, jobs, and their stations. I wanted to represent the pride and honor Coasties feel in being part of the U.S. military as well as the family that they truly are to each other. I hope that nothing I've written disrespects the honor and service of these men and women as I hold them in the highest regard.

The *Aurora Borealis* painting by Frederic Edwin Church is really owned and on exhibit at the Smithsonian Art Museum in Washington D.C. For purposes of the book, I had it on loan to The Metropolitan Museum of Art in NYC. Neither the Expeditions Exhibit nor the painting's participation in it are real.

The Hayes quote was sourced from Wikipedia: Aurora_Borealis_(painting). Most other quotes used in the story were sourced from www.BrainyQuote.com.

For the purpose of the book, I sped up some of the patellar injury cast and recovery timelines. I didn't do this to make Eli into a superhero, but because it was better for the book's timeline.

Early detection of breast cancer is critical to successful treatment. Please do not skip any of the regular exams (self or with your doctor) that are required to catch this ugly beast before it turns your life inside out. Stage 1 breast cancer, before in the lymph nodes, has a high rate of successful treatment if caught at that stage. For more information, please contact your doctor and the American Cancer Society website.

Any other errors I made, I beg your forgiveness, for it was done without intention and with the heart of the story in mind.

Acknowledgements

My first acknowledgement is to my husband, who I adore more than words, thank you for being the person to take me from my moments of seriousness and self-doubt to laughter. Thank you for not letting me give up on this dream of mine and for supporting it with your time, our money, and your own effort. I am so lucky to have you as my partner in this crazy thing called life. I love our life together. I promise I'll try to be back on my feet soon. I love you.

To my daughter who has begun her own creative path, thank you for being the best critic and line editor I could have. Thank you for not only helping me craft my words but encouraging me, for understanding my creative drive and allowing me to be a part of your own creative world as well. I am amazed every day by your strength, your love, and your own personal journey. You were the very best gift to have ever entered my world. I love you.

Thank you to my big sister who wouldn't let me quit till I published, for always being my first alpha reader, and for telling me when I'm being stupid. Isn't that what siblings are for, after all? Ego checks and ego lifts!

Thank you to my parents who have been so proud of me that they show my book off wherever they go. To my mom, thanks for loving all my words even when they were oh so bad when I was a kid. And to my dad, thanks for reading my books even when they're romances novel instead of westerns.

Thank you to Megan Keith at Designed With Grace cover designs for not only my beautiful cover, but understanding the creative need in all of us. For reading my words and sharing them with the world when that wasn't part of your job. I'm blessed to have found you.

To Jenn at Jenn Lockwood Editing Services, thank you for being a partner in my creative process and for showing your love and support for my books. I never thought I could find someone who would completely get what I was trying to say even as a I rambled. Thank you.

To the bloggers who have shared my stories with the world on your own time and your own dime, I cannot say enough. The independent book world would not be what it is today without you. An extra special thank you to these bloggers who helped me get this book out into the world: Rachel at NovelMomma, Launa at Energy Rae, Ashleigh at Page Once Turned, Candyce at The Book Dutchesses, Heather at Books and a Blanket, Stacie at Boren Books, and Sophie at Digital Dirty Girl, as well as a whole host of other bloggers.

To the other independent authors who have helped keep me sane on this journey including Kelsey Kingsley, Amanda Johnson, Clare Lesbirel, Katy Ames, and Lauren Helms, I have not enough words. Thank you for sharing and supporting each other in ways that I never thought possible…without jealousy *and* while truly holding each other's crowns up when they fall. Hugs to all of you.

Thank you to Amy Harmon for not only inspiring me with your words but with your kindness and generosity.

Finally, but certainly not least, thank you to my readers. To those of you that I've come to know personally and those that I have not. Michelle Fritz, you are selfless and beautiful in all you do for us authors. Dee Shelvey thank you for making me smile very day when I've been ill. Michelle Odland, you allow me to be weak and then show me how I am strong, thank you. To every one of you who have read even one of my stories, THANK YOU!

About the Author

Award-winning author, LJ Evans, lives in Northern California with her husband, child, and the three terrors called cats. She's been writing, almost as a compulsion, since she was a little girl and will often pull the car over to write when a song lyric strikes her. A former first-grade teacher, she now spends her free time reading and writing, as well as binge-watching original shows like *Ted Lasso, Wednesday, Veronica Mars,* and *Stranger Things.*

If you ask her the one thing she won't do, it's pretty much anything that involves dirt—sports, gardening, or otherwise. But she loves to write about all of those things, and her first published heroine was pretty much involved with dirt on a daily basis, which is exactly why LJ loves fiction novels—the characters can be everything you're not and still make their way into your heart.

Her novels have won multiple awards including ***CHARMING AND THE CHERRY BLOSSOM,*** which was *Writer's Digest's* Self-Published E-book Romance of the Year in 2021. For more information about LJ, check out any of these sites:

www.ljevansbooks.com

FaceBook Group: LJ's Music & Stories

LJ Evans on Amazon, Bookbub, and Goodreads

@ljevansbooks on Facebook, Instagram, TikTok, and Pinterest

Books by LJ

Standalone

<u>The Last One You Loved</u>

A single-dad, small-town romance

He's a small-town sheriff with a secret that can unravel their worlds. She's an ER resident running from a costly mistake. Coming home will only mean heartache…unless they let forgiveness heal them both.

<u>Charming and the Cherry Blossom</u>

A contemporary romance with hints of magical realism

Today was a fairy tale…I inherited a fortune from a dad I never knew, and a charming guy asked me out. But like all fairy tales, mine has a dark side...and my happily ever after may disappear with the truth.

My Life as an Album Series

<u>My Life as a Country Album</u> — Cam's Story

A boy-next-door, small-town romance

Spirited athlete's Cam's diary-style, coming-of-age story about growing up loving the football hero next door. She vowed to love him forever. But when fate comes calling, will she ever find a heart to call home? Warning: Tears may fall.

<u>My Life as a Pop Album</u> — Mia & Derek

A rock-star, road-trip romance

Bookworm Mia is trying to put behind years of guilt when soulful musician, Derek Waters, strolls into her life and turns it upside down. Once he's seen her, Derek can't walk away unless Mia comes with him. But what will happen when their short time together ends?

<u>My Life as a Rock Album</u> — Seth & PJ

A second-chance, antihero romance

Growly, trash artist Seth Carmen knows he's better off alone. But when he finds and loses the love of his life, he sends her a series of love letters to try and win her back. Can he prove broken is beautiful?

<u>My Life as a Mixtape</u> — Lonnie & Wynn

A single-dad, rock-star romance

Lonnie's always seen relationships as a burden instead of a gift, and picking up the pieces his sister leaves behind is just one of the reasons. When Wynn enters his life just as her world is disintegrating, their mixed-up pasts give way to new beginnings neither saw coming.

<u>My Life as a Holiday Album</u> – 2nd Generation

A small-town romance

Come home for the holidays with this heartwarming, full-length standalone full of hidden secrets, true love, and the real meaning of family. Perfect for lovers of *Love Actually* and Hallmark movies, this sexy story twines the lives of six couples as they find their way to their happily ever after with the help of family and friends.

<u>My Life as an Album Series Box Set</u>

The 1st four Album series books + an exclusive novella

In the exclusive novella, *This Life with Cam*, Blake Abbott writes to Cam about just what it was like to grow up in the shadow of her relationship with Jake and just when he first fell for the little girl with the popsicle-stained lips. Can he show Cam that she isn't broken?

The Anchor Novels

<u>Guarded Dreams</u> — Eli & Ava

A grumpy-sunshine, military romance

Eli's chasing a dream that he's determined to succeed at, no matter the consequences. He isn't looking for love, but when the free-spirited singer, Ava, breezes into his world, he finds himself changing his tune.

<u>Forged by Sacrifice</u> — Mac & Georgie

A roommates-to-lovers, military romance

Mac is determined to change the world. A life in politics is his future. The dream Georgie once gave up is finally in reach—a law degree. When her family's past makes his future an impossibility, they have to decide just how much they're willing to sacrifice for love.

<u>Avenged by Love</u> — Truck & Jersey

A fake-marriage, military romance

Travis's focus is on his Coast Guard career and his brother's future. But once beautiful, comic-loving Jersey crashes into his world in desperate need of medical care, he offers a marriage of convenience to help. But what happens when convenience turns to love?

<u>Damaged Desires</u> — Dani & Nash

A frenemy, military romance

Nash is all about honoring a promise to his dead brother, so accepting a challenge from the long-legged force of nature tempting him isn't in the cards. Not if he wants to keep his only remaining friend and stick to the code he grew up on. Several dares later, he has to decide whether to continue hiding in his past or face a new future.

<u>Branded by a Song</u> — Brady & Tristan

A single-mom, rock-star romance

Brady's come home to help the sister he left behind and find inspiration for a new album. What he doesn't expect is to discover his muse in a woman who's completely off limits and lost in the past. Can he help her find the strength to sing a brand-new love song?

<u>Tripped by Love</u> – Cassidy & Marco

A broody-bodyguard, single-mom romance

Cassidy is juggling her restaurant, a tiny human, and unrequited love. There's no time for her ex to try and derail her. Marco is determined to bury the feelings he has for his boss's sister, but that doesn't mean he's going to let the sniveling father of her child steamroll her. What happens when a little white lie changes everything?

<u>The Anchor Novels: The Military Bros Box Set</u>

The 1st three slow-burn romances + an exclusive novella

Guarded Dreams, Forged by Sacrifice, and *Avenged by Love* plus the novella, *The Hurricane!*

The Anchor Suspense Novels

<u>Unmasked Dreams</u> — Violet & Dawson

A second-chance, age-gap romance

Violet and Dawson had a heart-stopping attraction they were compelled to deny. When they're tossed together again, it proves nothing has changed—except the lab she's built in the garage and the secrets he's keeping. When she stumbles into his dark world, Dawson is forced to break old promises to keep her safe. But when the swells subside, will their hearts still be intact?

<u>Crossed by the Stars</u> — Jada & Dax

A second-chance, forced-proximity romance

Family secrets meant Dax and Jada's teenaged romance was an impossibility. A decade later, the scars still remain, so neither is willing to give in to their tantalizing chemistry. But when a shadow creeps out of Jada's past, seeking retribution, it's Dax who shows up to protect her. And suddenly, it's hard to see a way out without permanent damage to their bodies and souls.

<u>Disguised as Love</u> — Cruz & Raisa

A chemistry-filled, enemies-to-lovers romance

Surly FBI agent, Cruz Malone, is determined to bring down the Leskov clan for good. If that means he has to arrest or bed the sexy blonde scientist of the family, so be it. Too bad Raisa has other ideas. There's no way she's just going to sit back and let the infuriating agent dismantle her world…or her heart.

The Painted Daisies

Interconnected, slow-burn romances with an all-female rock band, the alpha heroes who steal their hearts, and suspense that'll leave you breathless. Each story has its own HEA.

<u>Sweet Memory</u>

An opposite-side-of-the-tracks, second-chance romance.

Trouble—that's what her sister calls him. But she can't resist, not even when his past threatens her world.

<u>Green Jewel</u>

An enemies-to-lovers, single-dad romance.

He did it. She'll prove it. Her body's reaction to him be damned.

<u>Cherry Brandy</u>

An opposites-attract, forbidden romance.

Being on the run with only one bed is no excuse to touch her…until touching is the only choice.

<u>Blue Marguerite</u>

A Hollywood-celebrity, frenemy romance.

She may have to work with him to save her sister, but he'll never have her body or heart again.

<u>Royal Haze</u>

An antihero, secret-society romance.

He was ready to torture, steal, and kill to defend the world he believed in. What he wasn't prepared for…was her.

Free Stories

https://www.ljevansbooks.com/freeljbooks

Perfectly Fine – FREE with newsletter signup

A Hollywood, second-chance romance

He's a charming, A-list actor at the top of his game. She's a determined, small-town screenwriter hoping for a deal. They form an unexpected connection until heartbreak ruins their future.

Rumor – FREE with newsletter signup

A small-town, rock-star romance

There's only one thing rock star Chase Legend needs to ring in the new year, and that's to know what Reyna Rossi tastes like. After ten years, there's no way he's letting her escape the night without their souls touching. Reyna has other plans. After all, she doesn't need the entire town wagging their tongues about her any more than they already do.

Love Ain't – FREE with newsletter signup

A friends-to-lovers, cowboy romance

Reese knows her best friend and rodeo king, Dalton Abbott, is never going to fall in love, get married, and have kids. He's left so many broken hearts behind there's gotta be a museum full of them somewhere. So, when he gives her a look from under the brim of his hat, promising both jagged relief and pain, she isn't giving in.

The Long Con – FREE with newsletter signup

A sexy, antihero romance

Adler is after one thing: the next big payday. Then, Brielle sways into his world with her own game in play, and those aquamarine-colored eyes almost make him forget his number-one rule. But she'll learn…love isn't a con he's interested in.

The Light Princess – FREE with newsletter signup

An old-fashioned fairy tale

A princess who glows with a magical light, a kingdom at war, and a kiss that changes the world.